Crossing
Burning
Bridges

Crossing
Burning
Bridges

One Woman's Amazing Journey

Cyndie M. Styles

Crossing Burning Bridges
One Woman's Amazing Journey
by Cyndie M. Styles

Published by:
CMS Enterprises
P.O. Box 8039
Van Nuys, CA 91409-8039 U.S.A.
Orders at http://www.cyndiemstyles.com

Library of Congress Control Number: 2005905677

ISBN, print ed. 0-9768170-0-4

Printed in the United States of America

First Printing 2005

This book is a work of fiction; names, characters, places and incidents either are the product of the author's imagination or are used fictitiously. Any resemblance to events, organizations or persons, living or dead, is entirely coincidental and beyond the intent of either the author or the publisher.

Many thanks to my friends, my niece, and my aunt for proofreading. Many thanks to Doris and Nadine for being in my life. And many thanks to Doug for your continual support in all of the crazy things that I do.

Cover Designer: Robert Aulicino, Pro-Art Graphic Design
                   http://www.aulicinodesign.com

For my beloved kids:

Killer (aka: Wiggle-butt), Foxy Lady and Sherlock

Part I

Beginning My Life

Chapter I

The Godsend

Dear Journal: I was ushered down the endless empty corridor while searching for the thoughts that would surround the night's events. As we turned a corner, I saw additional medical personnel waiting. They then guided me into a room that was dreary, sterile, emotionless, not at all like my everyday surroundings. I changed into drab hospital garb. They escorted me to a gurney, where I was lying while they strapped me to it. Shortly thereafter, a nurse came in and inserted an I.V. into my arm. The orderlies began wheeling me toward that room. The room of death, or the room of pardonable life.

There was never a question. I always knew this would be a possibility ever since the day I discovered the truth. But who knew I would be so calm about it? Goodnight Journal.

"Don't I at least get a cigarette or a blindfold?" I razzed as I felt the medication starting to take effect. The orderlies said nothing as they wheeled me closer and closer, with their stoical faces.

A million questions sprouted in my mind as I was lying there. What were they thinking about me? Did they think that I was the enemy? Was I too ruthless for them? Did I feel hatred for her because of my abandonment issues? Would they have forgiven me if I had rejected their request? Why did she...?

My thoughts were interrupted by him, a man I had seen earlier, who was now partially masked and peering over me. "Hello, Jordan. We're about to begin."

I nodded and everything faded.

As I awoke some time later, I looked around the room. I couldn't see much from my angle, but I could hear nurses buzzing about.

"What time is it?" I asked, wondering if I'd actually said it out loud. No one answered. "Excuse me. What time is it?" I reiterated.

"It's okay, just lie back down. Someone will be in shortly," claimed a nurse, not listening to my question.

"What time is it?" I repeated. No one answered me.

I was lying there for what seemed like hours before that man reappeared and stood over me, smiling. "How are you feeling, Jordan?"

"Okay, I guess. What time is it?"

"It's late. You should get some rest now."

"What happened? How many pieces am I in?" I asked, trying to hide my anxiety. "And what about...?"

"Yes, everything is fine. You need to rest now," the man answered as he cut in, then disappeared.

When I awoke again, I was in a hospital patient room on the forth floor. This room was rosy, with bright green curtains hanging alongside a window that looked out onto the hospital garden. It was daytime now. Because of the angle, I could barely see out the window but I was able to see people walking around, mostly people smoking.

As I spanned the room, I could see greeting cards on a side table, opened and standing erect. There were a few dozen lavender roses in a vase next to my bed with a card attached. I reached over and pulled the card from its holder. It read: "You are a Godsend. You saved our lives." There was no signature. I was so weak and groggy that the card slipped out of my hand and floated to the floor. I then noticed beeping and buzzing behind me but didn't have the strength to turn to see what was generating the noise.

The door was closed but I could see some activity in the hallway through a small window toward the top of the door. Someone was out there. I heard whispering. My hearing seemed distorted and echoey, and I couldn't quite make out what they were saying. "Who is that?" I thought as I slowly sat up in order to get a better look out the window of the door. I could hear people whispering something in disagreement, but I couldn't see who was out there.

Suddenly the door flew open, and the male angelic face walking toward me said, "Hellllo, JoJo." However, before I could return a greeting to him, everything faded.

As I looked around the room, I could see it was nighttime again. I waited for a moment while I examined my body to figure out if they had performed the operation on me. They had not, and knowing that, I lifted myself up and slid out of bed. I was hooked up to several tubes and probes. I started pulling them out and off, all except the I.V. in my arm. Then, when I noticed a slight chill toward the back of my gown, I slipped on the robe that was hanging from a hook on the bathroom door. "Yeah, that would make a good picture splashed all over the covers of tabloids," I thought. I grabbed my journal out of the nightstand drawer and a large glass of water from the table next to the bed, then shuffled my way toward the nurse's station with my I.V. stand trailing behind me. I paused around the corner until the nurses all had vacated the station. As I again moved forward, I looked around for paparazzi waiting to jump out at me. With the nurses absent now, I sifted through the charts piled on the counter until I found the one I wanted. I located her room number from the chart. I then shuffled my way down the corridor toward her room.

My mind was jumbled with questions. What would I say to her? What should I tell her? What would I want her to know? What would they not want me to tell her? I stood outside her room for a moment assessing possible nurse's movements to make sure no one else was in there, then entered. I didn't want any interference because we needed privacy. I dragged a chair from the corner of the room toward her bed, then reached for a spare pillow along the way. I placed the pillow on the seat of the chair and then just sat there watching her motionless body with all of those machines beeping, buzzing and flashing around her. Her room was cold, much more than mine. She didn't have a window, nor bright curtains. There were no flowers. There were slightly deflated balloons in the corner of the room including one with a cheery greeting. Not really knowing what to say, I nevertheless slowly began speaking in a whisper...

"Hi Zoë. You don't really know me; I'm your sister, Jordan. We are a part of each other now. We have an unbreakable bond. We have the same blood... well, more now than before. I knew it was risky, but there was never a question; I always knew I would do this for you, because you are *my* Godsend."

I took a deep breath before continuing. "I hope you can hear me because we have a lot of catching up to do. I know I should have told you of these things long ago; I make no excuses. If after you hear my story, you wish to banish me as well, then I will happily go away - just to have known you for this short time, and to have given you life. No one else need know about all of this, if you don't want them to know it. I guess I should start with the basics. I'm six years older than you, twenty-eight now, but you probably already know that. If you were older or I was a younger age, I'll bet we could pass as twins. And look there, we have the same red hair." I began to wonder if I was just rambling without a purpose.

"I suppose I'll give you some family history first. It may make it easier to understand the events that follow, knowing a little about my background." I leaned back as I searched for what to say next.

"Mom, Katia, was from a Russian father and a British mother. By the time Mom was in junior high, her father had retired. He was a carpenter and architect by trade, but I think he made most of his money investing in stocks and bonds. His name is Anton, but we all call him Gampy. My grandmother's name is Elizabeth, whose friends all call her Annie, and has always been a housewife. We call her Gamma. I've seen pictures of Gamma when she was my age, and she was beautiful. She has always had a lot of friends, and likes to play cards and give parties. She even enjoys volunteering down at the senior center. Gamma was raised in London until her family moved to America when she was around ten.

She grew up with wealth, old money, you know - just like you, I suppose. It was mandatory for her to have an education and Gamma chose a degree in Art History. She and Gampy only had one child. Mom grew up to be a very stunning woman, never smiled though - not in any of her pictures did she smile. She always had a wounded look about her."

I took a sip of water and another deep breath before continuing. "Dad, Ethan, was from a Chippewa father and a Scottish mother, if you can believe that combination. His grandfather's great-grandfather changed their surname from Waw-goosh, meaning Fox, to Walsh to fit in with their white settler neighbors. Dad, along with his younger brother, Uncle Red, had a middle-class upbringing - nothing really to write home about, I suppose. Their parents didn't practice the Native American ways, but I think that's why Uncle Red did, to be his own person. Dad has dark skin like his grandfather's great-grandfather, high cheekbones, black hair - the whole works. He calls himself a traveling *businessman*, which was laughable to those who knew him."

I briefly paused in order to decide what to tell Zoë next. "Neither Mom nor Dad attended college. They were high-school sweethearts from the same class and the same age, and it was no secret that she was pregnant when they were married. Their life together in Houston was a turbulent one, to say the least. She's an Aries and he - an Aquarius. She was controlling and he wasn't going to be controlled. Their wedding was no wedding. She had no formal wedding dress, no wedding cake or reception, no bridesmaids, no flowers and no friends were there. There was only one wedding photo taken, which Gamma snapped before they left for the courthouse. My grandparents were the only ones there - his parents, not Gamma and Gampy. The ceremony was treated as a technicality, like a missed detail from last week's schedule. I guess that's why I insisted on a big wedding, not that I really wanted all of the hoopla, but I didn't want my wedding to be like theirs. His parents died in an automobile accident two months after the wedding so I never knew them. Which brings me to me."

Just then, a nurse stormed in and interrupted me by saying, "*What* are you doing here? You should be back in your own room, in your own bed!" As the nurse finished scolding me, a loud beep from a monitor down the hall sounded and she ran from the room.

I turned back around and shrugged. "I'll bet she's a Capricorn," I said to Zoë before continuing. "I, Jordan Melanie Walsh, was born on the twentieth day of March. I don't love my name, but I don't hate it either. For a long time, I thought it was kind of masculine and I wanted a more girly name. Some had said that I had a great-great grandmother by the name of Melanie so that's how I got that part. Having my birthday on the first day of Spring, I can't tell you how many times I've thought back and was thrilled my parents hadn't named me Refresh, Floral, Spring, Warmth, Blossom or Bonnet. Rumor had it - some were actually discussed. I resemble Mom in many ways, as you may already know, and my hair is straight like hers. Only mine is red and hers is dark-brown like her Russian ancestors. I guess we both know why it isn't black like Dad's; I suppose that's just the mystery of DNA. I just wish I had gotten some of the height of my father, since I'm only five foot five inches tall."

I paused to reconstruct my thinking pattern. I wanted Zoë to learn about *me* first and not focus on our connection. "My toddler years seem to have been normal, from what I can remember of them. I was a little ignored, but my adolescence appeared normal for the most part. Except for one thing... I have no memories of Mom ever hugging me. There were no pictures portraying motherly affection, none where she was even pretending to show a closeness. In photographs, she'd always stand beside me with a blank stare on her face like you see in old Western photographs."

I was so immersed in telling my story, I hardly noticed when other monitors down the hall would screech out their deadly blare.

I started to drift back in time as if I were reliving my life prior to knowing Zoë. My consciousness was that of actually being in the past. While watching the rhythm from the lights flashing on her monitors, I was led into a hypnotic trance, and was sent back in time to retrieve my memories...

~*~¡~*~¡~*~¡~*~¡~*~¡~*~

I guess I was around eight when I started to remember the events in the world, and in my world. We lived in Houston in a small house that had three bedrooms. When we moved there, I had heard Mom tell the realtor that my bedroom was a little small but I thought it was just right. The house was plain, but it was clean for the most part. Mom made curtains for my room that were bright yellow with pink roses on them. She made most of the curtains in the house because we didn't have much money. My dresser was small, but it had legs that raised it off the floor to a point where I could hide things under it. I could hide all of my worldly treasures and no one would know. We had an average-size family room with a small color television set in it that Gampy bought for us. That's where Mom spent most of her time when Dad was away working. I so wanted a television set in my room, but that was completely out of the question unless "I could afford to buy it." And that was the basic theme of the house. I could never get anything extra when we visited the department stores because Mom said, "It wasn't in the budget."

One day as I was watching television, a commercial appeared on the screen for child models to do runway work. They paraded children down this red velvety walkway, twirling and pirouetting. Mom was on the couch sipping her *magic juice* (concocted with a little something she'd mix into her morning orange juice) when I swung around and peered at her in amazement, realizing that she had just uncharacteristically chuckled. I continued watching the commercial intensely and knew that's what I wanted to do. That's what I wanted to feel. I wanted to entertain. I wanted to make people laugh. I wanted to make *her* laugh. I wanted to *shine*. It made perfect sense; I am, after all - a Pisces.

After relentlessly pestering Mom to drive me to their talent agency for an audition, not only did I *not* get the job, they refused to sign me as a client. I was "not what they were looking for." I was seriously crushed. Devastated. Mom was seething from wasting her time on such useless nonsense and made sure I knew it.

"Not what they were looking for?" I was a kid and I could twirl; what were they looking for - Anna Pavlova? I spent the next few weeks sulking about it, trying to figure out what I did wrong, plotting how I was going to do better the next time, and how to prevail without upsetting Mom. I *wanted* this. All I knew was that it frustrated me, and I was not going to take "no" for an answer. I was actually grateful for that rejection. It gave me the motivation I needed to move forward and persevere.

Two months later, I got my first assignment from their competitor. It was a smaller agency, but at least I got my foot into someone's door. That's when I met Larry Wozowski, my agent. He's a short man, bald, and his office always smelled of cigar smoke, but he was nice and loved to make jokes. Dad wasn't there to sign the contract so I got Mom to do it. I caught her in a good mood when she was drinking her *magic juice* with her friends.

My assignment was to hold a sign with a store's name on it while walking around an outdoor mall and wearing the store's new children's fashions - from skirts to coats, anything they could resell after I wore it. They didn't pay me much, but Larry said it would pay off for me to get experience.

Mom never came into the store with me; she'd always just drop me off out front. She'd usually return four or five hours later to pick me up, after her girlfriends departed the cocktail lounge. For the times she hadn't returned at all, I'd have to ask the manager of the store to call Uncle Red to come get me.

Uncle Red is similar in physical build as Dad, yet he always tried to look different. Uncle Red was the only person who called me Joey. I liked it because it made the name special.

Anyway, I did that job until I got my next assignment working as one of Santa's elves at the department store during the holidays. Gamma came down and made such a fuss about it. She was taking pictures and pressuring Santa to vacate his chair so she could snap pictures of me in it. Old Saint Nick got ticked and that was the last day I wore the pointy ears. I never told Gamma.

Larry was ticked too. He didn't give me another assignment until three months later, the day of my ninth birthday. It was a job in the high school auditorium, returning props to the prop room after performances. I'd ride my bike over at lunchtime the following day to do the job because the performances would go on to nearly midnight. It was an unofficial job because the person actually in charge of the props approached Larry to hire someone to cover his position. That guy was a member of the drama club, and was much too distracted and involved with his *social* life to be bothered. So Larry had arranged for me to do it. The guy said they weren't paying him much to do this job so the pay would be low. We figured the truth was that my pay was low because of his *social* expenses. I did receive occasional tips from the crew, though. It was an excellent learning experience, getting to know my way around a theater. And even though the theater was old and musty, I was thrilled to be working there. When no one was around, I would go out on stage to bow and curtsy. I would imagine being a big star and holding roses while waving to the crowd that was gathering around the stage from the audience. It only took the embarrassment of being caught once, and I stopped doing that.

I also remember my ninth birthday vividly because that was the day I came home and saw Mom sporting a black eye and cuts around her mouth. I hadn't ever seen her like that before and didn't know what to say or think. Before I could comment, Mom gave me an explanation of how she fell down the stairs to the basement. That was odd, she never did that before no matter how many *magic juices* she would have.

During that year, was when I also found out mom would be having a baby.

That assignment continued for the remainder of the year, along with a handful of other temporary jobs, until it ended just before they began their Christmas production. The guy that hired Larry said his little sister wanted the job, so he'd have to fire me. No matter, I was ready to move on anyway.

Then on December 25th, my little brother was born. Thomas Ethan Walsh entered our lives as our *little Christmas miracle*, as Mom would call him. I was hoping for a sister. Dad wasn't there the day we brought Tommy home. Actually Dad was hardly there at all anymore, but the house seemed to run smoother when he wasn't around so it wasn't mentioned much. I began to see a transformation in Mom. Even though she still never smiled, I could see that she was happier - happy enough to actually hug Tommy.

And just around that time, amazingly, Mom realized that if I was old enough to work, I was old enough to do *her* work. She would make me clean stuff. Clean the bathroom, clean the kitchen, clean the basement, clean Tommy's stinkin' dirty diapers. I accommodated her demands, but felt like Cinderella in soot-covered clothes. And instead of the wicked stepsisters, it was a brother - *the crowned prince*. I daily witnessed Mom reclining with a *magic juice*, cooing at Tommy, and watching television while I was doing all of the work. Why did she choose this life as a housewife only to relinquish her duties onto me?! She and I began to have heated battles over all of it. Dad was no help, and didn't want to hear about it, but I'd had enough.

I decided I wasn't going to do it anymore, no matter what the consequences were. I knew she would threaten to terminate my contract with Larry so I had to figure out a way to circumvent that. I decided to offer a trade. She hated to cook, and she was terrible at it too. So I made an offer to perform all of the cooking from then on so I wouldn't have to clean anymore. And it worked. Mom didn't care so long as she didn't have to make the meals anymore.

Not only did I succeed, but I now knew how to work out a plan for negotiating. Dad, the schmoozer, was so impressed with my bargaining skills that he confidentially offered to send me to culinary classes. I told him to save that money for my acting classes because cooking was not my destiny. I was thrilled with how things had worked out; it was a great deal for me. Dad was rarely there, Mom only had toast with her *magic juice* for breakfast, and Tommy didn't eat our food yet. I frequently made my own meals anyway so it wasn't much different.

I asked Gamma to teach me more recipes and she was thrilled to show me. She and Mom never got along long enough for Mom to learn anything from her. I suppose it's true that the teachings come easier with one generation removed. Even Gampy helped out; he made me a step stool so that I could reach the stove easier.

Dad was away more and more; he would find anything to do that didn't include us. He wasn't even there for my tenth birthday. Occasionally, he returned for fresh clothes. He always had a deal going on somewhere, somewhere other than where we were. I'd watch him clicking his fingers, saying stuff like "I gotta go make things happen, get things done, wheel and deal." And off he went. Seems Mom tripped down the stairs less often when he was gone so she'd never complain about his departures.

I guess there's a reason I don't talk much about my friends. I didn't have many. None really, just the kids in my classroom. I tried making new friends in school, but I was working so frequently that it made it difficult to keep the friends I'd already made. I also felt that they would probably just leave me anyway the way Dad was doing again and again so most of the time I didn't bother. No matter, I preferred working over playing anyway.

I did small modeling jobs, presentations, or whatever was available. Only when rarely requested, did I have Mom or Larry with me at my jobs; otherwise, most of my bosses did not ask for an adult to be present. Larry coached me and said that I would be offered profitable acting parts if I knew how to sing because there were more musical productions produced than anything else.

Meanwhile, Larry sent me to an audition at the local community theater for my first real acting part. Well, almost real. I was auditioning to be an extra, one of the looney patients in *Harvey*. I was so short, that I could barely see the woman in the theatre's ticket booth. "Hi, I'm here to audition for the role as a patient in the play, *Harvey*," I announced to the ticket teller on my tiptoes.

"Take a seat," the woman replied as she continuously read her newspaper, as if she wished to be somewhere else, anywhere else but there.

I sat and waited in that theatre for what seemed like an eternity. I kept getting looks of annoyance from others in the room before realizing that I should probably stop fidgeting in my seat. It was taking forever and I had to get home. Mom was going to be worried.

After the audition, I sped my bike home in the dark, then ran into the house screaming, "I got the part! I got the part! Mom, I got the part!"

"Shhhh, don't you know your brother is sleeping?"

I whispered, "I got the part."

"What part?" Mom asked as she poured a glass of her *magic juice.*

"The part in the play, *Harvey*. You know, that guy with the rabbit. You're going to come see me, right?"

"Sure sweetie, whatever you want," Mom murmured, as she slumped down onto the couch and drifted off.

I skipped toward my room and when I reached Tommy's room, I stepped in to check on him. He was awake and playing in his crib. I leaned over him and whispered, "Guess what, your big sister is going to be a star. It's her time to shine." He gurgled and tried reaching for my hair. The smile on Tommy's face told me that he was proud of me. I tucked his binky around him before going off to my room to get ready for bed, but I couldn't sleep. I never wanted to forget this feeling. I wanted it etched in my memory forever.

I practiced the part over and over until I was actually doing it in my sleep so I was told. It was harder than I first imagined and that frustrated me. Just when I mastered the movements flawlessly, the director would whimper, "Oh, why don't we change this around?"

Oh, why don't we indeed? At that point, I wanted to change his face around. That aside, I loved being there. That's where I was christened JoJo. I used to hang around the elderly man (Isaac) who cared for the props. He stuttered and would call me Jo-Jo-Jordan. With everyone in a hurry and rushing around backstage, no one stuck around long enough to hear Isaac finish so everyone thought my name was JoJo. He's also the one who opened pandora's wonderful box of practical jokes for me.

Isaac and I would run-a-muck in the theatre with so many of our practical jokes, that it was a wonder we got any work done at all. One in particular was entertaining for me because I got to see the effects first hand. Isaac put black grease paint in the actor's cold cream jars, just beneath the top layer of cold cream. This joke didn't affect the show because the actors only used the cold cream at the end of the night's performances.

Opening night was exhilarating. What was I thinking? The dress rehearsal was exhilarating, but opening night was bigger than life, bigger than my dreams! I stepped through the looking glass that night. I'll never forget my first laugh. I did it. I got them to laugh! I now knew I had it in me and I could do it; I could make *her* laugh.

~*~:~*~:~*~:~*~:~*~:~*~

"Her? Don't you mean them?" asked Gladis, a nurse of African American descent standing in the doorway behind me. I was startled by the interruption, not knowing how long she'd been standing there. Gladis gave me a disapproving side glance, I assumed for being out of bed and in Zoë's room. Nonetheless, she put a blanket around me and headed for the door.

"Oh, um, sure," I answered, as I regained my composure and returned to my story for Zoë.

~*~:~*~:~*~:~*~:~*~:~*~

The curtain call was everything I imagined it would be, except it was for someone else. But that was okay; while I watched them bow and curtsy from stage left, I imagined myself being out there. I imagined them standing and applauding for *me*. The flowers were mine and the reviews were going to be great. I practiced my princess wave - of course, when someone saw me, I covered by saying I was just mocking them.

I sped all the way home on my bike that night, never sitting down on the seat. I was so excited about the evening, yet I was also worried wondering why Mom had never made it there. I was relieved when I found her in bed asleep and not on the basement floor. I glanced at her nightstand and discovered a half-empty glass of *magic juice.*

I sat up until the early hours of the morning with adrenaline still pumping through me. I couldn't wait to tell her of the night's events. From that night on, I was an actress.

About a month later during breakfast, Dad came into the kitchen and asked, "Hey Kitten, why didn't you tell your dear ole Dad you were a big stage actress?"

"I told you about the play last month when you were fixing the car, remember?"

"Oh, you know not to tell me things when I'm working on your mom's car. You know how it annoys me when she breaks things. I can't think about anything else at that moment."

I thought to myself, "No matter, the production closed last night." I finished up washing the breakfast dishes and skipped to my room to get my savings account book. I rode my bike to the bank to deposit my last paycheck from the production. I looked at my balance to make sure all of the money was listed and slipped the book back into my pocket.

During the next few days, I tried every way possible to persuade Dad to give me the money I needed for singing lessons, but he always muddled out some excuse - mostly blaming it on Mom's inability to budget. I knew I would have to forfeit my own money, even though it was earmarked for Christmas gifts. I had hoped this would be the first time ever that I was able to buy the gifts with my own money. I asked Larry for the name of a suitable singing coach, and he gave me the best he knew. I was excited to get started. I'd always wanted to learn to sing. I rode my bike to the bank, withdrew most of my money, and after returning home, I hid it under my dresser.

"Hey Kitten, what're you doing under there?" Dad asked as he popped his head into my room. I was startled by his interruption and didn't really hear his question.

"Hi Dad. I'm going to start singing lessons next week, any requests?" I hummed as I grabbed my hair brush and held it up to my mouth like a microphone. I acted as if I were already a singing sensation.

"I've always been partial to *Daddy's Little Girl*," he said teasing me.

We sat down to dinner that night and it was actually quite nice. Everyone was getting along and Dad was in a good mood for a change. Tommy was even cheery and not fussing like his usual self.

Monday morning came and I got ready for school. It wasn't until I was a little more awake and brushing my teeth that I remembered today was the day I would be starting my singing lessons. I hurried through making breakfast and rode off to school. The day seemed so long because of my excitement. I sprinted into the house with just enough time to grab the money, have a quick snack, and then ride on my bike to Mrs. Wesson's house for my first lesson. I reached under the dresser, swirled my hand around, but came out empty. I tried it again - *nothing*. I arched my head down and saw that the money was gone. A panic came over me and I trotted into the family room to ask Mom if she'd seen it.

"No sweetie, did you take it out and put it somewhere else and forget?"

"NO, I know it was there! I was all ready to go to Mrs. Wesson's. Is Dad home? Maybe he knows where it is," I questioned, then returned to my room to investigate further.

I could hear Mom's voice from a distance answering me. "No, he had to go on an unexpected business trip right after you left for school this morning. I don't know when he'll be back. You should call Mrs. Wesson if you're not going; it would be rude to leave her hanging."

After calling Mrs. Wesson, I felt humiliated. She must

have thought I was so irresponsible, so unprofessional. She was the best singing coach in town, and I was worried that she thought I'd just blown her off. I figure she'd never trust me enough again to ever agree to tutor me. And what about Larry? He said this training was necessary for me to get the prime acting roles.

As I sat there, I kept trying to figure out what had happened. I felt like calling the cops to report a robbery. "I know I left it there, didn't I? Now what am I gonna do?" I thought out loud.

The next morning, I got up and somberly rode my bike toward school, falling down and skinning my knee along the way. The scrape was bad enough that I had to go to the nurse's office and get it cleaned up. I couldn't believe what a klutz I was. I also couldn't help thinking about the great dresser robbery; the situation was still perplexing me. Were we really robbed after all? Did Tommy crawl into my room and eat it? He eats everything else that falls on the floor. I supposed that a big gust of wind blowing through my room was out of the question.

"Miss Walsh? Miss Walsh, I'd like an answer to my question," my teacher demanded as giggles from around the room drew me out of my thoughts.

"What?"

"No, *whooo*, Miss Walsh. Who was the first Indian to communicate with the Pilgrims?"

All of a sudden I realized that I was in class and my teacher was grilling me about history, and not about anything I knew. Since I had been too busy pouting over the lost money the night before, I forgot to study for the pass or fail oral quiz we were having that day. "Crap, and an Indian question too," I thought, "Dad's gonna kill me!"

"Any thoughts, Miss Walsh?" the teacher interrogated, tapping her pencil on my desk as if it were a ticking bomb. She turned away and posed the question elsewhere. "Okay Mr. Roberts, what's the answer?"

He stood and broadcasted, "Samoset was the first representative of the Indians that went to speak *in broken*

English to the Pilgrims, Mrs. Hudson."

"Brown-noser," I thought.

"Thank you, Mr. Roberts," our teacher vented as she scowled at me.

Needless to say, I got an F on the quiz and Mom grounded me for a week. She said that if I ever flunked another exam again I'd be grounded for the rest of my life. I spent the rest of the week with my nose in my school books. I'm not sure I was actually studying, but I wanted Mom to think so. It wasn't like I had anywhere else to go, not being able to afford my singing lessons. Now what? I figured I'd start over and just be more careful of what I did with my money. I guess, in a way, I got my singing lesson after all... I was sure singing the blues that week.

I had been set back to square one. Not only did I not have the money for singing lessons, I didn't have Christmas money either. I was forced to make gifts for everyone again that year, as I always had. Almost everyone said they liked those kind the best, but I still wished I had the money to buy them something. The only silver lining to that Christmas, was Gampy buying Gamma and I matching hairbrushes. They were *beautiful*. They were *magnificent*. The handles were scented with a lilac fragrance; hers was pink, and mine was powder blue. I knew I would cherish my brush forever.

I began begging Larry to put me to work doing anything so I could build up my savings account again. I continued to work, and by my eleventh birthday, I won my first primary-stage speaking role in *Little Women*. I did have to fight for the part though, since the casting director felt I might not be right for this play. She said my Southern accent made me sound like a hick - whatever that meant. No matter, I got it! I wanted the role of Beth because I felt I could show the depths of my work when she died at the end. But instead I won the role of Amy because of my age. Being in *Little Women* was the first time I was around a cast that treated me as an equal. I was one of them, not the extra who was bothersome and wasn't allowed to eat the food from the catering table. When I called Larry to tell him I got the part,

I asked what a hick was. He advised me not to listen to prejudiced people and just to focus on work - so I did.

After *Little Women*, I landed more theater roles effortlessly. I told Larry that all I wanted to do was work and make money. And that's what I did steadily for the rest of the year.

On my twelfth birthday, Ella came into my life. That was the first time I ever had something that was completely mine. I think of her as my first "puppy" love. Ah, *elephant* actually. She was the most beautiful elephant, well stuffed elephant, I'd ever seen. She was grey with pink ears and feet. She had a funny little tail and a pink bow around her neck. Her trunk was posed upward for good luck. Gamma gave her to me. Ella wasn't very big so I took her everywhere, inconspicuously hidden, of course. I didn't want anyone to think I was a baby. Ella seemed to be my lucky charm and I would prevail at everything when she was with me.

At that point, Gamma said she thought it was time I learned about good deeds. She said that since I had a lucky charm, I should share my newfound wealth with others by doing good deeds. I should do at least one good deed per day. It wouldn't have to be something like donating a kidney or anything, but a nice deed that I wouldn't normally think to do. Whenever I'd see Gamma, she'd want me to report my deeds to her.

I received so many more paying acting roles, that I finally got to take the singing lessons. It was hard work, but it was amazing. Larry even scheduled time in a recording studio for me, during the midnight shift, and I recorded various pop songs. They were far from reaching the top forties, but I was proud of them. That's okay, singing was secondary to what I really wanted to do anyway - that was, to be an actress.

I also continued to get grounded at home by Mom, primarily because I was spending so much more time studying lines than homework. Even during my worst semester in school, I managed to pull off a B-.

By the time my thirteenth birthday arrived, I guess Mom was tired of having me around so much because of being grounded, that she agreed to let me stay with Uncle Red for the weekend. More like *insisted*, actually. I loved going over there. During my stays, Uncle Red would divulge tons of details about the family. In fact, he was my strongest source of family information. Uncle Red would unleash many family skeletons from their proverbial closets. Richard was actually his given name, but he preferred others to call him what he considered to be a more earthy name like his Native American ancestors had. Uncle Red had a free spirit, and he was tired of living in Dad's shadow, being constantly compared to him. I always felt a little sorry for Uncle Red. He always seemed to be treated as an outcast, even though he was more educated, being an attorney, and more worldly. I'd heard others in the family say that their parents didn't acknowledge his achievements as much as their eldest son. So I suppose to compensate for it, he was more outgoing, charismatic, and friendly, which Dad wasn't. In short - a Leo.

~＊~:~＊~:~＊~:~＊~:~＊~:~＊~

After I returned to the present momentarily, I reached over and touched Zoë's hand to see if she was awake yet. She wasn't. I knew it was going to take more stories to awaken her so I continued.

"That was the time when I think I developed the first of my many idiosyncrasies. One of which was having to brush my long hair one hundred strokes before going to bed no matter how tired I was. That was also going to be a birthday that I would never forget. That was the first time I fell in love. Well, real love, and this loved one wasn't stuffed. Uncle Red introduced me to someone I would love deeply for the rest of my life."

~＊~:~＊~:~＊~:~＊~:~＊~:~＊~

Chapter II

Up in Smoke

As the end of our time together neared, Uncle Red wished me a happy thirteenth birthday once more and then drove me back home. That day had been my most perfect one thus far. It was the first time I'd fallen in love and she was beautiful.

When I returned home, Dad was in the family room reading his newspaper. I went in to greet him and tell him about Uncle Red's birthday present, but all he seemed to have time for was a grunt here and there.

"She's all I can think about, Dad. Perky personality, fluffy reddish-blonde hair, piercing white teeth, and a frisky energetic tail."

Dad looked up oddly at me from reading his newspaper and asked, "She? She who, Kitten?"

"My new puppy, Dad. Who did you think I was talking about? See here," I said as the furry fluff-ball danced around in a circle. "Uncle Red gave her to me. I named her Foxy Lady. She only weighs twenty-seven pounds, but she has a hardy bark."

"I don't like small dogs; they yap too much. Why didn't you ask your uncle for a German Shepard so it could at least protect the house?" Dad grumbled, as he sat back in his recliner and continued reading the newspaper.

"What do *we* have to protect?" I sniped, defending Foxy.

As I made my way to my bedroom with Foxy in tow trotting behind me, I heard Dad muttering something about insubordinate teenagers. He sort of brought me down by not admiring Foxy more, but I soon was cheery again with play from her. "How could anyone not like you? You are *so* cute. You look just like a fox, *my* Foxy Lady. And did you know that Foxy means irresistible?" I cooed at her.

During the next few weeks, I trained Foxy to do everything that I thought a well-behaved dog should learn. She was a hard worker and absorbed all of her lessons expeditiously. I sweet-talked Uncle Red into installing a fence around the backyard for her so Foxy would have somewhere to be during the day while I was in school. Mom did very little to help, but that was okay; I enlisted the assistance from others when I couldn't be there. Gamma was an enormous help, but I'm not sure I was comfortable with her coming by so often because she and Mom would get into shouting matches. I'm not sure what they were fighting about, but prayed it wasn't about Foxy.

Foxy *loved* her Champion Cheddar cheese crackers. She would try to steal the orange snacks every chance she got. She even tried to trick me to get to them. She'd jump around as if she had to go out for her walk so I would get up and walk to the door. When I'd get there, she'd dash back and snatch a cracker. *Clever girl.* She'd only execute that masquerade over those heavenly treats. She would never take anything else, not even if my dinner plate was sitting on the floor and I'd left the room. Of course, I would never be gone for more than a few minutes. I wouldn't expect *that* much from her. She would always snuggle up to me in bed too. I'm not sure that it was the best idea to let her up there because she would move around a lot when she was dreaming. Foxy would even bark in her sleep. I always thought she was dreaming about herding buffalo or something by the way she'd twitch her feet.

During that year, when I wasn't distracted by Foxy, I captured more theater speaking roles and would also earn my first part in a film. The movie part wasn't a speaking role, but it was in a major motion picture. Acting in a movie was different from the stage - boring actually. I'd stand around a lot doing nothing. I didn't have any lines to memorize so there wasn't much to do. I'd use that time to play my practical jokes.

So, by then, I had a film role I could put on my résumé. Larry thought that was significant because it would lead to bigger parts. And sure enough, it did. Larry snagged a number of them for me and began calling me his "little scene stealer." I wasn't sure what that meant so I just laughed along with him. I started getting film speaking-roles, and Larry said I was starting to get noticed. The newspaper reviews even began to call me, *Houston's Little Princess*.

~✻~¡~✻~¡~✻~¡~✻~¡~✻~¡~✻~

"But as I was about to learn, all that would have to wait."

Gladis coerced me into eating some fruit while she changed my I.V. Once she was done, I continued telling Zoë my story.

~✻~¡~✻~¡~✻~¡~✻~¡~✻~¡~✻~

This was another memorable birthday in my life. I was home with Mom and Tommy. Mom was entertaining her girlfriends.

"Jordan!" Mom called from the family room.

"I'm right here, Mom," I yelled back from the kitchen.

"Why don't you come in here and say hi to everyone? You're the birthday girl, the main attraction, the center of attention," she said with malice, mocking me. Mom was drunk once again, sloshing around her *magic juice* as she slurred her words.

"Stop it," I demanded as I retreated from the room.

"No, no, come on. Come on back here. It's your day. You're sweet sixteen today. Be sweet already," she blistered.

"Mom, I'm fourteen remember?"

"Fourteen, ya sure? Well, that doesn't roll off the tongue very easily does it?" Mom slurred as she encouraged laughter from her drunken girlfriends. They'd made a mess in the kitchen mixing their concoctions, and I knew I'd be the one who'd eventually have to clean it up.

"I'm going over to Uncle Red's, goodnight," I conveyed with disgust. I jogged to the phone, called Uncle Red, and he was more than happy to come get us - Ella, Foxy and I. I packed an overnight bag and was out the door before Uncle Red arrived. We swung by the grocery store and picked up a chocolate cake, ice cream, and some snacks. And, of course, Champion Cheddar for Foxy.

When we arrived at Uncle Red's, I discovered that he had a friend staying with him that evening; his name was Sam. This friend was a real nice gentle guy. He was not as tall as Uncle Red and he seemed younger, and more muscular. His bulk looked strange to me because he was a bit matronly, always tending to us and acting as if he lived there. Sam even knew where Uncle Red kept the cake platter that only came out twice a year.

We talked some about what had happened with Mom. "I'm tired of it all and just want to forget about it for one day, especially my birthday," I grumbled.

"Then it shall be, Queen Joey. Today is the holiest of days, and it will be published that only good thoughts resonate on this day, and until the end of time," Uncle Red stated as he bowed to me, the ruler of all Joeyland.

I donned my kitchen towel cape and accepted my monarchy and knighted both of them with a wooden spoon. We then talked about the future and we categorically solved all of the problems of the world. However, I was tired and said I could sleep for a week. I led Foxy outside for her royal nightly walk, gave her majesty a Champion Cheddar, then retired for the night in Uncle Red's spare bedroom.

When I awoke, I looked at the digital clock on the nightstand; it read 3:37 in big red numbers. It was a moment before I realized that I was awoken by Uncle Red's ringing telephone. I heard Uncle Red's voice as I tried hard to listen to what he was saying.

It sounded like "Hel-lo. What? Are you sure? Where is she now? Ahuh, ahuh. Okay, we'll be right there."

Uncle Red knocked on the bedroom door and I quickly answered, "It's okay. I'm awake, come in."

"Get dressed. We have to go."

"What? *Why*?"

"I'll tell you on the way."

"Okay, I'll be there in five minutes." I put Foxy in the utility room, and then told Sam - who had been sleeping on the couch - that Foxy would be okay to be left in there. Next, I quickly hopped into the car where Uncle Red was waiting.

"What's going on?" I asked as if it were the same old crap with Mom.

"Your mom has really done it this time. She's burnt down the house and is in the hospital."

"What?! Where's Tommy?!" I asked with a panic in my voice.

Before I could say any more, Uncle Red interrupted and added, "She's okay, just a little smokey, but there's more. The police were called, and when your mom is discharged, she'll be arrested for endangering a minor."

"Where's Tommy?" I asked in a calmer way, but more forcefully in order to know.

"Tommy's okay, he's with your grandmother. She stopped by the house after you left to give you your birthday present, and she didn't like the state your mom was in so she took Tommy home with her. But the police have witnesses saying your mom was drunk long before Tommy left the house."

I looked at Uncle Red knowing he knew what I was about to say. "You have to help her, Uncle Red. You know that, right?"

"I'll do what I can, Joey."

I was scared to enter her hospital room. Mom was hooked up to monitors and they were beeping, buzzing and flashing. The nurse nudged me in and explained what she was attached to and what every machine was doing. She told me that Mom's injuries were minimal and those monitors were there just to be certain nothing else was wrong with her. That information made me feel a little better.

"Why isn't she awake?"

"I guess it's because of how much she consumed.

She'll be fine in the morning," assured the nurse.

After sitting with Mom a while, I wandered out to the waiting room to see Uncle Red. "Where's Dad? Have you been able to reach him?"

"No, not yet."

"You know, you don't have to stay," I told him. "You need to get some sleep so you'll be rested when you talk to the judge in the morning."

"No, I'm not going to just leave you here all by yourself. What'ya crazy?" he teased, trying to cheer me up.

So we sat there together through the early morning hours until Uncle Red left to speak to the judge when the courthouse opened. I soon learned that the news was not good. Turns out this wasn't the first time Mom had been in trouble. I didn't know about the other times, but Uncle Red did. He said he wanted to spare me the circumstances.

"The judge wants to speak to you in his chambers bright and early on Monday morning to get things straightened out," informed Uncle Red.

"Me? Why? What things?"

"It's just a formality, Joey. Don't worry. I'll be right there with you. But the good news is, you get to spend the weekend with your grandparents, that's great, huh?"

The next morning, I rose to the smell of something heavenly that seemed to possess me to meander down the stairs where Gamma was already fixing breakfast in the kitchen. Tommy was on the floor crashing his trucks together. Foxy was outside gnawing on a bone given to her by Gamma. I could hear the television in the family room where I assumed Gampy was.

"Why didn't you wake me? I can do that," I said to Gamma.

"No, you don't have to cook when you're here, dear."

"I kinda like to. You taught me - that's why I like it."

"That's sweet of you, Jordan dear. However, I like to cook too and you need this time to do your homework. I never thought I would have to fight over the cooking duties in this house," she teased, as to take a jab at Mom's non-culinary skills.

It wasn't until she mentioned that, that it hit me. All of my stuff had been lost in the fire. It was the first time I was able to stop for a moment and visualize everything that I, and Tommy, lost from it. "Crap," I thought, "and all of my homework I'll have to do over again. And all of my photographs with Dad. And all of my school books. Ah well, maybe that's not so bad." But I kept inventorying, over the weekend, of what all was gone forever. The only good thing was that, now I wouldn't have to clean up the mess Mom and her girlfriends made in the kitchen. Tommy got out of the ordeal with some clothes and his binky. I - not so lucky. But I did have Foxy, Ella and the hair brush that Gampy gave me; basically what I had taken to Uncle Red's. "I can't believe Tommy still sleeps with that thing, but I could use a binky right about now," I pouted to Gamma.

When Monday morning arrived, I was chauffeured over to the courthouse by Uncle Red. We waited forty-five minutes to speak to the judge, which made my anxiety rise. I kept getting looks of annoyance from the lady behind the desk, before realizing I should probably stop fidgeting in my seat, which was starting to become a habit with me.

We entered the judge's office, exchanged greetings, and he asked Uncle Red and me to sit.

"Do you know why you are here today, Jordan?" asked the judge.

"Not really. I know what happened to our house and to Mom the other night."

"Do you know that she's been in my courtroom before?"

"Yes, I was told."

"Seven other times?"

I sat there in a daze. Seven? How could that be? "No."

"Yes, and each time your mother said she would stop drinking, that she would take better care of five-year-old Tommy."

That brought it all home for me - when he called Tommy by name, it put a personal spin on it. I nodded.

"I'm not going to be returning your brother or you to her custody. Do you know what that means?"

"We won't be living with her?"

"That's right."

"Who will we be living with?"

"We have a nice family that we'll place you with until your dad can be reached. Jordan, I want you to know that there is a good chance I won't be placing you or your brother back with either of your parents any time soon. Your dad has been here too, promising he would take care of the situation, but there are still problems. He is actually in contempt of court right now for not showing up for your mother's last arraignment when I ordered him to."

"What's that mean? What's an a-rraign-ment and a contempt?" I asked the judge, but glanced over at Uncle Red.

"Well, all that means is she was given some instructions to follow. And your father was suppose to be here to make sure she followed those instructions. Since he wasn't here, he is now in some trouble with the court and needs to answer some questions from us."

"Why can't we live with my Uncle Red or my grandparents?" I asked, turning to Uncle Red and asking him with my facial expression.

As the judge looked up from his paperwork at Uncle Red, he answered, "Maybe we'll look at that for you down the road, but right now you'll have to go where the courts indicate. These people have been assessed by the courts and we know they will be good to you. Your uncle may be a real nice person, but it's up to the courts to make sure you are safe, and we don't know anything about him yet."

I felt sick. I wanted to cry, but I wasn't going to let the judge see me do that, because he could take Tommy away from me too, if he thinks I'm such a baby.

Tommy was confused and it was a tearful separation from Gamma, Gampy, Uncle Red and Foxy. Gamma whispered to me how it was my duty as an older sister to watch over Tommy, just as I always had, but even more now. I held Tommy tight as we drove to our new home. He was so brave, probably because he was used to strangers caring for him when Mom wasn't able to. I cried more than he did.

Tommy and I moved in with the Burtons. They were a nice couple, but Mr. Burton was always trying to hug on me and it felt weird, phony, just icky. I couldn't wait for us to get out of there; the whole house smelled like moth balls. They put us in separate rooms; however, when the Burtons turned in for the night, Tommy would tiptoe into my room, crying, asking for his *Sissy*. A few times I heard the doorknob rotate late in the night and that was spooky so I'd push a chair up to the door after Tommy snuck over. I was so anxious to leave, that I only used one drawer in the dresser making it quicker to pack.

Since Uncle Red was taking care of Foxy for me, I wouldn't have to worry about her. But I missed her desperately. I missed how she'd snuggle up to me at night and try to steal pillow space.

Uncle Red told me that Dad hadn't come back to court when the judge told him to, once again, so after a week the cops handcuffed him and took him to jail. The judge was furious and invoked community service on Dad, where he had to clean up trash-covered streets all over town. Mom wasn't as lucky. She spent thirty days in jail and was given community service on top of that. Neither Mom nor Dad was allowed to see us until they completed their punishments.

Meanwhile, a social worker kept dropping by to ask us questions. The Burtons would coach us with the answers that they *expected* us to convey to her. Tommy didn't know any better so he told the social worker whatever they wanted him to say. I just kept my mouth shut and nodded responses to whatever she asked.

Finally, the best news came when they allowed Tommy and me to move in with Gamma and Gampy - as a temporary custody arrangement. We were *so* happy. I hugged Tommy as we both leaped into their car like fish flipping back into the water. We were finally settled down by dinnertime that night. I felt sick. I needed to sleep. I don't think that I had gotten more than three hours of sleep a night during the past month. As I laid down, Gamma stroked my hair. I took a deep breath. I thought, "We're home. We're *finally* safe."

Soon, Tommy was in a new school and was getting used to his new kindergarten class schedule. The courts approved Mom's petition to have supervised visits with us as long as she would stay on the schedule the courts provided. This was so she wouldn't wreak havoc on our school schedules or show up at midnight to see us. Tommy loved the days Mom would visit, but I kept my distance. No matter, she always liked him better anyway.

I found out that the courts wouldn't let us live with Uncle Red because he was a single man and I was a teenager. Not sure I understood, but we got to see him whenever we wanted. And Tommy and I were fine where we were.

When I did go stay with Uncle Red, Sam was there most of the time. Uncle Red mentioned Sam had moved in and that they were roommates. Sam and Uncle Red got along good, except for this one time I heard them arguing late at night when I visited for the weekend. Sam said something about asking Uncle Red why he couldn't tell his family because Sam had told his. I'm not sure what that was all about. Nevertheless, most of the time they were a lot of fun to be around so I didn't worry about it.

The bad part of staying with Gamma and Gampy was that they made us visit the dentist, which Mom never did. Gamma would bug us to brush our teeth morning, noon and night. She'd also ask me every day what my good deed was. That meant I couldn't fudge on it anymore. I liked doing the good deeds most of the time, but sometimes it was hard to come up with them.

The good part was, that Foxy got her own room when I was at school. Gampy built her a room in the basement so she wouldn't have to be outside all of the time. I put together a bed for her with old sheets and blankets and even some clothes with my scent on them so she would know I was close by. I even put Tommy's old binky down there, but never told him because he would have had a melt-down.

One day about six weeks after moving in, I stepped

into the family room where Gampy was watching television. All I saw was a bunch of people running around screaming and letters flying across the screen that didn't make words. It was confusing, but I was intrigued because Gampy was so uncharacteristically excited. I think that was the first time I realized that I liked figuring out puzzles and problem-solving. Gampy was sweet, even though I felt like a pest, and he tried to explain the basics of it. He promised he would quiz me every day on what the stock market was doing so I could learn slowly and not get overwhelmed. It was fun. He taught me what a PE ratio was of companies and quizzed me on material such as what a front-end load and a back-end load was. I think that made him happy to share that world with someone. He probably always thought it would be Tommy.

While two months has passed since we moved in with Gamma and Gampy, Dad had not been out to see us. Gamma remarked that it was because he disliked them and she tried to cover for him as much as she could, but I knew better. Mom appeared to be drinking less, but had her binges now and then.

After school one afternoon, I walked into the kitchen where I found Gamma fixing one of my favorite dinners. It always smelled like a home in their house, in what was now *our* house. Nowhere else on earth smelled as good to me, not even at the bakery, although that was a close second.

"Hello, Jordan dear. How was your day today at school?"

"Good. Nothing notable."

"Larry called."

"Oh thanks. Did he say what he wanted?"

"No, just to call him back when you get in. You know you can't do any more acting until your grades come up to a solid B, right Jordan?"

"Yes ma'am," I answered as I trotted upstairs to use the telephone.

"Are you sitting down?!" Larry asked with excitement in his voice.

"What? What's going on, Larry?" I responded, mirroring his enthusiasm.

"You're being sought after by a casting director who saw you in *Muddy Streams* last year. She admitted that she kept you in mind all this time until a role came up for you. She also said that you are perfect for this role and wants you to fly to New York for an audition."

"Wow, that's great - to New York?! What kind of a part is it? Oh, but Gamma isn't too happy about this line of work and it will be two more weeks before I get my grades. She won't let me do any acting until she sees them. But I know I'm doing well in all of my classes because they made me have conferences with all my teachers."

"That's okay. I'll apprise them of your *unavailably* until next month. That will make them want you even more," Larry responded, chuckling. Then he added, "Only condition, you mention me in your Acclamation Award acceptance speech." With that, Larry laughed again. "Call me when you get everything straight with the grandparents. Bye."

Things progressed as planned. I increased my grade level to a B+, and Gamma would allow me to fly to New York City with one condition - Gampy would go with me instead of Larry. Everyone was agreeable to that. Larry messengered over all the information.

This was exciting, my first airplane ride. The Flight Attendants gave us a safety demonstration, which I watched intensively, primarily because I thought they would quiz me afterwards. It was only a little scary when the plane ride started feeling bumpy, but Gampy told me it was just normal turbulence. The Flight Attendants were very nice and gave us lunch, plus they gave me *a whole can* of soda. They even gave us a bag of peanuts, dry roasted - my new favorite kind.

Everything went fine with our excursion. Gampy and I stayed at a very exquisite hotel and we had dinner in their elegant dining room. The next day at the audition, several people attended, but only three were there for the part I was up for. The audition was always the best part for me. The audition was the only time that an actor got to interpret the role and perform it the way they wanted to.

Gampy bribed the cabby to take a detour, and we drove by the New York Stock Exchange on Wall Street before returning to the airport. Gampy was explaining where everything was and who worked where. He was as giddy as a school boy the whole plane ride back, where we were upgraded to first class by the casting director. But it was good to be home, as it had been an exhausting trip. We found Gamma on the back porch with Foxy and Tommy.

"How'd ya do, little starlet?"

"Oh Gamma, I'm not a starlet - YET," I shouted as I showed her the production schedule. "We start filming this summer so I don't have to miss any school. Isn't that great?"

"That's a plus," she responded coolly.

"We'll film for six weeks, and the location is only twenty-five miles from here - that's great too, huh?"

"That's definitely another plus. Congratulations," Gamma expressed as she gave me a quick hug. Then she gave a quick look of disapproval to Gampy.

"They want someone who speaks like a Texan. This is a larger role than I've ever had before. I'm in almost every scene."

"What was your good deed today, Jordan?"

"I tipped the taxi driver in New York an extra dollar out of my own pocket, Gamma," I answered before trotting out to the backyard with Foxy.

Before I could get all the way out the patio door, Gampy commented to Gamma, "Annie, I think it would be good for her to get her mind off everything that's been going on around here."

After that, the film roles avalanched in. I was back on track again. At the time of my fifteenth birthday, Gamma reluctantly agreed to let me drop out of public school - but only if I could afford to pay for my own tutor and take the state-required tests. Larry was able to find a management company to look after my wages and expenses, which would also be monitored by Gampy. Mom still had legal control over the account since Gamma and Gampy were just our temporary guardians. However, Gampy told her that he was going to be the one who cared for it. I also had to pay for a chaperone while I was working on the sets. I ditched her most of the time though.

Looking back, I'd made four movies in less than two years. Two were musicals, and I got a chance to use my singing voice in one of the movies.

I continued to play my practical jokes for each of the productions and continuously evaded capture. I could hear the props lady squeal, knowing there were plastic spiders glued to jumping beans in the treasure chest. On the last film, I dusted itching powder onto the director's toilet tissue. He must have been a little upset because I could hear him hollering all the way to the mess tent. With all the drama going on lately, I needed some comic relief.

Larry was driving a Lincoln now and calling himself, *Mr. Larry, agent to the stars.* I had accumulated a nice nest egg of my own and was dreaming of the sports car I would purchase, when I got my license next week. Things were good and I was having fun again. I knew this birthday would be a good one.

"Happy birthday to you, happy birthday to you, happy birthday dear Jorrrrrdannnn, happy birthday to you!"

"Wow, thanks."

Tommy was jumping up and down, "Blow 'em out! Blow 'em out! Sissy, blow 'em out!"

"Whew." I knew that he just wanted dessert, but that was okay - so did I. It was Gamma's famous delectable chocolate cream pie with little pink roses made of frosting, my favorite. Even Foxy was jumping up and down, but for her Champion Cheddar.

Mom walked up to me and said, "You really are sweet sixteen today, sweetie. I'm really proud of you. You know that right?"

"Sure Mom." I gave her a quick hug and changed the subject. "Did you see Tommy's grades, all A plusses."

"He's my little Thomas Edison," Mom boasted as she tousled his hair and watched him eat his dessert.

"What's another name for futures?"

"Commodities - that was an easy one, Gampy. Try

again."

"Okay... what's the ticker symbol for Consolidate Acme & Associates?"

"Ah, I'll have to get back to you on that one," I responded as everyone laughed.

"HA, smarty pants," he teased.

"What was your good deed for today, Jordan?" Gamma inquired.

"You mean I have to do that on my birthday too?!"

"*Jordan?*"

"I'm just kidding, Gamma. Since I had some free time today after my tutoring session, I went by the senior center on my way home and donated my time by reading to them for a while."

"Good girl," said Gamma smiling at me as the telephone began to ring.

"Hel-lo. Hey, how ya doing? Long time no call. Okay, hang on - Joey, your dad."

As Uncle Red handed me the phone, I could see that everyone, except Tommy, was looking at me soberly. They seemed to be waiting to catch a glimpse of how I was going to handle speaking with him after such a long time.

"Hi, Dad, where are you? No kidding. Okay. Okay, when? Okay. Bye."

I didn't offer any information after hanging up the telephone, and no one asked for it. We resumed the party for another hour while I opened gifts, and then everyone said their good-byes.

"Thank you for my birthday party, Gamma," I said as I gave her a hug. "I'm going up to bed now. It was a good day today, wasn't it?"

"Yes, dear. Are you going to see your dad?"

I nodded as I left. I could tell she wanted to ask more, but I was excited about seeing him and didn't want any negative thoughts about it.

The next day, Dad drove by to pick me up. He told me to wait outside because he didn't want to talk to anyone else.

"Hi Kitten, how's Daddy's little girl?"

"Hi Dad. I'm not a little girl anymore," I said, noticing that he'd aged quite a bit.

"I can see that," he replied as he drove into the parking lot of a nearby café. Once we were seated, he said, "Guess what? Your dad's got his life straightened out with the courts, and he wants you to come back to live with him. What'ya think of that?"

"What? How'd that happen?" I inquired with caution in my tone.

"I returned to the courts and showed them that I was a good guy, and they said I could take you back."

"What about Tommy? You didn't mention Tommy."

"Oh, of course, I want Tommy too, but I can only handle one of you right now and I chose you. Isn't that great?"

I sat there with a blank look on my face, not knowing how to feel - much less what to say. I didn't want to be uprooted again. I didn't want to be separated from Tommy, no matter how irritating he could be. If Dad didn't want Tommy, would he not want Foxy too? And what about Mom?

"And what about Mom? You two getting back together?" I asked.

"Well no, not right now, Kitten. The courts won't return you to me if she lives with us. But I'm sure we can work something out, and it'll all get straightened out soon."

"Dad, it's been two years, and we've heard from you only a half dozen times and the last time was almost a year ago."

"Yeah, I know Kitten - but like I told you, I've been working real hard to get back on track so I can take you back. Don't you want our family to get back together?"

I could feel the pressure Dad was putting on me, the guilt I was feeling. Was I so selfish that I couldn't be a little charitable?

Well, the courts didn't give me any other option; they determined that I would be better off living with a parent than a grandparent. Since Dad was not petitioning for custody of Tommy, they didn't consider him. So I moved, *again.* We lived in a small one-bedroom apartment that had been converted from a motel room. Right away I noticed that it smelled funny. Dad set up a pullout sofa bed for me in the living room. When the court-appointed social worker would visit us, Dad would take me over to an *acquaintance* girl-friend's two bedroom apartment and say we lived there. The social workers didn't seem to care enough to investigate much; they just filled out their forms and left.

I asked Gampy if I could leave Foxy with him and Gamma for a while until I got settled. No matter, it only took two weeks before Dad tricked me into signing some forms to empty out my bank account, sold all my stocks, and then abandoned me for a business trip. When the courts found out that he'd left me there for over a week by myself, they reversed their order.

Apparently, that was Dad's only chance to make things right. He assured the judge that he was truly a changed man and also told the judge that he had a nice two bedroom apartment all lined up for us. When all of that didn't work, Dad threatened to make a big stink in the press if they didn't return me to him. Of course, I heard all of this from Uncle Red, who was, as I suspected, the little birdie who reported to the court that I was being left alone. Uncle Red never admitted his part in that though.

I was ecstatic to be moving back in with Tommy, Gamma and Gampy.

"Well, here I am, broke and unemployed again," I said to Gamma and Gampy sitting in the kitchen with them. "Guess I'll have to take the bus from now on, since I don't have any money for a car now."

"It's not your fault, dear. Don't even think for a moment that you had anything to do with this mess. And besides, you'll always be rich when you have the love of all of us - right Jordan?"

"You always know how to make me feel better, Gamma."

"What's the PE ratio of GE this morning, Jordan?" Gampy asked, desperate to change the subject. Not waiting for an answer, he added, "Annie, we have a future stock broker on our hands."

Soon after, Gamma and Gampy received permanent custody of me, and of Tommy. Mom finally divorced Dad. They hadn't lived together for over two years, since the night Mom burnt down the house.

"Little did I know, that wouldn't be the end of my troubles with Dad. I was in for a much worst time, and I'd have to fight for my life and for my freedom. But this time, Larry would be there to help me. This was when I learned how to be ruthless." I dramatically said to Zoë, trying to entice her to wake up and ask questions. She didn't so I continued...

~✳~¡~✳~¡~✳~¡~✳~¡~✳~¡~✳~

Chapter III

Divorce and Marriage

A few months after settling back into life living with Tommy, Gamma and Gampy, I stood looking into my full-length mirror. I was all depressed that I didn't have any money - no money to buy *anything* in order to pull myself out of my depression. As I looked into the mirror at my 5'5" frame and long red hair, all I could see was that I had no clothes to speak of, no car, no boyfriend, and not even a friend in sight. But I did have wonderful grandparents and a halfway decent brother. I figured that was enough for the time being.

I returned to work doing high-profile films. I was starting to get noticed in Hollywood and was offered main character roles. I was even popular enough to be mentioned in a tabloid, even though the article was mostly about Mom's *activities*. I'd had some fairly good roles and was able to turn down the ones I wasn't interested in. Larry said a *real* star was able to turn down roles. He was becoming more finicky about the scripts he presented to me to read.

I got my share of pressure from other agents who claimed it was time to leave the small town guy behind. They promised me everything under the sun, but I stayed loyal to Larry. Not only because I believed in him, but also because Larry was a hoot and I liked having him in my life. He never reminded me of a fast-talking schmoozer wheeler-dealer like Dad.

And speaking of which, Dad was continuing to make a mess out of his life, and as I discovered soon enough, he would again make a mess out of mine. During the week he'd left me alone in the apartment, Dad had signed a contract with a casting agency for my services. He was paid a huge retainer to sign me and then split with the money. And Dad had left me to clean up the mess. I had to pay it off if I didn't want to get stuck doing risque roles, to put it nicely, for the next five years. Larry was livid. We pooled our money to abolish the contract. We offered the sleazy casting agent half the amount and claimed we would expose them for producing child pornography if they balked. This was hard ball and it toughened me up. It was my first lesson about ruthlessness.

Larry and I counseled with Uncle Red. The two of them determined that the casting agency probably had no legal claim but we wanted it over with. Apparently the agency didn't want to take the risk because they accepted our offer and then threatened to go after Dad for the rest of the money. No matter, they were out of my life. I now owed Larry a bundle of money and knew I would have to work for a good long time to pay him off - but he had saved my life. So much for turning down roles.

One morning a week later, Gamma asked, "Are you ready?"

"Yes, I need to do this," I answered.

"Then let's go."

Gampy, Gamma and I met Uncle Red at the courthouse and headed into the courtroom, yet again. The session only took twenty minutes and then it was over. I trotted upstairs to the clerk's office to get my copy of the court documents "divorcing" me from having any financial responsibility to or from Dad ever again. A "divorce" from a parent was a bit unusual and somewhat drastic, but it would legally free me from Dad's villainous antics.

We stopped for pizza before returning home. As a family, we ate dinner - Gampy, Gamma, Tommy and I, and even Foxy snuck a little piece of crust.

"You okay?" asked Gamma as she cleared the table.

"Never bedda," I slurred, trying to sound as if I were

a Yankee, using the accent I'd learned from my last film. I think I was more mad than sad. That whole ordeal had been a hard hit on me financially. I was a little sad at what had conspired and how drastic it was, but I was now rid of Dad's shenanigans forever. The "divorce" took care of that.

A week had passed when Gampy stormed into the kitchen where the rest of us were hanging out, talking and doing homework. He seemed agitated. "What the hell is that? Outside, did you see it?" he blistered.

We all appeared shocked, as it was not in his character to be so emotional about anything - except his stock market. Even Gamma said she thought a bulldozer was sitting outside raring to mow down the house. We all raced outside to see what catastrophe was waiting for us this time. And there it stood. There it was in all its glory. A bright shiny red beauty. There was my new car. Okay, well it was six years old, missing the back bumper, and rusted out in various places, but it still had four wheels, and not bike pedals. It was an old red Chevy Impala and not the red sports car that I had wanted - but it was mine - and it was beautiful - and it was *freedom*. Gampy said he wanted me in a safe car - so this car not only protected like a tank, it drove and looked like one too.

Gampy rode with me most of the time to fulfill my learner's permit obligation because Gamma was such a back seat driver, that she would constantly be grabbing the dashboard anytime I was stepping on the gas pedal. She really wasn't doing her job having her eyes closed most of the time anyway, probably praying. Gamma didn't like to ride with us because Gampy and I would talk about the stock market, which bored her anyway. After I got my license, Foxy and I drove everywhere in *the tank*. Only down side, I now had to chauffeur Tommy around, but at least I got to drive. Tommy said it was cool to ride around with his 'Sissy.' He told all of his friends and I had to give them rides too. But mostly just to school and to their batting practice on the weekends when I was in town.

"No Tommy, don't get out on that side. Get out over

here so you don't get run over, 'kay?"

"'Kay, Sissy, bye. See ya lata, ali-gata." And off he ran into the school, dragging his bat, without looking back, or even to hear my "after-awhile-crocodile" comeback.

After the last ordeal, I just wanted to work. I started back acting at Houston's most prestigious theater just to get some applause, which helped to mend my bruised ego, after having let Dad walk all over me. When that production closed, I was ready for a movie role. Actually, I *craved* it. I wanted it more than ever. It was like a *marriage* to me, Gamma would say. I'm not sure I understood what a marriage was, especially after witnessing my parents', but I was devoted to acting, that was for sure.

The morning of my trip to the production site, Gamma came into my bedroom as I was packing and asked if I needed anything else for my trip. She gave me her little speech as she always did, as if I'd never heard it before.

"Make us proud, be polite, make them think we raised you properly. You have Ella?"

I nodded. "Of course, Gamma. I won't let you down."

Gamma and Gampy drove me to the airport and as I sat on the plane, I did some soul-searching, thinking about where to take my life from here. I knew I needed a distraction, someone I could be with, hang out with - a friend or someone more. What did I want in my life? "Less drama would be nice," I thought.

I was sixteen and everyone seemed to think I should have a boyfriend, except Gamma, of course. I didn't really know any boys. In fact, I didn't even have any friends for that matter. I was sweet sixteen and had never been kissed - how pathetic was that? Could I make some new friends during the making of this movie, maybe even something more? I wasn't sure I'd even trust another male with the way Dad had treated me. But Uncle Red and Gampy were nice, so maybe I would find someone like them.

My anticipation was growing to such a level, that I was already missing the new friends I hadn't made yet, and the boyfriend I hadn't met yet. I entered the production with growing optimism.

"Please don't go Frankie, I don't know what I'll do without you," I pleaded.

"I'll come back for you, I promise. After the war is over, we'll get married and build a house. Would you like that?" Frankie asked.

"Yes, yes Frankie, please be careful. Come back to me in one piece," I begged as we slightly kissed before he hopped aboard. I began walking along with the train. Then I stepped back and watched as the train sped up and it finally faded out of sight. I stood there motionless, waiting for a signal.

"Cut! That's a wrap, folks. Don't forget to return all the props to the props department before you go. Do not take *any* of them with you," I heard the director dictate as I swiftly walked toward my trailer. "God, I'm glad that's over," I thought. "I think he's eaten sardines every single day of this stinkin' movie."

"Hey JoJo, you going to the wrap party tonight?" came a voice from over my shoulder, trying to catch up with me.

"Oh no, Tim, I have to catch a flight back home tonight," I said to one of the grips as I hoofed it faster toward my trailer.

I played my final practical joke on the film crew. I put a picture of a baby's face on the rear view mirror of the humongous macho front gate guard's car. I wrote the caption, "You have the cutest little baby face," at the bottom. I also put a tape of a baby crying in his tape deck so that when the guard turned on his car, it would start playing. I finished packing my things including a box of Champion Cheddar for Foxy, put Ella in my carry-on bag, and headed for the airport.

I sat on the plane thinking about my life - *again*. My responsible side told me that I had to accept any role that came to us in order to pay Larry back, and it was killing me that I couldn't choose the roles that I wanted. I suppose I could have, but I felt obligated to pay him off just as soon as I possibly could.

"Hi Miss Walsh, can I have your autograph?" a little

face asked as I spun my head around in my plane seat to see who was talking to me.

"Of course you can. What's your name?" I asked as she handed me her autograph book.

"Annie," she answered.

"Wow, Annie, that's a great name," I said as it reminded me of Gamma. "What grade are you in and do you like school, Annie?"

She answered my questions as she retrieved the book from me, smiled, and stepped over to her mother who was standing close by. They returned to their seats.

"Wow. That was a first. Someone asking *me* for my autograph? I can't believe it," I thought, thrilled to have such a request. "I hope I was friendly enough. I hope I was smiling after the day I've had! I love this business, but sometimes the roles suck."

That flight was memorable for another reason as well - the turbulence was frightening, and I thought it would take me a week to shake the feeling and get the equilibrium back into my body.

I was returning home late and tried not to wake anyone with my notoriously loud clumsiness. I found Gampy still awake and fidgeting in his hobby shop. We exchanged greetings and chatted a while before I dragged myself up to bed.

The next month brought mixed emotions. I was excited, but I was apprehensive too. I knew that my next movie would be the most important one of my career. It was the moment I had been waiting for. This movie was what it was all about. I was finally in a comedy. "I hope those acting workshops pay off and I will have comedic timing," I thought. Plus, I was going to meet her - my idol.

"I've done so many dramas and tragedies, I don't know if anyone will pay to see me in a comedy," I worried, before Gampy tried to ease my nervousness by getting my mind on something else.

"What's the PE ratio of General Dynamics?"

"13."

"International Accounting Equipment?"

"24."

"You ready to go, Joey?"

"Yes, Uncle Red."

"What time is your flight?"

"Not for a few hours, but I want to get there in plenty of time. You never know what the traffic will be like."

The flight seemed to go by faster than I expected. I had butterflies in my stomach by the time I was making my way onto the production site. Not only was I going to meet her, I was really going to work with her. I kept thinking and wondering how much she made for her movies and giggled thinking it must have been millions of dollars. I mean, after all, it was *her*. I was shown to the trailer that I would be sharing with two other actresses. We made our introductions, then the three of us walked toward the reception room to check in. As we left, I remember thinking, "Today was going to be a Red-letter day in my personal history book. *Today* I would meet Lexy."

"Okay, be cool. Don't act stupid," I kept silently repeating to myself as I walked toward the rehearsal room. Nevertheless, that was not to be. I tripped and fell down right in the doorway as I walked in. No, not *too* embarrassing - only about twenty people saw it and laughed. I bowed and then hobbled over and sat down across from where my name card was. I could see many famous people around the large table and also others walking around the room. Everyone was schmoozing and shaking hands as if they were old friend and good buddies. I sensed a familiarity in it as I did with Dad's friends, and it made me uneasy and mistrusting of them. Then in walked Lexy. Many of those people just stopped talking and stared at her as if they were star-struck too.

We introduced ourselves around the table and announced the part we were cast in, until it was Lexy's turn - being last. Lexy stood there bigger than life, beautiful; I was in awe. Alexandria Sherman was her full name. She was fresh off the plane from London, which she called home being British and all. Lexy had dishwater-blonde straight hair, a fair complexion, and a slender body. She was a year and some older than me; I wasn't sure exactly how much. Lexy had the reputation of being a party girl, and also ambitious and competitive - but hearing her speak, I witnessed a teenager with a gentle and kind heart. Out of the corner of my eye, I spotted a tabloid that someone had folded under their arm. On it was Lexy's picture. I could barely catch the title, but it had something to do with "Celebrities, born rich."

As I watched the activities of the day, I observed everyone there and how I thought it would be to work with each of them. I tried to figure out what everyone's sign was, but there was one that I couldn't be wrong about. Lexy had to be a Gemini. I would stake my life on it.

After what seemed like hours of discussing the scenes, we finally got our first break of the day, and I wandered over to the catering table to get some food with my new roommates. I was famished because I was too nervous to eat breakfast. I could hear Lexy talking to someone as she walked up behind us. Suddenly Lexy abruptly turned to me and nearly shouted, "Hi Pookie, how are you?" as if we knew each other.

I was a bit taken back, but before I could say anything she looked me straight in the eye, leaned in closer, and whispered, "Pretend you know me and we're good chums."

I was startled, but without missing a beat I continued the skit. "Hey Lexy, no time no see. Weren't you suppose to call me last week? I've got so much to tell you; excuse us, we're going to go chat a while," I stated as I shouldered her away from her male assailant, and we walked away arm-in-arm to the ladies room.

"That was brilliant!" she roared, safely inside.

I smiled widely and bowed to her for my performance. "Thank you."

"Aw, bloody 'ell, I've been trying to get away from that bugger all day. He keeps looking down me blouse as if he's been in prison for the past twenty years."

"Why don't you tell the director? Get him thrown off the set."

"No, it's much more fun playing cat and mouse with him. Besides, I wouldn't have become your 'best friend' if he hadn't been here. We are going to have such fun on this movie. Rumor has it, you're somewhat of a practical joker - is that true? I'll bet everyone wants to be your friend so they don't get a joke played on them, right Pookie?"

"Well, if I told you that, I wouldn't be able to play any on you, now would I?" I humorously answered with a question. "I've never really had any girlfriends. I moved around and worked too much to ever keep any."

We talked a while more and then returned to the table. Lexy picked up her name card, brought it all the way down the table and then placed the card next to mine. The director gave us a scowling look, but didn't say anything. Suppose that's because Lexy was carrying the movie; she was the star.

"Well, you've had a 'ell of a life so far, ay?" she asked without any regards to how it may affect my feelings. But there was still something sweet about the way Lexy said it, so I didn't mind. I was also somewhat flattered that she was interested enough in me to have been watching my career, talking to people, and/or reading the tabloids to know about the events in my life.

During the filming, we became fast friends and played jokes on just about everyone. No one could really prove it was us doing them, though. "That's the way you need to do it; don't let them know. That way, you can continue doing them without getting busted," I explained to Lexy.

We sat up talking for hours every night, even though I was suppose to be studying what my on-set tutor had assigned me. I didn't let on that I already knew most of the information and that it was basically a review for me. Anyway, I discovered so much about Lexy that no one was writing about in the tabloids. For instances, she volunteered at an animal shelter back in Liverpool, and no one ever wrote about that. I told her about Foxy and about her Champion Cheddar addiction.

We ended the film with a huge wrap party, and Lexy

got so drunk that I had to carry her back to her trailer. I wasn't happy about that; it reminded me of Mom. The next day, she had an enormous hangover. I thought that was punishment enough and I didn't lecture her on the perils of drinking. I felt a little sad on the plane ride back home, my good times with Lexy were behind me, but I was anxious to see everyone at home again - especially Foxy. I leaned over and reached down to my carry-on bag to double check that I had Ella and a box of Champion Cheddar for Foxy. I then sat back in my seat and began to daydream. I dreamt of the time when I was such a big star that I would be able to take Foxy anywhere. But those thoughts were soon interrupted by turbulence so jolting that I was nervous for the remainder of the flight.

The next week was spent studying and taking the state required tests; equivalent to highschool midterms.

"How'd ya do, Jordan?" Gamma asked during lunch.

"Aced 'em," I answered, just before snatching Gampy's pickle off his plate. I dashed out of the room with it, but not before reciting the top five largest traded stocks for the week and what I did for my good deed that day. Of course, this was also before tripping on my way out and running into the wall.

"I swear someday you're going to put an eye out if you don't pay attention to what you're doing," Gamma squawked.

Things moved quickly that year and soon I had completed two more films. I paid Larry his last payment and instead of paying him interest, we agreed that I would pay another half of a percent in my contract for the next few years. It was business after all. I felt good about our agreement and it was a good deal. It was also good to get that off my mind and I was able to focus on the future.

We were now doing incredibly well financially, so well that I was able to make a downpayment toward a house in the Hollywood Hills, out West in Los Angeles, California. The climate was basically the same, except Los Angeles was less humid than Houston. Gamma and Gampy were hesitant to move, but agreed for me because of my acting career. Gamma reluctantly said good-bye to all her friends. Gampy didn't really care about leaving so long as he had a hobby room and could obtain his stock reports. Tommy didn't seem as though he even noticed a change; he usually rolled with the punches as long as he had his bat and baseball.

Larry was actually doing so much better financially that he too relocated his business to Los Angeles. He was thrilled to sign more *high-end* clients.

Mom came along with us and I bought her a cozy condo in a nearby neighborhood; it was nothing fancy, but she was happy with it. The courts forbade her from ever living in the same house with Tommy and me, as long as we were minors so separate housing would have to do.

Just before we moved, I heard the story of how Gampy had been giving Mom money to raise us. It started just after Tommy was born because Dad stopped giving her money. Dad always claimed that he didn't have any money and demanded that she go out and get a job. When Mom would ask who was suppose to watch us kids, he'd tell her to get a night job and that I was old enough at nine to care for an infant by myself while she was at work. No matter, that was in the past, and I had enough abandonment issues to deal with - I didn't need to fuel them with past stories.

Mom had been working odd jobs the past couple of years since Tommy and I left, but nothing that would support her for very long. She had never been trained in anything and Dad never paid child support, much less alimony so I made sure she had some money in the bank. I also instructed my management company to make monthly deposits for her bills. I knew there was a possibility she would drink it away, but I felt a sense of obligation. Gamma taught me about good deeds and she taught me to be charitable. No matter what Mom had done to us in the past, she was still our mom.

After she settled into her condo, Mom did find a steady job working part-time in the mornings as a receptionist. She talked about wanting some responsibility and a sense of accomplishment. Mom said that her alcoholic treatment sponsor gave her the advice, that she would feel better about herself if she could lean toward self-reliance. I do think working helped Mom to stay sober; she had something to look forward to every day.

I hired Eddie and Ruby full-time for the new house - he as the butler and my driver, and she as the housekeeper. I even hired a chef to cook only a few nights a week. Gamma gets all flustered when she doesn't get to cook; she doesn't know what to do with herself with all the extra time. I also think cooking was like meditation for her, a time to ponder the solutions to all of life's little problems.

Oh, and yes, I finally did buy that dream car - an Alfa Romeo. It was the dealership's sportiest model. It had leather bucket seats and a very shiny *red* paint finish. Foxy had her own little elevated booster seat on the passenger's side so she could poke her head out the window while her tongue flopped in the breeze; barking "hello" at all the dogs as we passed by. She even had a tray table for her Champion Cheddar.

Sometimes I would get a twinge of missing the old house back in Houston because it was the only place I had known that felt like a real home with safety and security. But the new house was beautiful, and nothing like I had ever seen before - much less lived in. But after Gamma filled the new house with the magical aromas that she'd filled the other house with, it felt like home. The property had a swimming pool which Tommy loved, and a Jacuzzi which I loved, and even a tennis court which everyone loved. Gamma adored the yard and it was so spacious that Gampy and I bought her dozens of rose bushes to fill the yard up. Well, the rose bushes were also bought to keep Gamma busy so she wouldn't miss her old friends so much. I especially liked the pink rose bushes; they had been my favorite since they were on my curtains as a little girl. I had a small solarium built where Gamma could also fiddle with her plants and flowers. Gampy found and hired a gardener who was absolutely fantastic. He'd do everything Gamma wanted and that made her happy. I think Gampy stole him away from one of our neighbors;

gardener-stealing was very popular in that neighborhood for some reason. Sort of like a sport, I think.

There were ten bedrooms in all; at least I'm guessing they were originally constructed to be bedrooms. We allocated three bedrooms for the four of us, and I insisted Gamma and Gampy have the master suite. There were two bedrooms for the staff and two guest bedrooms. Two of the bedrooms became hobby rooms, one for Gampy and the other for Gamma. She made hers into a sewing room. Plus we reconstructed one into a type of library and study room for Tommy and me. An odd thing I noticed was that the bedrooms were much bigger in Texas than California. But our new house was beautiful and there was plenty of space for everyone.

One thing that was definitely bigger was the kitchen. Gamma's face lit up when she walked into it for the first time. She was in her element. She couldn't believe how many cabinets it had and there were even refrigerated drawers for veggies and fruit that looked just like the cabinets. Gamma became overwhelmed and all flustered and said she would never be able to remember what she'd put where.

The garage had four spaces for cars and one for a limo - but we didn't have a limo, *yet*. For that matter, we didn't have four cars between us so Tommy commandeered a space for his bike, skateboard and baseball paraphernalia.

I bought all new furniture including new beds. My bed was heavenly. The family room was outfitted with every kind of electronic gadget there was, I think. Gampy was in his element so much so that I can remember Gamma complaining she hadn't seen him for days. But all you had to do was go into the family room and there he was, grinning from ear to ear. Foxy even got her own space. She had a considerable fenced-in grassy area outside for the times when we couldn't take her along with us, and for her potty place.

After we all got settled in, Lexy flew out to Los Angeles and stayed with us through my seventeenth birthday. We got into more trouble than I'd like to acknowledge. We went out every single night and Gamma expressed concern that we may be doing something illegal or immoral. I don't think she trusted Lexy much. That's when I started writing in a journal; mainly because before than I never had anything worthwhile to write about. I never admitted to anything about that week, but I titled it: **Two Teenagers Loose in Los Angeles**.

Dear Journal: Lexy and I had the time of our lives this week. I had my first taste of champagne. It was great, but the hangover wasn't, especially when Foxy was barking in my face to let her out. I know I'm going to have to watch myself with Lexy; she will be the death of me yet. We got into this night club and danced until my feet were swollen. We flirted with every guy there and they flirted right back. Three guys wanted my telephone number, but I didn't like any of them so I gave them a bogus number. Well, I didn't want to hurt their feelings by telling them no, did I? Lexy let a guy kiss her, scandalous! I wonder if that will be in the tabloids? Ha ha. Goodnight Journal.

Our fun was soon over, and Lexy returned home as I got back to work with the next of my many movies Larry had lined up for me.

As the holidays approached, I decided to take some time off. I needed to regenerate. We decided to have a gigantic party for Tommy's eighth birthday with a baseball theme because he was feeling a little left out with all the movie stuff going on. We wouldn't even celebrate Christmas that year until December 26th because the 25th was his day. I had to use all of my resources and popularity to get a magician to come out to perform on Christmas Day. We even had to hire child extras to be included on his guest list because most of his classmates were celebrating Christmas with their families, except a few of his Jewish friends. And, of course, Tommy would want me to mention inviting his friend, Anwar, who originally was from India. A Buddhist, I believe.

In February, I finished up another movie role. Even

though I had worked on some movies that were box office hits, which got me on the same level as Lexy professionally, I hadn't matched Lexy's level of popularity yet. The fans still recognized Lexy more than they did me. Turns out this worked to our advantage. The powers that be in the movie biz didn't normally team us up again with the same actors in a film so soon. However, since I was not that well-known in our first movie, I suppose they thought the union would fly. I was excited when Larry told me of the pairing arrangement and to be working with Lexy again.

The morning of my trip to the production site, Gamma came into my bedroom as I was packing, as she always had, to ask if I needed anything else for my trip. She gave me her little speech, as if I'd never heard it before. "Make us proud, be polite, make them think we raised you properly. You have Ella?"

I nodded. "Of course, Gamma. I won't let you down," I reassured her, as I giggled to myself knowing I would probably get into tons of trouble with Lexy nearby.

~✳~⦂~✳~⦂~✳~⦂~✳~⦂~✳~⦂~✳~

"I think I read about that 'divorce' in the newspaper back then," remarked Gladis. "I remember it because it was odd to see a child divorcing a parent. Did you ever see your father again?"

"You'll have to stay tuned," I answered, taunting her.

I looked over at Zoë and asked, "And just what do you think happened next? Yep, you're right, I was about to hatch the scheme of the century! You should have seen me, I was amazing. People were talking about it for years!" I bragged to Zoë who was still sleeping. Gladis sat back in her chair and appeared to be reading her magazine, but I suspected she was just pretending and was actually listening to my story.

~✳~⦂~✳~⦂~✳~⦂~✳~⦂~✳~⦂~✳~

Chapter IV

The Monkey Murders

I just knew that the next film with Lexy would be a blast. We always had such a good time together on our "*holiday*," as she would call our vacation, but they never lasted as long as we wanted them to. We both had very busy schedules and other people depended on us for their livelihood. I was feeling good going into this movie for other reasons too. I had paid Larry what I owed him, got Mom set up in a place she could call home, bought a beautiful spacious house for the four of us, and finally had some money back in the bank. I even started reinvesting in some of the stocks that Dad had sold, or rather, had stolen from me. My financial burdens were gone, Tommy and I were safe, and my mind was free. As I sat on the plane on my way to the production site, that's when the conspiracy plan hit me. That's when I concocted the *Monkey Murders*.

Not only was it a practical joke, but one I could get someone else to take the fall for and to take the heat off me from past suspicions. And it involved a murder mystery too! Several members of the last crew had accused me of pulling all of the stunts, but they never had any proof. They were suspicious though, so this time I needed to get someone else to take the blame. And I wasn't sure about including Lexy this time. She was always so squeamish about breaking into places to plant evidence so maybe not. I know she'd kill me if she found out I'd left her out, though. But this practical joke would be different from the others. It was possible that I could make it look as though someone else was setting me up, so Lexy would be thrown off too. That was great because it would validate my innocense even more to have Lexy convince everyone it wasn't me. I just needed to figure out who was on this crew that was on some of my others. Millie! Ooo, yeah, Millie. She always blamed me for losing props and disheveling her sets. She was often the ringleader who pointed the finger at me for past pranks; of course, that time she was right, but still, I had to seek revenge. And since she was the set designer she had access to more of the site than anyone else.

I was getting excited just thinking of all the possibilities. I'd never done a practical joke so elaborate before. This would take some planning, yeah nefarious planning.

Once on the site, I discovered that my trailer was right next to Lexy's. "Who misplanned that detail?" I thought. Didn't they know we wouldn't get any work done, being so close? Of course, we wouldn't anyway no matter how far apart we were so maybe they were thinking after all. *This* trailer was considerably different from the one I had the last time Lexy and I worked together.

"Whew, how nice is this?" I said, as we stepped inside.

"You get a maid too, Pookie," Lexy bragged.

"Even nicer. Did you get a golf cart too?"

"Sure, it comes standard with all these films. Beats walkin'. Get used to these perks, girlfriend - you're in the big league now."

"I'm not sure about that."

Lexy shrieked, "Aw, bloody 'ell! Look! That's the same bugger from our last film together. Now I'm gonna have to sew my nipples to my blouse so he doesn't constantly ogle them." Lexy and I laughed as we peered out the window at him.

"You don't think he learned his lesson from the last joke we played on him? He'll never look at a cactus the same way again."

"Can't say 'e'll look at burritos again without stocking up on toilet tissue, either, ay?" giggled Lexy. "Did you see what Jennifer Appleton was wearing at the Acclamation Awards last year? How embarrassing for her! And she actually thought that looked attractive?"

"Ooo, Lexy!" I giggled. "What'll you wear this year?"

"I don't know. What do you think we should wear?"

"We? I'm not going - do you think they'd invite *me?* I'm not *Ack Award*-inviting material. Well, YET!" I screamed like a teenager.

"Well, I'm not going without you, Pookie. Have you seen Dirk Matthews? He is soooo hot, I could die, and his family is rich beyond belief," Lexy cooed as she flipped through my teen magazine.

"Dirk doesn't do anything. He's only popular because of his Dad's wealth. He's just a playboy that gets into trouble to make himself famous. You know, you should have him invited to one of those Beverly Hills parties you go to so he could fall madly in love with you."

"Then I could dump 'em."

"Ooo, Lexy! You are so bad. What'd you think of the script? Any thoughts on how you want to play this?"

"We won't get a chance to play it how *we* want; the director will have the say. But I do like the monkey we'll be working with - he is sooo hot," she wooed scandalously while rolling on the bed kissing Ella, mocking me for the Dirk Matthews comment. I couldn't help but laugh.

"That's a *girl* elephant, ya know," I said, knowing it would get back at her.

She laughed and tossed Ella to me.

The first day of taping proceeded without any problems. We worked with a stuffed monkey in the rehearsals so we wouldn't squander the day away if the real monkey wouldn't hit his mark. They shot the monkey's scenes last in the day, and were mostly just shots of him to add into scenes, as cutaways.

I wasted no time getting things rolling. First, I needed a distraction for Lexy. I would get her involved in another practical joke as a diversion to the Monkey Murders. When she was off setting up the foundation for that ruse, I would be off setting up mine. My first task of the series was getting six identical, or as similar, to the prop monkey as I could find. I located them at a nearby toy store, then visited the hardware store, then stopped by the local bank and finally ended at the stationers. And, of course, I wore a disguise and paid cash. The next step consisted of getting a hold of the original prop monkey. For that task, I brought along a pen, duck tape, that day's newspaper and an instant-developing camera.

During our first scene the next day, Millie screeched as we were about to shoot. "Okay, who took *Millie*?" she demanded. "Walsh, was that you?"

"Excuse me? Who?"

"The monkey! Yeah you, did you do this?"

"Do what?"

She presented a photograph of the prop monkey with its eyes duck taped and a newspaper propped up against it. The handwritten caption on the photograph read, "Six million in bananas or the chimp gets it."

"This," she answered. "Very funny, where's my monkey?!" Everyone laughed. "That's not funny! You know what I meant!"

Lexy looked at me and mouthed, "Did you do this?"

I looked back and just shrugged my shoulders indicating I didn't know what was going on. I didn't really want to outright lie to her. Okay, it was a fine line, but I had to continue the plan.

"Ah, I don't even like bananas - why would I ask for six million of 'em?" I asked innocently while others laughed.

"Very funny. Have that monkey back to me before the end of the day or *someone here* is gonna get it!" Millie screeched as she stormed off.

"She named the monkey, *Millie*? *Millie*-the-monkey?" I asked Lexy, as we both laughed. "Typical."

Early the next day as we assembled for the first shot of the day, *Millie II* - the first of the replicas was found in the director's chair. It had black electrical tape Xs over its little eyes with a banana-handled letter opener looming out of its chest. A note was hanging from its foot, like with a toe-tagged corpse and it read, "Five million in bananas or the chimp gets it - again."

"Oh, cute. Okay, stop monkeying around," Pete, our director, joked as everyone laughed. He tossed the toy to Millie and added, "Here ya go. Don't let it out of your sight this time."

As Millie pulled the tape off, she looked closer and declared, "This ain't it. This ain't *Millie*." Everyone laughed still not used to its name.

"What?" Pete blistered.

"This AIN'T *Millie*."

"What difference does it make what the monkey's name is?" he asked, mocking her.

She stormed off in a huff. Lexy and I joked about it all night, and she still had no idea it was me - or maybe Lexy did, but she wasn't saying. The two of us ran lines for the next several hours until we passed out.

Millie made us use the stabbed monkey for rehearsals, but wouldn't let it out of her sight. We nicknamed it *Norman*, from the film *Psycho*.

Three days later, the next *Millie* was found in the mess tent. It had the consistent Xs over its eyes. This one was propped up against a bottle with a picture of skull & crossbones taped onto it, which were sitting on the dessert table next to a mysterious banana-creme pie. Paul, the sound guy, was having a birthday the following day, and there was a caption written right on the pie, "Happy B-day, monkey boy Paul - 4M or else." There were candles stuck in all around the outer edge of the pie. Everyone laughed, except Millie, and they continued to eat their dinner not bothering to move it. Paul eventually cut a piece of the pie and ate it. Others followed suit until it was gone.

During all of the excitement, we did manage to get some acting in. But then, finally, the day I'd been waiting for came. A secret lynch mob was assembled by Millie. She demanded that they search for any more monkeys on the site. Her mob looked anywhere they could get into - the trailers, cars, bathrooms... even the director's office. "When we find the monkeys, we'll find the thief who stole *Millie*," screeched

Millie like the Wicked Witch in *The Wizard of Oz*.

I wasn't that stupid to leave the evidence in my trailer. I always knew my goal was to frame Millie so I had purchased one more monkey than I needed. I hid that extra one in Millie's trailer on the first night I had them. That way, I could frame her, but continue my ruse if I wasn't finished by the time they found that monkey. I hid the rest of them in plain sight behind other props we'd use later in the filming on the top shelf in the props room. No one even thought to look there.

"Hey, I found it, I found it! Look here guys, I found it!" yelled one of the grips. "I found it in Millie's trailer."

"NO you didn't," Millie cried.

"Yeah, it was hidden pretty good too. I had to pull the slats off your bed to get at it. I spotted it through the air ventilation holes on the side of your bed. Yeah, no tape on this one - yet," he expressed accusingly.

Everyone gathered round as the grip hurled it into the air like a trophy. Millie profusely denied any involvement for the next two days, until the next one was discovered. Discovered in *my* trailer by Lexy.

On that Friday, I invited some teenagers on the set back to my trailer for a pizza fest. I had to establish an alibi so I climbed out of my window and knocked over the lamp as I did. Then I snuck around the back and waited for them to assemble. After a while, I came running up to the trailer as if I forgot about the event. Many were already inside playing music and chatting. I knew Lexy would be the first person to use the bathroom, to primp.

"Aw, bloody 'ell - look at this," she announced as others gathered around. "This one's been electrocuted in the shower with a hair dryer. It has the same Xs over its eyes too. They're demanding three million in bananas this time. What is this - kidnapper's discount bartering? Soon it'll be a shilling or two. And look Pookie, your bedroom window is open and the lamp is on the floor. You've been targeted!"

I grilled everyone about it, asking if they had discovered anyone coming out of my trailer as they arrived there. The rest of the evening was spent dressing up the corpse and pinning curlers to his head. Lexy even put makeup on him, except for its eyes - of course, which were still taped.

Even with all the fun, I was a little homesick and I called Gamma to share my adventures with her. Everyone back home were doing fine - Tommy was trying out for softball something or another, and Gamma held Foxy up to the phone so I could hear her breathing. That made me miss Foxy all the more.

"Tell her I have a box of Champion Cheddar all ready and waiting for her. I may even send home a case."

"No, no, she's got enough of them to make her sick for a week," Gamma replied. "You hurry home safely. Make a list of those good deeds you're doing in your journal, and we'll see you soon."

The next murdered monkey was found in the street, in the flower bed, and in the bushes. There were no Xs over this one's eyes. There were no eyes. This monkey had been blown to bits - stuffing everywhere. A massacre.

"Aw, bloody 'ell, it's the scarecrow all over again," shrieked Lexy, pretending to be weeping, dramatically holding one hand over her eyes as she pulled the empty monkey carcass down from a tree branch with the other.

"Anyone find the note?" came a voice from the gathering crowd.

"There it is, hanging from a branch!" yelled Pete as he retrieved it. "Same ole crap, 'cept they're down to two million in bananas."

Everyone joined in to help collect the monkey's remains.

After the weekend, Uncle Red called to see how things were going. I told him of my "monkey" escapades and he laughed, claimed he was jealous of all the fun I was having and that he missed us since we moved.

"I know, but you could come out to Los Angeles to live. We have a room in the house just for you."

"Can't Joey, I have a law practice. Such as it is, it's better than starting over again."

"But I make enough that all of us can live from it. We are now, what's one more?"

"Maybe someday, but I'll have to pass for now."

"Okay, I'll come see you when I get back. Can Foxy come too?"

"Of course she can! Silly girl."

The final monkey corpse was found hung, swinging from the light bulb over the keg at the wrap party like a pinata with its shadow dancing around the room. Everyone laughed and just watched it swing, the monkey seemed to be swinging to the beat of the music. It was a while before someone spotted *Millie* sitting on top of a crate of bananas. She was in perfect condition with a banana in one hand and a bank book in the other, with a deposit slip sticking out stating **one million bananas** on it.

"Ah ha so it was you all along, *Millie,*" I accused as I pointed at the monkey. "You staged your own monkey-napping and killed all the other monkeys to show you meant business and to collect your million bananas. Take her away officer," I announced mockingly as I stared at Millie taunting her.

"Very funny Walsh, I know it was you," Millie declared as everyone laughed. The partygoers began sporadically chanting, "Yeah, sure, we know who was caught with the evidence."

The crew danced into the night and when the morning came, our time together had ended, again. "I'm so sad that we have to say good-bye, Lexy," I said to her. We tried to be brave, but wailed anyway.

"Aw, bloody 'ell Pookie; there goes my makeup," Lexy whined.

"I'll see you again at the premier Lexy. We'll have a great time," I sniffled.

When the editing was finished, the promoters called us to invite us to the premier. That event was just the next excuse for Lexy and me to go shopping. We made a week of it and headed for Rodeo Drive every single day. Lexy was a star even while shopping. Everyone loved her. I swear one woman thought I was her personal assistant and demanded that I hold her jacket and purse while that woman had the male sales clerk take a photograph of her and Lexy. I laughed and just said, "Yes ma'am, no problem. Can I get you a cappuccino too?" This woman was so star-struck with Lexy that she didn't answer. And that was fortunate for me because she probably would have put in her coffee order otherwise.

The premier was dazzling. The people were cheering. Lexy was beautiful and working the crowd. I was a mess. It was my first major premier and I didn't know quite what to do. I just stayed close to Lexy and waved when she waved. I was even more of a nervous wreck when we were viewing the movie. I wondered if the audience would laugh at all the right moments during my scenes. That would be the deciding factor whether they thought I had comic timing - that was what it was all about for me. And they did laugh, for the most part. I thought some scenes were funnier than they did, but I was happy with the overall results. Lexy teased me relentlessly for being worried, but that was okay. I wasn't offended. That was just Lexy's style.

The next few months were spent promoting the movie. I was asked to appear on Danny Kellerman's show. He grilled me about the Monkey Murders, but I exclaimed that *Millie the Monkey* was caught with the evidence. And Mr. Kellerman was frustrated that he couldn't get anyone from the film to own up to it. He was a funny man and I liked the audience. It was almost like being in a stage performance - you could hardly see the audience because of the bright lights, but you could hear them laughing.

The tabloids were in my life full-force now. They were writing about everything they could get their hands on. Mostly it was stuff that they had just made up and that wasn't true. One article hinted that Gamma had been a madam in a whorehouse back in Texas and her card-playing girlfriends were actually the girls who worked for her in the bordello. Another wrote that Tommy was autistic and didn't know how to spell his own name even though he was the captain of his baseball team. It was all stupid stuff, I just don't know how they invented some of it. Not even much was about me, just the family. I'm the one who's famous;

wouldn't you think people would read their rag for information on me and not the family?

We tried to hide the news from Gamma, but reporters marched right up to the house and asked her about it.

But they did finally write about something that was true. That's when I found out Uncle Red was gay. Uncle Red said he didn't know if I would understand what that meant so he wanted to wait until I was older to tell me. Sam wasn't a secret anymore, which made Sam happy, but Uncle Red thought it might hurt his law practice if people knew.

Uncle Red said I could sue the tabloids for the stuff they lied about, but it probably wouldn't do any good. He said as long as the papers used the word *alleged*, they could say just about whatever they wanted and the judge would normally rule in their favor. It had something to do with first amendment rights, but I still couldn't see how that applied when they were mostly lies. Uncle Red explained that they taunt celebrities in order to get a rise out of them so they will do something stupid, and then when they write about that, the tabloids are vindicated.

The tabloid madness was mind-boggling, so Lexy and I took another *holiday* - plus the laughing withdrawals had become too severe. We also needed to get ready for the next big event. We laughed about the Monkey Murders all over again, and Lexy told me her stories of how all the interviewers wanted to know who did it.

"Aw Pookie, it's the year's major *who done it*!" she revealed as she laughed.

Next, I went to spend a week with Uncle Red. I hadn't realized how much I missed him until I saw him and Sam at the airport when they came to pick me up.

"Hi Sam! How are you?" I asked as I kissed them both hello.

"Good. How is everyone settling in at the new house?" Sam asked as he returned my hug.

"Great and you should see it - it's bigger than any house I've ever been in."

The three of us spent the week chattering like magpies, nearly nonstop, but I knew I had to return to my life and to my job.

~✳~¡~✳~¡~✳~¡~✳~¡~✳~¡~✳~

I paused and looked over at Zoë, who was still dosing. By this time, I had an audience of three - Gladis, another nurse and Zoë.

"Don't stop. Did Lexy ever know that it was you who put on the Monkey Murders?" asked Gladis.

I chuckled. "No, afraid not. I wanted to tell her, but thought she would be hurt that I hadn't included her - not to mention, used her as a decoy when I sent her off on another ruse unrelated to the Monkey Murders *and* had her find one of the monkeys. I suspect she had her suspicions."

"How did you get the bank book that you left with the last monkey at the wrap party?"

"I told the teller that I was on a scavenger hunt with a local youth group and a bank book was on my list. I had a list to show them, ya know, of the things I really needed for the ruse so they believed me and gave it to me. Not a big deal - it didn't mean I had money in an account or anything because nothing was stamped inside of it."

"What about the banana cream pie?"

"I had ordered it in town when I was doing my errands the first time. I told the baker it was for my bratty brother that I was making fun of with the monkey boy message written on it. I had it delivered to the mess for that day."

"What about the crate of bananas?" asked the other nurse.

"I made up an excuse to ride into town with the caterer on the last weekend we were shooting, and I had the grocer deliver the bananas on the day of the wrap party. When the front gate received the order of bananas, they just assumed they would be for the party because that was the only event we had going on."

"*Clever girl*," the nurse said smiling. "Don't you think you should call it quits for the night?"

"No, no, I'm just getting to the good stuff." I turned to Zoë and whispered, "Sorry about the comments from Lexy and me about your brother, Dirk." And I continued with my story. They sat back and listened.

~✱~:~✱~:~✱~:~✱~:~✱~:~✱~

Chapter V

I've Arrived

Lexy and I giggled our way down the walkway of the Acclamation Awards. All I could see were bursts of lights around me. All that flashing made me disoriented and I had trouble walking in my three-inch heels - let alone how clumsy I was normally. But that's okay, it felt great to be five foot eight inches tall; well not really, but I was that night. Lexy and I had exercised for a month to look good in our designer dresses - not that Lexy really had to workout, she was already gorgeous. But we were both lookin' good - toned and tanned. I wore my hair down and it nearly reached my waist. Lexy talked me into adding a little more of a vibrant red hair color with temporary occasional shimmering burgundy streaks down each side. The two of us loved the new trendy fashions from London that year, but for the awards ceremony we only trusted Gemi - one of the most prestigious clothing designers in New York. It was a big moment for me. This was the first time I'd been at these awards, and I was presenting - that's big! Larry said I would get great exposure for doing this and he prepared me all week. Lexy and I were bombarded by tons of people with microphones.

"Who are you wearing?!" shouted the crowd.

"Happy Birthday, Jordan. They want to know who you're wearing?" asked Marion Hunter from the *Amusement Today* TV program show.

"Oh, thank you, Marion. I'm wearing Gemi attire and Rosabella jewelry. Lexy is also wearing an original Gemi," I answered as the crowd cheered at my willingness to stop on the red carpet to chat. I gave a quick wave to the fans while the organizers nudged us inside.

"We have to get you rehearsed for your presentation, Miss Walsh," declared one of them.

I promised Larry I would speak in the most sultry voice I could muster; he had always told me that was my best feature, even though others said it was my smile. Tonight I planned to exploit both. I walked out on stage from one side and Barry Mallee, an up-and-coming actor who was my co-presenter, walked out from the other. When we met in the middle of the stage, we reached out, held hands and continued to the podium. The crowd cheered. I had to almost scream to be heard over the crowd so I abandoned the plan to use my sultry voice. "Good evening, ladies and gentlemen. We are here to present the award for Best Actor in a Supporting Role."

"Each one has demonstrated an excellent performance," Barry added.

"And the nominees are," I rendered on cue. We stood there as the monitor in back of us lit up and ran the list of nominees with short clips of their respective movie roles.

"And the winner is..." Barry taunted and then made a drum roll on the podium with his fingers.

"Daniel Becker!" I announced. We stood back as Daniel took the stage and Barry handed him the award. After Daniel's speech, we all walked off together. I could hear Lexy in the second row whistling a piercing tone. I'm not sure how long I was standing back stage, but Lexy's nomination was next. I stood in the wings of the stage and impatiently waited for them to announce the winner of the "Best Actress" award. Lexy was up for a role in a smaller film. I was so nervous for her, all I could remember hearing was the part "And the winner is."

"Alexandria Sherman, ladies and gentlemen!" I paused for a moment because I wasn't used to anyone calling Lexy by her given name, except her mother. But then I started screaming, jumping up and down and clapping my hands. I must have looked like a lunatic, but I didn't care. In fact, I didn't even notice my feet were swelling from the three-inch heels. Lexy waltzed up on stage so cool and calm; *I* was the basket case. She gave a beautiful speech and thanked her family and then her friends as she looked over at me. I started crying like a little baby. Lexy almost ran off the stage and then we jumped up and down together.

Later, she let me hold her award and I pretended to give my acceptance speech with it. The whole night was spent celebrating her win and my eighteenth birthday. It seemed we hit every night club in Los Angeles. Early the next morning, I put Lexy on a plane for London. She was exhausted, but still as beautiful as the night before. "How does she do it?" I wondered.

When I got home, I was exhausted and spent a good portion of the morning in bed until Foxy'd had enough and wanted to go outside. So I got up and walked with her. We spent the whole day together and I drove her over to the dog park in the Valley. She had the best time. The park was full of other dogs and the ground was a nice green grassy haven. Foxy would roll over and over, wiggling upside down in the grass. I got all kinds of pictures of our day together. I'd toss a Champion Cheddar at her and she'd jump real high to get it. She even shared them with some of her new friends.

Gamma had a cake baked for me later on that night, and as a family, we quietly celebrated my first adult birthday. I was feeling content and life was good - well, as good as it could be with this family. I was an adult now and that gave me reason to review my life, where I'd been and what I wanted for my future. Well, in the immediate future anyway.

The truth of the matter was - I wanted a boyfriend. I dated a bit, but no one really impressed me. I was even seen out with Barry Mallee and the fans seemed to love the match, but there wasn't anything there for me. Not even enough to kiss him, not that he didn't try. Gamma said that I just wasn't ready, but I think she only said I wasn't ready because she wanted me locked up in my room until I was forty.

For the most part, Mom had settled into life in Hollywood. She was going everywhere in loud outfits trying to be noticed, just so she could tell people a famous movie star was her daughter. Mom would have her drunken slips now and then. She even did a few stints at alcoholic treatment centers, but mostly that only lasted as long as it took to find the closest bar. She loved diamonds, her birth stone so I bargained with her and agreed to buy one nice piece of jewelry for her a month if she would stay sober. This worked most of the time because that seemed to make her happy. Then she'd go back into her bottle, moaning about her life, but I refused to listen to that. I'd lecture, "If you don't like it, then change it, but don't stew about it. Only *you* have the power to change your life." It wasn't until I was older that I realized Mom was a housewife because she had no choice. She was trapped. Mom wasn't strong enough to actually divorce Dad, so she was stuck in that turbulent relationship. The whole ordeal had made her stronger and wiser that she could now live on her own - without him. Keeping Mom's limitations in mind, I had more patience with her.

I'd hear from Dad now and then. Most everyone advised me not to speak to him, but I thought that was too harsh. He came into town last month with "the flavor of the month" dripping off his arm. He would guilt me into lending him my Alfa Romeo saying that his car was broke down. After I found some of their clothing items left behind, I had it fumigated and refused to let him use it again. That current woman tried to win me over; however, after I informed her that "whatever he promised you Doll, he doesn't have control over my finances" - she was long gone. I suppose that was the way he'd pick them up, by dropping my name. One woman actually stayed for two weeks until I paid her some money and enlightened her, "that's all you're ever gonna see, Doll." She was more than happy to take it and left. It wasn't until I was older that I realized other women were in that equation the whole time. Mom said Gampy had something on Dad to force him to stay in the marriage, that's why he never left, but she never knew what it was. She never told Gampy that Dad was beating her, that's why he never used the information against Dad.

I knew from a very early age that, unlike my parents, I wanted to do something different from just the same thing day in and day out. I watched Mom and Dad incessantly, every chance I got when I was growing up, and wondered why they did what they did when it made them so unhappy. It also taught me to treat people differently than they did - better actually. I could have treated them as they treated me, but what good would that have done? Yes, I'd feel good for the moment, but then feel like crap the next day or the next time I'd see them. Then what? You're the one who has to live with whatever feelings come from your actions - not them. If you felt guilty about what you've done, then you're the one who lives with the guilt.

This was a good time in my life. I'd reached adulthood in relatively one piece. I pondered questions to the universe and got most of my answers. I even dealt with most of my abandonment issues and concluded that Mom and Dad did the best they could. I felt successful in my career and was financially independent. And I was happiest at home with the family and my friends.

~✻~¡~✻~¡~✻~¡~✻~¡~✻~¡~✻~

"Yes, life was good and it was about to get better," I teased.

"Don't suppose I can talk you into taking a break?" Gladis asked.

"Not a chance, I haven't mentioned *him* yet," I smiled wickedly as I looked at Zoë, "All in good time, Zoë." I turned to Gladis and asked, "Why doesn't she have flowers in here? I bet that would cheer her up."

"Can't. Still water promotes bacteria," she answered. I looked confused, which prompted her to add, "In other words, the still water sitting in the vase becomes laced with bacteria and that could infect a patient who has had incisions."

"Oh, so that's why she has balloons," I responded.

Gladis changed my I.V. and left the room. Zoë and I were alone and I resumed my story.

~✻~¡~✻~¡~✻~¡~✻~¡~✻~¡~✻~

Chapter VI

Making Contact with *His* Soul Mate

Lexy and I had fun at the Ack Award, but it was now time to get back to work. We still had contracts to fulfill, careers to build, families to feed, pranks to execute, and people who counted on us for their livelihood. But I was a teenager and all I could think about was going on another *holiday*. The next occasion when Lexy and I had time off to hook up was five months later.

We decided to do something different from what we normally did so Lexy and I flew out to Indianapolis to watch a race-car event. She had always said those drivers looked hot in their driving suits, and that was enough for Lexy to nominate this event.

The minute we stepped off the plane, we were mobbed by fans and tabloid reporters. When we finally got to our hotel, I called the only person who could help us. Larry arranged for a couple of bodyguards to drive us to the event. They were able to sneak us through the back hallways, avoiding another clash.

I watched the event with excitement; it was the most exhilarating sports event I'd ever seen. Everyone was running around working on cars, and some were yelling for others to get out of the way. I thought it was going to be boring just watching cars go around in a circle, but I was pleasantly surprised.

After hearing Lexy whining about being mobbed, the group of people around us became our protectors. They wouldn't let anyone annoy us and even shunned the hot dog guy, which was a pity because I was starving.

We spent most of the day trying to decide which driver Lexy liked the best. I liked them all - every one of them seemed fascinating and liked living on the edge. There was one that I did like a little more than the others, but I knew not to say anything for fear I would be teased beyond humiliation by Lexy. As the day progressed, the event promoters displayed a gigantic trophy bowl onto a table down front, and Lexy kept threatening to go over and drink champagne out of it.

When leaving, Lexy and I were escorted through the same route and it worked fine - that was, until we got to the locker room area. We were confronted by an aggressive mob of fans in the hallway that were waiting for the drivers to emerge from the locker room to sign autographs. Lexy freaked and started running in the opposite direction down the hall. I didn't know what else to do so I ran along with her. We turned a corner and Lexy started turning knobs on any door she could find. She finally found one unlocked, opened that door and pushed me through it. Only problem was, that this was the backdoor into the men's locker room. Being in such a big hurry to get away from those people, Lexy and I hadn't looked where we were going. I crashed in and tripped over someone, which sent both of us hurling to the ground in a mass of arms and legs flailing about. I could hear Lexy laughing hysterically over us.

"Lexy, help me up!" I screamed as I straightened out my dress.

"Yes Lexy, by all means - help her off me," demanded someone below me with an Italian accent.

I looked down to see who I was laying on top of and couldn't believe my eyes. It was *him* - Jack Rebello, the most amazingly beautiful man I'd ever seen. Along with a gorgeous wavy dark-brown thick head of hair, he had deep dark rich mysterious eyes that drew you into his soul. I'll bet hundreds of women have lost themselves in those eyes. My stomach was flipping all around just looking at him. I was lying over his 5'11" athletic frame staring at him while he was staring right back at me. I wasn't sure what Jack was thinking, but he was now smiling. His smile was sexy and effortless. I could tell he had given that smile to a million people who probably melted from the sight of him. I was one of those melting people - well, until I realized that others were pulling me off him.

"Sorry," I hollered back to him as Lexy began pulling me from the room. Jack and I gave each other one last smile.

"No, pro-blem-o," Jack remarked, as I continued to admire that smiling rugged chiseled face.

Lexy and I continued running.

"Wow Pookie, you like him," Lexy teased, "Can't believe you even noticed a guy. You've never shown any interest in any *one* guy before. You never even looked at any single guy long enough to tell me what he was wearing. He is rather cute. Do you think you two'll get married?"

"Shut up, Lexy," I giggled, elbowing her to stop teasing me and get moving out of there.

After Lexy and I got back to our hotel, we ran into our room, and then dropped onto the bed - exhausted. Relentlessly mocking me about Jack, Lexy kissed Ella like she had on our last film.

"I'm beginning to think I should plan a wedding for you and that elephant," I teased as Lexy laughed, and then picked up the telephone to call room service. But that's okay, from the first moment that I laid eyes on Jack Rebello, I was sure I would love him for the rest of my life. Or at the least lust after him in a big way.

I suppose one could argue that I was a true klutz - skinned knees from bike-riding accidents, falling down a lot, spilling on myself, and now tripping over Jack. But in my defense, *I* was pushed.

The *holiday* was over before Lexy and I knew it, but we both had a schedule to keep. I flew home and got back into my routine. Larry had another film role waiting for me. I was on location for three weeks before running into Jack again. This time, I didn't actually *run* into Jack as the time before, but saw him at a party an actress acquaintance was hosting. We made meaningful eye contact and exchanged our hellos, but we never got a chance to chat. This was mainly because the hostess of the party was all over him. And who could blame her? Plus I had an early call so I couldn't put in the time to pursue him.

Soon, my next film was ready to wrap, and I was packing my bags to leave. But I wasn't going anywhere before performing my final practical joke for the picture. This one, on the director. Uncle Red had previously sent me some *enhancements* for my ruses that he thought I could use - exploding pens and shock pens. I finally found the perfect time to use them, and cleverly stuck one into the director's pencil holder in his office. It was hit and miss for him to grab the right one at any given time. I don't remember which one I used, but I could hear him in his office cussing when I was leaving - all the way from the front security booth. I never looked back and told the driver to "step on it."

I flew back home, gave Foxy her Champion Cheddar, and life got back to normal in Los Angeles. One day, Gampy treated Tommy and me for lunch at Valentino's, while Gamma was at the stylist's having her hair done. That was the next time I saw Jack. As Gampy stepped over to give the parking valet our ticket, Tommy and I were standing in the foyer of the restaurant. I looked over and was excited to see Jack walking over to me.

"I must thank you for not dropping into my lap while I was eating my soup," Jack bantered, teasing me as I smiled. "I could thank you properly by taking you to dinner next week. That way I'd be able to keep a better eye on you flailing about."

I screamed "YES" on the inside, but answered "sure, I'd love to" on the outside. While giving Jack my telephone number, we made conversation. Jack said he was in town racing in an event in Long Beach - just south of Los Angeles, but by the way he was stammering about the subject, it seemed he was making it up. I think he didn't want me to know he was there to find me. Jack and I said good-bye, and then Gampy drove off with Tommy and me to pick up Gamma.

Of course, after Tommy witnessed all of this, he was

relentless and wouldn't stop chanting, "Sissy and Jack, sittin' in a tree, K I S S I N G," all the way home. It was somewhat annoying, but secretly I was chanting it too.

That was the longest week of my life. I must have gone completely through my closet seventeen different times. The housekeeping duties for Ruby that week entailed her running around the room trying to pick up everything I would reject and toss aside. Finally exhausted, Ruby just shrugged and asked, "Can I get you a shovel, Miss Jordan?" And off she went. I laughed, but continued searching for that *perfect* outfit.

Gamma walked by my room, just shook her head from side to side and sighed. She was probably thinking, "Teenagers! And we have one more of these to go."

I called Lexy every day asking her what I should wear, how I should style my hair, and what should I do if he tried to kiss me? Okay, that one was a no-brainer, but I needed help with the rest. We decided to go natural. Lexy figured that Jack was constantly bombarded by glitzy females, and if he hadn't had a long-term relationship with any of them, that wasn't what he was going for. So, natural it was, and that was good because I knew how to do that. That was, well, natural for me.

It was so cute, for our first date, Jack took me to an Italian restaurant he'd found that reminded him of home. The reception for him was like an event; it took twenty minutes just to say hello. The owners and waiters were like his American family, having Jack taste everything and waiting for his opinion to authenticate it. When some of them dragged him back to the kitchen for a moment, I got a chance to talk to some of the waiters - alone. They gave me more information about him, admitting they knew he had women throwing themselves at him, but the waiters thought he was more interested in his profession than the partying lifestyle. That was good so did I. I was a little surprised when they told me he'd never brought anyone there before, that he had always arrived alone.

As we sat together eating at a dimly lit corner table for two, I found out so much about him. I was drowning in Jack's charm and hardly noticed that we were sitting at a table with a red-checkered tablecloth and three white daisies in a small clear vase. His accent wasn't so deep that you couldn't understand him, but enough to where it was sexy. Every now and then, Jack would throw out an Italian word and I just about melted.

His full name is Giovanni Rebello. Giovanni meant John in English so his American friends called him Jack. However, he said no one back home called him that. He had a loft in New York and a small villa in Italy on his parent's estate. Both of his parents are Italian. Jack came from money and his Father never wanted him in the racing life, but rather in the winery business with him. His parents made Jack attend college and he has a degree in Italian History, but I suppose over there they just call it history. Jack said he thought his Father imaged he would sidetrack Jack just long enough with going to college that it would get racing out of his head.

I could see Jack was down-to-earth, no matter what was written about him. They also wrote that Jack takes chances that he shouldn't on the racetrack. After gently asking about it, Jack said he knew what he was doing even though he had gotten into some dreadful crashes. I remembered hearing someone mention at the racetrack the day Lexy and I attended, that a driver was killed in one of Jack's accidents. I asked him about that too and he said they never could determine who was at fault. Jack said he wasn't, and I could see he was telling the truth. Anyway, the driver knew that fatal accidents were a chance they faced when racing. Furthermore, Jack's uncle was in the racing field and had taught him everything he knew about auto racing. His uncle once held the title for the fastest time in the world.

Jack said he'd always wanted to settle down and get married, but had never found the right girl with the same dreams and interests. He wanted to fill his villa with a thousand children. However, before he did all that, Jack's lifelong dream was to sail around the world.

Jack seemed too good to be true. His only down side was being an Aquarius - like Dad. Still, that was okay; I felt even with my outrageous stunts and wild side of being a Pisces, it could mix with this calm down-to-earth Aquarius. After all, he also had his Italian hot-bloodedness, which kept him in the game.

Our time together was short, but we shared some quality time and I got to meet some people who were special in his life.

"When can I see you again?" he whispered while having dessert, leaning in close to me.

"I'll be free for the next few months," I whispered back.

We made plans to get together during the next month when he wasn't racing. Jack and I then walked to his car, and as he opened my door, he leaned toward me and gave me a passionate kiss - the kind you could really sink into. After that, I could barely walk; my legs just didn't seem to want to work - more than my usual klutzy-self. Good thing I was already at the car. After he drove me home, Jack walked me to the front door, and we were kissing again until the porch light turned bright. Soon we could see Gamma peering out at us through a window. We laughed and I whispered, "Goodnight."

I was driving everyone crazy stirring around the house waiting for my next date with Jack so I decided to cut them a break and flew to London to visit Lexy. It was my first overseas flight, and I found it to be way too long. I read a while, then I watched the movie, then I wrote in my journal, and when that was done, I was bored again. I just didn't know how Lexy did it so often - and looked so good doing it too. I was a mess when I got off the plane.

My visit with Lexy was short lived. She apparently wasn't expecting to run into her father at her favorite watering hole in a plush downtown hotel. Well, not "run into" exactly. We saw him walking into one of the elevators with someone other than her mother. Lexy was shocked to say the least.

"Lexy, go say hi," I suggested while nudging her.

"No, that wasn't my mummy in the lift with him!"

"So, maybe she's a client. You don't know the whole story until you ask."

"Working up in a hotel suite, Pookie? Not blooming likely. More like *he's* the client for a bang. Aw, bloody 'ell; did you see her dress? I'd be surprised if she didn't get a chest cold with all that exposure."

"In or out ladies?" hailed a voice from behind us.

I pulled Lexy out of the way of the people trying to get into the adjacent elevator, dragged her to the lobby bar, and sat her on a bar stool.

"What'll it be, ladies?" asked the stocky bartender.

Lexy stared into space, seemingly in shock, and didn't answer him.

"Um yeah, Lexy's having an embolism right now - could you give us a minute?" He left for the other side of the bar and washed bar glasses. Lexy and I talked a while and she admitted she wanted to go home. I then decided to fly back home to give her some time to find out what was going on. She called me three days later. Turns out her father was having an affair with an unknown British actress Lexy dubbed "Chippie."

When Jack returned to L.A. for our date, he stayed in a spare bedroom at the house with us. Since Gamma wanted to protect my virtue against someone of Jack's worldliness, she kept her eye on him the whole time he was there. I don't think she got much sleep. I was expecting to find her perched in the hallway with a shotgun in her lap. No matter, I had no intention of doing anything more than kissing at that point.

My time spent with Jack in Los Angeles was adventurous and fun. Jack spent time talking to Gampy about the world's economy; actually, arguing was more like it. But I could tell Gampy was invigorated by it. He didn't say so, but I think he respected Jack for the way he stuck to his point and wasn't swayed by trying to impress him - because of me. My heart would skip a beat every time Jack would walk into the room.

At first, I pretended to know all about auto racing; I wanted Jack to think I was interested in his profession. But then after he suspected I didn't, I confessed that I knew very little. He smiled and tried explaining the details to me. Jack told me what they were doing to the cars when they brought them into the pits. I must have looked dazed during his explanations because Jack laughed a lot. He said the most important races of the year were in Indianapolis, scheduled in the summer months.

Jack and I spent three whole days basking in one another's company, and our time together was just right. It wasn't too long to kill the mystery and the yearning to see each other again. And it wasn't too short for us to feel as though we were still strangers.

We said our good-byes at the house because we didn't want the paparazzi to intrude on our concluding moments together. Of course, being at the house meant Gamma was lurking about.

After Jack had left, I announced to Gamma making dinner in the kitchen, "Don't worry, Gamma; my virtue is safe."

"Oh Jordan!" Gamma squealed.

I could hear Gampy laughing all the way from the family room.

Gampy stepped into the kitchen and uttered, "Oh Annie, leave her alone, she's a good girl."

"It's not *her* that troubles me," she remarked and quickly changed the subject. "Did you get the brochures I left on your dresser, dear?"

"Yes Gamma, they were on my dresser," I teased, gently mocking her as I stole tastes of her wonderful concoction.

"If you don't decide soon, you'll miss registration for the fall semester." She paused. "What do you think?"

"I think I'll look at them later and if I don't, I'll miss the registration for the fall semester," I mimicked while running out of the room before she could snap me with her dish towel.

I ran to my room to read a note Jack wrote to me. He requested me not to open it until he had left and I was alone. It was a poem. It read:

> To my love, to my soul mate
> To be with you, is my fate
> You are my dreams of fulfillness
> I awaken in breathlessness

I read it over and over. Then I slipped it in back of a framed picture that was sitting on my dresser so no one would find it. I'd smile and giggle every time I looked at the picture.

I registered for college and started classes that next semester at the University of California, Los Angeles. Lexy kept asking me why I wanted to go back to school. I told her it was never an option; I always knew I needed to get a college degree. I have to admit, there was an instant when I thought, "Why, I don't *have* to go, I'm wealthy enough," then thought of Gamma being disappointed in me. I knew it would be harder to take her disappointment than to just go.

I knew it wasn't going to be easy. Sometimes I would be exhausted just thinking about my schedule. The next four years would consist of homework, homework, and more homework. I was also planning to make movies, but only a maximum of two per year. And, of course, I would try to see Jack whenever possible. Just the thought of it was overwhelming.

I signed up for all of my required classes, figuring that I would get them out of the way in the first year - especially since I hadn't selected a major yet and didn't know which direction I was headed. I also signed up for a drama class. Except, on the first day, the professor announced he was dropping me from his class. I was in a huff and decided to go see him during his free period to ask why.

"Jordan, you'll ace my class and you will have learned nothing. Wouldn't you rather spend your time and money on actually learning something new for yourself?"

"I don't think that's for you to decide."

"As a matter of fact, it is. Part of my job is to access

the qualifications of the students, granted mainly because they're under-qualified to be in my class - but in this case, you are overqualified. If you persist, I suppose I will accept you, but I don't see where that would benefit you in any way."

After I pondered the situation, I let it drop. I wasn't going to waste my time fighting a small battle like this one. I was upset though - it was the principle of it. It irritated me that the professor had made that decision for me. Here again, someone else was trying to control my destiny without involving me first. And someone else was taking something without asking me, just like Dad. Now I had to register for another class to replace it. By then, most of the classes were closed so I had to take the only thing that was available. Business Fundamentals - ugh. How boring. Still, Gampy would be proud that I secured a seat in that class. I only hoped that I could stay awake long enough to learn the name of my professor, much less what was on the exam. No matter, it was done.

Every weekend I'd try to catch a glimpse of Jack on the sports channel whenever I could. I'd watch his interviews and the cutaway shots of him talking to the fans, especially blonde female ones, which he seemed to enjoy. However, I was confident of his interest in me. Lexy was scarce these days too and I missed seeing her. I knew that I was busy with school, but I told her she could come over to stay as much as she wanted.

Jack and I got together when we could, but usually only for dinner or to attend a sporting event while he came to visit me in Los Angeles. We got together during Spring break that year; which was also around the time of my nineteenth birthday. During that time, was when Jack and I made love for the first time. For my first time. And it was amazing. I was glad we waited; it was worth waiting for.

For our special week together, Jack rented a villa in the south of France and it was quaint and beautiful. He actually rented two villas so as to not put pressure on me. It was absolutely the best time of my life, thus far. When I returned home, I had to write it all down in my journal about our time together.

~✳~¡~✳~¡~✳~¡~✳~¡~✳~¡~✳~

As I sat there with Zoë, I read my journal, but to myself and not out loud - it was just too personal.

Dear Journal: Jack and I were together. Our first time together. It was romantic, it was sweet. We were seldom more than a few inches from one another for our entire stay. We slid into a hot tub and talked about our future. We drank champagne and ate strawberries. We returned to bed and made love some more. And as the sun came up the next day, we made love again, but more aggressively and more intensely each time. It was exhausting and it was pleasurable. He seemed to know what felt good to me without even asking. We somehow did get in some other activities as well while we were in France. One day we SCUBA dived and found a magical wonderland of sea life deep below the surface of their beautiful cliffs. Jack said he never wanted to leave. I will always remember this time in my life as spiritual. We slept on the plane ride back home, which was about the only time we did. Even after the time we spent together, the kiss good-bye was passionate. I love you, Jack. Goodnight Journal.

I continued my story for Zoë.

~✳~¡~✳~¡~✳~¡~✳~¡~✳~¡~✳~

It was hard to concentrate on school. The days would drag on as I sat in class thinking of Jack and our time together. When I had any spare time, I would fly to wherever Jack was to be with him. I would sit track-side and watch him race. I watched how excited the fans were to get his autograph, along with the sexy female ones too. I sat staring at them thinking, "He's with me, sister - so back off!" Jack wasn't as friendly with the children fans as I hoped he'd be and that reminded me of Dad. But I felt he would be more interested in our children, since he would fantasize out loud about us having them. Jack and I always found a good Italian restaurant wherever we were. After dining together, we would go back to the hotel and make passionate love. My homework just had to wait. Acting took a back seat too. I barely pulled a 3.4 grade point average out of my first semester and Gamma commented that I should quit. I was shocked.

Then she continued. "Yes, you should quit if you're not going to take it seriously. Why waste your money?" Needless to say, I did better the next semester. Gamma's shunning was too hard to take.

Since I hadn't worked in a while, I decided that would be a good time to take a break from everything and everyone at home. That summer I chose to work on a smaller project - a horror movie; something that I had never done before. It was refreshing and fun. Lexy came out to visit on the set and even played one of the corpses, inconspicuously, of course. The production couldn't afford to pay Lexy the salary she usually received, so they didn't show her face onscreen. Lexy used an alias for her credits and donated her *extras* paycheck to charity. Since the movie was staffed with all union members, she hadn't violated any union rules.

Jack and I agreed that our lives would be easier if he had a place in Los Angeles. That way, he could be around me when he wasn't working. I could devote more time I'd normally spent traveling to study time. I missed being with Jack at his racing locations though, but I knew that this was the best scenario for the time being. I also didn't like not being there when I knew those other women were pawing at him.

I was the one who actually purchased the condo that Jack would live in because Jack said that there was some sort of problem with his credit or the bank transfer - I'm not sure which. Jack said there was also a mixup with the title on the condo and they put it in his name instead of mine. I'm not sure what happened, but I trusted Jack not to steal it from me and to get it straightened out.

Another good thing was that Lexy was around more often. She came out to visit and stayed with me a while. But Lexy was Lexy and she had to party even when I couldn't.

She'd go out and party several times during the week, and I stayed home to study. I knew I needed to finish school and not procrastinate anymore. So it was good that Lexy was preoccupied, but bad that she drifted from one guy to the other in a very short time. She was "desperately in love" one minute and "madly in love" with someone else the next minute. I wasn't sure what to do for her. Lexy would stay for a day or two, then she'd get restless and abruptly depart to places unknown. I'm not sure how much of my being happy with Jack played into it. I think it was mainly because Lexy couldn't handle her father's affair. She said she felt guilty about something, and I guess it was for not telling her mother. She didn't talk about it often. She did stay in Los Angeles with me after the last breakup for a stint long enough to take a class on interior design. She didn't stick with it for very long afterwards, but I think it gave her a sense of accomplishment to finish the class.

That was also the year that Lexy dropped out of sight from the public for a while; she said that she had to go get her head together. I flew out to visit Lexy at her vacation site and even stayed with her for a few weeks during that summer.

During my third year of school, Jack proposed. He had a decorator garnish the condo with what seemed like a million kinds of flowers, including red and yellow roses, but no pink. They ran a string of twinkling lights around the terrace, lighting up the area. It was all so romantic. I had no idea that Jack was even thinking of this. Jack got down on one knee and said he had loved many women, but none like me. Then Jack claimed that he would perish off the earth if I didn't agree to marry him. After I said YES, he presented me with his great-grandmother's engagement ring dangling from one perfect long-stemmed pink rose. Not to mention a box of tissues. We danced on the terrace with no music playing. We made love for hours, it was hot and steamy. We made love on the terrace, then in the den, then in the shower.

When I got home that night, Gampy was sitting in the

middle of an orchard of pink roses. They were surrounding him in his easy chair in the family room. When I walked in, Gampy glanced up from his newspaper and all he said was, "So you think we should get some flowers to spruce up the place a bit?" And then he returned to reading his newspaper. I laughed hysterically, partly because Gampy was teasing me and partly because he looked so comical in the middle of all those flowers. I showed him the ring, but he wasn't surprised. A little birdie had told him of Jack's plan.

Gamma glanced at the ring the next morning and then went back to her kitchen duties. She didn't seem to be impressed. I'm not sure that she had warmed up to Jack yet, but she did love me and I suppose that's why she never said anything bad about him to me. I did know that she and Jack had a *discussion* a week ago. All I knew about it, was that it was heated and their discussion had something to do with a prenup. I'm not sure for whom - him or me. No matter, they seemed to have put it behind them because neither Jack nor Gamma would tell me what it was about.

The following week after Jack proposed, we had a small engagement party. Before the festivities began, he spoke to Mom - alone. Jack's an old-fashion guy and he wanted to ask Dad for my hand, but had to settle for asking Mom. I wasn't sure how to advise him with that. Maybe he should have asked Gampy or even Gamma - they were the ones who actually raised me. No matter, Mom was impressed. Lexy was a basket case during their conversation, which didn't help me any. She kept saying, "Aw, bloody 'ell - would they hurry up already. I'm dying to find out what they're chatting about."

"Lexy, hush. I can't hear anything through this door with you jabbering." What was Mom telling him? Would it be something embarrassing? Then I sprinted away as they came out laughing. I tried to be cool, but Jack knew I was nervous and gently teased me about it. We danced and laughed all night, and as the party was ending, Jack stole me away for an Italian ice - just the two of us. We ended the evening by making love back at the condo before he brought me back home. I decided not to spend the night at the condo, even though we were engaged, out of respect for Gamma's traditional values.

After we made our public announcement, the tabloids kicked into overdrive writing, "**Sultry Redheaded Actress to Wed Playboy Daredevil Racer**." They wrote that Jack's only goal in marrying me was to use my popularity to further his career and acquire more sponsors for himself, since he was having trouble keeping them. Gamma wasn't amused, but I liked the headlines and I tore off the tabloid's front page before slipping it into my journal.

Jack and I agreed that we wouldn't get married until after I graduated. We set a date and released it to the media after notifying the family. I didn't waste any time. Lexy and I started planning the wedding for the end of June - three weeks after graduation. We bought every bride's magazine sold and then complained when they didn't have the new issues on the stands early enough for us. Eventually it became too much for me to handle; along with school and working, I was exhausted. I finally just hired a wedding planner, a woman named Toni.

The summer after my third year in school, I made the flight out to Italy to see Jack's world, to meet his family and to see where he grew up. His parents were very nice and his father looked as if he ruled with an iron fist. They had miles of land and a vineyard that went on forever with a very prestigious label. Jack didn't have any brothers, and he told me his father was upset that he hadn't carried on the family business.

They had a very nice engagement party for us, and even though I couldn't understand them most of the time, I could see that they were happy for us. Jack did his best to translate, but everyone kept stealing him away. Later that night, Jack and his father got into a heated argument, but I'm not exactly sure what it was about. Father and son stuff perhaps. And maybe it just seemed heated to me because they were a passionate sort of people. I did hear someone whispering, in English, that they were fighting over money and sponsors, but I don't know if that was just for my benefit, why else would they be speaking English? Maybe next semester I'll take Italian.

After Jack and I returned home, Larry presented me with a script that he said was perfect for me. I wasn't sure if he had just said that to get me back to work or if he had truly felt that, but I could not see the connection. Nevertheless, I decided to do it for him, and spent the rest of the summer working on the film. This time on the set, I would be alone. Lexy was MIA and would not be there to cheer me on. Jack was working and everyone at home had their lives to live. I felt somewhat lonely and homesick. No matter, we soon wrapped and I headed home again and returned to school for my final year.

Finally, another milestone in my life was behind me. I received a business degree from UCLA and graduated with honors. It wasn't the highest of grades, but Gampy was so proud that I swore I spotted a tear in his eye at graduation. Gamma cried like a baby and didn't care who saw her. Mom was there, but sat in the back. I didn't even know she was there until the press told me when they were asking me for a statement. It wasn't too difficult to pick out the soccer team's players. Even though Tommy was into baseball, he was impressed with the comradery of all the soccer teammates huddling around like they were on the field celebrating their triumph for graduating, and he didn't notice much else. Foxy wasn't there so I said I wanted to hurry through it and go celebrate with the *whole* family.

When Gamma asked me what my good deed was for that day, I handed her my diploma while saying, "I got this for you." She sniffled all the way home.

Jack hadn't been able to be there either. He said something about having to help an old friend, actually an old *girl*friend, but the details were sketchy. No matter, he assured me it was platonic and I chose to believe him and didn't make a big deal about it. I got a call from Uncle Red gushing and teasing me about going to law school next. I also got a telegram from Lexy congratulating me and that was just like her to be dramatic and mysterious. I didn't hear from Dad.

We had refreshments at the house. Gamma made my favorite; chocolate cream pie. Foxy had her Champion

Cheddar. I opened presents and it was a good day, except for not hearing from Jack or Dad. Before turning in, I tried calling Jack, but he hadn't returned home yet.

~*~!~*~!~*~!~*~!~*~!~*~

Zoë was still unconscious. I reached out and touched her hand to see if she would awaken. When she didn't, I added, "I later found out that Jack had an admirer in Italy. Jack told me that person lied about what his father had said to Jack about fighting over the money and sponsors. They came up with the idea to tell the lie when they read about our wedding announcement in the tabloids. It was told just to make me doubt and break up with him. That's why they spoke in English, just as I suspected."

I knew I needed to eat something and take a break from my storytelling; I was feeling a little weak. Gladis walked me back to my room and sat with me as I ate my meal. I sat in silence thinking about what I'd told Zoë so far and how I left out the part about Lexy having a high-profiled relationship with her brother, Dirk. She probably already knew anyway so no big deal. But Zoë probably didn't know that it was because of Dirk that Lexy dropped out of sight for a while. But that's another story and that wasn't *my* story to tell.

It was still dark out, and I knew I needed to finish telling Zoë my story before morning. By then, everything would be different and they would take her away from me. I didn't know if I'd ever get this chance again - to tell her about my life and what they robbed from both of us. I hurried through dinner, also because I didn't want Zoë to think I'd abandoned her.

~*~!~*~!~*~!~*~!~*~!~*~

Chapter VII

Practically the Wedding of the Century

As the wedding date approached, I was getting more excited. I'd never been involved in an event so big before. Toni, our wedding planner, got everyone involved - even Foxy. Foxy was to be our flower girl, with the rings pinned to a pillow she'd wear on her back. The plan was that she would trot up to us when I called her, and Jack would take the rings off. I practiced with Foxy for hours when we'd go to the dog park.

Jack's best friend Buck, a racing buddy, was to be his best man. The two of them were off fishing in Acapulco and due back about a week before the wedding; this left me to do all the dirty work. Jack said to just tell him where and when to show up and that would be his part. But that was okay; I was having the time of my life and Lexy was in her element.

Toni had snagged the most beautiful reception room at the Deluxe Holiday Resorts Hotel in Los Angeles with plenty of space for our two hundred guests. The hotel had huge spectacular chandeliers flowing from the ceiling and stunning pastel-blue carpeting. Toni was decorating the reception area with tiny clear icicles with pink streaks in them. She told me about the rest while I was drifting away in my own fantasy spinning around the dance floor like Alice in Wonderland, so I didn't hear another word. That was okay; I trusted her to make it beautiful.

I had asked Lexy, of course, to be my maid of honor. And who was not so secretly planning my Bridal Shower/ Bachelorette Party, with male strippers no less. She planned it to take place three days before the wedding; that way, it wouldn't interfere with the rehearsal dinner and the other activities we had scheduled. Lexy's dress was beautiful; I let her select the style herself. I wanted her to feel comfortable in it because nothing was worst than a bad bridesmaid dress you had to wear for several hours in front of hundreds of people. The only condition was that it had to be pale pink to match the flowers. We sought out Gemi to design it as we did for our Acclamation Award treasures and she outdid herself.

Tommy would be one of the ushers, a duty which he took very seriously. I once walked by his room and spotted Tommy practicing holding out his arm for the women who he would walk to the seating area at the ceremony. I couldn't help but snicker a little. I was just happy that we could get the baseball cap off him long enough to see Tommy actually had hair.

No one could reach Dad, but no matter; I wanted Uncle Red to walk me up the aisle anyway.

Even Mom sobered up long enough to help plan the wedding. She tried selecting her own dress, but Toni about had a meltdown over what Mom chose. So as difficult as it was for Mom to put aside her controlling personality, she allowed Toni to select the dress for her because Mom knew it would make me happy. That was one fire put out. I figured that if this was as bad as it got, I could handle it.

My dress was also designed by Gemi. It was a strapless white satin and lace masterpiece with embroidery from the waist up and a lower portion that flared out. Gemi sewed tiny pearls along the waist and up the back. The dress included an embroidery Victorian design choker with diamonds dripping down from it. My veil was a simple design of medium-length mesh, as we didn't want it to overpower the ensemble. My shoes had embroidery on them as well and were three and a half inches high. I didn't know how in the world I was ever going to walk in them, but Toni said it would present a better portrait since Jack was almost six feet tall.

The invitations were simple with gold lettering on

ivory-colored paper. We didn't know exactly how to write them, because we couldn't locate Dad and didn't know if he'd even bother showing up if we did. So we didn't include any of the parents' names. This saddened Jack's parents, but he told me that they understood. I wasn't sure if he was telling the truth, since I only heard Jack's side of the conversation via the telephone, and that part was in Italian. Jack and his parents were fighting about something while he was telling them so I don't know for sure if he said that just to spare my feelings.

Toni had a heck of a time trying to find two hundred antique picture frames for our wedding party favors. We started in antique shops around Los Angeles and just bought up what they had. Then we found some at antique clothing consignment shops, but the bulk of them came from antique shops in Paris. We had them flown in. None were over the size of five by eight and that was perfect. I saw so many that I wanted to keep myself because they were so beautiful. I made sure Gamma and Mom got their first choice. We planned to send a wedding photo of Jack and me to everyone after the nuptials.

The cake design was three-tiered for the guests, plus a top layer for our first anniversary. It had white frosting with pink strawberry batter inside. All around the outside were pink roses made of frosting and on the top the roses looked so real, I thought they were. Jack insisted that it have pink roses on it; that color was significant to both of us, so it wasn't just because pink was my favorite for roses. The groom's cake was chocolate with raspberry frosting. We had champagne flutes prepared with our names engraved on them. Slightly smaller flutes were engraved for Buck and Lexy. We selected a Gelato Italy dessert dish for Foxy because it sits low to the table so she could reach it easily, and not knock it over. It too, was engraved with her name. These pieces all had wedding theme wine glass charms dangling from them, even Foxy's.

My bouquet was simple, with one perfect pink rose in the center of two dozen white roses. It was accented with lace and baby's breaths. Buck would wear a single pink rose and Lexy would carry a bouquet of pink roses and baby's breaths. The flowers on the tables were white roses with a single pink rose, similar to my bouquet. We didn't want to go overboard with the pink.

We planned the "something old, new, borrowed, blue" because Toni didn't want any last-minute surprises. Gamma gave me her set of beautiful diamond earrings that had been handed down from her grandmother for my "something old." Gamma got Foxy to give me a linen handkerchief for my "something new." Mom gave me one of the diamond bracelets that I bought for her sober encouragements for my "something borrowed." And finally, Lexy gave me a beautiful blue-embroidered lace garter for my "something blue," along with a blue negligee she tried to get me to wear under my wedding dress.

"Aw Pookie, you don't want to waste any time when you get to the honeymoon suite, do you?" she teased. I laughed and admitted I'd be wearing a corset-inspired bustier under my dress though, with silk stockings and not nylons. Lexy fired back with, "Ooo, La, La," in a French accent as Lexy and I giggled, and Mom and Gamma smiled at us. It was a nice moment.

When Gamma asked what my good deed was for that day, I said I was allowing the man of my dreams to marry me. Everyone laughed.

Jack's tux was stunningly handsome. He didn't want anything over-the-top fancy so we kept it simple. Black tux, white shirt, with a black cummerbund and a simple single white rose for his lapel. Since I was going to wear his great-grandmother's wedding rings, we searched and found a ring for him that would match mine. I thought the ring was perfect, I was just happy he was going to wear one to ward off his female admirers.

Jack was planning the honeymoon, but wouldn't tell me where we were going. However, I did overhear him talking to someone on the telephone one day. He implied to whomever he was talking to that he "couldn't wait for the first time to see her in a bikini under her SCUBA gear." Also something about motion sickness pills. I'd always hinted that

I'd love to dive the barrier reef off the coast of Australia so I thought maybe that was it. And since I didn't really like to fly long distances, I figured that's what the pills were about. I also speculated that maybe we'd go back to our villas in the south of France. Or maybe sail around the world like he'd always wanted to. At some point, though, I had to stop thinking about it or I would have driven myself crazy trying to figure it out.

I planned to have my makeup done professionally the morning of the wedding by one of the makeup artists I knew, a friend who owned his own props store and was very well-known for his work with special effects on the movie sets. I knew I would be too nervous to handle that on my own. I also hired a hair dresser, but still had no idea how I wanted to wear my hair. I was worried my red hair would clash with all the pink. Toni reassured me, "No worries - don't panic. It will be fine." So I was trusting her.

My bridesmaid's gift to Lexy was a gold-lined compact cosmetic mirror that lit up when opened. I had an inscription engraved inside; "To Lexy, my best friend who's never left my side for one minute, Love Pookie." Jack's best man's gift to Buck was a remote-controlled race car. That wouldn't have been my first choice, but boys will be boys. Jack teased he was going to have it engraved.

Gamma and her enlisted helpers made up pouches of bird seed instead of rice so it would be environmentally safe for the animals. They set up a table for assembling them at the house, and I think Foxy helped too because she was over there a lot. Maybe she was just a part of the clean up crew.

I wasn't particular about the menu. I preferred that Mom work it out with Toni. Mom felt good that she had tasks to do and that I wanted her involved. The only stipulation I had was that we set a place at the bride's table for Foxy and have Champion Cheddar for her.

One week before the wedding, I was ready with planning the details, but *I* was a mess. The wedding was the biggest event of my life and Jack wasn't around. He was due back shortly, and I needed him. I was starting to get butterflies in my stomach and he always knew how to divert my fears.

"What if I drop my bouquet?"

"Then you pick it up," Toni answered.

"What if Foxy runs off with the rings?"

"Then we shoot her in her tracks."

My eyes popped open like saucers, and I looked at Toni with my head tilted in disgust.

Toni rebounded, "Okay so we'll bribe her back with a leg of lamb."

"Or a Champion Cheddar?" I suggested, smiling.

"Ooo Kay, a Champion Cheddar then," Toni said patronizing me. "You need to look over this wedding photography layout list and circle what you want so we can arrange for them with the others..." Toni was cut off by the ringing of the telephone.

"Hello?"

"Hi Joey, honey. I need to talk to you - do you have a minute?"

"Hi Uncle Red, I always have a minute for you. As a matter of fact, take two."

"First, I need you to find a quiet place to sit down."

"Why, what's going on? Now what?" I asked as if Dad was up to his old shenanigans again.

"Please, can you just sit down Joey, honey?"

"Okay, I'm sitting."

"Joey, I just confirmed through my sources down at the police station that the plane that Jack chartered has lost radio contact with a Mexican air-traffic control tower. They said they lost radar on his plane a moment after that. Now, they don't have any news, and they don't know for sure what happened - so it's important that you stay calm."

A surge of fear streaked through my body like lightning. With my head in my hands, I uttered in a monotone voice, "I'm calm, Uncle Red. When have you ever known me to panic?"

"Good girl," Uncle Red said. "Let me come get you, and we can fly down there together to talk to the Mexican authorities."

"Ah no, you're closer to Mexico; I'll come to you. I'll be on the next flight. I'll call you from the airport with my flight information."

"Okay... will you be alright to travel?"

"Yes," I answered with a bit more collectiveness.

I asked Larry to go with me to the airport. Eddie chauffeured us, and by the time we arrived at LAX, the details were all over the news. There was a mob of people out front at the drop-off curb holding microphones and wearing earpieces, waiting for me. There was every news organization imaginable present, from reporters to gossip columnists, with their station's trucks lined up at every terminal. Larry and I pushed past them, and after calling Uncle Red, I got on a flight to Houston. By the time I arrived in Texas, Uncle Red had spoken to several people concerning the missing plane. He updated me with the details during our flight to Mazatlan, the closest city to Buck and Jack's last known location. All we knew at that point was that their plane stopped transmitting, which didn't mean it had crashed. The authorities informed us that they had sent a search party out to look for Buck and Jack, but they didn't have any news yet.

When Uncle Red and I disembarked, we were greeted by an escort. He drove us to a private airport that housed several helicopters. We then flew with several officers up above the location where they thought the plane might be located. Hours passed as our helicopter traveled around the area, but we didn't find anything - not even a crash site. We then returned to the police station to wait for any new information.

Assessing the day I discovered - not finding a crash site was the good news, but that was also the bad news. Where were Jack and Buck? Where did they go? And what happened to the plane?

"You can't just lose a plane," I thought out loud, trying to make sense of it all.

"We'll find them, Joey."

About a minute later, one of the Federalies came into

the waiting room and said, "Señor, Señorita, we've just heard from the United States and they have your friend. But they only have one of your friends, and he is alive. You can reach him at this number."

"Oh, thank God," I said. "Uncle Red, you call."

As Uncle Red spoke on the telephone, I could see the look on his face change to anguish. The "friend" wasn't Jack. Buck had returned on his scheduled flight, but Jack was a no-show. Buck said that Jack wasn't feeling well and just before they boarded, they got separated. And that's the last he saw of Jack. He just assumed Jack would take the next flight home when he didn't see him board the flight. Buck called the police after he heard on the news that Jack and he were missing. Buck informed them of what he knew, which wasn't much.

After hearing about these developments, Uncle Red and I went back out with the authorities and searched every daylight minute of the next three days, but there was no plane, no crash site, no evidence, no Jack. I called Toni and told her to notify everyone that the wedding was on hold until I found Jack. We continued to fly out every day searching the ground for any evidence of Jack and his pilot. Also, I called home every day to see if Jack had called or if anyone had information we weren't getting in Mexico.

Inside of the helicopter was cold and biting, but I welcomed that sensation to take away the pain I was feeling. After the first week, I started to feel sick and knew I had to eat more to maintain my energy.

After three and a half weeks of searching, Uncle Red convinced me to take a break and return home. He said that as much as he loved me and wanted to help, he had to return to his life and law practice. People were counting on him for their very lives. Sam missed him too. I understood.

I reluctantly agreed to take a break, but only to gather fresh supplies then return. Gamma begged me not to return to Mexico; in fact, I had to practically peel her off me to get out the door. What was I suppose to do - just forget about him? I just couldn't think of anything other than helping Jack.

I brought Foxy back with me and took her every day on the search. I hired Poncho, a helicopter pilot from the private airport in Mexico, for most of the search excursions I took. I rented an apartment nearby the airport with only a bed and table in it. Since I didn't spend much time there and knew I wasn't going to stay, what was the point of furnishing it? It wasn't home. I was going to find Jack and we were going home to get married and we were going to live our perfect life together and have a thousand babies like he promised. I had learned long ago not to take no for an answer or give up on what I wanted.

My daily routine was to get up in the morning while it was still dark, shower, drive to a private airport, charter a helicopter and pilot, and look for Jack every daylight hour. Every night, I would go to the same café and order the same meal. I'm not sure if that was because I didn't feel anything anymore and the taste of food didn't matter or if I was just superstitious. At first, I would sneak Foxy in under the booth table, and I'm sure they knew, but the waitress never said anything. I would then go back to the apartment to review and map out new possible places to search, retiring for the night around eleven or twelve o'clock. I would get around five hours of sleep during the night, and get up to do it all over again. My routine was mundane but my mission of finding Jack motivated me. The only variations to my days were when I gave Foxy a bath once a month and called home once a week to give them updates. There wasn't much to tell because there weren't very many updates.

"Hope," I whispered each night before drifting off. "That's what we'll name our first daughter, Jack. Hope."

At one point, I had an annoying confrontation with my nosey and insufferable apartment manager in Mazatlan. The guy claimed he had just discovered that I had a dog in the apartment. He declared, "No pets in the apartments; it's against the rules."

"So what's your price?" I asked with a huge sigh.

"Excuse me?"

"What's your price to overlook that rule?"

"I don't have a price; no pets in the apartments," he responded.

"Everyone has a price, amigo. So let's take a moment and visit the best case scenario here, shall we? I'll call my accountants, buy this dump, fire your ass, and then eliminate the rule. How's that sound to you, Mr. Management? Cuz, that is a real possibility, especially with the mood I'm in," I vented coolly with a deadly glare toward him.

I'm sure he sensed my anger and ruthlessness because that's when he reconsidered. "Hundred bucks more a month and I don't see nothin'."

"Acceptable - now stay out of my room from now on. I know you've been in here. If I find you in here again, I'll kick you in the crotch so hard you'll need a tracheotomy just to relieve yourself, comprehenda? Now get the hell out of my doorway and don't come back." I'm sure there wasn't a pet rule; there were animals all over that place. That guy just wanted to be a big shot, to have control over someone's life, and to make them feel indebted to him. I couldn't help think, "Dad would be very proud of him." I was bitter knowing yet another man was trying to control my life.

At first, the Mexican Federalies sent out a "search and rescue" team to help find Jack, but after a week and after Uncle Red and I went back home, they renamed it to "search and recover." I didn't or wouldn't believe Jack was dead and that was why I hired my own search team. After a month of Jack being missing, the Federalies stopped going out altogether. After that, they didn't care. They gave me every reason they could muster for not continuing, everything from they didn't have the money, to he probably got cold feet about the wedding and returned to Italy, or his plane probably glided for a while under radar and then crashed into the ocean.

In searching for Jack, I would have my map and coordinates ready each morning. Poncho had a buddy who would ride along with us to provide another pair of eyes to help spot any wreckage. Much of the terrain that would go on for miles around Mazatlan was flat and deserted, thus easy to view. We also tried flying east toward the Sierra

Madre Mountains thinking it would be an easy place for Jack's plane to get lost and hard to spot wreckage there. Some days we'd stay close to Mazatlan thinking maybe the Federalies were right about Jack being near the ocean when the plane went down. Flying over the beach reminded me of the honeymoon Jack was planning for us and about the comment he made with me being "in a bikini under her SCUBA gear."

Lexy came down every once in a while, but said I'd changed and she couldn't reach me in my depths of depression anymore. Lexy said she just couldn't bear to see me suffer. But that wasn't entirely true because she kept coming back. I understood and said I would be better soon, better when I found Jack.

When the days were not favorable for flying, I'd hire an interpreter and we'd head into town to ask questions. I got to know my way around most of the seedier areas of the city. They seemed to have more information there, but it was sketchy at best. Most didn't like answering questions and others just shrugged. Oftentimes, no one recognized me, but sometimes they did and it wasn't always good. Especially when I acquainted myself with the Mexican underground - they were a little scary. But I proceeded with caution and learned how to find informants who knew more than their share, and *would* share - for a price. A *big* price. After I'd pay, they typically wouldn't know as much as they thought they did. Again and again, however, I could sense they wanted to tell me more about what they knew, just as much as what others were trying so intensely to hide. The whole experience was frustrating, especially since I didn't *feel* Jack was dead.

Somewhere in the sand of the hour glass, I was drowning. I had dropped out of sight in Hollywood and spent a year and a half searching for Jack, but I couldn't find him. I was numb. My life seemed to stand still. Everyone was sympathetic at first, but then told me I needed to get on with my life. What life? I didn't have a life without Jack.

After nineteen months of searching for Jack, I returned

home broken. The nights were hard and I would cry a river of tears lying awake for hours. I spent my days helping other people and trying to get the focus off me. It seemed to help when I could help someone else, since I couldn't help Jack. I used helping people for my good deeds, but in reality, they were helping me.

Gamma didn't know what to do for me. She wanted to have a birthday gathering for my twenty-fourth birthday, but I didn't feel like celebrating. I agreed, only because it seemed to give her joy to do something for me.

I instructed my management company to sell Jack's condo. I figured that would be a good place to start in getting on with my life. They informed me that the condo was not in my name and I couldn't touch it, even if Jack *still* owned it. Nevertheless, he didn't. Turns out, the condo had been sold two months before Jack disappeared. The only reason the management company knew this, was that's when the homeowner's association returned my checks for the dues, stating they were no longer required due to the sale of the property. I wasn't sure what that was all about, but I really didn't care. It was just one less thing that I had to do to erase Jack from my thoughts. The money was never a concern, and I assumed his parents received the proceeds from the condo sale along with Jack's possessions. I had thought that my management company had been paying for the expenses even after Jack disappeared, but they said no. I guess with me being out of town for so long, along with not really caring about what was going on with my business affairs when I was searching for Jack, it didn't surprise me that I didn't know the particulars.

It was peculiar though, that he had sold the condo. I assumed he did this because he wanted to save me the hassle. He knew we wouldn't need it anymore, since we planned to live in the Hollywood house after we were married.

I started going to a counselor to help me put a face on my loss, but it was impossible to move forward. She said that the more I felt abandoned, the more I wanted to be alone, so no one could leave me again. And with that, she advised me to start dating again so I gave it a try and went out on a few dates. They were total disasters. If my dates weren't asking me about Jack and what I thought happened to him, I would be talking about how my life sucked without him. That sort of killed the mood.

I would lie in bed at night wondering where Jack was. Why didn't he want to come back to me? How could he possibly be dead? He was an athlete, young, prime, strong - invincible. "You didn't keep your word, Jack - you said I could plan the wedding and your only part was to show up," I'd whisper to him, feeling that he was out in the world somewhere.

All of my abandonment issues started creeping back in. I felt completely and utterly alone. Not even Foxy could fill this void for me this time. I'm not sure I got through all the five steps of loss, especially in the order they say we should, but I went through something. Denial was definitely one. Anger was a big one, especially after I returned home. I suppose I just needed all of my energy for the search instead of feeling anger at the time. Bargaining - well, I don't think I bargained. I yelled at God a lot, but I didn't bargain especially since I thought I was strong enough to help Jack on my own. Depression - absolutely. Acceptance - well, I don't know about that one yet. I have moved on with my life, but only because I've had to do so. Life was moving on around me.

I sort of felt sorry for Gamma; she had to dispose of the wedding paraphernalia the best way she knew how without me being there to instruct her. She kept some of it stored in the attic not knowing if I'd be angry that she discarded it. As if to say, "This wedding will never happen." A few months after returning from Mexico, I had every last bit of it removed from the house. I donated my dress to charity - anonymously since no photographs were ever taken of it. I didn't want that beautiful work of art that symbolized my hopes and dreams with Jack to become a circus free-for-all for the tabloids. I sent the ring back to Jack's parents. I think that was when I finally realized that I was not going to marry Jack. That was a hard day. And if that wasn't enough stress for me to deal with, Mom was drinking again. She said something about not being able to help her little girl so she used that as her excuse-of-the-month. This made me mad, that she would use *me* as her latest justification to jump back into the bottle, and I was set back again - back to *depression*.

~*~:~*~:~*~:~*~:~*~:~*~

I squeezed Zoë's hand, but there was still no response. "Jack and I were all ready to walk up the aisle. I cried the tears of a grieving widow for him. I tried to move forward, but something kept holding me back. Everyone said it was just that I didn't want to accept what was obvious to them - that he was gone. My condition was almost like being an alcoholic, and for the first time in my life, I understood what it was like for Mom. Not that I knew for sure that she was an alcoholic - rather, that she just liked feeling numb. But I had such a craving for wanting Jack back in my life that I ignored everything else around me."

~*~:~*~:~*~:~*~:~*~:~*~

Chapter VIII

Pookie Productions

Most of my family and some of my friends assembled together one day to perform a kind of intervention on me, I suppose you would say. They basically told me that I needed to get back to work. "You haven't worked in three years, and you need to get back to your first love." I guess no one had the courage to complete that sentence with, "since your second love died."

Larry was thrilled to see me return to work, even for reasons other than making his commission. I didn't feel as though I was ready yet, but did it nonetheless. I threw myself into it full force and made three major pictures the first year after coming home from Mexico. I made sure Larry understood that I would not do interviews or promos for the films. I knew the reporters and TV commentators would ask about Jack's disappearance. I hadn't anything to say, and what *could* I say? I didn't know anything about Jack.

Larry said I thrived in adversity, but that I was also becoming overexposed in the industry. He instructed me to retreat a bit and become more discriminating in my role choices. But now that I was back, I wanted to work. I needed to stay busy, exhaustingly busy. I knew that Larry was right about being overexposed, and the critics were crucifying me for it, but I still needed a distraction to fill all the other hours in my life. That's when I formed my own production company. I finally put that business degree to work as the Executive Producer of Pookie Productions.

I chose that company name because Pookie was Lexy's

pet name for me, and also, because it had a fun chime to it. I was ready for a little fun again. I wanted a fresh new start for the fresh new company, with a fresh new name, and that's when I came up with my new pseudonym, Mel Kobach, to use when I was producing. Mel came from my middle name, Melanie, and Kobach was Gamma and Gampy's last name. The production company opened for business just in time to celebrate my twenty-fifth birthday.

Pookie Productions soon found some scripts to produce and had six movies in production at one time. The work was hard, but exhilarating. I had never known how much fun it was on this side of the business, and began to think that maybe I was meant to be there all along. I still planned on acting in two movies per year, but producing was becoming my niche.

As if all of that weren't enough, Gampy thought of another good distraction for me - to build a house. Gampy teased that I also needed to spend some of the wealth behind my *dynasty*. He said that he would oversee the construction, while I stayed busy planning the interior. I agreed - for two reasons. First, I could never say no to him, and secondly, I could hardly bear to live in *that* house anymore. That's where Jack and I were going to live happily ever after - after we were married. I think Gampy could sense I needed to live somewhere else too because I was barely there anymore, and when I was, I never slept in my bed. I think it was Gamma who told him I always slept on the couch in my room. I knew she was suspicious and I didn't want her to worry so I would mess up the bedcovers to make it look as though the bed had been slept in. She wasn't fooled though. My relocation also made Foxy a bit confused. She used to snuggle up to me in bed, but now we both couldn't fit on the couch together. After that, she usually slept on the floor just to be close to me.

The construction was fast, and the new house was shaping up to be a superb fortress. It would even have a mote. Gampy said something about Feng Shui'ing it with water swirling around the entire house. Who knew he knew about that kind of stuff? Gampy continually surprised me.

My "castle" now sits on ten acres on the Palisades cliffs overlooking the Pacific Ocean. The house is so enormous, that Tommy joked it made the nine hundred room Deluxe Holiday Resorts Hotel in Los Angeles look like a trailer park. Gamma teased Gampy, saying we'd need a newsletter just to let everyone know what we were having for dinner. The interior of the main house ended up having five separate suites of rooms. Each suite has two bedrooms and a living area. There's only one kitchen though; Gamma insisted that everyone still eat together. I told Uncle Red that when he was ready, we had a suite ready just for him and Sam.

Back before completing the blue prints on the house, Gampy asked Uncle Red to return to court and obtained a clarification on Mom's court order. The court ruling stated that as long as Mom didn't live under the same roof as Tommy, she could live on the same property. So Gampy designed the house with one detached suite, just for her. That way, we abided by the laws and Mom could be close enough to live as a part of the family again.

It was now my turn to make decisions on the interior, however, I relinquished most of these duties to Gamma and Lexy. Since Lexy had some interior design knowledge, I thought it would be fun for her to be involved. Unfortunately, they couldn't agree on anything and squabbled constantly - even Foxy couldn't get a bark in edgewise. Gamma was conservative and Lexy... well Lexy was Lexy. So when I needed to, I'd step in and chose a medium of whatever it was they were disagreeing about. We ended up with a beautiful mix of ideas, very eclectic. The final design included huge walk-in closets in each bedroom and an attached bathroom.

It was Gamma's idea to have a family room where everyone could meet at the end of the day to have refreshments and some hors d'oeuvres. She included a saltwater aquarium in the room, closer to one end. It was Lexy's suggestion to turn the family room into an amusement haven. So we included a billiard table, dart board, and a poker table.

Lexy also recommended the romantic open-pit spherical fireplace area at the opposite end from the aquarium.

Gamma contributions included the wine cellar, walk-in pantry, and tennis court. Lexy proposed the workout room with tanning beds and an electronic games arcade. I added the music recording studio and, of course, my Jacuzzi. Gampy was happy with his hobby room and the media center where he watched his stock market channels. Tommy had his outdoor batting cages and a full-length Olympic-size swimming pool.

On top of it all, we included Lexy's own bedroom in the architectural design, even though she didn't really live there with us. This room was hers exclusively whenever she wanted to come visit. Our house wasn't going to be anything like her home; she lived in a bona fide castle just outside of Liverpool. Poor Lexy, she was so touched by us including her that she cried and got mascara all over her new Gemi designer cashmere sweater.

Our estate has way more than four parking spaces as the other house. We hired a contractor just to plow a parking lot for the party area we affectionately dubbed "The Party Barn," which has its own dining room, an electronic games arcade and disco. Despite the name, this party section is very elegant and looks nothing like a barn. We built a parking garage for the family, where Gampy also designed a taller and wider stall for his airstream bus - his new toy, and pride and joy. He gutted out the whole inside of the bus and refurbished it to be this very plush luxury lounge on wheels. I teased that the next one he did was for me to take on location, instead of living in those drab production trailers.

Oh, and yes, I finally did get that limo. Foxy has her own little elevated booster seat in the back of that one too so she can look out the window. And, yes, we even added another tray table for her Champion Cheddars.

We drove to the local pet adoption center and adopted a truckload of animals to fill the house - including three more dogs and five cats. The dogs were a rottweiler mix and roamed the grounds freely. They were high-spirited and Gampy called them his *little babies;* it was so cute. He named them, "Larry, Curly and Moe." They slept in Gamma and Gampy's room at night. The cats were all sorts of breeds. Gamma had a heck of a time keeping them straight. I even brought six bunnies home, and the dogs kept them tightly corralled since they couldn't keep track of the cats either. Tommy got an iguana he named Iggie - ugh, I wouldn't go near it. Sometimes he'd bring it to dinner with him crouched on his shoulder. Everyone would refuse to come to the table until it was gone so Gamma would have to yell at Tommy to take it away. Gampy also found two beautiful horses, one of which I named Poncho. That was the name of my helicopter pilot in Mexico, and I liked the name. The other one I named CoCo because of its color.

Gampy had staff quarters built for the additional live-in staff members we hired. Eddie, in addition to being my driver and our butler, was promoted to Chief of Staff of all personnel. And along with Ruby, our housekeeper from the old house, we hired another housekeeper, a chef, my personal assistant (Brandy), and three security guards for the grounds and front gate. I also upgraded my personal security and hired more bodyguards for round-the-clock personal security. Tracy's the one who was designated to travel on location with me.

Finally, the house was completed just before my twenty-sixth birthday and it was perfect. I stocked it with everything imaginable, even all new furniture. I donated all of my old bedroom furniture, including my bed, and almost all of my clothes to charity. I wanted a fresh start, and I felt comfortable in the new house. I also was soon bored again and that meant trouble. I'd sometimes drive by the old house dreaming of what could have been - that is, what could have been *with Jack*. I finally looked at myself in the mirror one day and said, "You have way too much time on your hands, and it's time to get busy doing something else." That prompted me to get back to work.

As the Executive Producer, I often journeyed to the locations to check on how a film's budget was enduring. It was nice to be reacquainted with some of the people I'd worked with in the past. It was even nicer to be able to pull my pranks and smile again. I asked Brandy to make accommodations in Phoenix for Tracy and me, and off we went.

Paul, the sound guy on this film, was someone whom I hadn't seen since the Monkey Murders. "Hey, monkey boy, how are you?" I laughed and hugged him hello.

"Hi, Miss Walsh, what are you doing here?" he inquired. I gave him the short answer and we continued to reminisce about how fun the "old days" were. I'd laugh, but it wasn't a real laugh. I figured if I fake-laughed enough, it would be easier to reclaim my laugh for real.

About the third day on the set while joking around, I started to have a flashback that hit me like a brick. One of the boom boys was screeching down the street in his new sports car and that brought it all back for me. I was seeing Jack in his race car. I could hardly contain the wave of sadness I felt and I left, rushing back to the hotel.

The next day, as Tracy and I headed for the airport, I felt that I must have made a fool out of myself by departing so abruptly. After we took off and as I sat on the plane, I tried not to let the turbulence bother me, but it was gnarly - the worst I've ever experienced. Coupled with my emotional state, I just about lost it. Sleeping was out of the question for several reasons. For one, I could no longer sleep on planes since I had developed a phobia of sleeping in public. The problem was that my dreams of Jack were so bad that I would sometimes wake up screaming. I wasn't sure that the Flight Attendants would understand that the crazy screaming lady in 3B was just having a nightmare, and wasn't actually trying to hijack the airplane. I thought I would write in my journal to help with the anxiety of the turbulence and also the pain of remembering Jack. I felt that maybe if I wrote my feelings down, I could release them from my mind and my memory.

Dear Journal: In my Phoenix hotel room this morning, I was putting on the last touches of my makeup and making sure my outfit was spotless when the telephone rang. I picked up the receiver and started to give a greeting when I was interrupted by a recorded message. "This is your wake-up call! Have a nice day." Well, I guess two hours late was better then no call at all. I just hate those impersonal recordings. I gave one last glance around the room to make sure I hadn't forgotten anything and stepped out into the hallway where I met up with Tracy. My mind began to drift. I started walking down an endless empty corridor searching for the thoughts that would surround the day's events. A balcony opened in our path and I could see the sun rising up from behind a distant mountain with palm trees waving effortlessly. My spell was ended by a blurred figure in a business suit dashing past us showing no enthusiasm in response to my greeting. Tracy and I walked toward the main lobby as the wheels under my luggage clicked on the bricked paved sidewalk, like firecrackers against the silence. The lawns were green; the pool, crystal blue; and the perfectly groomed bushes surrounded us. As we proceeded to pass the parking lot with all the fancy sports cars, I thought of "him." The front desk checkout was so dreary, I found myself suddenly outside waiting for the limo, not totally remembering the conversation of "Hi, how are you this morning, Miss Walsh?" from the front desk clerk. They all seem to say the same thing like that irritating recorded message. My thoughts quickly switched to those of Phoenix, how hot and dry it was and how Gampy liked that sort of climate. I wondered if they had scorpions here like they did in Houston, but bigger I suppose, and if any really did get into the rooms like rumor had it. My thoughts rambled, touching on anything just to keep myself from going crazy from the boredom and to keep me from thinking of "him." My thoughts were interrupted by the limo pulling into the pavilion. As we got in, the driver was reporting in on his CB radio. The drive took longer than I remembered the first time, my mind still rambling on about everything, including how alone I felt. My face scowled as we passed a car dealership with their sportiest model up on a hoist. I once again thought of "him." The black muscular man behind the wheel asked if I had a good stay. I told him yes, but it was much too short. I guess I was secretly referring to the incident with the boom boy's sports car. The driver said he would like to travel sometime but, as he spoke, my mind drifted away again. Moments later, he pulled me back into the conversation by asking where I was headed. I answered, except

I didn't feel much like having a conversation. This never seemed to bother our driver at all and he kept right on chatting. We were driving the last lengths to the airport, when I spotted a gorgeous Jag, one like "his." I felt even lonelier. Tracy and I got out of the limo and walked into the terminal. Again, I started walking down an endless empty corridor searching for the thoughts which would surround the day's events. Goodnight Journal.

Would there ever be a day, a moment in time, that my mind wouldn't go to him? Would I want it to? I did know that I wanted this ache to fade. I wanted so desperately to laugh again, and mean it, and for it to come naturally - not forced just because others think that I should "get-over-it-already." I couldn't help feeling a sense of hopelessness and I thought, "No one knows how I feel."

I didn't mention my emotional episode to the family; they were already worried about me. And I decided not to go back onto a production site for a while, assigning most of the hands-on tasks to my associates. That was, until I noticed that we were producing a movie for Pete, the director, and another of my buddies from the Monkey Murder days. I felt I had to redeem myself and face my fears, and hoped that I'd be able to handle things better this time. So I told Tracy to get ready for the trip, packed up Foxy, and we hopped a flight to see Pete in San Antonio, Texas. I was also anxious to be in Texas again. San Antonio was only about two hundred miles from Houston and that meant I was close to home. While Texas was no longer my actual home state, it gave me comfort to think of it that way.

We arrived and checked into our rooms at a hotel near the location shoot. We then drove over to the production site, where I waved at Pete to let him know that I was there.

"Hey JoJo, how ya doing?" he asked as I introduced him to Tracy and Foxy.

"Wow, no one has called me that in years. I never knew how much I missed it."

"I heard you ran into some bad luck with that whole wedding cancellation and all, sorry to hear that," Pete stated as a matter-of-factly. "What are you doing these days?" he asked, as he moved on with the conversation. No matter, I didn't want to talk about it anyway.

"Thanks Pete. I'm mostly producing, including with this movie."

"No kidding. I've been working with the crew over at Pookie Productions and I thought some guy named Mel Kobach had this one."

"You're looking at *him* or rather her, that's me," I added with a smirk. "A name I came up with to keep the acting and producing worlds separate. You have been dealing with my associates. I have been tied up with other projects so I delegated," I explained, not admitting the real truth about why I was staying away from production sites. I continued, "But I'm still doing a role every now and then." I wanted to change the subject off me, so I asked, "Tell me - is your biggest movie to date? Any Ack Award talk yet?" I asked, actually teasing Pete, knowing this wasn't as big of a film as he usually directs.

"Yeah, I'm doing it as a favor to a friend. My *friend* was suppose to direct this film but dropped out at the last minute and didn't want to get a bad rep for bailing, so I stepped in for him. And yes, we'll be receiving the award for the worst romantic comedy in history."

"Ah Pete, this is a romantic drama."

"Yeah, I know that, but I can't get my leading woman to have chemistry with my leading man."

"Ever thought it might be the leading man's chemical deficiency," I bantered, defending my gender.

"Yeah, okay, *someone* is deficient and I have a movie to get made. Any thoughts?"

"None come to mind, but I can think it through for you. I'll need to see them in action. Where are they now?"

"Try the mess hall."

"Okay, catch ya later."

I walked into the mess hall and observed the leading man and leading woman at opposite ends of the room. She was sitting at a table close to the door with several other crew members, and he was standing on the far side of the room talking to three guys. It didn't take much deciphering when I saw the leading man. He was an Adonis. No chemistry? What was she thinking? I wondered how I should approach this. What would Lexy say to do, being the big romance goddess and all? She would probably just roll around on my bed kissing Ella and mocking me. "Hum, sometimes people just don't connect. I'll start with her," I whispered to myself.

"Hi, I'm Jordan," I said to her.

"Yes, you are," she stammered as she began to admire Foxy.

"And you are?"

"Myra, Myra Burns. I've seen every movie you've ever made."

"Really? Which did you like?"

"Oh, they were all great."

"Great, and which one did you like the best?"

"Well, they were all so good that I couldn't possibly name just one."

"I only ask that because most people can't name two that I've been in when I ask - they just like meeting actors."

Myra quivered with a slight panic in her voice as she asked, "I hadn't heard... I mean, are you in *this* movie?"

"No, no, I'm the Executive Producer. I just pay the bills."

"Oh, that's good too," she expressed with relief. What'd she think - that I was there to replace her?

We continued our conversation and I came to the conclusion that, although a bit flighty, Myra was perfectly capable of handling her scenes. I went back and spoke to Pete about our exchange. Then we decided to meet back in the mess for dinner at six.

By that time, the Adonis had disappeared from the area so I went in search of him. I found him rehearsing for an upcoming scene in a barn that the set designer had built for the production. That Adonis looked serious about his role - so much in fact, that he refused to take telephone calls or have distractions of any kind while on the set. Seeing this,

I decided to sit and watch a while. Foxy had been a big hit on the set and I hoped that no one started cooing over her during his rehearsal scene.

Just as I was thinking that, someone behind me whispered, "Hey JoJo, how's it going?"

It was someone from one of my first movies - Cody from *Muddy Streams* who was the surfer-dude type - blonde hair, but not young and always somewhat distracted. "Hey Cody, right back at ya," I whispered.

Knowing the importance of quietness on the set even in rehearsals, Cody continued his job of testing the sound and refrained from speaking during the remainder of the scene.

I watched as I was swept away by the physical movements of Adam, the Adonis. He was graceful even with his tall height, which I was guessing to be around 6'1" or 6'2". His deep voice was gentle and whispery. Adam spoke with a slight accent; I was guessing it to be Cherokee like Elvis or maybe Chippewa like Dad's ancestors. He had black shiny straight hair that fell midway down his back. There was an angry edge to him, not anything mad or threatening, but more of a look of hunger. That look most actors have just starting out in this business. Adam's face wasn't that of a boy. He had intense lines and a more weathered look for someone of his age, which I presumed was a few years younger than me at about twenty-two or twenty-three.

After the scene was completed, I waited for most everyone to leave before approaching Adam.

"Hi, I'm Jordan. Most people around here call me JoJo."

"Hello," Adam said softly with his very deep voice, waiting for me to state my business.

"I'm working on the movie - well, *with* the movie actually."

"Yeah? So am I," he demurely committed, smoothly smiling at my awkwardness - somewhat poking fun at me while he continued to pack up his script and assorted paraphernalia.

"I thought I would come visit the set to get to know

some of the people and how everything was progressing."

"And you thought you would start with me? I'm flattered," he said jokingly exaggerated. His stance was not domineering, yet not wimpy. His eyes were kind and he had an angelic look about him. I could tell instantly that he was a quiet sort - aloof, who would alluringly draw you in with his bruting nature. I actually wished he would talk more because I couldn't get enough of his accent.

"Well, actually I know Pete and Cody and some of the others," I said as I slightly turned to point toward the direction of Cody's exit. As I turned back around, I wasn't sure what he was thinking, but he was now totally checking me out.

He then nodded and said "Well, then I guess I'll have to settle for being number fourteen on your list."

I smiled and silently thought, "Okay, now what?" Usually I had the experience that it didn't make much difference what you said; it was enough to just make contact and the conversation would flow. But it wasn't flowing. What was wrong with me? I felt a little intimidated. Then I finally said, "Are you rehearsing or shooting anything else today?"

"No, that was it. Why?" he asked as he seemed a bit shy.

"Pete's having a little gathering at his trailer tonight; I thought maybe I'll see you there."

"Maybe," Adam said, before smiling, tipping his head, then walking away. My stomach seemed to flip a little when I watched him walk away - admire was more like it. I don't know why exactly, but the word *beefcakes* came to mind. I was one of those admiring people - well, until I realized that Cody was standing next to me asking a question.

"Well, what do you think?" Cody asked.

"What do I think about what?"

"The party, I heard you talking about a party when I came back in to get some equipment. Is the crew invited to this kegger too?"

"Ah... yeah sure Cody, but don't spread it around to too many people - it's not my *bash* and I shouldn't be presumptuous in inviting people. Okay?"

"Yeah, no problem. See ya there." Cody seemed happy to be included.

I left in search of Pete. I stopped by the office to view his schedule and found him there.

"Pete! You have to throw a little gathering at your trailer tonight."

"What? Why?"

"Because I told someone you were and now you have to."

"Aw JoJo! This isn't one of your practical jokes again, is it? I'm not going to wake up tomorrow with a dead monkey in my bed, or worse, am I?! If I give you access to my trailer, there's no telling what I'll be charged with," Pete blistered sarcastically.

Wide-eyed innocently, I asked, "You think *I* was involved with the monkey murders?"

Pete tilted his head, smirked and looked at me as if he knew I was the perpetrator of the hoax.

"Yeah, okay, that was then," I said admittedly, then trying to move on. "I need you to do this because the someone is your leading man, and I'll need to focus on him in a social setting to evaluate the problem. You still want to know the problem, right?"

"Yeah, okay, but you'd better be telling me the truth," Pete answered, giving me a side glance. "I'll be hiding all the sharp instruments in my trailer *and* the hair dryer, just in case."

"I wouldn't have dreamed you'd even have a hair dryer, Pete," I said, poking fun at his balding head just before jumping out of the way of his swat. I learned early on in life that if you have a sense of humor like mine, you'd better know how to move quickly.

I wasn't entirely sure that I needed to see Adam in a social setting to evaluate him, but I knew he seemed stiff on the set talking to me, even with no one around. I also think that secretly, I wanted to talk to this Adonis again to see if my nerves were based on him or the situation on the set.

Pete had the little gathering and Adam arrived after

most of the others were there. I thought, "Lexy would love him; she was always fashionably late, making everyone anticipate her arrival." I tried working my way over to talk to him, but Cody seemed to jump out of nowhere and started talking a mile a minute. Adam played it cool though. I observed him glancing over at me now and then while he was talking to one of the cameramen. I wasn't sure what he was thinking, however. Did Adam wonder if I was on the set to cause trouble? Did he think I was there as Pete's girl-friend? Since it did sound a lot like I was asking him out, did he think I was trying to pick him up? Did he think I was trying to steal his props?! What?! And why did I care so much?

Finally, Adam walked over and asked, "Cody, isn't that your car out there with the lights on?" And Cody ran out the door like his hair was on fire, all the while Adam never taking his eyes off me. "So you wanted me here... I'm here," he commented coolly, but with a sexy smile on his face.

"Yes *I* did."

"So do you want to talk to me alone?" he asked while glancing at Tracy lurking nearby.

"We *are* alone, as alone as I get," I said glancing over at Tracy then back at Foxy while snuggling Foxy to add levity into my statement.

He nodded, ignored Tracy, tousled Foxy's ears, and then we filled the rest of the evening with conversation. Adam talked mostly as I listened. It was good to have something to do again - a project to keep my mind off of my heartbreak. We spent hours together talking that night. After Adam and I said our goodnights, I remained behind to speak to Pete in his trailer.

I began my summation for Pete. "I believe that Adam is still new to his acting profession and wants *very much* to do well. He may just be a bit too serious at this point and just needs to loosen up and relax. I have noticed that he is also somewhat shy and not overly confident."

"Okay," said Pete, before adding, "With that in mind, I know of a few maneuvers that we can try to get him out of his shell. We're shooting something other than romantic scenes tomorrow and that will give us time to remedy the situation." Pete and I discussed budget matters for a while, and then he thanked me before Tracy, Foxy and I left.

As the days passed, I found myself waiting for Adam to finish shooting so we could continue our discussions where we had left off. We talked about everything. He knew a plethora of information about the stock market and even taught me some stuff. He seemed to know a lot for his age, about life and loss, and what's most important - family. Adam told me about his family back in South Dakota and about his daughter, Dakota.

"You don't want to reconcile with Dakota's mother?" I asked, somewhat fishing for relationship information.

"No, her mother and I have done our best, but we were never meant to be together. We got together in the first place for all the wrong reasons, and so we didn't have a chance. Our families decided it would be a good match, and we went along with it, not even knowing each other," Adam explained. Adam never asked me about Jack, and that was good - I wasn't thinking about Jack when Adam and I were together. And that was good too.

When Adam wasn't filming, we took in the sights of San Antonio. I had been there a few times and I knew a little about the town so I played tour guide. He found the local people to be friendly as he said they were in South Dakota. I escorted him to their famous romantic Riverwalk, and we stopped in at various outdoor cafés and shops. I found out that Adam loved Mexican food so we made a day of just sampling assorted cuisines. I told him about my roots in Houston, and he continued to tell me about his family.

Adam's mother was from the Lakota Native American tribe. His father was Irish, but had passed away. His mother raised Adam to respect four cardinal virtues in life: bravery, fortitude, wisdom and generosity. He had an impoverished upbringing on a reservation.

I began liking Adam more and more. I had almost forgot that I was there to help Pete with his dilemma because I was having such a good time with Adam. He seemed to only have one down side - that was being a Pisces, just like me. Two Pisces usually don't mix well together, except in the bedroom, and that's not what I was initially looking for. But that's exactly what found me. The night before the last day of shooting, Adam came to my hotel room. We didn't need to say anything; Adam and I both knew exactly what he was there for. And it was amazing.

After our lovemaking when Adam had drifted off to sleep, I was laying there a while, but couldn't sleep. I had mixed emotions and had to write in my journal. So I slipped out of bed and stepped into the bathroom. I sat on the floor with Foxy, who was nibbling on her Champion Cheddar.

~✳~¡~✳~¡~✳~¡~✳~¡~✳~¡~✳~

As I sat there with Zoë, I read in my journal, but once again to myself and not out loud. I knew that this was way too personal to tell any other living soul.

Dear Journal: I was there alone with him. He's tall, sturdy, not bulky, but tight. Not ruggedly handsome like Jack, but still very nice. Not that I should be comparing him to Jack; it's just an observation. The room was dim, but not dark. He undressed as I watched his silhouette change to a hardened form. With each piece of his clothing removed, I removed mine, until we were unbound. He slowly stepped toward me, towering over me with his six-foot two frame until he was touching me. He kissed me and we slowly stepped backward until we were lying on the bed. Our naked bodies pressed firmly together. Then my lips tingled as they pressed against his. I thought of nothing but the rhythm of his moves and how that affected me. We fondled for the next few hours, I don't know exactly how long... I lost track of time. There nothing wrong with our chemistry. Goodnight Journal.

I continued my story for Zoë.

~✳~¡~✳~¡~✳~¡~✳~¡~✳~¡~✳~

After Adam and I woke the next day, we stayed in bed and chatted a while.

"You tossed and turned a lot last night; I hope I wasn't

the cause of it," Adam said.

"No, no."

"Did you not sleep well?"

"I'm sorry, I didn't mean to keep you up. I don't ever sleep well, I have awful haunting nightmares."

"About what?"

"I'm looking for something and I can't find it. It's crucial and I can't breathe without finding it."

"Finding what?"

"I don't know. I never know what it is that I'm looking for so I never find it. But I think it might have something to do with finding Jack. I won't assume you know so I'll tell you. Jack was my fiancé who has been missing for four years. Sometimes he'd come to me in my dreams and tell me to keep looking. I'm sorry, I don't mean to talk about him... here... now."

"That's okay - we all have our demons. Go ahead. I want to know why you don't sleep."

"I suppose I've always blamed myself for him not being found, not coming home. There are so many 'what ifs' in my dreams. There is so much guilt. It's hard for me to close my eyes sometimes."

"Can I tell you a story - one that might help you?"

"Yes, please do. I can't tell you how many times I've wished someone would actually understand what it's like to be in my skin. Please tell me your story," I said as we turned to face each other in bed.

"I *was* in your skin. I was a kid when it happened to me. I was only eight. I thought I was responsible for my father's death, but I'll spare you the gory details. It took me a long time to move past it, and with some help from my mother, I did. When Dakota was born, I didn't want anything to do with her and I couldn't understand why because I love kids. I had lost all respect for myself for ignoring Dakota. But I made it through it - and enough to love Dakota more than life itself. Mother told me that all I had to do is love myself again. That was the key - self-love and forgiveness. I was worth saving and she taught me that. I hope you can take this story with you and find some peace with it."

Adam seemed brokenhearted when he told me his story, and I sensed that there was something deep within him that he wasn't sharing.

We talked a while longer, but he had to return to the set. He kissed me tenderly and whispered, "Have mercy on my heart. I haven't loved many women, and I just know you have the power to break my heart into pieces." Then he left for his last day of shooting, that crucial love scene with his co-star. But before he left, Adam asked to see me again, and so I gave him my telephone number. I also said that I might be at the wrap party, depending on what was happening back at my production office.

My last thoughts before Adam left were that he was a good kisser and that I liked kissing him. It was nice - and it was sexy.

~*~:~*~:~*~:~*~:~*~:~*~

Gladis understood that I needed a while longer with Zoë, and she didn't bother trying to force me from the room. She stepped out of Zoë's room as I tried tempting Zoë out of her slumber.

"I never, in my wildest dreams, thought I would meet someone like Adam. My time with him was special. I had been lonely for a man to touch me again, and he was the only one who I let get close to me. I had built a wonderful house, felt good about my family, and now someone found me and wanted to be a part of my life. But I was still scared and didn't know if I wanted to be in a relationship yet. Not that I knew it was a relationship at that point. But then someone *else* found me. Any thoughts as to who?" I asked Zoë, teasing her. "Well, I was in for the shock of my life. Never, did I think that would happen to me, not after what happened to Mom."

~*~:~*~:~*~:~*~:~*~:~*~

Chapter IX

Moving on with My Life

After Adam's big scene with Myra, Pete called the hotel and said, "It couldn't have been steamier!" That made me smile, and I hoped that Adam was thinking about me when he did the scene. I called the production company and said, "Another one's in the can."

I decided to skip the wrap party and Tracy, Foxy and I headed home. This was mostly because I wasn't ready to make anything public or to even hint at having a new relationship I was willing for others to see. It's awkward enough at the beginning of any relationship, but ten times over when you're famous and everyone wants to know your personal business. It seems some people think it's their *right* to know your personal business if you're a celebrity. I wasn't sure at that point if there *was* anything to make public - for him *or* for me. Adam did ask to see me again, but some guys just say that at the awkward part of saying good-bye. I didn't yet know which one he was. And if he was sincere, I certainly didn't want to hurt Adam's feelings if he cared for me and I decided that I didn't want to continue.

The publicity shyness excuse wasn't entirely true, more of a copout I suppose. We could have gone somewhere quiet with no one else around, like Jack and I used to do. Running away seemed like the best solution at the time. I wasn't even sure how I was feeling. Mixed. It felt good to move forward, and from what I knew about Adam so far, he was a great guy to move forward with. But even with that warm feeling of being close with someone again, an overwhelming feeling still nagged at me - guilt feeling. Cheating guilt. Cheating on Jack.

Lexy came out to stay with me for a while. I didn't tell her what had happened with Adam. I didn't want Lexy to get her hopes up, to think that I had someone new in my life again. I mostly just listened "like a little kid" to all of her travel stories. It was like we went back in time, back to when I first met her and was in total awe of her. I felt jealous that Lexy was having fun. She was still the same old Lexy and I just felt *old*. I felt my time to be happy and in love was over, and I was still in my twenties - how pathetic was that? Lexy was seeing someone special this time, and she had left behind her guilt feelings about her mother from her father's affair. While I felt proud of her, I also felt envious of her for being able to move past it. I couldn't help secretly wishing for a relationship with Adam, but it was selfish of me because it was just to feel love again with someone - anyone.

In the next couple of weeks, Adam called several times. Sometimes I would take his calls, but I would keep it brief, and other times I would just listen as he left a message. The tone in his voice gave me reason to believe he wanted more than just sex, but I was scared to see him. I was scared that I would have more feelings for him than I was willing to admit to myself, especially after seeing him face-to-face again. I knew I wasn't over feeling guilty about leaving Jack behind. I didn't even know if I had anything else in me to give anymore, after loving and losing Jack. At any other time in my life, I would have been thrilled that a guy, especially like Adam, would have wanted me in his life. Still I chose to do nothing.

A little over a month had passed since my night with Adam. I was feeling better about my feelings of guilt. I could look back on our time together fondly, but that's all it was - something from the past. There was just too much that I had to deal with during that time, and too much time had gone by, that I felt Adam had lost interest in pursuing me. By doing nothing, I had chosen *for* him, and for us. I was a little sad about the "what if," but I needed to put that aside and focus on other things or I would be right back where I started from - guilt-ridden.

One day soon thereafter, I was sitting in my office at the production company mentally planning my *holiday* to Maui with Lexy and her boyfriend, Brad. We were going SCUBA diving. I flipped through the pages of my datebook, laughing to myself, thinking back to the CPR class Gamma forced us to take right after we announced we were taking SCUBA lessons. Gamma was so afraid Lexy was going to get us both killed. It didn't help matters when she heard my story of how Lexy was making out with the dummy, pretending it was her boyfriend at the time.

"Doesn't that girl ever take anything seriously?" Gamma squawked.

I kept flipping through my datebook, but I couldn't find what I was looking for. That's when a surge of anxiety and fear came over me in an instant. I could feel my face turning hot and flush.

"Where the hell is that damn entry?!" I thought out loud. "This can't be right. This can't be happening to me. OH MY GOD! Oh my God. How can this be? I was so careful."

I flipped to the back of my datebook to my telephone numbers. I picked up the telephone and placed a call. "Hi, yeah, this is Jordan Walsh. I need to set up an appointment with Dr. Easton. Yeah, okay, that would be fine. What the appointment is for? Um... a check up. Thank you, okay, I'll see you then, bye."

Things moved in slow motion over the next few days. When the day of my appointment finally arrived, Eddie drove me to the doctor's office. As I sat there in the waiting room, I was reminded of how Dad felt - trapped with a relationship and family he didn't want. Those feelings of entrapment destroyed Mom's life. Logically, I knew the scenarios were different; I wasn't forcing anyone to do anything, but I was too close to the situation to be completely rational. I couldn't help but to feel a responsibility not to ruin another person's life. How could I do that to someone? How could I bring someone into this world who never asked for all of these problems and just dump it on them nonetheless. I knew first-hand what it was like to feel you were the reason so many people were unhappy. Would this child feel abandoned? Lost? Always wondering why people didn't love them? I couldn't let that happen.

I thought about the other women sitting there - how many were thinking the same thing, were in the same predicament as me. Many of them seemed happy and full of life. "Full of life - now there's a profound statement in the middle of a gynecologist's office," I thought. I tried to put the possibility out of my mind; it wasn't true until Dr. Easton said it's true.

It *was* true. Dr. Easton confirmed my suspicions. After the doctor finished examining me, she added, "Congratulations, you're about six weeks along, Jordan."

"I know. I know exactly when it happened," I uttered in a monotone voice.

"Not a planned pregnancy?" Dr. Easton asked, as she helped me up from my exam position.

"It wasn't even a planned night of passion. I don't understand - we were careful, we used protection every single time."

"Well, not all of them are a hundred percent effective. And I'll need to tell you a few things about your options. Get dressed and meet me in my office where we can talk."

After dressing and walking down the hall to her office, I paused and stood in her doorway. Dr. Easton was sitting at her desk writing on a prescription pad when she glanced up and motioned for me to come in and sit down. "First, do you think you will be having the baby? Because if not, I can recommend another physician for you to see. I cannot perform the procedure myself."

"BABY?" I thought. Actually hearing the word for the first time put a realization spin on it, bigger than just the peanut I was imagining. "And options?" My head was spinning. When I came out of my funk, I asked, "Procedure? Oh no, I didn't mean... I mean, I didn't even think in that direction."

"You need to know what all of your options are,

Jordan. You should take some time to consider every option available to you, including adoption. Let me know what you decide, but don't take too long - the procedure needs to be performed soon if you decide to terminate the pregnancy."

I envied her ability to string more than four words together at that moment without stuttering. "Well, I can let you know right now," I cooed, rubbing my stomach. "My choice is to have the baby and raise it myself. I may not have planned for it, but I can love and protect it just as much as if I had."

"Protect?" she asked.

"Oh, slip of the tongue. It's a long story - many issues, you don't want to know, trust me."

She prescribed vitamins along with light exercise before we concluded the office visit.

Eddie brought the car around and picked me up out front. I sat back and stared out the window, looking shell-shocked, I assumed. I tried to act normal, but Eddie finally asked, "Everything alright, Miss Jordan?"

"Never bedda," I replied.

I didn't know how to tell everyone so I didn't. I was getting good at that running away thing, but I knew I couldn't run or hide forever. I figured I'd keep it to myself until I got used to the idea, or maybe I was just chicken. Well, I did finally tell someone - I told Foxy. She did seem happy for me, or maybe it was just the Champion Cheddar I had in my hand at the time. I called Lexy and bowed out of our SCUBA *holiday*, promising I would catch her up later as to the reason why.

"Wonder what Gamma would say about my good deed today?" I thought. This was a doozy.

I started searching my feelings about all of this, as much as I could with all the hormones bouncing around, and decided to write in my journal.

Dear Journal: What am I going to do? What am I feeling about all of this? How would Foxy handle not being my one and only baby anymore? I laughed knowing she would be just fine and that would be one more person for her to love. I know I want, more than ever, to be a good mother. I want more than ever not to let what happened to me happen to it. I can't let that happen. I want to raise my baby differently than Mom raised me. I know I can't blame her, because Mom did the best she could with what she had. But I am not her. And she is not me. And I have the resources to do this by myself if I have to.

As I sat there writing, I realized that I didn't like referring to the baby as *it*. I needed to start treating *it* as someone, as he or she or just to give it a temporary name. I thought of the name Hope, and how I wanted Jack's firstborn daughter to be called Hope. But that wasn't fair to this baby or to Adam. That was the past and I was carrying living proof of my future. How about just Junior? That way, I wouldn't get attached to any particular name and *it* wouldn't be an *it* anymore. I continued to write.

I know it would be better for Junior to have two parents. I know I could love Junior enough for two, but would that be fair to him or her? Would that be fair to Adam, not knowing his child? When I think back to the way I felt when Dad scurried off on his excursions and didn't want to be a part of my life, it makes me wonder if any man who didn't plan for a child would do that. To promise to be there and then not be. I really don't know Adam well enough to know if that would happen with him. But maybe I do. I know he treats Dakota well, I can see it in her smile in the photographs that he has shown me of her. Knowing that will be enough for me to try to include him in his new baby's life. Goodnight Journal.

I think Gamma became suspicious when I declined to go on a riding jaunt on my horse, Poncho. I knew I couldn't lie to her so I stayed busy in order to give my hectic schedule as an excuse. But I also knew that wouldn't fly for long so I had to get busy with the business of telling Adam.

I was beginning my third month of pregnancy when I decided it was time to stop procrastinating. I was feeling tremendous guilt for not continuing the relationship as Adam wanted, but I had to speak with him. But how would I do it? I didn't know how *I* felt so how could I tell Adam? I needed clarity.

I sat down that night and starting writing out all my thoughts and all my feelings about Junior and about Adam. I was surprised to find I had more good feelings than I thought. Whatever it was, I liked what came out. I began organizing the words into a poem and before I knew it, I had a song. Our song. I went over to the music studio in the house to put notes to it and to hear what it sounded like. I couldn't believe it, it sounded good. I didn't know if anyone else would think so, but I liked it. I put a title on it, folded it up, and slipped it into my journal.

It wasn't until the fourth month into my pregnancy that I got the courage to just show up at Adam's location. I called around to find out where he was shooting his current film. Alone, I jumped a flight with my carry-on, along with a few barf bags in hand. I checked into a nearby hotel, rented a car, and arrived at the production site. I wasn't expected and the inattentive front-gate guard requested my pass from me. When I didn't produce one, he looked up from his magazine. I smiled at him. The guard must have recognized me because he hopped to his feet and opened the gate to let me pass without saying another word. In fact, he must have been a fan because he was smiling and watched me the whole time it took me to drive through the gate and around the corner to the production office. The attention made my ego feel good, as bloated as I felt even though I actually hadn't started showing yet.

My first stop was to see an old friend, a rival in the production business - Charlie Brooks. Charlie was known for being brash and brutally honest. I didn't mind that, actually I preferred people to not blow smoke up my skirt and to just get to the point. He was sharing a small smoke-filled trailer office with the director. I could barely breathe and was about to toss breakfast so I kept it short. We chatted briefly about the glory days and then I asked about Adam.

"How's he doing? I've heard things aren't going well with filming."

"Not great, it's off and on. He's having difficulty concentrating on his part. We've had to stop filming a few times because he hasn't memorized his lines. I can't imagine what's wrong. I viewed a rough cut of him in *Romancing Running Deer* and he was brilliant."

That was the film we were shooting the last time I saw him. "I'm sorry to hear that. Maybe I can help figure it out for you."

"I'm not sure if I should let you. You aren't going to steal him for one of your productions, are you? And what are you doing here anyway, and why didn't *you* produce this picture?" he asked, teasing me.

"I'm here for moral support," I answered vaguely. "I'm going to the mess for some tea. Care to follow me around to make sure I stay out of trouble?" Giving him one last smile, I hopped out of the trailer as I was dying for some fresh air.

As I walked into the mess, I spotted Adam. A flood of feelings came over me as I watched him make his way through the line.

"Hey pretty lady, are you a part of this picture?" asked a voice from behind as if he were the cops. It was Cody.

"Hey, what'ya stalking me?" I teased. I gave Cody a hug, and he sat me down at the nearest table. He brought me some herbal tea and we chatted a while.

"It's great to see you. How long will you be here?"

"Not sure, I just arrived so I'm playing it by ear." As we sat there talking, Adam turned to the sound of my voice, our eyes met, and he grinned. He was talking to someone, but didn't stop so it would seem obvious to others that he was happy to see me. I looked at Adam while saying my good-byes to Cody and sort of backed out of the room. I hoped Adam would get the message that I wanted him to follow me. He did.

"Hi," Adam said as he stood there with his angelic face all lit up. I didn't know how to react. I knew I didn't want to lead Adam on, but I was glad to see him. He was more magnificent than I remembered. Maybe it was the hormones, maybe it was because I had been so lonely, but I didn't care - I was smiling.

"Hi, how have you been, Adam? I was hoping you

would follow me out; I came to the set to talk to you."

"Okay, we can go back to my trailer - if that's okay with you."

"Yes, that's fine," I agreed.

He motioned me over toward his trailer. "Ah, this is a nice trailer," I said ineloquently stammering out my words, not really meaning it. I knew I wasn't very convincing yet I tried not to be rude.

Adam laughed at my effort. "Yeah right, not like your trailers, I'll bet. When I'm rich and famous like you, I'll get the fancy accommodations."

"And I have no doubt that you will," I said sincerely, with a soft smile on my face.

We made small talk for a while until Adam asked why I was really there. He knew I wasn't involved with the picture. I was scared. I didn't want to hurt him, and I didn't want Adam to feel trapped like Dad.

"Are you still with me? Where did you go? I know you're still in there," he teased when I hadn't responded.

I chuckled, but then softly smiled. "I'm pregnant," I seemed to have just blurted out. No, I hadn't just said that. No, not like that, I hadn't just blurted it out. Yep, where had that sixty thousand-dollar education gone to? Could I not have thought of something better to say?

He looked confused as if I were speaking Chinese. "We're pregnant?" he asked. I guess that was Adam's way of confirming that he was the father without being cruel by outright asking if he were.

I nodded.

"Oh, have mercy on my heart" was all Adam said before having to excuse himself to shoot some scenes, but not before asking me to wait in his trailer until he returned. I was finishing up telephone calls to the family when he returned. Adam still looked shell-shocked, but he was now speaking in complete sentences. That was an accomplishment and better than how I handled the news. "I didn't get to eat when you saw me in the mess, are you hungry?" he asked.

"Are ya kidding me? I'm always hungry and I now eat like a linebacker on steroids. This month I'm in the middle of craving Mexican food; I can't seem to get enough."

"Remember our trek around San Antonio eateries?" asked Adam.

"Remember? I fantasize about it daily. Ah, the food I mean," I answered grinning.

"I think we have some Mexican food at the mess. It's not like San Antonio's - but with a little imagination and a lot of antacids, you'll satisfy your craving."

"Mumm, can't wait. What flavor are the antacids?" I put on my serious face again and said, "I need to say something before we go. It's important for me to tell you that you don't need to do anything here. I mean, to support me in this, I mean, support *us*, financially. I'm strong in that area and I can do this on my own. I have past issues in my life that makes me have to say this, which doesn't have anything to do with you, and I hope you know that you can be as involved as you want to be. Or not?" I could feel myself babbling so I just stopped talking and looked into his angelic face.

Adam reached over, touched my arm, then leaned in real close to me and asked, "Great, does this mean you're buying dinner?"

"Yes, yes, that's exactly what it means," I said unconvincingly trying to cover my blunder. "I'm so glad you could get that from my ramblings."

We meandered over to the mess to have dinner, and we had a nice time. Adam and I didn't talk about Junior or anything heavy, and that was nice. When we returned to Adam's trailer, the conversation turned awkward and I quickly announced that I should probably go.

"No, I'll bunk in with Cody. You stay here, no problem."

"No, that's crazy. I'm the one who just showed up unannounced. Besides, I already have a hotel room nearby."

"No," Adam insisted, "I don't want you out this late at night."

I reached down and rubbed my belly. "Thanks, we appreciate the hospitality, good and kind sir." His offer felt good; the truth was that I didn't want to go anywhere. I was feeling comfortable with Adam. He tucked me in, *us* in, and he slept on the floor in the front room instead of going to Cody's. In the morning, he lightly kissed my forehead and promised he would be back after shooting.

I made a few telephone calls before he returned.

"Do you feel like talking a little?" Adam asked, a short time after getting back.

"Okay, I'd love to."

"It's been about four months since we were together, and to some, that would seem like a long time," Adam began. "I'm guessing you have had concerns about telling me. Since it has been so long, you must have decided what it is that you want to do. Where is it that you see this going?" Adam had asked, as though he were fishing for how I felt.

"Yes, I was a bit scared to tell you. Petrified, actually. I've seen this very thing happen to someone in the past, and it wasn't something that guy wanted to hear. I know all guys aren't the same, but that was the only example I witnessed. And it wasn't a pleasant experience. The only thing I know for sure is that I'm going to raise this child with as much love as it will let me give it. I can only speculate as to what you want, and I'm sure you will tell me what that is, in time. I know you are a great father to Dakota; I can see it on her face when she's with you in your photographs. So I know you will be a great father to this one too, if that's what you choose to do."

"Yes, I would. I mean, yes, that's what I choose. I want that. I want to be a part of its life. And financially, as well. I know you 'have it covered,' but I take my responsibilities seriously. I want to support it."

I reached down and pulled his hand up to my belly and said, "Junior."

"What?"

"Junior - that's what I'm calling *it*, instead of *it*. Just because I was tired of calling it *it*. Get it?" I teased.

"Have mercy on my heart, woman," Adam said, smiling with his angelic face while shaking his head. He then asked, "What would you say to being wooed? I know we didn't start out dating or being madly in love, but there is still that option of becoming more than just two single parents. Seems fate, also known as *Junior*, has brought us together, and I'd like to explore that - what'ya say?"

"Okay," I said, as I seemed to have just blurted it out, yet again. Where did that come from? Did I really mean that or was I just caught up in the excitement of being wanted by a man? Maybe deep down I knew it was time to admit I needed someone. Whatever it was - I didn't care, all I wanted right then was to spend more time with Adam. And without even thinking about it, forcing it or faking it, I was happy.

We dated openly during Adam's filming. We did the whole dating ritual: holding hands, making out and he would give me flowers. It felt like I was a teenager again and in love for the first time.

Most days when Adam was filming, I sat in his trailer and conducted production company business. On the first day of the second week I was there, I had just hung up the phone when I heard a female voice ask, "Hi, who *are* you?"

I turned toward the door a bit startled and asked, "Hi, who are *you*?"

"I asked you first," declared the trespasser.

"Okay, we seem to be at an impasse. I'll start - I'm Jordan."

"Yeah, I can see that you are. I meant who are you to be sitting in Adam's trailer alone?"

"Ah, his girlfriend? And you are...?" I responded sarcastically.

"Kelly, the scheduling coordinator on *this* picture. And Adam doesn't have a girlfriend. A friend of mine who worked on his last film said you two were 'seeing' each other at that time, but he dumped you."

"Well, on all *my* films, being the scheduling coordinator didn't give anyone the right to just barge in someone's private quarters unannounced. Since no one dumped anyone, I'll have to remind Adam to send you the memo regarding our *personal* relationship. We'd appreciate a knock in the future." I'm seldom that rude, but I didn't like her tone. She spoke of Adam like property and that bugged me. Okay, blame it on the hormones *again*. "Since you didn't ask for him, I have to assume you knew Adam wasn't here. So why are you here if you knew he wasn't?" I asked accusingly.

She just gave a quick fake smile and left in a huff, slamming the door behind her. Okay, hormones were all *over* the place! I couldn't wait for Adam to return so I went looking for him. I found him in the mess taking a break. Before I approached, I took a deep breath so I wouldn't sound like a *psycho jealous girlfriend-from-hell* so early in our relationship.

"So why didn't you tell me I had some competition," I teased in the softest voice I could muster at the moment.

"Hi JoJo," Adam said sweetly. He lightly kissed me before asking, "What are you talking about?"

"Kelll-eee," I said sarcastically, but still jovial.

"What? Kelly's not competition; she's a friend. Are you hungry? Can I get you something from the counter?"

"An overprotective friend from what I just witnessed. A friend you didn't tell me about. She walked into your trailer without knocking, about gave me a heart attack," I said uncharacteristically ignoring his offer for food.

"You wouldn't be a little jealous, would you?"

"Well, yeah! Have you seen her? An attractive blonde with a tight little body. A body I used to have, a body I seemed to have left in my other pantsuit," I said pouting as I looked around my body, pretending to search for my lost figure even though I hadn't started showing yet. "She just comes waltzing into your trailer unannounced and unencumbered about knocking, like she's living there. She's *not* living there, is she?" I said half-teasing him.

"No. Not a problem," he laughed. "We're just friends, and I'll talk to her about knocking, happy?" he teased, as he gave me a little hug.

"Yeah, okay. So where's that food you promised me?" I said, bantering back to him. We sat there a while together before he went back to work.

I figured I should start asking around about Kelly and

whether she was after Adam. So I approached Cody first. He said she'd taken the previous week off and was now back on the set. As far as he knew, she was probably just chasing him, but Cody thought they were just friends. He suggested maybe Adam hadn't realized what Kelly really wanted. I can't say that I'm a suspicious person naturally, but Jack used to tell me not to worry about all the women he always talked to - not sure I really believed Jack's explanations.

I felt a little jealous, but I knew Adam was devoted to giving our relationship a try. And so what if he'd had something with her in the past - he was now with me. I had a past too. Let the past stay in the past. So I tried to put her out of my mind. Our relationship moved forward, until about the third time she walked in on us in his trailer without knocking. This one particularly bothered me because it was nine-thirty at night.

"Oh sorry, didn't know you would be here or I'd of knocked," she mocked sarcastically toward me, as if I were about to vanish like a puff of smoke in the wind and out of Adam's life. Kelly was also letting me know that she felt she wouldn't have had to knock if I wasn't there. "Did you get the new shooting schedule, Adam?"

I just sat there fake-smiling at her. Just the gooshy way she said his name infuriated me. Nevertheless, I thought I would stay out of it and let Adam handle her. If nothing else, it would show Adam how mature I was, even though I wanted to gouge her eyes out with a chainsaw and puck every dark-rooted bleached-blonde hair out of that bubble-headed hatrack with a hand axe! But, I'm calm, no bouncing hormones here.

"Yes Kelly. Was that all?" Adam asked.

"It was for tomorrow so I wanted you to have it."

"Yes Kelly, you gave it to me this morning - remember?"

"Okay, I'll see you tomorrow, Adam. Bye," she said ignoring what he just said. Kelly then smiled at me as if she had just slam-dunked the winning basketball.

I looked at Adam with my continual fake-smile. Before I could say anything, he said, "I'll talk to her."

"Nooo, I have a better idea," I interrupted. "I'll have Eddie drive Gampy's Air Stream trailer out here and we can stay in that. It's plush up to the ceiling. She'll never have the nerve to barge into someone else's trailer, no matter who is in it. And honestly, who could really blame her; have you seen how hot you are?" I teased. I paused and smiled, then continued. "She doesn't threaten me, I know you're devoted to this working out between us. Kelly just has to learn there are a few boundaries that she has to adhere to. Besides, I want Foxy to come out anyway - I miss her."

"The trailer sounds like a great idea," Adam said excitedly. "I'm going to have to watch you though. I've heard about your practical jokes and now I've seen first-hand how smart you are. That's a scary combination."

"You know nothing, I admit to nothing, and you can't prove a thing," I goaded him. Adam started tickling me, pinching my behind, and we rolled on the floor with laughter. We were making memories.

I called Gampy, and Eddie drove the trailer out to the site. Adam dropped Eddie off at the airport and the chauffeur hopped a flight back to Los Angeles. Adam told me that Eddie would fly out when we were ready to leave, to drive the trailer back home.

I was so excited to see Foxy and she was rolling over and over with joy, wiggling upside down on the floor. Gamma included a case of Champion Cheddar for Foxy in the trailer, plus some of my things, like Ella, which made me happy. Tommy had threatened to include Iggie, and I was so glad he didn't. Adam teased me about Ella, but I didn't care - I had missed her too.

After that, not only did Kelly stop barging in; she stopped coming by altogether. Charlie was thankful they got to save money on the production, by giving Adam's trailer to someone else.

That maneuver may have stopped Kelly from barging in, but she was still on my case every chance she got. She'd still snipe comments like "Didn't you used to be an actress?" or "What are you doing here anyway, don't you have a production business to run?"

I would fire back, "I'm smart enough to hire competent people so I don't have to be there 24/7. And speaking of competency, where's the new shooting schedule Adam ordered from you yesterday?" I wouldn't let Kelly answer and always walked away acting like I spotted someone I knew. Cody was amused by the disagreements, and he was always there to talk to me when I needed him. Adam was concentrating on the film and was mostly oblivious to the whole exchange. I played a few, *crueller than usual* practical jokes on Kelly, thinking, *"Mess with me,* will ya?" I even included the itching powder in the toilet tissue joke. And while I was in her bathroom, I decided that her foundation makeup tube was the perfect place to slip in some black grease paint.

Perhaps deep down, I knew all of this was just the hormones talking and that I needed to get back to what was important, but it was fun anyway. The bigger picture was that I had a goal - I needed to figure out what I was going to do with the rest of my life, and if Adam and I were going to raise our child together.

We hadn't made an announcement yet because I hadn't told the family about Junior. I knew I needed to accomplish that soon. Adam and I agreed that we needed to tell them before a reporter got a hold of the information. I called Gamma and Gampy and apologized for telling them over the telephone. I explained that I needed to tell Adam first, and since I wasn't returning to Los Angeles for quite some time, the telephone was my only option. They were thrilled with the news and promised to tell Mom and Tommy. We talked a while longer, until I heard Gampy in the background saying, "Annie, put it in a letter. It's costing a fortune!"

"Gamma, tell Gampy I can afford it now, remember?" I said, teasing him.

After hanging up, I called Uncle Red and he was thrilled for us. Uncle Red reminded me that he was still a little sad that we were out living in Los Angeles and not just around the corner anymore. I reiterated my offer for him and

Sam to move in, but again he declined. I think Uncle Red just likes to be reminded that he was still important in our lives, even being so far away from us. Even more so, because there would be one more of *us* to miss.

Lexy was next. She cried and told me how happy she was that I found someone - meaning Adam. Lexy also said she was jealous that I would always have someone in my life to love - meaning Junior. I told Lexy I missed her desperately and invited her out for a visit with us on the site. However, she said that Adam and I needed this time to be together *alone*, just the two of us to bond. I knew Lexy was right, but I missed her and told her that. She also gave me a few practical joke ideas to play on Kelly. They were *good*.

Midway through the production, they hired a band and had a party to blow off some steam. They rented a kicker joint for the night, and we all went to have some down-home Southern kicker fun. Now, this was right up my alley. My Houston roots were crying out to have a great time. Adam, to my surprise, also knew how to two-step. We danced and had so much fun. I laughed until my face was numb. It was good to just kick back and forget about everything for a while. Kelly tried various ploys to get Adam's attention throughout the night, but he never took his eyes off me.

I turned to Adam and said, "You look very nice tonight in your handsome cowboy duds, Mr. Maguire."

"Thank you."

"Okay, now it's your turn to say something nice about me. No, on second thought, I'd rather you put your mouth to work over here," I said, as I pulled him close to kiss me.

About two hours into the night, the band took a break and so did we. There wasn't any music playing at all, and everyone was looking for someone to entertain them. Cody began clapping his hands and chanting, "JoJo sings, JoJo sings." Adam encouraged me to get up on stage and sing something.

I was very reluctant because I hadn't sung or preformed a song for what seemed like forever. But I took a deep breath and agreed. I summoned the drummer back so he could play backup for me and gave him some instructions for the song. I took a guitar from the stage and sat on a stool in front of the microphone. I tried to keep it light as I eased my way into it.

"Okay, I hope you know what you're asking of me. I haven't done this in a while. Confucius say, 'Be careful of what you wish for.'" I started lightly strumming the guitar as I said, "This is a song I wrote a few weeks ago for a special someone in my life. This is a song about being lost and finding my way back with the help of this special person. He taught me that all I had to do is love myself again, that this is the key - self-love. I only know a few guitar cords so bear with me. So far, I'm calling it *The Wisdom of This Man*."

♪   There's this rush that's come over me,
         Since you entered my life I can see
         That future I thought I wanted, was not to be,
         You found a way for me to be free

         True happiness comes from within,
         Until then my heart you can't win
         I endlessly searched to find that key,
         Then I found you, who shared it with me

         A feeling tells me, that I can, ann ann,
         A feeling tells me, that I can, ann ann
         A feeling tells me, that I can, ann ann,
         Trust the wisdom of this man

♫   You handed me back my happiness,
         That I thought was lost in the abyss
         Then you showed me what I needed to do,
         To trust the wisdom of a man like you

𝄞   Until I felt love for myself again,
         I wouldn't find true love with any man
         You understood my pain and my sorrow,
         Because of you, there'll be another tomorrow

True happiness comes from within,
Until then my heart you can't win
I endlessly searched to find that key,
Then I found you, who shared it with me

A feeling tells me, that I can, ann ann,
A feeling tells me, that I can, ann ann
A feeling tells me, that I can, ann ann,
Trust the wisdom of this man

♫   *A feeling tells me, that I can, ann ann,*
A feeling tells me, that I can, ann ann
A feeling tells me, that I can, ann ann,
Trust the wisdom of this man

Everyone paused for a moment and then busted out with applause. Adam inconspicuously wiped his eye. I walked over to him and put his hand on my stomach, and Adam stood up and hugged me, saying, "Have mercy on my heart." I knew things would never be casual between us ever again. We were now exposed; it was out there. We put it out there and we couldn't take it back.

Another good thing that came out of this, Kelly never even spoke to either of us again for the remainder of the filming.

Adam and I would talk for hours lying in bed together at night, when we weren't making love, of course, and I found out so much more about him. He was fascinating. Adam would tease me about my idiosyncracies, but I found out that he had a few of his own. He'd only eat green vegetables, no corn, and the vegetable juices couldn't touch the meat on his plate. He'd only wear cotton shirts. And those were just some of the sane ones.

Adam told me how he had lived in the wilderness for two years, living off the land through the knowledge of his Lakota teachings when he was searching his feelings about what had happened to his father. He said he would visit a recluse in the hills of South Dakota, and this Native American man taught him how to meditate, to allow the spirits within to speak to him. This man also taught Adam how to fight. Silently... deadly... the hand-to-hand combat kind of stuff you learn in Nam. He taught Adam how to fight using a knife. Adam studied and perfected the teachings in his seclusion. He hated guns, though. Adam wouldn't go near them.

"Maybe someday I'll tell you about the time I wrestled a buffalo," he bragged, jokingly.

"Buffalo? Wrestled? No, I don't believe you - you'll need to show me how you wrestled this buffalo. That is sooo hot," I teased, as he laughed.

Adam was a diamond in the rough, but he was sensitive and kind. I wanted to be the one who he made memories with.

Earlier, in the first month of filming, someone leaked that Adam and I were an item to the tabloids, but the article only appeared on an inside page. I thought, "I guess I was losing my popularity." But then when someone leaked the baby news, the tabloids had a field day with it, and it showed up front and center. "I guess I'm still popular after all," I remarked to Adam, as I pitched a copy of the tabloid in the trash. I think all of the media attention made him a little spooked since he'd never had this sort of publicity before.

The film ended, and Adam and I headed for the airport with Foxy in tow. There was a mob of paparazzi out front of the airport asking us a million questions. I advised Adam to stay close to me and not get distracted by what they were asking or doing. I explained that they do crazy things just to get an unflattering photograph in order to sell their magazine. I decided to answer the only civilized repeatable question I heard; who asked, "Jordan, would you like a boy or girl?"

I answered teasingly, "Well, we've definitely decided that we'd like one *or* the other."

I flew back to Los Angeles while Adam flew to see

Dakota to break the news to his daughter. I couldn't wait to meet her. Then the two of them came to Los Angeles. I was nervous. She was nervous. Dakota and I both laughed when we told each other. We quickly became fast friends, even though she was only seven. Anita, Dakota's mother, was understandably apprehensive about letting her child travel so far from home so I called to try to ease her fears. It didn't make Anita any less nervous, but she was thankful anyway. Dakota got to stay four days before returning home. Adam escorted her back like a good father.

When Adam returned to Los Angeles, he moved from his Studio City loft into the house. I planned to remodel our suite to suit both of our tastes and needs. It was tough at first, but I reluctantly compromised and made room for his clothes in my closet. Adam laughed when he saw how much stuff I had piled up in there. Gamma took on the challenge of sorting it all out for me. She also took on the challenge of redecorating the bedroom, but it was my idea to have chiffon drapes over the canopy bed which promised to be very sensual and romantic. Of course, Gamma didn't waste any time decorating the nursery as well.

Gamma also threw a huge welcoming party for Adam and he was touched. He met all of the family except Uncle Red, Sam and Dad, and everyone seemed to love him - Gamma most of all. I suppose she never did like Jack and overcompensated by wanting Adam to feel like a part of the family. He and Gampy didn't seem to have as much in common as Jack and him, except maybe the stock market, but it was still early yet. Tommy loved hearing Adam's stories of living in the wilderness. And Mom was just happy that I was happy. Foxy was already in love with him, especially since Adam learned early on while filming what she really loved - her Champion Cheddar. She was a little unsettled when we moved her booster seat, that was in my car, to the backseat, but besides that she adored him.

One day while we were sitting by the pool, I'm not real sure if Adam was feeling some sort of vibes from someone there or not, but I was a little surprised when he started questioning me about Jack and how he had fit into our lives. Adam had always seemed more self-assured and confident than that so something must have spooked him. Or perhaps he was just curious. In either case, Adam asked, "Did Annie like Jack as much as she seems to like me?"

Tommy happened to be buzzing by us on his skateboard when Adam posed the question and responded, "NO way, she hated the dude."

"Well, hate is a strong word, but clearly she didn't like him. If you are good to people and do good deeds, then Gamma will love you. And you already do that Adam, so you are way ahead of the game with her."

"Wasn't Jack a nice person?"

"I don't know, maybe not to everybody - but he was to me. I guess that's why Gamma never really told me that she didn't like him - but clearly, it was implied."

That discussion compelled me to analyze the differences between Adam and Jack. It seemed that I had always chased Jack around the country and was the one who called him to get together, but with Adam it was different. It felt good to be the chasee for a change and not always the chaser. That didn't mean that I didn't want to be with Adam or that I felt any less attracted to him in any way, but just that it felt good to know someone wanted to spend time with me without begging them to be there. Adam was also content to just sit back and talk to me wherever and whenever, whereas Jack always had to be doing something or be on the move - kinda like Dad. Maybe it was just what Jack did, like racing, but it seemed as if he was always bored by just sitting and talking.

Adam and I spent hours together talking about our future and our baby. On my next OBGYN visit, Adam came along with me. While in her office, Dr. Easton informed me that I had perfect hips for giving birth, and that it was my destiny in life to have lots of babies. I told her I wanted to know the sex of the baby, but Adam did not. We flipped on it and, well, "It's a girl."

"Not only is it a girl, but it's twins," the doctor added.

"What? Have mercy on my heart!" Adam bellowed as he stepped back clutching his chest.

"You! You did this to me," I teased and everyone laughed.

"But Jordan, if you don't stop eating, the next time we weigh you we'll all be down at the harbor's loading docks," Dr. Easton warned, teasing me.

"Oh sure, it doesn't help when you put that big jar of Malamars out in your waiting room," I said, then added poutingly, "oh, but the cravings are so intense."

"Loading docks," repeated the doctor.

"Oh, okay, I'll see what I can do," I said as I was thinking about the Mexican food Adam had promised me after our doctor's appointment.

Adam expressed concern that I would soon be replacing our sex life with Mexican food, due to the way that I would make yummy noises while eating. Not that I made yummy noises while making love, but I was truly enjoying my food. But as he soon found out, that was the furthest from what he experienced. I would have cravings for him as well. In fact, Adam decided that he wanted me pregnant for the rest of our lives.

Adam and I were together every day, with Gamma hinting around about "wedding" plans, until Adam went back out on location three weeks before I was due. Adam was shooting near where Dakota lived and that made me happy, but I was also nervous about him being gone, and so far away. I tried to show a brave front and told Adam to go anyway.

"I'll only be gone ten days, then I'll be back for three weeks while they shoot around me," he promised, affectionately pinching my behind. Next, he whispered, "Then we'll celebrate Valentine's Day when I get back, okay?"

"Okay, I'll be here," I pouted.

"Okay, so you'll be here?"

"Yes, I'll be right here and nowhere else," we continually bantered, like an Abbott and Costello act. I guess that's the hazzard of being involved with an actor.

Two days after Adam left, I started to feel peculiar. I'd never had a baby before, much less two so I didn't know what was going on. I knew it wasn't normal though, so I called Lexy and told her I needed reinforcements. She jumped a flight that same day. I'm not real sure why I chose her for my coaching partner; Lexy tended to be more emotional than I was. And *I* was the one with all the hormones bouncing all over the place. I called Adam, but he couldn't be reached - the operator told me something about trouble with the telephone lines. That shook me to my core. I was nervous enough as it was, and now I couldn't communicate with him. For a moment, déjà vu struck me like lightning. It took me back to the time when I couldn't reach Jack. I began feeling all of those abandonment issues creeping back in. Then I saw how Lexy was freaking out, and it made me laugh. I was okay. She was a basket case, but I was okay again.

Early the next morning, something drew me out of bed like a flash. I couldn't believe my nose, it was stirring me directly toward the kitchen. I sat, drooling at the kitchen table, while I watched Gamma fix a breakfast that included her delicious frosting-topped cinnamon buns. For the first time during the pregnancy, something other than Mexican food actually smelled good. More than good - heavenly. I had to move the flowers on the kitchen table, though. That aroma was iffy. I couldn't believe how much I ate. More than that, I couldn't believe that it stayed down for once. That's when I knew something was wrong. Something was different.

After we finished eating, I made an announcement to everyone, "I think it's time." Everyone looked at me like I was joking. "No, really, I think it's time," I said.

"Jordan Melanie, you'd better not be pulling one of your practical jokes," Gamma screeched as she cleared the table.

"No, I just didn't say anything until now because I was hungry and didn't know when I was going to get another decent meal."

Gampy was the worst. He ran around like a chicken with no head, not knowing what to do. I sat back and smirked at them all. They finally got it together enough to actually get me into the car. I screamed, "Ella, I have to bring

Ella." I wanted to pass her along to my babies, and she was still my good luck charm. Foxy licked my cheek for luck and off we went.

"Gampy, please keep trying Adam - he needs to be here when his babies are born," I pleaded as they wheeled me into the delivery room.

~*~:~*~:~*~:~*~:~*~:~*~

"Of course, Ella had to be in a plastic bag, but at least I got to bring her into the delivery room with me." I added, as Gladis smiled. I turned to Zoë and said, "Adam loved his song. He had me record it on a tape in our studio at home, and he plays it in his cassette player when he jogs. Oh, sorry, Adam doesn't jog, he *runs*. I guess that's a guy thing."

Zoë wasn't responding so I thought I would intrigue her with "I didn't know what I was getting myself into - a whole lot of trouble for starters. Just keep thinking, *the more, the merrier*, Zoë."

~*~:~*~:~*~:~*~:~*~:~*~

Chapter X

The More, the Merrier

"How are you doing, Jordan?" asked Dr. Easton, walking into the delivery room after my twenty-seven hours of hell, I mean labor.

"Never bedda," I answered with transcendent sarcasm. "I feel like I'm gonna explode."

"No, don't do that, we just mopped the floors," she joked.

"Okay, where are they? Are they out yet?" I continued to banter as I peaked under the covers.

"Not yet, but we have two teams here - one for each of them, Jordan," Dr. Easton informed as she examined me. "Well, you're at ten centimeters and we're ready, Jordan. It's time to start pushing."

"Push, Pookie, push," screamed Lexy all flustered, her arms flailing everywhere.

"Lexy, calm down - you're a basket case. I need you to focus," I instructed, wanting to throttle her.

I pushed so intensively that I thought my small intestines were going to squirt out. And then there she was. She was here. I could hear her screaming. One team of nurses took her over to the bathing table to clean her up.

"Well, here comes the other one Jordan - start pushing," instructed the doctor.

"Push, Pookie, push," shouted Lexy, but this time she sounded like a cheerleader chanting. "Push, Pookie, push."

I pushed just as intensively as the first time, then I heard something - another cry. Dr. Easton instructed the nurse to take the second baby over to the bathing table to clean it up. I turned to look at the bathing area, and there they were - they were here! I could hear them screaming, even over Lexy's screams. The doctor rolled her chair backwards and said she was taking a quick look at the babies. Then all of a sudden, one of the nurses shrieked, "Doctor, come here, quickly," as she stood looking at my private area. Dr. Easton rolled her chair back to look at what the nurse was all excited about.

"What? What's going on? Someone tell me something," I demanded.

"Um, well, we're not done here yet Jordan. Let's do this again."

"Aw, what'ya kiddin' me, doc?" I blistered.

Lexy screamed, "Aw, bloody 'ell, I don't think I can go through this again."

"No, I'm not kidding," chuckled the doctor, "you have to do it again - push Jordan."

After they cleaned me up, I got a chance to breathe. I was wheeled into the Neonatal Unit to look at my daughters - all three of them. They were beautiful, they were perfect.

Lexy was crying worse than the babies. We stood there for the longest time staring and cooing at them. And when things were silent, except for Lexy's sniffling, she asked, "You're gonna name one after me, right Pookie?"

I laughed with emotion and answered, "Yeah, of course, I'll name her Basket Case."

Just about that time, the press appeared from nowhere, and before security could get a handle on escorting them out, one of them asked, "How ya feeling, Jordan?"

"Never bedda," I beamed.

Adam finally arrived and he had Dakota with him, which was perfect because I had something to ask her. Almost everyone was there at the hospital with me now - Gamma, Gampy, Tommy, Larry, Mom, Uncle Red, Sam, Lexy, Dakota, Adam, and, of course, the girls, along with Tracy. Even Foxy was there, Uncle Red snuck her in inside a baby carriage that he put a blanket over so no one could see in.

He gave Foxy a rawhide chewstick to keep her from jumping out. Someone in the elevator even commented what an active child he had. Dad was a no-show.

I asked for a few minutes alone with Dakota and Adam before everyone gathered together around me. Dakota came into my room and motioned that she wanted to sit on the bed with me. However, when she saw my I.V., she backed away.

"Hi, Dakota honey. That's okay, you can sit up here with me - you won't hurt anything. So how does it feel to be a big sister?" I asked.

Dakota smiled, shrugged and said she didn't know yet.

"I've got something to ask you. I was wondering if it would be okay if I borrowed your name. I mean, if I could use it. You see, the oldest girl doesn't have a middle name yet, and I was wondering if you'd share your first name with her - would that be okay?"

She teared up, flailed her arms around me, and announced smiling, "Yes. I would love it."

"That's my girl," Adam said smiling, then added, "have mercy on my heart, you two."

After Adam and I signed the birth certificates, and just then realizing that it was Valentine's Day, everyone joined Adam and me in my hospital room. The nurses brought the girls in and retreated. Everyone started cooing at them.

"Everyone, we would like to introduce you to the newest members of our family - our sweet adorable Valentine's gifts. This is Stephanie Dakota Maguire," I glowed as I winked at Dakota. I was pointing at each baby as I spoke. I continued introducing: "Bethany Katia Maguire," turning to Mom and smiling, "and Tiffany Alexandria Maguire," while squeezing Lexy's hand. Lexy was still a mess.

After the applause subsided, I turned to Gamma and announced to everyone, "They are all actually named after their great-grandmother, if you'll notice - all of their first names end with *Annie* even though it's not spelled the same," I said as Gamma started to cry.

"We're the Maguire Sisters Singing Group," blurted Dakota.

Everyone laughed.

"Well Gamma, I did three good deeds today. How'd I do?"

She couldn't seem to get an answer out and just smiled.

It was a good day, but it was also an exhausting one. At the end, we exchanged good-byes to everyone and Gamma took Dakota back to the house with her. Even Larry had wept a little from being included in the family event. Before Uncle Red took Foxy back to the house, I hugged her so tight that I thought I was going to squish her. After begging Dr. Easton, she gave her permission for Adam to stay the night with me. I drifted off as Adam sat next to me, with one hand around my shoulder and the other on the bassinet gently rocking the girls.

The nurse came in and woke me during the night. She announced that she was wheeling the girls back to the Neonatal Unit. I stationed Tracy there for their protection, mostly because of how easy it was for the press to get access to that floor. I thought for a moment that I was feeling overprotective of them already, but Adam agreed and we felt more at ease about the girls being away from us.

After the girls were gone, I drifted off again. When I awoke a few hours later, I reached for my journal and began writing. I knew I wanted to express every feeling and thought I was experiencing while it was still fresh in my mind.

Dear Journal: Today tied with the best day of my life. My babies were born today. They are the most beautiful beings, along with Adam, that I've ever seen. My other best day - the day I met Adam, the man who bestowed this special gift onto me - these beautiful babies. The first born and the last born have Adam's coloring, dark Native American skin with black hair. The second born has red hair like her Mommy, but a little darker which makes it auburn. The girls all are a beautiful mix of both of us. They are not here right now, but in the Neonatal Unit and I miss them already. The nurse just came in and told me that they are doing fine. She also agrees - they are beautiful. I can't seem to stop writing that. They are beautiful. They are also so small. Stephanie was the biggest, at five pounds seven ounces, Bethany was five pounds two ounces, and little Tiffany was only four pounds one ounce. When I look at them, I don't see how small they are, I see how beautiful they are. If I didn't know first-hand that they came out of my body, I'd say Adam had them all on his own, as much as they look like him. They all have his eyes, but I think Tiffany will have my smile - just a hunch. They are beautiful and I love them. I love Adam. Goodnight Journal.

The next day, we got the fright of our lives. After a doctor told us that Tiffany was having difficulty breathing, I stole Adam's line and said, "Have mercy on my heart." But the good news was that it was treatable with medication.

The doctor released me the day after they were born, but the girls all stayed in the hospital for three more days until they were strong enough to come home.

With all of the happiness we were feeling toward the girls coming home, we almost forgot about the tabloid reporters hovering outside the hospital. Adam and Tommy devised a plan to divert them. I didn't know what they had planned and didn't ask, but it seemed to have worked for the most part because the members of the media were scarce when we were leaving.

"You didn't kill 'em all, did you?" I sarcastically asked Adam and Tommy.

They both looked at each other mysteriously and then looked at me. "It's best you don't ask too many questions," Adam teased as if they had just pulled off the performance of the century.

The girls' homecoming was special and sweet, and everyone was there to welcome them. Gamma had decorated their nursery with every shade of pink imaginable. All the way around their room there was a huge mural painted in numerous pastel colors. The mural featured a bunny trail with all of their critter friends around the outside of the trail cheering them on to hop down the bunny trail. I wanted to stay in there with them forever; it was a wonderful fairyland.

Before a month had passed, I'd bought the hospital some new Ultrasound equipment with a note attached. It read; "Hey doc, this might help with counting fingers and toes," teasing them for not detecting my third baby.

Somehow I had gotten the notion that I could take care of all three of them all on my own, but I couldn't have been more wrong. Every time I thought I had things under control, someone would start crying, or someone would lose breakfast. The situation was getting out of control, and Adam, dear sweet Adam, gently convinced me that I couldn't do it all. That's when we hired Clara as our nanny to help with the girls. She came very highly recommended and was a gem. I was amazed at how much energy she had at her age of forty-something. Clara was my early twenty-seventh birthday present from Adam. And for his birthday present, I let him hire her. But Adam was also busy living in his own fantasy world. He hired a contractor to build a playground for the girls. Adam claimed it was for Dakota, but he kept saying "them" a lot when we'd talk about the project. I smiled and let it slide.

Adam and I talked about getting married, and about three months after the girls were born, he formally proposed and I accepted. I did all the planning this time and only included family and close friends - about fifty people in all. It would be held in the Party Barn. It wasn't my parent's wedding, and it wasn't the wedding I had planned with Jack. It was *just right*.

We also planned the baptisms of the girls for the evening before our wedding. We thought that was a perfect beginning for our new family, *and* we would have everyone there, having arrived to attend the wedding. I wanted our wedding on July 4th because it mainly signified initiating our independence from tyranny of past apparitions. Adam was thrilled to celebrate our marriage with a good ole-fashioned down-home fourth of July Texas barbeque for our reception. The wedding's style was laid back and easy-going, that was Adam, that was us, and it was fun.

Of course, I asked Lexy to be my maid of honor. Adam asked Tommy to be his best man, and he was thrilled to be so involved. Tommy was a bit nervous about the best man's speech, but Gamma said he rehearsed it perfectly. Adam went to get Dakota and they flew back together. She was to be our flower girl, and I don't think Foxy minded one bit. Adam's family regretted that they couldn't make it out to our wedding, even though we offered to pay for all of their expenses. That made Adam sad, and so that made me sad.

My wedding dress was simple, mostly white-crepe material with embroidery down each side and around the bust area with a floral design. It was strapless; the wedding being in July, I wanted the gown to be very light weight with no train attached.

Adam would wear a double-breasted black Armani suit with a black vest underneath. He looked incredibly handsome in it.

We went together to pick out our wedding rings. Adam said he didn't really care what we chose, but he did prefer the white-gold bands over yellow-gold ones - so we went with that. He had three diamonds on the top of his, and mine had five diamonds around the top of the wedding band. My engagement ring featured a beautiful four-carat Asscher-cut diamond in the center, with two smaller diamonds on each side. With completing that, the major preparations were done.

The night before the wedding, after the baptisms of the girls, I sat out by the pool while everyone was playing games in the house. I began to think about Jack, about what would have been. I'm not sure if it was just cold feet, but I was feeling hesitant. I kept thinking about the heat Jack and I shared, sometimes it was almost out of control. It was exciting.

I then tried to focus on Adam. Adam was sexy and soft-spoken, and made love in a more loving and gentle way then Jack. It was still exciting, but wasn't intense. Our time together was fun, and Adam didn't focus on sex as much as Jack did. We were completely comfortable with each other, more of a best-friend feeling. I loved that about Adam, but also missed Jack's fiery of passion. That began to scare me - would I be bored with Adam in time?

I set any doubts aside for the sake of the family, friends and children, and we said our "I do's" and had our celebration. We were married outside under a canopy of red and white roses, highlighted with blue ribbons - not a pink one was in sight. Uncle Red walked me up the aisle, and when the minister asked who gives this woman to be with this man, all the guests answered, "We do." Adam and I two-stepped our way into our first day of marriage together. We were a family and we were happy.

I was nervous about leaving my babies for the first time, but Adam needed to take Dakota home and I wanted to accompany them. When we escorted her back to South Dakota, Adam and I stopped in to visit his mother. Turns out that they had a surprise wedding reception planned for us that night. This was the best news ever and Adam was ecstatic. I guess they wanted to have one for us and that's why they didn't attend ours. During the reception, Adam's mother gave me my own Lakota name as her gift to me, and her way of welcoming me into her family. I was now known as *Hopa Tokala* to his family from then on, which meant "fox of beauty." His mother said the name was selected because of my beautiful red hair color. I don't think Adam knew, therefore, couldn't tell her about Dad's family name of Waw-goosh, which was Chippewa for Fox.

I loved and cherished my new name from his mother. I also discovered that she called Adam, *Waeco Wawate Ca*, which meant "gentle actor."

While we were there, I told Adam that I wanted to provide Anita with money for Dakota, but he said she wouldn't take it. I felt as though we should at least offer so I called her. Sure enough, Anita said she felt strange about accepting it. She was suspicious and declined the offer initially, then asked why I wanted to provide money for Dakota. I told Anita that I wanted Dakota to have financial security, and that Dakota might think we love her less than the other girls if they all didn't receive equal portions. I also told Anita that I didn't care who received the credit or praise - I wanted Dakota to have the trust fund no matter what the circumstances. Anita said she would think about it, but in the meantime, she invited us over at the insistence of her daughter.

After talking to Anita face-to-face, she agreed but said that we would all be equally acknowledged for contributing to her trust fund even though the monetary amounts were not equal. Dakota's trust fund would also allow her to attend a private school that she had been wishing for. She was thrilled and hugged all three of us. That was worth every penny.

When Adam and I returned home, I contacted my accounting management company and instructed them to make a two million-dollar deposit into an investment fund account for Adam to use as he wanted. Even though he had his own money, Adam wasn't making the big paychecks yet of a leading man. I wanted him to have enough so he didn't feel as though he had to ask *the wife* for money all the time. There was never any mention of a prenup; that suggested mistrust and I didn't have any where Adam was concerned.

Adam spent less time away on location and more time at home with the girls and me. I don't know if he felt guilty for not being there when they were born, but I didn't complain or overanalyze it. We flew Dakota out to Los Angeles whenever Anita would allow her to visit. We negotiated vigorously for Anita to relocate to Los Angeles with Dakota, but at no avail. We also included into the negotiations, payment of all their expenses, including a condo for them to live in, but Anita had strong ties to South Dakota and didn't want to leave. She seemed self-assured, level-headed, and sincere so I trusted that it wasn't to keep Adam from his daughter.

Meanwhile, Tommy had done so well in high school, pulling out nearly all As, that he graduated a year early at seventeen. This was despite the fact that Tommy had actually started school when he was nearly six. He excelled in chemistry and mathematics, but his main focus, apparently, was in sports. I'd heard Tommy speak of, for the umpteenth time, how he wanted to play professional baseball someday, but I never really gave it much thought. I'd seen him out back in the batting cages, and Mom claimed he was out there every waking hour, but I still didn't think Tommy was serious. Little brothers always think they're going to be baseball players, firemen or astronauts. Tommy was no different. But Tommy *was* different. He was becoming a very good baseball player and was so good, in fact, that he received two bona fide offers in his first year of college from major leagues - just a few months shy of his eighteenth birthday.

Later that month, after Tommy spoke incessantly with Uncle Red, he signed with the Angels for the upcoming summer season, and dropped out of college. Gamma read him the riot act about needing an education in life, but Tommy somehow always charmed his way out of things with her. I could never do that, and I wasn't about to let him forget it. I planned on Iggie iguana later being my accomplice for that.

We planned the most extravagant party ever for Tommy's eighteenth birthday. Gampy even helped with the festivities, and he was just as giddy as he had been the day we cruised by the New York Stock Exchange in Manhattan - the day Gampy and I went for my first big audition. Gampy even named the event. "The World Series of Birthdays Extravaganza," and he had a gigantic banner made for the Party Barn area.

When the idea was born, I asked Gamma humbly, "Is there any way you can help plan the event this time, since I have my hands full with the girls, and the production company, not to mention my acting career I need to get back on track."

She responded, "Okay, okay, I get the picture - you're busy. Yes, I would love to plan this for Tommy."

"Well, I mean *help* plan it. Do you think you could include Lexy in the planning?"

Gamma sighed and reluctantly agreed. "Shall I expect big purple pom-poms to float down from the ceiling when he enters?" she teased, making fun of Lexy's somewhat eccentric tastes.

I just smiled and answered, "Could be, with Lexy you never know." That didn't instill much confidence in her, but Gamma took another deep breath and dialed her number.

A full week hadn't gone by, when they were fast at work planning the event. The invitations were sporty, but also reflected Gamma's exquisite taste. Since no one would probably attend on Tommy's actual birthday, Christmas Day, they planned it for two weeks before. Each time we'd plan a party, we would incorporated a theme. That was so we could sponsor a charity for the event. We chose Big Brothers and Big Sisters for our charity on that day because I thought that fit into our family's theme too. Speaking of fitting in, I worked out every day until the party so I'd be able to fit into my party dress. Despite the recent birth of our girls, I finally did. That was a true testament that we were ready.

On the night of Tommy's birthday party, I gave most of the staff the night off, except my personal security, plus Clara to watch the girls. Gamma hired a staff supervisor who oversaw the direction of all the party personnel. We watched in amazement as everyone buzzed around doing their respective jobs and my head was buzzing too trying to keep them all straight.

No one was allowed in the main house; all the activities were in the Party Barn area. There were several guards stationed throughout the house, including one outside of our suite where the girls and Foxy were. We instructed the guards to permit access to the household members and staff, but not before viewing a security badge designed and laminated by Gamma. The front-gate security checked invitations before the guests were allowed entry onto the grounds. Even a professional lifeguard was hired for safety, in case one of the guests decided it'd be a great idea to get drunk and then go for a swim.

Adam took one look at me in my skin-tight dress and smiled, saying, "Have mercy on my heart, woman!" And he looked me up and down before pinching my behind, or trying to because my dress was so tight, he couldn't. I returned the compliment before we headed into our girl's room to say goodnight. Adam and I stood over our daughters and smiled proudly, arm in arm. It was a tender moment, and I was happy. We kissed tenderly and waltzed in to join the others.

"You look wonderful, Gamma," I beamed. "Everything looks fantastic; you outdid yourselves," I said to both Gamma and Lexy.

Gampy was handsome in the suit that Gamma made him wear. He fidgeted, but knew better than to complain. Tommy was wearing a suit with the tie untied and hanging off his neck. Gamma tried to catch up to him to tie it, but he eluded capture.

"Hi Mom. You look beautiful," I said greeting her. "How are you feeling tonight? Any qualms about being around people who are drinking?"

"No, I'm sober and that's how I'll stay no matter what happens, sweetie," she responded. "At least for tonight, anyway. I can only go one day at a time. And I'm strong today; I can make it through tonight." Mom sounded as if she was affirming her alcoholic treatment affirmations.

"Good, I'm proud of you," I said, and kissed her cheek. I knew Mom wasn't good with emotional stuff like this, but I felt okay about it because I was. I didn't let Mom's lack of emotional attention stop me from showing her how proud I was of her.

As Adam and I walked through the Party Barn area, I held onto his arm tightly so I wouldn't trip, as klutzy as I was. We were pleasantly surprised that they had executed a perfect party atmosphere. There were tables lined up outside under a canopy, and games arranged on the grounds for those who could brave the cool night air. Even though, technically, it was a birthday party, there was a definite baseball theme going on. They had birthday and baseball decorations inside the disco, the dining room and the arcade. There was a videographer moving around the dining room, with two still photographers snapping at everyone as they entered. The arcade was fully stocked with liquor, and the champagne was flowing faster than Foxy could catch an orange Champion Cheddar cheese cracker. Catering offered everything from prime rib to ballpark-style hot dogs. They even gave out baseballs as party favors with Tommy's name signed onto them.

"I certainly hope Gamma didn't make Tommy sign all of them personally," I whispered to Adam. "He'd never be able to pick up a bat again after all of that."

Before half the night was over, I decided it was time for one of my practical jokes, and it was Tommy's turn. I instructed a staff member to place an empty fruit-punch bowl on the dessert table, where shortly thereafter, I placed Iggie inside of it. That *slimy* lizard kept trying to get out, but it was too slippery and she kept falling back down inside of it. When a female guest screamed after seeing her, Tommy ran over to calm her - Iggie, that is.

Adam laughed and acknowledged my brilliance, "That was good."

I smiled seductively, raised one eyebrow, and whispered, "It's not my first time."

Adam leaned over and said, "I thought you only did these on the set."

"Why should tonight be any different?" I revealed with a nefarious-looking face.

"Oh, and by the way, thanks - I'm just grateful that I wasn't your target tonight," he added before kissing me to prove his gratitude.

"Oh no, *thank you* because you *are* partially my target. Tommy will probably blame you for this because he knows I'd never touch that wretched thing," I added before I quickly moved away prior to him wanting to retaliate by trying to pinch my behind.

But it wasn't to be that Adam would take the blame for me. Just then, Tommy yelled, "Sissy!" And I tore out of there faster than Gamma could snap me with her dishtowel.

It was a fun evening, but Adam and I were tired so we snuck out of the party with Tracy trailing behind. We checked in on our daughters before going off to bed. The night ended passionately.

By the time Adam and I got up the next morning, the

extra maid service Gamma had hired was around and busily doing their work. The morning was brisk so the two of us nestled ourselves together under a blanket and sat out on the patio. We sipped our coffee while watching the ground crew take down the canopies from the night before. I chatted with Adam and occasionally glanced at my current script. I was happy and life was good.

Then Uncle Red and Sam came up, sat down and told us they needed to tell us something. They had wanted to discuss it for about a week now, but waited until after the party. Uncle Red said that he got a call from a police buddy of his and was told that Dad died in a bar fight about five years ago back in Houston. That was just about the time I graduated from college. Dad had a fake ID on him with another name. When the police saw my picture in Dad's wallet, they just assumed he had a picture of a movie star in there. The authorities didn't know who to contact so they let the state bury him and closed the file. After they made the connection, purely by accident, the police figured Dad changed his name to escape from paying back the money he owed to that raunchy casting company, along with dozens of others. Dad died just how he lived his life, alone.

I didn't know how to feel. This news was confusing for me. I felt somewhat responsible since I didn't pay the casting company the full amount so they went after Dad. He raised me, but I didn't really know much about him. And what I knew was distasteful to me. I tried searching my feelings. Guilt set in. I tried to feel loss, but I found that I had already mourned his passing years ago when Dad hadn't included himself in the events of my life. Not just the birthdays or holidays or opening nights, but the losing of a tooth, or the skinning of a knee. Even when Dad was there, he wasn't really there. How do you miss someone that your heart has never touched? I wanted to cry, in fact I felt I was obligated to cry, but I couldn't make the connection to feelings of loss. I think I felt more pain from him teaching me about mistrust and deceitfulness when he stole money from me than anything else. Plus there was anger over how he used me as a pawn toward his revenge on Mom. And the anger about his stealing my opportunity to have a real father. He stole that from me, he stole away a loving father I could have had. Mom stole a childhood from me, but somehow I forgave her. I helped turn Mom's life around and I could have turned his around too. I now needed to forgive Dad in order to move on with my life and not have the burden of anger fill my heart. I hadn't saddled Adam with any of the past details of Dad's actions nor the way that I was feeling about it. I just wanted our time together to be positive.

Uncle Red said to look into my children's eyes and forget the pain and confusion Dad had caused me. And Uncle Red said that I was not like Dad and believing that would relieve any fears I had about not raising my children on the right path. I told Uncle Red that he was more of a father to me, and no matter how far I would search the world, I wouldn't find a better one. Uncle Red was silent, then remarked he had to go do something or another, but I knew better.

Tommy didn't say much when we told him. However, later that day, I could hear sniffling coming from his room. I knew Tommy would be embarrassed if I saw him crying so I just let it go and decided I would do something extra nice for him later in the week.

I asked Uncle Red if we could exhume Dad's body and have it moved closer to us. He advised against it and asked if I'd just let him be. So I did.

That night Adam and I walked into our children's nursery and just sat with them a while. They were sleeping and didn't even know we were there, but we knew. Neither of us spoke much. Just being there together with the girls said volumes. *Time*. That's more than Dad ever gave me. For that matter, that's more than Jack ever gave me either. "My children will never feel abandoned," I thought out loud. Adam didn't respond. I don't think he really knew what I was thinking with that comment.

A week after Uncle Red left, he called and said he just couldn't tolerate my pestering anymore - and said he had decided to move to Los Angeles with Sam. I jumped up and down like a kid and told Uncle Red that was the best news I'd heard in ages.

About a month later, Adam and I sat in the terminal at LAX waiting for their flight to arrive. I began to reminisce to Adam about my adolescents with Uncle Red. "He is a brilliant attorney who bailed me out of more jams than I care to admit that I was foolish enough to get into in the first place. He's always had a good heart and took on lost causes, which didn't bring in much money because of it. His parents withheld their attention from him, partly because he didn't use his profession to extort money from people. Instead Uncle Red liked helping others by not swindling them like Dad did. I don't know why, but Dad always got all of the attention from their parents."

"I'm glad you had a positive male role model growing up. That's why you treat me so good," Adam teased.

Uncle Red and Sam finally arrived. I hugged both of them so hard that Adam had to pinch my behind to get me to move away from them. We took them out to a nice dinner. Then Eddie drove us back to the house and we got Sam and Uncle Red settled into their new suite. The next morning, we woke to one of the saddest days of my life.

~❋~¡~❋~¡~❋~¡~❋~¡~❋~¡~❋~

"Yes, I woke to one of the saddest days I would ever have in my life," I said to Zoë. "My first love, my first soul mate would leave me. Little did I know that this would also be the most joyous time of my life. It was very confusing for me to feel the worst I've ever felt and joyous at the same time. I was turned upside down. And what's worse, I couldn't turn to the most important person in my life, because he was a million miles away on the other side of the world." I started to tear, and with that, Gladis left the room.

~❋~¡~❋~¡~❋~¡~❋~¡~❋~¡~❋~

Chapter XI

Departures and Returns

"Did you bring 'em?"

"Yes, Joey honey, I got them."

"Do you think she'd like this?"

"I think she'd love this. Not only does she get her very own box, but she gets her very own case."

Adam was trying to steady me as I was wobbling and shaking. "I don't know if I can do this. What do I say, what do I do now, what am I going to do without her? She's been in my life for fourteen years; I can't possibly find any words that would express the joy she brought into my life."

"Why don't you just say what you just said to me? That was nice," said Uncle Red.

Earlier that day, Adam and I had selected a nice place for a burial plot, which was positioned at the edge of the property. I stood at the foot of Foxy's grave, tears streaming down my face. I looked around at the small crowd of people that I personally had invited to be there with me. Slightly shaking, I began to speak. "I'm not sure what to say, I'm not sure what I'm able to say at this point. She was so happy. She was so brave. She was so loving. She was my savior more times than I can count. What can I say about a loved one who has been there for me like that? I remember the day Uncle Red brought her into my life. When all things seemed the bleakest in my world, she'd pull me back. She'd lick my face til I laughed. I know she wasn't human, she was closer than that to me. She was always there to cheerfully greet me no matter how long I'd been gone. She was always able to perk me up no matter how down I got. I'm not sure which she loved more, me or Champion Cheddar. And y'awll know about her obsession with her heavenly snacks. In honor of her today, I thought she would like it if each of us tossed a handful of them in with her so she will have a nicer trip up to heaven."

Everyone opened a box from the case and took out a handful of crackers. Each of us tossed them in, one at a time, into the grave with Foxy as Gamma read from her scriptures. I stared as the crackers seemed to float down in slow motion, like orange rose pedals swirling around in the wind. Her tiny coffin was blanketed with them.

"Thank you all for loving her as I did." I turned and looked up, then whispered, "Bye Foxy Lady, I will always love you." Adam held my shaking hand as we walked back to the house.

Later that day, I sat on the bed staring out the bedroom window for what seemed like hours. My mind wondered, but mostly came back to Foxy. Uncle Red had always been there for me when I needed him to be. I was glad he was closer now.

"Hi, Joey honey. How are you doing?"

"I'm okay, I just needed a moment to let everything sink in. I miss her. The ironic thing is that I'm sad because she's gone and I always turned to her when I'm sad."

"I know, but have comfort in knowing she died in her sleep, snuggled up to you last night and wasn't in any pain," Uncle Red said, consoling me. "Foxy was right where she wanted to be. And she's right here now, very close any time you want to go talk to her."

I nodded, but couldn't seem to get any words out. I sat there for a moment, then choked out, "Where is everyone?"

"Well, your grandparents are in the family room, Lexy passed out in her room, Tommy's in his room, your mom is in her suite, and Sam is in ours. Dakota was depressed about Foxy so Adam told her that he would have some fun stuff for them to do - so he took all the girls to the zoo. Adam said he told you."

"I don't remember, did he? He took them all - all by himself?"

"No, he took Clara," Uncle Red chuckled softly.

"Oh good - she's the best. That's good," I whispered, sleepily. I gave Uncle Red a small hug and told him I was going to sleep a while. I watched as he left the room and then I stretched out on the bed before everything faded.

When I awoke, everything seemed foggy. I didn't know how long I had been there. I looked around the room and then it came back to me. She was gone. I took a deep breath and staggered into the bathroom to wash my dried-out face from my salty tears, and that's when I heard them. I heard whispering. It was coming from the hallway. "Crap, I can't quite make out what they were saying. Who is that?" I thought as I slowly opened the door to the hallway. I could see Gamma and Uncle Red whispering something in disagreement.

"Plotting to take over the world?" I asked, startling them. "Or just maybe overthrowing the government of a small country?"

"Oh hello Jordan dear, what are you talking about?" Gamma asked nervously.

"What'ya doing out here?"

"Dinner will be ready soon, dear. You should lie back down until I call you."

"That's not what I asked you," I said, getting back to the point. "What'ya doing out here whispering in the hallway?"

"Well, we were just trying to come to an agreement on something."

"Yeah what?" I asked.

"Joey honey, we have something to tell you."

"NO, we don't," blurted Gamma.

"Okay, either you do or you don't - which is it?"

"She's going to find out anyway, and it should come from us."

"Just let her have some peace for a while - is that too much to ask?" Gamma asked tearfully.

"Okay, that's enough. Can't you see that whatever this is, it's upsetting her?" I asked Uncle Red, protecting Gamma with my arm around her. "Let's all go and have a nice cup of tea and we can sort through this," I said democratically and somewhat proud of myself for being cool about it.

As I was nudging Gamma toward the kitchen, I could hear other voices coming from the family room. Voices? No. A voice. A familiar voice. A voice that was hauntingly familiar. A voice that haunted my dreams. I didn't seem to have control over my legs; they were drawing me closer and closer to that voice. I was mesmerized by the sound of it. Yes, of course, I knew that voice. I knew that haunting voice; it had echoed in my mind for years.

They were all looking at me as I stood staring into the family room from the doorway. I thought, "What am I doing here? I was sleeping and this was the weirdest dream ever - so with what I was seeing, it couldn't be real." I stood there staring for seconds, then minutes as I tried to rationalize it in my subconscious. The scene didn't make any sense. I had to wake up, I had to snap out of my slumber. I wondered if my hallucination was because of losing Foxy. Maybe I was having a stronger reaction to Dad's death than I was admitting to myself - and this was the only way I could deal with it. I had heard that sometimes tragedies made dreams more vivid. Yeah that was it. But no, that didn't make any sense either because what did that have to do with this, why would Jack be standing in the middle of the family room talking to Gampy? Jack doesn't have anything to do with this house. My dreams of him were always in the Hollywood Hill's house. And beside, they were diminishing... so why was Jack here and so real to me now?

Suddenly, I heard Lexy's high-pitched scream coming from behind me. I spun around to look at her and then back at Jack. Everything started to fade.

"Jordan? Jordan, are you alright? Jordan dear, can you hear me? Someone get some water. Call 911!" Gamma screamed.

"I'm okay, Gamma," I said groggily. "What happened? Why is everyone in my bedroom?"

"Jordan - you're not in your bedroom, dear. You're in the family room and you've fainted."

"What?" I asked as I slowly sat up still on the floor. "Where's Lexy? I thought I heard Lexy scream, or was that in my dream?"

"Lexy's fine, dear," Gamma told me. "She's, she, she stepped out for a moment."

I brought myself to my feet and wobbled over to the couch. I looked up and there he was again. I stood up and walked over to him. I looked straight into Jack's eyes and reached up and touched his cheek. I felt weak and backed up until I was sitting on the couch again never taking my eyes off him.

"I don't understand. Why won't I wake up?" I asked in a monotone voice staring at Jack.

"You're awake, Joey. Yes, that's him - we can all see him. Would you like some water?"

I suddenly, without thinking, ran over to him and hurled my arms around him. "You're alive? Did you know we thought you were dead? You're alive," I confirmed, laughing emotionally. Then I instantly realized, he was alive so where had he been all of this time? "You're alive and you didn't come back to me. Why? Why didn't you come back to me, Jack? I prayed every night that you would come back to me."

"Jordan, I didn't have a choice. I was detained," Jack answered.

Hearing his voice for the first time and now knowing I wasn't dreaming, I asked heatedly, "DETAINED? Detained where?"

"I was held against my will."

"You expect me to believe that?" I asked, getting madder at him, at the situation, at feeling abandoned with all these feelings rushing back to me.

"It's true. I would like to tell you the story. Can we sit down and I will tell you everything?" Jack and I sat across from each other as everyone stepped closer. "Can we have some privacy?" Jack requested from everyone.

I couldn't take my eyes off him. I looked at every crease on his face and every new wrinkle. Jack's face was older, much more than five years worth. He was tanner than in the past. He had a weathered look, as if he spent four years in the desert. I watched his every move. I barely even noticed everyone leaving the room. "Where were you, Jack? I tried to find you. I looked everywhere - where were you, Jack?"

"I was in a Mexically prison that was built underground and well hidden from the outside world. That's why you couldn't find me. Buck and I were suppose to catch a flight back to the states together, but I became ill so I went into the men's room. When I came out, the flight had departed with Buck on it. So I tried to find another flight. The only way out I could find was on a chartered twin-engine plane, so I booked it and hired a pilot who was hanging around the terminal. I was headed home when the pilot announced that we had to make a quick stop. We landed on what seemed to be a rarely used runway. I didn't feel good about it at all, but I had no choice except to go along with it. When we got on the ground, a jeep drove up with several heavily armed men in it. They blocked us from leaving in the plane. These men claimed to be Mexican Federalies and they were there to make a bust. It was then, that I found out the pilot was there to pick up a cargo of marijuana. Since I was with him, they contended that I was in on the transaction too."

"That's not true, Jack. I spoke to the Federalies. I spoke to them every day that I was down there looking for you. The Mexican authorities claimed that they didn't know where you were and that you were probably dead."

"The guys who kidnapped me weren't the Federalies. They lied so we would cooperate, not that we had a choice with all that firepower. When I got to an underground prison, they took everything from me - my passport, my wallet, everything. I told them who I was, but they already knew. They weren't interested in any marijuana cargo - they were interested in me. When I finally escaped, I flew back to Italy and my family told me that these people were extorting money from them and promised they would release me if they paid. These people threatened that they would kill me if my family made it public or told anyone because that would destroy their scam. From what I understand, the kidnappers were very well financed and had a good operation going on there, and that's why no one knew it was there. The real Federalies probably didn't know about these guys or they lied to protect them because they were getting kickbacks. I found out that they had lured the pilot to land with a setup with the marijuana as bait so they could abduct me in the middle of nowhere. I was gift-wrapped and hand-carried to them."

"But what happened to the plane? They had to do something with the plane."

"I don't know what they did with the plane."

"How did you escape?"

"I watched and learned their routine and struck when they were most vulnerable. I hitched a ride to the border and crossed into the United States along with a truckload of illegal aliens. I contacted a friend to help me secretly get back to Italy."

"Where's the pilot? Why didn't he help you?"

"They killed him sitting in the plane. That's when I knew they lied about the bust, because they don't just go around killing suspected drug smugglers. I never knew for sure why they killed him until I returned. It was simply because they didn't need him; he wasn't worth anything to them. My father paid three million dollars and they still wouldn't release me."

"Oh, that poor man. When are they going to tell his family?"

"They already did."

"How long have you been back?" I asked, just realizing this wasn't even his second or third stop if he had all this information.

"Over a month," he answered as my eyes got wider. Then Jack continued, "We had to keep my return quiet in order for them to think I was killed escaping. That way, we could shut them down and make them pay for what they did."

"And did you?"

"No, the Mexican government went in to clean out that facility, but they said it wasn't there. I escaped at night and couldn't remember exactly where it was. My main priority was to get out alive and move as fast as I could. It was in the middle of nowhere and I didn't know exactly where I was or how far I had traveled. The Mexican authorities apologized, but stated that all they could do was try to find it. Without an exact location, it would be difficult - especially underground. They probably won't ever be able to prove that the officials you spoke with were involved. And we really don't know that they ever were."

"I don't know what to say, Jack," I said. "I'm sorry for not looking for you harder. I was down there for a year and a half trying to find you, but I should have looked harder. I wished every night that I had found you. I don't even want to think about what it was like for you. I'm so glad you are alive, Jack," I reiterated as I hugged him again.

"I wished you had too, but it's not your fault - you couldn't have known about all of this. I don't want you to feel guilty. I'm grateful that they didn't kill you for asking too many questions to the wrong people. I came here because I wanted you to hear this from me and not the press. My family and I are going down to make a statement when I leave here. I knew telling you about this would be the hardest thing I'd ever have to do so I left it until now." Jack sat there looking at me for a moment before saying, "I almost forgot how beautiful you are. I sat there every day thinking of being with you again. You saved my life. Thinking of you every day was the only thing that got me through that miserable ordeal."

I smiled as I gazed into Jack's eyes. I was emotionally drained, but felt energized at the same time. He was alive and Jack had finally came back to me.

He kneeled down close to me and whispered, "We can be together again, just like before. All you have to do is say the word. It will be very easy - all you need to do is pay off the prenup and we can get married like we planned. We can do all the things we pledged that we were going to do with each other. We can build our house, grander than this one, and we can have that life we promised each other. You can even give him custody and we can start our own family that we dreamed of, Jordan - we can be happy. We've waited long enough... it's our time now, it's our destiny to be together, Jordan."

My head was spinning and I wasn't sure that I had heard everything he said, much less understood it. All I could seem to get out of my mouth at that moment was "You're alive."

"Hi, we had a great time at the zoo. Dakota, tell Annie what we saw." I heard Adam's voice in the distance and he was talking to Dakota and Gamma.

"Adam," I thought.

Citing an appointment with the press, Jack left abruptly. From the distance between us, I could hear Gamma briefly filling Adam in on what was going on. Adam walked into the family room and found me crying on the couch. Adam knelt down in front of me and said he was there if I needed him.

I whispered to him, "I'll always need you, Adam."

We hugged.

The next day, the headline read, **Jack Rebello Returns from the Dead**. I read the article from start to finish. I knew the story, but needed to read it over and over for it to sink in. My head was still spinning from what Jack had told me, mostly his plea to me. Adam didn't say much. He listened mostly. I didn't say much. I couldn't. I didn't know what to say, and even if I did, I was too numb to verbalize my feelings. Did I really hear what Jack was suggesting or was I just interpreting it because I wanted an easy clear-cut answer to all of this?

I couldn't eat, and I felt sick. Gamma tried to get me to eat something. I may have taken two bites, but mostly just moved the rest of the food around on my plate.

It was strange seeing Jack again. Strange like being in a fog, or like I was dreaming awake. Sort of like waking up from a dream so vivid, that you were convinced it was real.

"If you need anything, I'll be in with the girls," Adam

said, interrupting my thoughts as he squeezed my shoulder and then left the room. He seemed to be a million miles away, and my arm just didn't have the strength to reach out to him. I just sat there - I couldn't move, I couldn't do anything. I wasn't much good to anyone. I tried playing with the girls for a while, but they were distracting my thoughts and I needed to think about this - about Jack.

The next day, Adam escorted Dakota on her flight back home. He said he was going to stay for a few days, a week at the most, to get Dakota settled back in at home and to see the rest of his family. We exchanged good-byes and he left.

I spent my days playing with the girls and riding Poncho. I locked myself in the recording studio reenacting the night I sang the song that I wrote for Adam, but nothing kept my mind off Jack for very long. That was also fueled by Jack calling a dozen times a day. When Gamma would answer Jack's calls, she'd hang up on him - accidently, of course. When I would answer, all he wanted was to know if we were getting back together. I had no idea what to say to him. How could I hurt Jack if I said no? I had waited so long for him to come back to me. How could I demolish any hope of having my dream of a future with him - something I dreamt about for so long? It wasn't Jack's fault that they had kidnapped him and held him captive. And he would have to accept the girls, no way I was going to just give them away. I'm sure Jack didn't mean that. And what about "Hope?" Hope had a face of a little girl that looked just like Jack. She had a soul that I mourned when Jack was lost and when I knew he wasn't coming back. She could now be resurrected, like Jack.

But how could I hurt Adam if I said yes to Jack? I'd grown to love him, but was he my destiny? We had a family together. We had built a home and not just a house for all of us. He was tender and loving and I was comfortable with him. We had similar interests, and our everyday life wasn't filled with drama, like it was with Jack. I just wanted the confusion to stop. And the only way I knew how to do that at this point was to put the whole thing aside and not think about it.

After glancing at my datebook, I realized it had been three days since Adam had left. I grunted and shuffled into the bathroom when I heard it again - whispering in the hallway. "Oh, now what?" I said out loud.

Not so slowly and quietly as before, I stepped out to see what was going on. Gamma and Lexy were conspiring something.

"Oh, hello dear," Gamma greeted cheerfully. "Why don't I run you a nice bath - would you like that dear?"

Looking suspiciously at them, I answered, "No Gamma. Except for my occasional dips in the Jacuzzi, I'm a shower person, remember?" I turned and shuffled back into the bathroom.

"Well then, why don't we leave you to that dear," said Gamma. I observed their fake smiles while they backed away and closed the door.

I could hear Lexy through the door suggesting, "Don't run any water! We want to encourage Pookie to stay in the shower as long as the hot water will hold out. She's gonna need a fifteen minute soak, minimum."

"No truer words have ever been uttered," Gamma remarked, astounding me by her bluntness, and the fact that they could actually agree on something.

As I stood there feeling the warmth of the water flowing over me, I let my thoughts try to catch up with reality. I loved Jack, and I wanted more than anything to have him back. But everyone told me to get on with my life and so I did. I had a wonderful family. I loved my family. I loved Adam and the girls. I loved my home; I didn't want to leave and build a *grander* one. I loved having the rest of the family living with me; I couldn't just leave them. What was Jack thinking?

Later that day, Lexy and I had a tearful good-bye and she flew home. She was missing Brad, now her fiancé, so I put her on a plane. Adam was coming home in a few days and I wanted to be able to communicate my feelings to him. I thought, "I need some help with this, I need some clarity.

I need to talk to the only person who's been there in this situation. I need to talk to Mom."

~*~¡~*~¡~*~¡~*~¡~*~¡~*~

Zoë was still lying there immobile. The sun was creeping up slowly so I had to hurry before visiting hours arrived. I could feel that she was waiting for what was coming next, what she had been waiting for all this time. The answers to a thousand questions that came down to one word. How?

As I sat there alone with her, I told Zoë, "In order for you to understand the next part of my story, I'll have to tell you how I discovered the secret. Our secret, of *how* we became sisters."

I took a deep breath to calm my nerves. "Mom got drunk one night a couple of years ago when she was all depressed about not being able to 'help her little girl' when I lost Jack, and she told me a story. Mom hadn't realized she told me because the next day she denied ever seeing me. That night Mom told me that she was dating Dad in high school, but that she'd always had a crush on this boy who was a few years older than her. She said the Matthews family was quite wealthy and powerful in Houston. Mom claimed this boy asked her out one night and she was more than willing to go. She wanted to have a relationship with him and thought because he wanted sex that he loved her. I guess since she was immature at sixteen, Mom didn't know any better. Afterwards, the boy announced that he wasn't going to call her again and that if she told anyone about that night, no one would believe her and everyone would think she was a floozy and a gold digger. But Mom didn't listen to him, and told someone after finding out she was pregnant. Mom told his then girlfriend at the time, thinking that she was the reason he didn't want to be with her; she hoped to sabotage their relationship. Since Mom was also sleeping with Dad at the time, Mom claimed she never really knew who the father of her child was. I suspect she did after I was born and I looked nothing like Dad. She told me that this ruined her life. Since that story, I've suspected that Dad found out right around my ninth birthday, the time he started beating her. Before then, Dad had never touched her, as far as I knew. That was the version she told me. Since Mom had been drinking a lot, who knows how much of it was true. After learning this, I did an investigation of my own. I found out I wasn't Dad's daughter. In doing this, I remembered an old jacket that he had left behind in my car while borrowing to seduce his 'flavor of the month' girlfriends. I submitted a hair sample off his jacket, and once the lab had determined that they were male hairs, they performed the DNA test. I had to assume that there were only the two boys involved so that left your father. A chromosome comparison DNA test has never been done, to my knowledge, but after matching our rare blood types, I guess we can assume we're sisters - blood sisters. The whole blood thing is a bit complicated. We have what's called the Bombay phenotype. We inherited two recessive alleles of the H gene so we do not produce the H protein that is the precursor to the A and B antigens. With you having Bombay phenotype blood groups, you could only be transfused with blood from another Bombay phenotype person, and that would be me."

I didn't want to tell Zoë, but around the time Mom told me her story, I had filled Tommy in on what I knew about my background. I didn't tell Zoë because I felt she would be uncomfortable with knowing someone else knew before I had told her. I had figured that Tommy had a right to know that, technically, I was only his half-sister. I'm sure he didn't think anything about it, since Tommy has never made reference to it since.

I continued with my story for Zoë.

~✳~:~✳~:~✳~:~✳~:~✳~:~✳~

Chapter XII

Best Friends, New and Old

On some level, I already knew the answer to my question about Jack and Adam. I knew what was truly in my heart, but I wanted to hear from someone who'd been there. I didn't get my nerve to speak with Mom until the day Adam was expected back. I had put it off long enough.

"Hi Mom. What'ya doing?"

"Hi sweetie, come in. I'm just watching some television. How are you, and how are my beautiful grandbabies doing today?"

"You should come over to the nursery to see for yourself; they'd love to see you. You always make such a fuss over them, that they smile for hours after you leave. Tommy wants to know if you're still going to go watch him play ball on Saturday."

"Yeah sure, I'll talk to him later. So what brings you by?"

"Can't I just come see my mom?"

"What's wrong? Something's happened - I can see it on your face."

"Yes, okay Mom, something's happened and I need your help." I swear she almost started to cry when she heard me say that.

"You need my help? I'll do what I can for you. Would you like some tea? I can make us some tea."

"No Mom, I need you to come sit down and listen."

"Okay, sweetie."

She sat as I started to tell her about Jack, about what

happened to him and about what to do next. Mom said she'd seen something about it on television, but thought it was a tabloid hoax and didn't want to upset me with it.

"That wasn't anything like what they were saying. I just couldn't believe what that Lydia Hodges said about you in her article of that rag she calls a magazine, and about all of us. What's it called? Newsmonger Magazine? Simply appalling. They implied you had already left Adam and were cohorting with Jack again. Do they just sit at their desks and make that stuff up, or do they pay someone to sit outside our gates and write whatever pops into their heads when they see someone here?"

I interrupted Mom's tantrum about the tabloids and reminded her about what she had told me about Dad and the boy she had a crush on. I asked her not to deny the possibility existed that Dad was not my father, that I needed to know the truth about everything and I would be counting on her to tell me. Mom admitted the story was true and she started to cry. "You must think I'm so awful."

"No Mom, I don't think that. And if that's the worst thing that ever happened in my life, I'd be grateful. But now I need you to tell me something else." She looked up at me and wiped her tears. "Mom, I need you to think back. You were dating Dad and you had a crush on this boy. If the boy had wanted to marry you, knowing what you know now about him and his family, would you have done it? Would you have left Dad to be with him?"

"Yes, I would have," she answered to my surprise. "But that would have been the biggest mistake of my life. Even bigger than not telling your dad right away about that night. I didn't love that boy, I know that now. I was a stupid little girl with a big crush. I loved your dad, and no matter what he may have done in the past, I know he loved you very much. He would talk for hours about how he was going to raise you, what he wanted to teach you, and how proud you would be of him someday."

"Thanks for saying that Mom, but my point wasn't how Dad felt about me - it was about choices. I don't know where to go from here."

"You've never had trouble making decisions before sweetie - I know you'll make the right one."

"Yes, but this isn't your everyday run-of-the-mill choice, now is it Mom?" I asked sort of teasing her.

"I think the point is that this boy used me, humiliated me, and then threw me away. He didn't give me what I wanted or needed, but your father did when I needed it the most. If given the choice, I think he still would have wanted to marry me and raise you. He may not have treated you right in the past, but I think that was more of a sickness and that was his demon - it didn't have anything to do with him knowing about where you came from." Mom paused before asking, "Remember when you performed in the play *Harvey*? Which version was true? Was Harvey-the-rabbit invisible or imaginary? Elwood staked his freedom on his convictions of Harvey being invisible. Veta thought identically about her convictions that Harvey was imaginary. Don't let anyone try to change your convictions. Search deep inside of your own heart, sweetie. Only you can decide which version is true for you. Does that make sense?"

I nodded. "Thanks Mom, I knew I could count on you."

As I left, Mom was teary and commented she hadn't felt that good in years - to be able to help her little girl.

When I got back to our suite, Adam had returned and he and the girls were playing on the floor. I stood in the doorway for a while and just watched them play together. He was so good with them. "Patient, loving, fun - nothing like Dad," I thought. It was a while before Adam noticed me standing there. Actually it was Tiffany who snitched on me, holding her arms out for her Mommy.

"Hi, how was your trip?" I asked Adam.

"Good, I got to see my family, and that was good."

"Good."

"Where've you been?" he asked without an accusing tone, as if not to pry.

"Mom's."

Adam looked up in surprise, "Why, is she okay?"

"Yeah, I just wanted to see her," I answered as I got down on the floor to play with the girls too. Things were tense and a little forced, but any time than with Adam was a better time with anyone else.

Adam seemed to be making small talk to lessen the tension between us. "Did you see Stephie?" he asked. "She can crawl faster than any of them. I still can't believe how different they are. Beth is the best eater, and little Tiff can scream the loudest."

"Yeah, why do you think Tiffany is Lexy's namesake?" Adam and I both laughed, but it soon grew silent again. I felt that even though Adam and I had moments of silence between us; we could still be in a room together and still have communication.

I spoke to Mom later that night, and I was glad to know she was still sober after our emotional talk. I told her I was proud of her for staying sober through this latest drama. I'd learned through the years that Mom was just as vulnerable to alcohol during extremely high highs, as she was with extremely low lows.

I was exhausted from all of the emotional trauma of the day, and I retreated into the family room where Gampy was watching television. I just needed a distraction, something else to wrap my brain around for a while. He looked at me as if to ask, "What's wrong with you?" And I gave him back a look as if to answer, "Don't ask."

So we sat there in silence until Eddie entered the room an hour later and asked, "Can I get you anything else before I turn in, Miss Jordan?" I shook my head from side to side. I soon walked to our suite to turn in for the night, and slipped under the covers of our bed.

I must have looked like hell because Adam - being the third person that day - asked me, "You okay?"

"Never bedda," I answered, staring up at the ceiling. After Adam climbed into bed, I skooched over next to him, but he wasn't interested in snuggling and went to sleep. Adam had always been my pillow and I couldn't sleep well without him being there for me. Needless to say, it was a long night.

The next day, everyone was sitting down and eating breakfast when I got a call from Lexy. She was hysterical - so when wasn't she? Lexy claimed Hollywood was roasting her the following month in Las Vegas, and she wanted an ally. She wanted me to get up and say a few words on her behalf. I said I was honored that she would think of me in her time of desperation. Actually, this was perfect, as I needed some comic relief. I asked Brandy to make our hotel accommodations in the best suite at the Bellagio, where the roasting was taking place.

As her night approached, Lexy was a basket case and called me three times a day asking what she should wear. We had to go through her closets four times over, via the telephone all the way from Liverpool.

Adam and I flew to Las Vegas the day before Lexy's event to get in some gambling and to see a show. Basically, just to have some fun.

Lexy's big night began, and after visiting the bar, we walked into the room. As Adam sat down in the audience, I walked up to the main table and sat down across from my name plate. Lexy was sitting at the middle of the table talking to the MC. Her parents were sitting in the first row, and her mother was sobbing with pride while they were introducing Lexy and starting the festivities. After a few people got up to speak and totally annihilated her, I could see her sinking down into her chair.

As I got up, I pulled some notes from my pocket, then I walked over to the podium to speak. Lexy screeched, "Aw, bloody 'ell, now I'm a goner." Everyone laughed.

Then I grinned as if I were going for the jugular and began. "What can I say about Alexandria Sherman? Just that she was there for every single main event of my life. Lexy was more than just there; she was a sister. Lexy was there for my first big movie role - of course, she got me in so much trouble, that we almost got kicked off the movie set. Lexy was there the first time I attended the Acclamation Awards - of course, she only needed me there to carry her Ack Award statue home so she wouldn't smudge her nail polish. Lexy was there with me when the monkey murderer was on the loose - only so I could protect her and shield her from him."

Lexy broke in and added, "Or her."

I laughed and looked at her mischievously before continuing. "Lexy was there for countless birthdays, always reminding me that I was getting older and it was time for me to start wearing night cream. Lexy was there when my girls were born - yes, right there in the delivery room coaching me on. Of course, we had to resuscitate her a few times, but she was *there*. One of my daughters even bares her name, but we still have reservations about naming our child, Basket Case. Lexy was my maid of honor when I married my husband, Adam, of course, she tripped over the caterer and landed on the cake because she had to be first in line. Lexy always used to bring my dog, Foxy, her favorite snack box. Yes, just the box because the contents were empty by the time she handed it over. She has *never left my side for one minute*. Thank you, Lexy, for being there."

I ended with a smile for Lexy. As she already knew, that was also the inscription that I had engraved into the gold-lined compact cosmetic mirror I gave to her as a maid of honor gift from my almost-wedding with Jack.

The four of us - Adam, Lexy, Brad and I decided to spend the rest of the evening partying and having some fun. And that's what we did, until around midnight when we spotted Jack at one of the roulette tables. He was lurking about and repeatedly glanced over and smiled at me. When Adam discovered him doing this, he clenched as he fake-smiled back at Jack, then turned to me. My face hadn't changed and I hadn't smiled back at Jack, and it seemed to put Adam more at ease to know I wasn't playing along with Jack. We decided, as a group, to ditch Jack and we snuck out. The four of us jumped into a cab and headed to another casino to continue the evening. Adam was still a little distant after seeing Jack there.

When we got back to our hotel room, I asked Adam if he wanted to talk a while, about Jack and about him stalking us, but he declined. He stepped into the bathroom and took a shower, alone, uncharacteristically with the door closed.

Early the next morning, Lexy called and asked if we could stay another day or two. I woke Adam and asked if he would be agreeable to that.

"Why, what's going on?" Adam asked groggily.

"Lexy, what's going on?"

"We've decided that since everyone is here now, we're going to get married!" she screamed.

"Really? That's great, but you don't have anything planned, Lexy," I said while sitting up in bed. "It's going to take days just to plan a small Vegas wedding. Why don't we wait and have a big shindig at the house and we can do it up right?"

"That would be great, for the reception, but we want to tie the knot this weekend. And who knows when I'll get my parents back in the same place again. I don't want anything fancy for the ceremony; we can leave that for the reception."

"Not fancy, since when?" I teased.

Just then, Adam cut in and asked, "Can you call her back in a few minutes? We need to talk about it."

"Lexy, let me call you back in a few." I hung up and looked at Adam. "What?"

"We've been here for three days already - three days away from our daughters," he said looking at me, waiting for me to respond.

"And you've spent two weeks away from them at a stretch when you're working. So what's your point?"

"I just think we need to spend as much time with them as we can and not be off gallivanting around the world."

"We're not gallivanting around the world; we're three hundred miles away spending a little time on *holiday*. We can do that, you know. We're allowed to have some time together away from the family, and they are perfectly safe where they are without us there. And this doesn't have anything to do with the girls and you know it. I'd appreciate you not putting them in the middle of our disagreements like that. Why are you dancing around the subject? This has to do with Jack, and the fact that he's here, and you want to get me as far from here as possible."

"Fine, let's suppose for a moment that it's about him. Is he always going to keep showing up wherever we are?"

"I don't know, maybe - you'd have to ask Jack. I didn't invite him here Adam, and I don't know why I'm getting blamed for it. I've done nothing to encourage this behavior from him."

"You've done nothing to discourage it."

"Should I have gone up and slapped him in the face for smiling at me? That may have worked a hundred years ago, but I don't think that's very civilized nowadays. Were you not listening to the speech I gave last night? Lexy has been there for me countless times. I can't even imagine how I'm ever going to repay her for her friendship, but I do know of one way - I can do this small favor for her. Lexy has no big agenda to get me back with Jack. She isn't staging her wedding just to do that. Can't we just put this aside and deal with it when we get home?"

"It seems you're always putting this aside. I want some answers; I think I'm entitled to some answers here."

"Just last night you said you didn't want to talk about it, and now you're demanding answers? I don't know where you are sometimes. You are a million miles away when I want to talk - but now when I'm needed by someone else, you demand an audience. For an actor Adam, you're timing sucks."

Adam got out of bed and started getting dressed. He pulled out his suitcase and threw his night clothes in it. "Fine, we can put this off yet again. I've given you a million miles of space to get through this and that didn't work. I've demanded answers and that didn't work. Nothing seems to work. I'm still frustrated with the situation, and you've done nothing to simplify it. Sure, what's one more day of hell for me with *whomever* lurking about?" With that, I could tell he didn't even want to say or hear Jack's name anymore.

"Faith," I said to Adam.

"Excuse me?"

"Sometimes you just have to take a leap of faith, Adam. I love you and I want you to trust me that I do love you." We paused arguing for a moment, then I continued. "I need to do this for Lexy, Adam. You can stay or you can go. But if you go, I won't tolerate any accusations about *whomever* when I return home."

"You want me to go?" Adam asked as he stopped packing.

"No, of course not. I want you to stay here with me. If you stay, we can spend more time together, and wouldn't that show *whomever* a united front? Do you honestly want *whomever* to see us divided? That wouldn't be my plan of action, Adam," I said as I walked over and put my arms around his waist. "If you remember, not too long ago, I had a hurdle named Kelly, and I chose to stay and fight for you. Aren't I worth the same consideration?"

Adam smiled, not wanting to, then pushed his suitcase back in the corner with his foot.

"And besides, you don't know how to leave me," I said, before he smirked back at me. Even so, I could tell Adam was still somewhat agitated by the way he pulled away after we kissed.

I returned Lexy's call. "Sure, that sounds great Lexy - we'd love to stay and help."

"Everything alright, Pookie?"

"Never bedda," I said, winking at Adam. Lexy and I talked on the telephone at length planning the small event.

Adam didn't say much else about Jack or about leaving, and I felt he was just going along with everything for me. I was grateful. I was also grateful Brad had never met Jack and that he and Adam got along well. This was more for Adam's ease knowing Jack was there, than to keep him occupied while Lexy and I planned her wedding.

Adam and I met Lexy and Brad for brunch and made last-minute preparations, then headed for the wedding chapel. Lexy's parents showed up a short time later. Lexy was beautiful, even in her somewhat unorthodox outfit for a wedding. The bride wore a white bridal mini-shirt with white knee-high boots. She also wore what looked to be a corset. I never could figure out what this piece of clothing was, but it covered what it was suppose to, so I never commented. Nonetheless, it was a beautiful service with the six of us in attendance, and the ceremony was performed by *Elvis*. It was everything a bride like Lexy wanted in a wedding. Lexy was also happy seeing her parents there together, even though her father did not look happy to be there with her mother.

After dinner, Adam and I decided to stay behind for a nightcap. That was about the time that Jack showed up at the restaurant and sent over a bottle of red Italian wine to our table. That infuriated Adam, to say the least. He got up, grabbed the bottle by the neck, and walked over to the bar where Jack was sitting. I thought for sure Adam was going to bash him in the head with it, and a panic came over me. As mad as I was at Jack at that moment, I knew it wouldn't be good for anyone to have Adam finish him off and end up in jail. I knew Jack was just taunting him to have a showdown. Jack was capable of orchestrating an attack from Adam just to get him out of the picture. But all Adam did was slam the bottle down in front of Jack and suggest that it was time for them to go outside and settle this whole thing like men. I ran after Adam and urged him to drop the issue, saying it was time for us to leave. I knew Adam could literally kill Jack with a few blows. When Jack didn't stand up and walk outside at Adam's suggestion, Adam stepped back at my request. Then when we left the restaurant, I spotted paparazzi skulking around in the lobby. That's when I knew Jack had set this up and wanted Adam to do something stupid so he could humiliate him with the public and with his fans. I didn't mention this to Adam, figuring it was best to drop it all. Adam and I went back to our hotel room. We didn't say much else that night.

We arrived back home and settled in again. Adam didn't seem to want to talk about Jack after all so we didn't. I could see that Gamma knew there was something wrong between us, but she didn't ask. Instead, she told me the most shocking story I'd ever heard from her. She said that years earlier, right after Gampy had returned from overseas during the war, he confessed to having a brief affair while over there. Gamma said she forgave him, partly because she loved him very much and partly because she wanted him to always feel indebted to her for making that sacrifice of forgiveness. But mainly because she'd had a short affair of her own and she was ashamed. Gamma never told him about it. She never came out and admitted why she told me the story, but I suppose it was because Gamma wanted me to know that there wasn't much anyone could do that was unforgivable.

Gamma outdid herself for the girls' first birthday. For starters, she rented a pony. We tried telling her that they were only one-year-olds, but she wouldn't listen and had every kind of amusement for them. Magicians, clowns, pony rides, games - you name it, Gamma had it. The girls just sort of gazed at it all. We put their individual cakes down in front of them, and they dove in - literally. Cake was everywhere, even in Stephanie's ear. I could see that Adam loved the day and that made me happy, but he was still not really speaking to me - more just speaking at me and that frustrated me.

The next day, we got the fright of our lives. Tiffany was wheezing so we took her in to see her pediatrician. After hearing that Tiffany had asthma, I stole Adam's line and said, "Have mercy on my heart." But the good news was that it was treatable with medication which could be administered as needed. The doctor said she probably developed it because Tiffany was so small at birth - and also told us that there was a good possibility that Tiffany would outgrow it when she was around three or four. An oral corticosteroid was pre-scribed, and we rotated between Prednisone, Albuterol and Cromolyn to see which worked the best for her.

Tiffany's asthma was heartbreaking to watch. The thing that bothered me the most was that some of the medication took up to three hours to begin working. The side effects were also heartbreaking. Tiffany was hungry all of the time and even though she started out being the smallest of the three, she gained the most weight. Since her body held onto extra water, she would look puffy and her face appeared round and swollen. She would also have many mood swings, with high highs and low lows. She could be very happy, very sad, or very mad. The medication also made her blood pressure rise.

We were very worried about the long-term effects of these steroids. If taken for years, Tiffany could develop a high-blood pressure problem, and it could make her bones weak and easier to break. On top of that, she could have weakness of the muscles, grow slowly, and develop cataracts.

The pediatrician told us that it was basically a waiting game to see if Tiffany would outgrow the asthma or not. In the meantime, she would not be able to play and get winded like normal kids. I felt bad for her, not to have the best opportunities in life, and we prayed Tiff would outgrow it. Since the girls were fraternal and not identical, we were grateful for no other complications among them.

The next month, Gamma tried to get Adam and me closer by combining our birthday celebrations together. She planned to make it festive by having a tropical theme, but nothing would bring Adam out of his depression. He said that he just wasn't in the mood for a party. We wrapped things up early, and I ended up sleeping in the girl's room that night.

Dear Journal: My twenty-eighth birthday party was a bust. Adam hasn't touched me in months. I'm not really sure if our marriage is over. I don't know where to go from here. I'm tired of being punished for something that I didn't do. When I ask Adam to tell me what he's feeling, he shrugs or sometimes just doesn't bother to respond and walks away. I don't know what else to say or do to show him that I love him. I miss holding hands and snuggling when we think no one is watching. I miss the connection, the closeness, the touching. I don't know if we will ever get that back, or even could at this point. I suppose there are a lot of couples who stay married for the kids' sake and have minimal to do with one another, but I'm not sure that I can do that. Adam didn't do that with Anita for Dakota so I'm sure that wouldn't work for him either. This is a big house and maybe we could live separate lives and still be close to our children. In any case, I'll keep my distance from now on. He won't have to shun me away anymore. Goodnight Journal.

I filled my days with helping Lexy plan her reception and taking the girls places. But I was just going through the motions. I was missing a deeper life with my daughters because I was so immersed with the pain of losing Foxy, the pain of losing Jack, and now the pain of losing Adam by him pulling away from me. I needed to get away, I needed some distance from everyone and everything to get some perspective on what I really wanted. I needed a distraction.

Two days later, I walked into the nursery where Adam was playing on the floor with the girls. "I got a call from Larry today, and he wants me to go talk to some guys about a production he's trying to staff. If we can get this project off the ground, Larry will have signed six actors to it and that's significant for him. I owe Larry and really want to help him on this if I can. But I have to fly out and talk to them before I agree to anything."

"Why do you feel that you owe him? He made his commission from you didn't he?" asked Adam.

"It's more than that - he's helped me big-time in the past."

"That was just his job, JoJo - they all *help* us," Adam said with sarcasm.

"Adam, if it wasn't for Larry, the best I would be doing now are porno flicks," I snapped as Adam looked up at me in surprise. Then I walked over and sat down across from him. "When I was sixteen, Dad signed me to a casting company. The one that Uncle Red mentioned as he told us about Dad's death. They were doing child pornography. Dad signed me only to get his hands on some fast money, and then he took off with it. My own father didn't care or even consider what would happen to me as a result from it. It was Larry who bailed me out. Larry and I combined our money, well mostly his, and cancelled the contract. He did *not* have to do that. He used his own personal money to help me. Without Larry, I wouldn't be doing the kind of films I'm doing or I would be out of the business altogether."

Adam looked stunned. "How long will you be gone?"

he asked with caution in his tone, seemingly because of how emotional I was about the story.

"Just overnight - a few days at the most."

"Are you taking Tracy?"

"No, not this trip. I want her to stay with the girls."

"Are we still going to Tommy's ball game tomorrow?"

"Sure, I'll make my plane reservations for tomorrow night," I answered as I got up to leave the room. "I'll go let Clara know my schedule and have Brandy make my reservations."

I made it to the door before Adam asked, "And just so I know, is Jack going to be out of town with you?" Adam was still looking down and playing with the girls.

I didn't answer him. I acted as if I didn't hear the question as I left the room.

~*~¡~*~¡~*~¡~*~¡~*~¡~*~

At first, I had tried to keep the mood light for Zoë. "Lexy was squirming at the Roast and I had them all laughing so hard, that they were crying by the time I was finished."

At that moment, Gladis entered the room and gave me a look of, "better hurry up."

That's when I decided to pour it all out for Zoë, "Well, with that story about Mom and how I came to be behind us, we can move forward. Those were their choices in life, not ours. Let's not let their choices come between us. We can be strong. It really doesn't have anything to do with us being sisters, Zoë. The next few days would change my life forever. And that's where you come in." I went on as I was about to conclude my story for Zoë.

~*~¡~*~¡~*~¡~*~¡~*~¡~*~

Chapter XIII

Boy Bashing

Adam and I decided that it would be better to leave the girls at home with Clara while we attended Tommy's baseball game. They were too young to enjoy any of it anyway. Everyone else would be there. Gamma, Gampy, Uncle Red, Sam, Adam, Mom and I all piled into the limo, and Eddie drove us to the stadium. Adam and I sat separately with almost everyone else between us. That was the best for now. At the game, Adam looked as if he was having fun and I didn't want to spoil the day for him. I tried to put on a brave face, but I was hurting inside. But besides our current relationship difficulties, it was a good day. We drank beer, had hotdogs, cheered and laughed. And just when we thought it couldn't get any better, as Tommy was pitching, we heard the most amazing thing; "Hey batter, batter - your grandmother wears army boots," yelled Gamma at the guy up to bat. We all looked at each other in silence and then snickered.

Gamma thought a nice good deed for me that day would be to sign autographs for charity. I was reluctant because it was Tommy's day, but the stadium promoter thought it was a great idea. I admit I was sort of grateful for the distraction to escape all of the tension with Adam. I only spent an hour doing that because I didn't want to upstage Tommy.

Tommy beamed all the way home. His family got to see him pitch a shutout game, bringing his team to victory.

After dropping off the gang at home, Eddie drove

Adam and me to the airport. I was sure the only reason Adam went with me was to conceal our problems from the family. He never repeated his question about Jack meeting me there, I guess because he really didn't want to know the answer or maybe he thought my silence was his answer. For that matter, he didn't say much at all. He barely kissed my cheek as we said good-bye and just suggested that I should get on the plane. And as I sat back in my seat on the plane and thought about our good-bye, I realized that Adam hadn't secretly pinched my behind as he always had when we parted.

The flight was exhausting, primarily because I stayed awake thinking about how angry I felt about the whole situation with Jack. It wasn't fair what had happened to me... finding Jack to spend my life with, then losing Jack... finding Adam to spend my life with, now facing the possibility of losing him because Jack had returned into my life. And now I felt like I was being punished all over again.

"I know the answer lies with me, and I will have to get on with the business of clarifying it," I said to myself like one of Mom's affirmations. After stewing about it on the all-nighter flight, all I wanted to do was sleep. So I checked into the hotel and did just that.

Later that morning, I made my way from the hostess podium in the restaurant toward a table where four rather large men sat. As I approached the table, the man with his back toward me, made a quick glance my way before returning to his menu. He boisterously vented, "There you are, Kitten - any chance we can get a cup-a-coffee before the next millennium?"

Startled from the unexpected outburst, I instinctively responded, "Excuse me?"

Still not looking at me, he answered, "Coffee, you've heard of it right? That black stuff people drink."

"I'm sorry..." I was beginning to explain who I was, but he cut me off.

"That's okay Kitten - no time for apologies. Just put a wiggle in it, would'ya?"

I began to feel the hair on the back of my neck starting to prickle and my blood pressure surged a bit. I hated that word. *Kitten.* Dad used to call me that just before he was about to steal something from me. And with my anger about my life being a mess, not to mention grumpiness from having minimal sleep, I knew I was volatile. I took a deep breath as I pitched my coat and briefcase down on a chair at an adjacent table, and without missing a beat, I replied, "Forgive me sir - anything else for you?" The sarcasm out of my mouth was so thick that everyone else from the table peered up at me - except for the rude man who still had his back to me.

"NOOOO, just coffee," he replied impatiently, as if I had a hearing impediment or learning disorder.

With my hand on my hip and my head cocked, I added, "No problem, sir, and while I'm over there getting your coffee, I may as well pick up my standard-issued penis so I can join this little boy's club of yours. And I prefer Pookie. I'm not as merciful as a *kitten.*" I glared down on him without blinking as the man quickly turned and looked up at me. I stuck out my hand to shake his and added, "Mel Kobach, Executive Producer, Pookie Productions."

By that time, everyone's mouth was gaping open as they sprang to their feet. The man rose quickly in shame and shook my hand gently and rapidly, saying nothing.

In a mellower voice, but still with a sarcastic tone, I added, "I was told someone here requested a meeting. Was I misinformed?"

"No, no, Miss Kobach, you weren't misinformed," one of the other men sheepishly replied. With a slightly nervous chuckle, he added, "We were expecting a man, I guess... well you know, because of a guy's name like Mel."

"Oh, okay, that makes sense. That explains why you treat women like subservient peasants."

"No, no, not at all," he chuckled while desperately trying to change the subject. "Please - here, sit down. Take my seat. How was your flight?"

I could see the waitress out of the corner of my eye. She was alternating between laughing and having her hand over her mouth in amazement from my performance. She contained herself long enough to take our order with no further rude temperament from the table.

"I've come a long way for this meeting to accommodate you gentlemen," I said after the waitress took our food orders. "Please, let's get started."

Attitudes settled down long enough for us to proceed with the meeting. "Certainly, Jord... I mean, Miss Kobach. Let me take this opportunity to introduce everyone. My name is Mike Livingston and I am a Director with sixteen years experience with a degree from the University of Massachusetts." He continued around the table explaining everyone's participation in the project and what experience they were bringing with them. I was not very impressed and was still fuming from the display of chauvinism, but I listened patiently to his presentation. "This is Benny Canter, a Set Designer with seven years experience and a degree from the University of California. Drake Sans, a Director of Photography with eleven years experience. And Reese Fleeceman is the Screenwriter for this project. We would like to make this movie with the help of your company. We see this as a great opportunity for you..."

The director continued blowing smoke up my skirt with talk as if it were only going to benefit my company to have these buffoons running things. Did he think this was the first time I had been played? I already knew no other production company would touch this risky project. Can't say how many times I've had men try to put-one-over on me. As an expert at seeing this from Dad, I was amused by their attempt.

As silence loomed over the table in their effort to get me to commit to the project, I replied, "Sounds good. Pookie Productions will have final cut, reimbursement on expenses plus ten percent of the gross."

Grumbles emerged from the table before the director declared, "That may not be possible, Miss Kobach. We will have a lot of people to pay and we will have to clear it with our investors. And I normally have final cut."

"I completely understand, Mr. Livingston. Thank you

for your time today, gentlemen," I replied as I started to stand.

"BUT... we can certainly discuss this further, and I'm sure we can come to a resolution," the screenwriter, added quickly, as he respectfully motioned for me to be re-seated.

I sat back down before proceeding, "That's my offer, gentlemen. I can see that you have a lot to discuss and I'll leave you to that. I also want you to know that when I begin a project, I view everyone as a new friend. That way, we can all say what's on our minds without worrying about editing our thoughts. I'm a 'bottom-line-it' kind of gal, and as you have witnessed - I am *no* shrinking violet." As we all stood up, I leaned over to the photography director so that only he could hear me, put my hand out to shake his, and added, "Just a personal footnote - if I ever hear you speaking to another female the way you spoke to me, especially a waitress, I'll cross you off my Christmas card list. Friends?" I fake-smiled, let go of his hand, and turned away without waiting for a response. I was sure he heard me loud and clear. I was a powerful person in Hollywood now, and if I wanted him to be blacklisted, he could expect it.

When I reached the hostess podium, our waitress giggled. "You are my idol - I would love it if I could say that to some of these chauvinist pigs."

I smiled with contentment as I swiftly stepped into the limo. I rode back to the hotel and spent the rest of the day making telephone calls. I spent a quiet evening with a room-service dinner; I wasn't in any mood to be in public. After making some production notes on my tape recorder, I wrote in my journal. A few hours later, I received a call from Mike, the director. "It's a go on our end, Miss Kobach."

I called Larry and told him the good news, and he was happy. It felt good to see someone happy. I also called Brandy, told her that I was coming home in the morning, and asked her to make my flight arrangements for me then call me back with the information. I figured that Adam wasn't interested in hearing from me, but if he wanted to know my schedule, Brandy would have it.

I was lying in bed wanting to fall asleep, but I was

wide awake. That was about the time when I received a startling telephone call from a reporter. It wasn't startling just because they knew the exact room number I was in *or* that it was nearly midnight, but from what they had offered to me. Due to the nature of the topic and the intrusion of what they were proposing, I agreed to let them into my hotel room for a brief conversation. Prior to their arrival, I secretly planted my tape recorder to document our chat. After they left, it was even harder to fall asleep.

The next day arrived and I was happy that I was going home. I missed the girls and couldn't wait to see what they had learned while I was gone. They were getting so big that I barely recognized them if I'd miss a day or two. As I sat on the plane, I instinctively reached for my carry-on bag to check to see if I had a box of Champion Cheddar for Foxy. Then I was depressed again.

I kept myself busy during the flight by writing in my journal, making a list of all the things I wanted to do with the girls when I got home, and daydreaming of better times. I tried not to think about Jack; I was just mentally exhausted from it all. The next thing I remember was them announcing we were landing soon in Los Angeles. So I returned my carry-on under the seat as I placed my journal and tape recorder in my fanny pack, then strapped it around my waist. I wondered if Adam was going to be there to greet me back home when Eddie picked me up from the airport. "No, probably not - if he could avoid it," I thought. My ruminations were immediately interrupted when we reached approximately thirty-five to forty feet off the ground. That's when the plane dipped severely to the left side. Something seemed to be pulling us over, dragging us, and the plane wouldn't straighten out. Then suddenly the tension was released and we spun back to the right side with a tremendous force. When the plane's right wing hit the ground, it pulled the left side of the plane forward. I felt a surge of fear flood my body. As we tumbled onto the earth, my body violently thrashed about. My vision was blurred from my body shaking wildly. I could hear people screaming. We began rolling sideways down the tarmac, over and over repeatedly, tearing off the wings before coming to a stop. The sound was horrendous, being the loudest noises I'd ever heard in my life - deafening. And the smell was worst. Jet fuel was everywhere. Everything was in disarray and broken. Wires were hanging down into the cabin. Metal objects had been tossed about. Seats were torn from their bolted chassis.

I was disoriented, and I didn't know which way was up - literally. I could feel the blood rushing to my head. The sound was then silent. Eerily silent. I couldn't hear anything for a moment and then I heard people shouting. The Flight Attendants were shouting evacuation commands for everyone to get out of the plane. I reached down and unfastened my seatbelt, but the plane was upside down so I slid to the ceiling, which was about three or four feet below me. I started to feel intense heat rushing up from behind me like a flash. As I swung around, I could see smoke and a ball of flames speeding up faster than I could run so I leapt out of the aisle and ducked between the seats. As I covered my head with my arms, I could feel burning around my body so hot, I screamed for it to stop. Amazingly, I was patient enough to wait until the rush of heat had dissipated. I cautiously stood and looked around the cabin. No one else was within sight. That scared me. I wondered how long I had been down there. I was beginning to wonder if I was still alive, or was this what it was like to be dead. I started walking toward the exit when I realized that I was hurt. "Oh, thank God, I feel pain," I thought. "I can't be dead if my leg hurts." I was bleeding. It didn't seem to be so bad that I couldn't walk so I hobbled to the exit. The door was ripped off and the ground was right up to the opening so I just stepped over the wires and got out. As I felt the fresh air rushing up to me, I could feel my eyes burning and I had shortness of breath.

I walked away from the plane for what seemed like miles because of my leg, but it was only about twenty yards. That's when I saw them. People were everywhere. Bodies were everywhere. People were rolling on the ground moaning. I walked back, back onto the airplane, and started pulling blankets from wherever I could find them. I brought them out and started covering people who were shivering. I thought the jet fuel was the worst smell I could ever imagine, but that was now surpassed by the smell of burnt flesh.

Up until that moment, everything had been moving in slow motion. Then for some reason, it began to move faster and faster; maybe because I came out of my shock and realized the urgency of the situation. I could hear the ambulances now. I could see the Flight Attendants going around trying to help everyone. A Flight Attendant came up to me and asked if I needed assistance. I told her that I was alright and that I was able to be a helper if they needed someone. She nodded, then said she needed to bandage my leg first. Then the Flight Attendant gave me a first aid kit and asked if I would tour the area for others in need of minor assistance. She advised me to get everyone I could to run away from the plane, since it could still explode. I bandaged, I calmed, I consoled, and I even whispered prayers for those people I couldn't help.

Most people were in need of some sort of help. Then a man staggered over to me, grabbed my arm, and held onto me as he was about to topple over. The guy looked me dead in the eye and said he was going to puke. I realized that he was drunk. I pulled the man off my arm, gave him a once-over to make sure he wasn't hurt, and left him there to throw up.

That was about the time when I heard a middle-aged woman screaming wildly over someone. I hobbled over, and the someone was a young woman lying on the tarmac who looked to be in her twenties. She appeared to have stopped breathing. By instinct, I reached down to check her pulse. None. I then began CPR on her. A different Flight Attendant came over and did the breathing for her as I tried to restart the young woman's heart. I barely noticed the sounds of ambulances screaming around us. I thought of nothing but my count of compressions to her chest. A paramedic was waved over by the Flight Attendant. He ran up to us and assessed the young woman's condition while I stopped the compressions long enough for him to listen for a heartbeat.

"No pulse!" he shouted and I continued.

Another paramedic ran up with a gurney and I paused as they both lifted her onto it. The first paramedic was then called away by another injured passenger. The second paramedic asked me to continue the compressions as he wheeled her to the ambulance with the middle-aged woman trailing behind us. That paramedic shouted toward the Flight Attendant and me over the sounds of the screeching sirens, "Can you go with her?! We are very inundated with casualties and could sure use the assistance!"

I nodded as he then pushed her inside of the ambulance. I knelt down beside her. The Flight Attendant departed with us, and we maintained the CPR. The ambulance quickly pulled out and that's when I lost sight of the middle-aged woman who had been with her.

When we arrived at the hospital, they instructed me to kneel on top of the gurney so I could get a better angle to continue the compressions than the medical attendants could get from the side. A medical attendant used an Ambu bag to continue the breaths for her. They wheeled us into a temporary triage prepared for the airplane crash victims. I briefly noticed the press there, but they apparently didn't spot me going into the hospital. Someone inside the hospital announced, "We'll take over," but I explained that I didn't think I could get down because of the wound on my leg. Just then, someone reached up and pulled me down, then carried me over to an examining table. To my surprise, it was Jack.

"What'ya doing here, Jack?" I asked, baffled. There was a large digital clock on the wall of the triage that read 3:27. I hadn't realized how much time had passed. It seemed like only a moment ago we were running from the plane.

"The television news anchors announced that an airplane had gone down and said that you might be on it. When I heard the news, I drove over here from my hotel."

"You were in Los Angeles? Why?"

"To see you."

"Jack, we can't talk about that now," I said. Then suddenly I realized that if he heard it on the news, then the family would have too. "I have to call home. I have to tell them I'm okay," I shrieked as I tried to get up.

"No, no, you stay here," Jack insisted. "I'll call when someone gets off the telephone." He didn't leave my side and kept looking over toward the telephone booths and then back toward the entrance door.

When I was lying back down again, questions flooded my thoughts. Why was Jack here and not Adam? Wasn't he at the airport to pick me up? Surely, Eddie would have called to tell them my flight did not arrive or had crashed, wouldn't he?

My thoughts were interrupted when I looked up at Jack looking at the entrance door again. I turned my head to the side to see what he was looking at and I got a quick glimpse of Adam talking to someone on the other side of the room, however, there were so many people in the room, I couldn't see him for very long. It was chaotic. "Adam?! Adam, where are you?!" I screamed.

"Here, right here," Adam answered as he stepped out from behind someone in his path to kneel down to kiss me. "Are you okay?"

"I am now," I answered, looking straight into his eyes. "Please don't leave, don't leave me," I shuddered as tears came to my eyes for the first time during the ordeal.

Adam took and held my hand as Jack stepped back and out of the way of the doctors working on me. Adam then said, "Have mercy on my heart, I love you."

"It doesn't seem to be life-threatening, Miss Walsh, but your leg is bleeding at a steady rate," a doctor declared. He then turned to a nurse and gave her orders; "Classify this as urgent, but not immediately life-threatening." He turned back to me and advised; "Once we suture you to stop the bleeding, we'll dress it. We'll give you a tetanus shot and let you get into a room upstairs. We'll want to monitor you overnight for any internal bleeding. You may want to seek the opinion of a plastic surgeon once you return home." Then he left to assess someone else.

I could see everyone flying around the room out of the corner of my eye. I didn't stop looking at Adam, I didn't want him to leave my sight. When they finished with my leg, I sat up and I asked a nurse about the young woman who had received the CPR.

"Yes, Miss Walsh, you saved her life," answered one of the nurses smiling at me.

"Oh, thank God," I whispered, as I slumped back down. "Adam, you have to call Gamma. And you have to call Lexy - she's gonna be a basket case." Adam smiled and promised that he would call everyone as soon as I was admitted into a hospital room.

Adam looked me in the eye and asked, "You ready? The press is out there and we'll have to go through them to get to your room. You okay to handle it?"

I took a deep breath, smirked at him, and answered, "Never bedda."

Adam smiled back with his angelic face as he helped me hobble into a wheelchair. The reporters were right at the door as we left.

"Miss Walsh, what was it like to be in the airplane when it crashed? Where are you injured? They're saying you saved a woman's life - is that true? We spotted Jack Rebello here; can you tell us if you'll be reuniting with him? Miss Walsh, are you going to sue the airlines?" It seemed like a million people were shouting a million questions at once. Adam was trying to get them to move as the nurse wheeled me along. As we were about to enter the reception area, I turned and replied, "I'm fine - all I want to do is heal and go home... home to my family."

Adam held my hand tight all the way to my room, and he wouldn't let go even when we got there. I could feel his anxiety.

I reassured him with "I'm okay... it's okay... we're okay." Then I paused waiting for him to release my hand. "But Adam honey, I'm gonna need that hand to sign these forms."

He looked perplexed at my request, then said, "I can't seem to let go."

"I'm not going anywhere."

He smiled asking, "Promise?"

I nodded. I signed the forms, and he made a call home and then to Lexy. I began changing into a hospital gown left on the bed by a nurse when I realized that I was still wearing my fanny pack with my journal and tape recorder in it. I removed the fanny pack and stuck it into the nightstand drawer.

After his phone calls, Adam tucked me into the bed. "So you wanted me here... I'm here," he commented coolly, but with a sexy smile on his face, as he did the first day I met him.

"Yes *I* do," I replied, smiling at him. Adam sat down on the bed next to me. I put my head on his shoulder, and teased, "You know, if you think about it, this is all your fault."

"How do you figure?" he asked, surprised.

"Because you didn't pinch my behind when I left, and that's always been my good luck charm."

Adam smiled, pulled me closer, and pinched my behind.

I looked up at him and said, "God, I've missed you."

Adam teared and whispered, "I'm sorry - I'll never leave you again." I felt him hold me tight and I felt secure enough to drift off to sleep.

I awoke and sat up. Somewhat startled, I looked around the room, and it took me a moment before I remembered where I was. Adam had moved and was now sleeping in the chair next to the bed. I picked up Adam's watch he had placed on the table next to the bed to see what time it was. It read 8:30pm. I returned to a reclined position, and began to recall the details of the horrifying airplane crash when someone claiming to be a hospital representative entered my room requesting a sample of my blood for a possible donor match, claiming it to be of an urgent nature.

"We have another patient from the airplane crash that needs a rare blood type that you have. Will you donate?" she asked.

"Ah, sure but how did you know that I have a rare blood type? No one has drawn any of my blood for testing yet."

Just then, a man walked in and introduced himself as a doctor on staff with the hospital, performing surgery on a patient with the same blood match as me. I informed him I already knew the hospital needed some of my blood, and I agreed to donate. I raised my hand to point to the hospital representative who had just been there, but she had vanished. Adam awoke to the sound of his voice and sat up to listen.

"No, Miss Walsh," he interrupted without concern of her whereabouts, "what I may need is more than just your blood. My patient has suffered internal damage, and I'll be performing exploratory surgery to find out the severity of it. There is a possibility that she'll need a liver transplant, but I won't know that until we are in there. Time is of the essences and I need to get your consent now and prep you in case my patient does need the transplant. I'll need you to be waiting in the next operating room. Will you be willing to donate, Miss Walsh, if you are a Bombay phenotype match?"

Adam looked at me in a panic, but didn't say anything.

"Adam? Talk to me," I prompted.

"You're the boss," he replied.

I turned to the doctor to ask, "How did you know that I had the same rare blood type as your patient?"

"A nurse called my office and told me that. Is that not true?"

"No one has drawn my blood or tested it since I've been here so I can't say. I'm guessing they just suspected. I do have Bombay phenotype though."

"We'll draw some and have it tested; we'll have to do that anyway to find out if you are an organ donor candidate. There's several different tests involved."

I agreed to the organ transplant along with the blood donation, strongly sensing that I would be a match because I now suspected who it was that needed my help.

Adam sat with me while they took the blood samples to run the compatibility tests. By the time they were finished, it was midnight. They drew more, but this time it was for the liver donation, and that's when I knew for sure that I was a blood match. It was a very long two hours later before they came back to take me away. They wouldn't allow Adam to accompany me to the operating room so we exchanged "I love yous" declarations and kisses. I made a mental note of my next journal entry.

Dear Journal: I was ushered down the endless empty corridor while searching for the thoughts that would surround the night's events. As we turned a corner, I saw additional medical personnel waiting. They then guided me into a room that was dreary, sterile, emotionless, not at all like my everyday surroundings. I changed into drab hospital garb. They escorted me to a gurney, where I was lying while they strapped me to it. Shortly thereafter, a nurse came in and inserted an I.V. into my arm. The orderlies began wheeling me toward that room. The room of death, or the room of pardonable life.

There was never a question. I always knew this would be a possibility ever since the day I discovered the truth. But who knew I would be so calm about it? Goodnight Journal.

~※~:~※~:~※~:~※~:~※~:~※~

"For *your* life, Zoë. You were that young woman lying out on the tarmac who needed my help. This is it, Zoë - we've reached the end and I can't put it off any longer. I have to tell you everything. The woman posing as the hospital representative who came into my hospital room and asked if I would donate blood to you was the same woman screaming over you on the tarmac, and the same woman who was your father's girlfriend all those years ago. The woman Mom confessed to... it was Lillian... your mother, Zoë. She has known about me since my conception. But don't be mad at her; she's not the only person who knew. If you have to be mad at someone, there's plenty of blame to go around. I also knew when Mom drunkenly unfolded her secret to me. Far as I know, Lillian has never told Joseph, ah - your dad that I was the product of Mom's night with him. Maybe he's just never made the connection; he only knew my mom for one night. I was afraid to do anything about the situation. I had my own fears of rejection to deal with. Since the time Mom told me, I've asked myself a million questions. Has she ever told him the truth? Doesn't he have to at least suspect? Does he not care? Mom said he threatened he would get his family to ruin hers if she told anyone about their night together, but that threat was probably just the ramblings of a scared kid. And what right did I have to judge anyway? I did the same thing. Well, nearly the same when I made love to Adam and then discontinued the relationship. I had my issues, but who's to say your father didn't have his at that time."

I took a deep cleansing breath, relieved that my confession was out there. Notwithstanding, I knew someday that I would have to reiterate my story for Zoë while she was awake. "You are *my* Godsend Zoë - you saved my life. You brought this family together, and it's all going to come out now. You brought us together as sisters, something I've always wanted and I'm happy it's you. If it weren't for you, I don't think I'd ever have had the courage to come forward with what I knew. Even if I walk away alone today, I have you to thank for abolishing my abandonment issues."

After finishing my story to Zoë, I returned to my room and laid down, exhausted. I was still feeling guilty though. While I'd told Zoë a lot of what happened, I hadn't told her everything. I wasn't sure she was strong enough to hear *everything*. I told her some scandalous things about her family - about her mother keeping my existence a secret - about her father using then threatening Mom, but that was not the worst of it. Someone else found out - an *outsider* from a tabloid. They never did reveal how they uncovered the information when they brought their knowledge to me while in my hotel room the night before last. They wanted to expose the story about my conception, but with a sinister slant to it. They wanted to run it in their tabloid, but hadn't yet - I suppose because of something that I had said to them.

As I sat there alone, I fidgeted with my tape recorder. It still enclosed the tape of the conversation with the *outsider*. I sat in thought for a moment before pushing the play button. **Click**. I began listening...

"Have you ever been tested to find out for sure?"

"No. On some level, I don't want to know. There's no real reason for me to know."

"Only a fortune. That family is rich and you are entitled to some of it. And you could probably blackmail them into giving you more if you were to remind them that she was underage."

"Not a chance. And I have enough money - thank you."

"Why not? You have the proof; you have it in your blood."

"It would hurt too many people in my family."

"No, I think I can write this story without hurting anyone in your family."

"This would hurt Mom. It would make her out to be a liar and would brand her as a tramp. She'd go back into the bottle for good. I can't take that chance."

"But it's rape, statutory rape - because she was underage and that would turn the whole story around. And he needs to be accountable for what he did."

"Okay, let's put that aside for a moment and focus on something bigger. So let me get this straight. You're going to go to the head of the most powerful family in this country and accuse him of being a rapist? How long have you had this death wish? He's now the Governor of Texas and a strong presidential hopeful next in line for the presidency, some say. There's men around him who won't let anything like this happen to him."

"I know I'm right."

"But that doesn't *make* you right. I hope you get a lot of money for the story because your family is going to need it for your funeral."

"But it's the truth."

"And your point is? What's the truth got to do with anything? And that's just *your* truth. You don't have any proof. Let's visit the best case scenario for a moment, shall we? You get the DNA evidence you need. You prove your theory. You publish your story. You make a million dollars. Do you think for one minute that those wealthy people are just going to let you call him a rapist and allow you to walk away? Even if they don't kill you, they'll finish you financially. And don't think for a moment I'm talking about being sued in court. They have so much money that they will ruin you, your life, your brother's life, your kid's lives when they're grown, your gardener's life - anyone you've ever met. Am I painting a vivid enough picture for you? Oh, but you're right. Where does that get you when you're dead?"

"You won't back up my story?"

"I can back up your story all I want, but you'd still be dead. Are you willing to die for this story?"

"I think it needs to be told."

"You didn't answer my question."

"Are you willing to let me have your DNA tested, legally?"

"No way in hell. Mom gave up her happiness because of this knowledge."

"Doesn't that make you mad? Don't you want revenge for what he did?"

"You bet I do, but I won't get it. He's too big. And she let this ruin her life, no one else did. No one said she had to drink herself stupid; no one said she had to be depressed for over twenty years of her life. Nevertheless, I'm not going to tarnish her reputation no matter what the benefit."

"Dirk Matthews is your half-brother."

"Yes, I know that."

"Does Alexandria?"

"No."

"I think everyone will benefit from it."

Click.

I returned the recorder to the nightstand drawer, slid out of bed, and shuffled back into Zoë's room and sat down again. I wanted to wait for her to awaken, no matter how long it took.

Chapter XIV

Crossing Burning Bridges

I was delighted that my face was the first face Zoë saw when she awoke. Zoë smiled while squeezing my hand and whispered groggily, "Hi Sis, I'm so glad you're here. And look, we have the same Irish red hair. I had the most fantastic dream about a cute little dog, and people going to parties, and three little babies, and about a man who came all the way back from the dead just to be with her."

I smiled.

Then Zoë asked, "Where's Tommy?" She dozed off again before I could inquiry about her puzzling question.

Only moments lapsed before Gladis escorted me back to my room and I climbed back into bed. I fell asleep and when I awoke, there was that male angelic face again staring at me, face to face, grinning. "Hi, JoJo," Adam said. "Shall we try this again? You must have been dreaming, you have a smile on your face."

Out of the corner of my eye, I could see Gladis checking my machines and monitoring me. "Adam," I said smiling and sleepily. "I was just dreaming about you. I'm sorry I passed out on you yesterday. I guess I was still groggy from all the blood loss. Or maybe it was from all the drugs I stole from the supply cabinet and that's also why I must be smiling," I said, teasing Gladis who I knew was listening in on our conversation.

"Hum, we'll have to get some of those to take home with us," he whispered, teasing me, and continuing to tease Gladis. She gave us both a side glance for our performances.

I chuckled at him. "I was dreaming and my dream came true - you're here," I said, then asked, "where have you been? I've missed you."

"When I was told that they didn't need to do the transplant, I went home for some sleep and to check on the girls. Gamma wanted to come down, but I convinced her to wait until you were awake. I guess seeing my smile was enough to calm her. I came back yesterday morning and that's when you snubbed me," he said, teasing me for passing out. "So I went back home to be with the girls and let you have some snooze time. I told the nurses to call me when you woke up. I guess they forgot," he said, while peering up at Gladis.

Just then, Eddie interrupted us by walking into the room with a picnic basket full of snacks, and set it on the table. "Is there anything else I can get for you, Miss Jordan?" Eddie asked, as if we were just lounging around the family room.

"No thank you, Eddie," I answered, snickering, knowing that he must have commandeered the hospital because he was so protective of me. I watched as he quietly stepped into the hallway.

"Miss Jordan? Why did he call you, Miss Jordan?" Gladis asked, without regards to interrupting a private moment with my husband.

I smiled at her impetuous curiosity and explained, "Oh, he's been calling me that for years. My staff and I came to an agreement early on. I wanted them to call me Jordan and they insisted on calling me Miss Walsh. I thought that was just too formal, especially since we're all living in the same house so we settled on Miss Jordan."

"Have these been approved, *Miss Jordan*?" Gladis asked as she sifted through my basket, mocking me before she left us alone.

I turned my attention to Adam. "Sorry again for the other day. I guess with not sleeping the night of Tommy's game, and then not sleeping much the night I spent away from you - not to mention all of the trauma to my body, the blood loss, and all the drugs in my system - I was exhausted."

"Understandable, and as Uncle Red would say, 'you've given a compelling argument, Miss Joey.' I'll forgive you this time."

"Thank you, sir - you are so kind. By the way, who were you talking to yesterday outside my door? I could hear whispering."

"No one."

"No really - talk to me, Adam."

"It was Zoë's mother wanting to dump all her guilt onto you and I wanted you to rest. She wanted to apologize for snubbing you all these years, and I didn't think you were strong enough to deal with her guilt after everything you've been through."

"Ha! Maybe you should have let her in. I would have enjoyed seeing her actually acknowledge my existence," I replied with sarcasm. Then I said solemnly, "But I'm sure she's grateful. I would be if someone saved any one of our daughters. I wouldn't care if it was the Boston Strangler; I'd owe them everything." I said, to emphasize the extreme measures I would go to for my children. I then reached up and stroked Adam's hair while adding, "But that's all behind us, and it's time to go home. It's time to be alone together."

"Well, we're alone, here, now," Adam said in a sexy tone as he looked around the room.

I giggled, "Adam! Has anyone ever told you that you're a hopeless romantic?"

"No, but worse - hope*ful*," he said as he kissed me. Then he teased, "We've never had a honeymoon, you know. This looks as good of a place as any, don't you think?"

"You're incorrigible, but thanks for being you," I said as I lightly kissed him.

He kissed me back, then put on his serious face and asked, "Have you done any DNA tests before?"

I knew Adam did not know the complete story of my origin, but had knowledge about some of it. "No. I was always too afraid to change things. Up until now, there's been no real reason for me to know. Mrs. Matthews has known for quite some time now, but I'm not sure she's ever told her husband."

"And Dirk is your half-brother."

"Yes?" I said - partly answering and partly asking, wanting to know where he was going with the statement.

"Have you ever told Lexy?"

I shook my head from side to side, and said, "No."

"Rumor has it from a tabloid, that during the time she was missing in action in Hollywood, she was off having a baby. His baby?"

I didn't respond.

Sensing I wasn't in the mood to talk about it, he changed the subject. "Tommy's here."

"Tommy? I thought we agreed everyone would hang out at home until I got there?"

"Yep, don't know what's up. All morning he's been pacing all the way down the hall and back."

I thought to myself, "Tommy knows what Mom told me, so maybe he's just curious about Zoë. And she did say something strange to me just before dozing off. She asked where Tommy was, but I thought she was just repeating what she heard in her *dream*." Then out loud I said, "Maybe he's just more worried about his Sissy than he can express - you know how guys can be." I smirked while teasing Adam about his gender.

"Maybe," Adam said shrugging and smiling.

Later that morning, I was released. Tracy was waiting in the hall for us to exit my hospital room. Eddie snatched the grips of my wheelchair from the nurse as she snarled at his abruptness. I smiled. Tommy had disappeared, and did not meet us back home until a few hours later. When we asked where he went, he just shrugged and welcomed me home.

As the days passed, I was still weak from the blood loss, including the plastic surgeries to restore the damaged skin on my leg from the plane accident. I was dying to ride Poncho again, but my leg was still sore so Tommy was kind enough to exercise him for me.

I was also starting to have bad dreams again. This

time they were related to the airplane crash. I wanted to play with the girls, but I was too weak from both the blood loss and from the sleeplessness. I just couldn't keep up with them. I loved watching them play, though. And I made sure they heard me laugh - it was important for them to hear my laughter. Mom would come over and help with them. She would play with the girls for hours. And that's when it happened for me, that's when I finally realized it. That was the first time I had ever heard Mom laugh and mean it. When she would make the girls laugh, she would laugh, and that would make me laugh. I was healing.

Adam was so good with them too.

Adam was so good to me; and he held me when I awoke from my bad dreams. Adam tried asking about my nightmares and I got a sense he thought they were about Jack again, yet he would never force the issue if I couldn't remember exactly what they were about. Actually, I'm not sure what most of them were about. But I do know that I searched for Jack for a very long time, and it's hard to just forget the pain and the huge amount of time that was taken from my life because of his disappearance.

Other than that, things around the house got back to normal, as normal as possible with three toddlers running the show. Mom tried teaching them to say Babushka, which was one term in Russian for grandmother. But it came out Babu so that's what they chose to call her.

I started thinking a lot about Zoë and all the others from her family. Some of the same questions kept popping back into my head, along with a million new ones. Should I try to contact them? Would they want to know me? Would they be okay with the tabloid articles? Actually, they should have been used to them, they had plenty of their own dirty laundry written about through the years, even though they tried to put on a facade of being pure. I wondered if Zoë remembered all of her *dream*, or if she just focused on the positive parts. I couldn't help remembering what Zoë had said about the "man who came all the way back from the dead just to be with her." Was she trying to tell me that I should go back with Jack? But I decided that the Matthews would have to wait - I had to get back to my life, to my family, and to clarify my decision for Adam.

Adam and I talked about our life, and we finally talked about Jack. He asked again if I had gone to see Jack, and I told him that Jack didn't show up until he heard about the crash on the news. But something kept nagging at me. I knew if I waited too long to resolve this, it would all drift away from me and I could lose the love of my life forever. This thing between Jack and I was still not over. I hadn't solidified anything yet. I called Jack, and we made plans to meet. I went to tell Adam what I chose to do.

"You know I have to go," I said to Adam.

Adam nodded solemnly, and all he said was "Have mercy on my heart."

Eddie opened my car door for me and I got in. As I left the house, I felt excited about my new life. I had peace for the first time in a long while and knew exactly what I wanted. A calm came over me and I wasn't apprehensive anymore. We drove up to Jack's hotel, and I could see him waiting for me outside. I got out of the car, and Jack and I walked to his hotel room together, stepped inside and sat down.

"Would you like something to drink?" he asked.

"No, thank you," I answered. "Jack, I loved you so much, and I thought I was going to die when you didn't come back to me. I missed you terribly." I paused when he reached for my hand. I pulled mine back, then continued while shaking my head. "I don't miss you anymore, Jack. I have made a life for myself after you left. No, it's not fair, but since when is life fair? I understand that your parents had to keep the secret from the press because it would have endangered your life, but they could have told me that you were still alive. That would have made all the difference in the world to me. I would have waited for you forever - but instead, I *grieved* for you. I have a family now, and I'm not going to just leave them. And it's more than that, Jack. I've discovered that I don't want to leave them, any of them. I am so grateful to you, more than you will ever know. You made me realize just how much I want them in my life. Adam may not have been my *first* true love, but he will be my last."

As I walked back outside alone, I realized that I was also closing a door from the past with Dad that day. I wanted so badly to please Dad and have him treat me like his daughter instead of someone he could use. I realized that I had just replaced Dad with another symbol of him - one that I could touch. Jack was everything Dad was - a schmoozer, philanderer, and someone whose behavior made me feel I needed to prove that I was worthy of his love. I had nothing to prove to Adam; he loved me unconditionally and never asked for anything from me, not even to make a choice.

As I sat back in the cushiony limo seat as we pulled out of the hotel driveway, I said, "Eddie, please take me home."

He grinned, nodded and replied, "Absolutely, *Mrs. Maguire*."

That made me smile.

When I returned home, there were no big parties being thrown. There were no marching bands playing. There were no flowers being given. There were no press releases. However, there *was* a family waiting by the front door to welcome me home. There was deep love. There was comfort. There was familiarity.

Adam and I celebrated our second anniversary in private, just the two of us in our bedroom. Gamma, along with Gampy, Uncle Red and Sam, took the girls for the night, and Adam and I celebrated our love into the early morning of the next day.

That was also when Adam told me that Jack had met him at the door of the hospital before I even arrived and told him that I had died in the airplane crash. Adam said that - because of the lie, Jack had done him a huge favor by making him realize just how much he loved me and wanted me in his life. Enough to straighten out his attitude. Enough to start showing me his love again. Adam said he was frustrated about Jack lurking around in my life and didn't know how to deal with it so he shut down his emotions to make the hurt go away. But then Adam discovered that the hurt was still there, especially when he thought the possibility existed that I was gone forever. Adam said he didn't tell me what Jack had said because he didn't want anything to influence my decision about whom to choose. If it was him, and not Jack, he wanted my decision to be based on how much I loved him, not on how mad I was at Jack for lying to him.

I wanted a new beginning with Adam. I began by telling Adam roughly everything I knew about everything. Some things were harder than others. I even told Adam about why Lexy dropped out of sight for a while years ago. I told him about what Mom had told me about herself and the boy she had a crush on - the whole story of my conception as I knew it. I let Adam listen to the recording from the *outsider*. I explained my abandonment issues. I told him about all of the guilt I was feeling after our first night together and how sorry I was I couldn't have given more to him at that time. Adam never asked for any information from me, but I felt I owed it to him to be forthcoming and not have those demons between us anymore. I opened up completely, and it's a good thing that I did. I would need every ounce of trust that I could get from him to see me through the next catastrophe.

Who knew that this was just the beginning. I would soon have my own daughter to rescue, the smallest of my babies. She's frailer than the others and she needs her Mommy. She needs her Daddy. She needs her family. But most of all, she needs her lifesaving medication.

There was a sense of urgency, and the clock was ticking...

Part II

Taking Back My Life

Chapter XVI

The Intruders

Larry was heading out my front door when he turned to reiterate, "Remember, *no* press from you is damaging press. This is your opportunity to clear up the misconceptions, not to mention, do damage control on your family's reputation that the tabloids trashed. They will print *their* version of the story if you don't do this, Jordan."

"There are so many other reputable reporters out there, why her, why the one who just wants to print gossip and not anything that's newsworthy?"

"Because if this interview goes well with her writing it, then people will know that you aren't that bad person they wrote the trash about. You need to focus on the bigger picture here. Make it interesting, dramatize it, embellish a bit so they will want to make a movie of your life so we can make another billion dollars."

"Another? *Who's* made a billion dollars? Talk about embellishment. And don't you think it's interesting all on its own? My life? Where have you been for the past twenty-some years, Larry? Beside, wouldn't you think they could check out any fallacies I gave them?"

"Okay, well then, spruce up my part and they can make a movie about me," Larry said chuckling as he turned to walk away.

"Fine, they're in for the ride of their lives. And who says you'll even be mentioned?" I rhetorically asked just to torment him as I watched Larry walk toward his limo.

Most everyone was out of the house that morning;

they understood we needed privacy. I sat down on the couch in the family room, and was surrounded by lavender roses. Adam gave them to me and said the color meant love at first sight - my new favorite. I pretended to read the latest script I unwillingly received from Larry while waiting for the reporter to arrive, fidgeting in my seat. What should I tell her about my life? What would people want to know? What should people *get* to know? It's not like I even had a choice; they were going to write the story anyway without me, and with all of the facts distorted. Talk about blackmail. And they call *me* ruthless? What was Larry *thinking* when he set this up? I didn't care what they wrote about me really, I just wanted them to stop hurting my family.

Eddie ushered the woman into the family room, her hand out to initiate a handshake before introducing herself. "Hi, I'm Lydia Hodges from the Newsmonger Magazine - it's good to meet you, Miss Walsh. You have a beautiful home. I hope we can include some photographs of it with the magazine article. I think the fans would love to see where you and your family spend your time. So, let's get started." She plopped herself down in the opposing chair to the couch without an invitation, clicked on a tape recorder, poured herself a soft drink from the tray on the coffee table, and began writing on her notepad.

Observing her warily, I slowly leaned back in my seat across from her, thinking, "I'll bet she's a Virgo."

"Now, we'll do an article - maybe a series if there's enough material. Wouldn't it be wonderful if we had enough for an entire book?" she inquired nefariously, as to capitalize on my misery.

"Jordan," I clarified, finally getting in a word.

"Excuse me?"

"You can call me Jordan. You want me to start with the first day of my life when I bit the doctor on the nose as he yanked me from my mother's womb?"

"Is that what happened?" she inquired with intrigue.

"No."

"Why don't you decide. Just start where you feel most comfortable. And just to get my information straight, how old are you now Jordan - twenty-seven, twenty-eight?"

"Twenty-nine and a half."

"Oh," she said with surprise.

I took a deep breath and reluctantly began. I knew the details of Joseph were what the reporter wanted, and that she probably wouldn't listen to the story at the beginning of my life if I started with him. I disclosed a brief summation of my first twenty-eight years, but not as detailed as I had with Zoë.

I told her of how I wanted to become an actress at a very early age. I told her briefly about Dad and his *adventures*. I didn't include most of his shenanigans, nor did I mention Mom's drinking binges. I didn't want the story to be mostly negative. I did tell her that Mom had a problem with alcohol, but said it was now under control. And I revealed the part about Mom burning down the house. I had to include divorcing Dad as a parent, but I didn't mention why. I thought I'd be most forthcoming where there had been previous articles or documentation. And yes, I even told her Larry was the most wonderful agent anyone could ever have and said she could quote me on that.

I told her about Tommy and how I cared for him in our foster home. About Gamma and Gampy coming to our rescue and adopting us. I told her about my amazing Uncle Red who always looked after us and rescued me more times than I could ever repay. I told her all about Foxy and her love for Champion Cheddar. I even told her about Ella. I told her about how Gampy taught me everything related to the stock market and Gamma taught me how to cook and do good deeds. And I also said, "No, my grandmother wasn't a madame as was previously printed in your magazine."

I told Lydia all about having Lexy as a friend and also about my practical jokes. I told her about our first house in the Hollywood Hills and, of course, about loving Jack. I kept my input about Jack brief though, along with the part about searching for him. I didn't want that to take the focus from what was really important - Adam and the family. I told her about having Adam in my life. I didn't want to give her too much information because the tabloids always turns stuff around and I didn't want him to think I was "kissing and telling." But knowing Adam, he'd probably be okay with anything I had to say.

I told her that the pregnancy with my girls was a surprise, but the best surprise I'd ever been given, rating equality with the surprise of meeting Adam. And contrary to what had been written in a tabloid, I'd never given one thought to terminating the pregnancy. I told her about the song that I wrote and sang for Adam when we were on location. I told her how one of my three babies was a mystery guest the day of her birth. I told Lydia how I named them after the loving women in my life. I told her of the very sad day when Foxy said good-bye. And about the horrid day of the airplane accident. And then about the very wonderful day when I got to save Zoë's life for her in the hospital. That was one of the greatest gifts I could have received. "Yes, I received a gift that day - a sister."

After about two hours of disclosing my life's event for Lydia about my first twenty-eight years, Eddie interrupted us by walking into the room with a fresh tray of drinks and some snacks. He set it on the coffee table before asking, "Can I get you anything else, Miss Jordan?"

"No thank you, Eddie," I answered as I watched him quietly retreat.

"Why did he call you, Miss Jordan?" she asked.

I smiled thinking back to the day when I said good-bye to my demons and the only time Eddie had ever called me *Mrs. Maguire*. I told her the explanation I had told Gladis.

"Would you like to take a break?" Lydia asked as she took liberties in preparing a plate of food for herself.

"No," I said, leaning back as I searched for what to say next. I began explaining the past sixteen months when my world became a nightmare, as if I were actually reliving it, almost in a hypnotic trance as I did the re-living of my entire life for Zoë.

~❋~¡~❋~¡~❋~¡~❋~¡~❋~¡~❋~

Because of the plane crash, Adam and I decided to

spend more time together as a family. We knew that life was too precious to take for granted. I told Larry I was on hiatus until further notice and not to send any more scripts for a while. But that didn't stop him from doing so. I also hired a replacement Executive Producer for me at the production company to work with my associates. Even though I needed to take some time off, I didn't want to end the business that I loved and built from scratch. It was also helping to support our lifestyle.

Soon thereafter, we got another brief fright when Gamma became ill. Gamma knew she wasn't feeling well, but didn't say anything to us because she didn't want to worry us. But that secret came to an end when she fainted onto the kitchen floor. We drove Gamma to the hospital and demanded that she submit to a complete set of tests. Turns out, she was just iron-deficient and everything else turned out fine. She was prescribed a high daily dosage of iron until her levels were normal again.

We also decided to make some time to go see Tommy play his baseball on a regular basis, but only at his home games. He was amazing and had a great year. Tommy had all the ladies wooing after him, but he seemed to have found someone nice and doesn't want to date anyone else. He hasn't brought her around yet so we don't really know anything about her except what he's willing to divulge. I'm not sure why, but he seemed a little shy about it so we didn't push. Tease, absolutely - but not push.

Mom was doing so much better. She hadn't had a drink in over a year. She'd had her slips in the past four years, then she decided it was time to get serious about not drinking and about getting her life together. Mom's not cured, even after a year of sobriety, and says she knows she has to work hard at it every day.

At the beginning of that year, I decided to do one more film before my hiatus officially began. I poured everything into it that I had to give. Adam was very supportive and played Mr. Mom while I was on the set. Of course, they all came out and had to live in a production trailer until we wrapped. I knew this was going to be one of the last films I would make for a while because I wanted to focus more on raising my children and being together as a family. And it goes without saying, I played the mother of all practical jokes because it would be a while before I could play another one. I don't know what everyone was so up in arms about. It wasn't like I moved anyone's house or anything. Just the production site trailers, about a mile down the road from where they originally stood. When they came back from shooting the second day, they stared at a vacant lot. Of course, I made sure ours was at the most prime location of any of the trailers. I guess that was my downfall, and that's how they knew it was me who did it. Adam was greatly impressed and just a little scared at the speed at which I executed it.

We celebrated Adam's birthday on location, and I had brought his present with me before leaving the house. I had a ring made for him. It was sterling silver with a triple stone setting of his aquamarine birthstones with diamonds around the outside. The aquamarine stones were flown in from Zambia. He loved it.

When we returned home, I mentioned to Gamma that I was missing Foxy terribly so she decided it was time that I adopted another companion from the animal shelter. Gamma knew we could never replace Foxy so she found a different kind of dog - a Poodle and Chow mix. I named her Pasta because she looks like a big bowl of curly white noodles. She has a black nose that looked like a big black Greek olive. Her obsession - toes. We've become a sock family now. Pasta can't seem to walk by anyone's bare feet without stopping to lick them. It's like an open invitation when you haven't donned socks. Pasta likes toes so much, she'd pull the socks off the girls just to lick their feet. Now that's a whole lot of toes. I guess she figured they were the easiest socks to get off. So Ruby's housekeeping duties expanded to include searching for socks, which would be from one end of the suite to the other.

Gamma also adopted a dog with a mixture of Bichon Frise and English Toy Spaniel breeding. I named her Snuggles because she reminded me of the way Foxy used to snuggle. And because I loved hearing Adam call her that. A big 6'2" macho-looking kind of guy calling for *Snnnuggggles*, it was the cutest thing ever, and I giggled to myself every time he said it. Of course, I never told Adam why she had that name. Snuggles is a reddish and white spotted beauty. *Her* obsession was with this small rubber ball that Tommy had played with as a boy, a few years after we moved in with Gamma and Gampy. She wouldn't let it out of her sight for very long. I've had to go buy three more, just because she wears them out. Snuggles doesn't chew on the rubber balls; she just carries one around. I had a heck of a time trying to find replacements after so many years.

Gamma couldn't decide between the two dogs for me so she didn't. They are both about the same size as each other, and the same as Foxy was. They were my twenty-ninth birthday present from Gamma.

Lexy came to visit often during this time when she wasn't doing great things with her acting career. I missed the *holidays* we'd take, but I had a family now and couldn't just take off as I did when I was younger. Lexy understood so she'd come to the house and we pretended to be on *holiday*. We had great parties, including my "youth mourning" bash - something they surprised me with. Lexy and I commandeered the Party Barn almost every weekend in March. That was also where we were planning to have Lexy and Brad's wedding reception so we would tell everyone we were planning that. I'm sure everyone knew better, that we were just gabbing about old times and past *holidays*. It seemed that Lexy was always busy doing something else, that her reception planning was always on the back burner.

Adam was making his movies and was receiving more main character roles. He was excited about an upcoming film he was making with a friend of his. He insisted that the girls and I come along with him, especially after he missed seeing their first steps while he was on location. Adam said that he wasn't going to miss anymore of their "firsts." I'm sure that had a lot to do with Dakota too. Adam once told me that he had missed almost every single "first" that Dakota had as a baby.

I began thinking of the Matthews family. I again started reassessing my life with the possibility of having these new people, or rather family, in it. If they were to be a part of my life, I would need to research some information to find out for sure if I was related to them. The blood match between Zoë and I aside, I still hadn't any physical proof. I started with acquiring a basic understanding of the study of Quantum Physics with DNA structure and chromosomes. I found that chromosomes are a threadlike linear strand of DNA with proteins in the nucleus of eukaryotic cells that carry the genes of hereditary information. A strand of DNA contains the hereditary information necessary for cell life. We receive twenty-three chromosomes from each parent. So if I match twenty-three of Zoë's chromosomes, we had one parent in common.

I began daydreaming about what it might have been like to have Joseph in my life growing up. The person I only knew as the biological one. What would he have been like in my life? Would I have not persevered as hard to make my life what it is today if I didn't have such adversity?

I decided I had waited long enough to talk to Zoë. She was out of the hospital and back at home in Houston by then. I called and I think it was Lillian who answered because she seemed a bit nervous. Lillian said Zoë wasn't there, and she took a message without identifying herself. "Whatever," I thought, "Zoë will never get that message."

Meanwhile, the tabloids were hinting around about a possible connection between "the woman I saved" and myself. They quoted Joseph denying any connection in his statement and that I was "just a donor." That was about the time when Mom received a message from Joseph requesting a meeting. Mom was clearly upset and said that she just couldn't handle seeing him again. I feared she would start drinking again so I offered to go in her place. I decided to wait a few weeks until Uncle Red was making a trip to Houston on business so we could travel together. I was feeling apprehensive about flying alone after the airplane crash because this would be my first flight since the accident. Since Uncle Red was going with me, we decided that

Tracy would stay with the girls.

Poor Uncle Red, I may have done severe tendon damage to his arm on the flight over there. Fortunately for him, it was only a few hours before we were there. Uncle Red and I agreed that we would meet back at the hotel after our respective meetings. I began to develop a few butterflies in my stomach, even more than I had on the flight. I arrived at Joseph's ranch and was ushered into his study. Joseph's personal assistant asked if I wanted a refreshment, and I declined. The personal assistant then instructed me to be seated as she sat at a desk. As I fidgeted in my seat, I could see history all around me in photographs hanging on the walls of the room. Joseph began his political career as the mayor of Houston, then won the governorship of Texas. As I walked around the room looking at the pictures, I could also see him posing with two former presidents.

After about thirty minutes, Joseph instructed her to let me into his office. He walked over to greet me at the door and put his arms around me, hugging me. "Jordan," he said, "welcome. Come sit down and let's talk a while. I hope I didn't keep you waiting too long. How was your flight?"

Joseph was a tall man, probably around 6'1". That in itself was intimidating. He had a Texas accent that he tried to conceal. You could tell Joseph was used to others following orders when he spoke, just from the way he addressed his personal assistant. Forceful, but not overbearing. He was the kind of man who knew that he never had to raise his voice - just his tone and demeanor were demanding enough.

"You look just like her, Jordan," he said while sitting. There was a kind of spooked look in Joseph's eyes, like he'd seen a ghost. "A pair of dark glasses and you could have passed yourself off as her," he added, chuckling.

"Thank you, I'll take that as a compliment," I responded with a smile. "Katia is her name, in case you'd forgotten - I know it's been a while. She wasn't up for making the trip."

"Well, I hope she feels better by the time you return home," he said. "I wanted to see your mother to ask why she never told me about you. It was never my intention to intimidate her in any way."

"She'll be fine, thank you," I replied. "I can't answer that question. I don't know why she never told you, but here I am and it's a done deal now." Then I added humorously, "Don't worry - I'm not here to ask for back allowance."

"Well, that's good - I'm rich but I don't know if I'm that rich," he said chuckling and sort of bragging. "Well, while we're here, I'd like to talk to you about all this before we make any announcements to the press. We're both public people and we should approach it with a certain decorum."

"What's there to talk about?"

"There's much that needs to be decided, such as the way we'll go public with it. This is a delicate situation, and it'll need to be explained gently."

"Whatever way you think is best," I said. I figured he could handle the press better than I could. "How will you approach it?"

"Since I'm a public figure, I do have to approach these things carefully. I'd just like you to trust me on this for a while," Joseph said as he smiled.

"I'm not good at trusting," I admitted. "I have serious trust issues I learned growing up, but I'll let you have this one. How long would you need?"

"I'm sorry to hear that," he said. "I wish I could have been there for you when you were growing up."

My abandonment issues began to creep back in with him wanting to put me off. I asked, "Is there anything you want me to do?"

"Yes, you can let me be your dad and trust me to take care of these new responsibilities," he answered.

I rose while saying, "I've taken enough of your time; call me if you need anything further."

We said our good-byes and I left.

"Well Uncle Red, that was interesting," I said quietly in the lobby bar of the hotel. "No big welcome wagon, but he was nice enough. Joseph needs a little time to get his ducks in a row before going public with it so I'm giving him that time."

"I'm glad things worked out - you deserve a good father, Joey," Uncle Red said sincerely. "Maybe after the publicity dies down, you'll be even closer. He's probably just a little preoccupied with his demanding job right now."

"Are you hungry? I'm famished," I said smiling, trying to change the subject. "Why don't we go out to a fancy restaurant and spend an ungodly amount of money on ourselves?" I didn't know exactly how I was feeling and I needed to take some process time to figure it out. I didn't want to do that at Uncle Red's expense, while we were spending time together, knowing I felt like a daughter to him.

~※~¡~※~¡~※~¡~※~¡~※~¡~※~

"We were looking forward to Adam's next movie because we would all be together, and he was going to work with an old friend of his - Quincy," I told Lydia. "Life was beginning to look good, but that was just a mirage. It would actually be Adam's next movie that more troubles began for us."

I took a sip of water and another deep breath before continuing for Lydia.

~※~¡~※~¡~※~¡~※~¡~※~¡~※~

Chapter XVII

An Intruder

Adam and I rounded up the girls, Clara and Tracy, and then Eddie drove us all to Adam's next film location in Nevada. We took our new recreational vehicle that Gampy had reconstructed for us. It was plush from one side to the other, back to front. Eddie loved driving it. Clara loved it too, as it helped with her nanny duties. It had dressing tables, high chairs and even built-in crib type beds for all three girls that were too tall for them to just climb out of. I guess Clara figured this would help her keep track of them easier. It had three private sleeping areas for the staff and a main bedroom in the back that was for Adam and I.

We settled in and began life on location again. It wasn't long before trouble found us though. There was an Italian actor on the set starring opposite to Adam. He was a last-minute replacement for Quincy. The replacement introduced himself innocently enough, but began finding excuses to run into me without Adam being around. It made me uncomfortable, not only because he was a dead ringer for Jack, but also because I felt he was up to something and it wasn't anything good. He then began openly flirting with me in the presence of other people on the set, and someone told me that he was starting rumors that we'd "hooked up." I confronted him a few times about it, but he denied any involvement in the rumors. He used the confrontations as vindication that something was going on between us, for others to see. He progressed by acting as though we'd been caught doing something when we were anywhere near other people.

Of course, all this got back to Adam and he was livid. He even confronted this guy himself and told him to stop bothering me. The guy insisted that it was all *my* idea, and that I was the one who was following him around. I told Adam that he was the only man I loved and that there was no contest with anyone else. I knew Adam believed me deep down, but if someone had set this up, they would have made a great choice for Jack's identical twin.

Nothing seemed to be stopping this guy and he continued to ruin the time Adam and I were spending together. He was so malicious and disgusting to me, I wouldn't even mention his name. I told Adam I would return home if that would make him feel better. He said it wouldn't, that he wanted the girls and me there with him and that no one, especially this guy, was going to spoil his time with his family. Adam said he understood, but I could feel his frustration growing. I did feel a little better when Eddie *accidently* dumped a tray of Bloody Marys all over the Jack look-a-like. All Eddie said was "Pardon me. May I get you a lime or stalk of celery with that, sir?"

When the movie wrapped, our family headed home. We decided that it would be fun to make a *holiday* of driving down off-the-beaten-path roadways on our way back. The countryside was beautiful. The trip was so romantic, that Adam and I grew close again. I just wished our good adventures would last longer than our next difficult moment in time.

One night in the moonlight, Adam and I danced to the music of chirping grasshoppers as our daughters wobbled in a circle around us. Adam would occasionally secretly pinch my behind.

The next morning, we showed our daughters rainbows. We put hopping frogs in their hands to let them know what it felt like when they jumped off. Well, that was more Adam's idea. We put daisies in their hair and made bonnets of tiger lilies. There seemed to be magic all around us like a fairy-tale. If I could have, I would have stayed there in that moment in time forever. I thought of Dakota and how I wished she could have been there with us.

Of course, klutzy me, I had to show the girls what it was like to fall into the river fishing for fool's gold. I think they thought that was the best part of our *holiday*, by the way they all laughed.

"Have mercy on my heart woman. One of these days, I'm going to die laughing with you as my assailant," Adam chuckled, teasing me as he helped me out. I retaliated against his comment by wrapping as much of my soaked body as possible around his, so that I could get Adam just as wet as I was.

That night, Adam and I snuck away around midnight for a walk in a field of golden wheat. There, we made love under the stars with a scarecrow looking on. Well, not after Adam put the scarecrow's scarf up over his eyes at my request.

When we returned home, there was another message from Joseph saying that he wanted to meet with Mom. Again, I needed to go see him since she wouldn't. Mom wasn't going to see Joseph for any reason, and I needed to make sure he wasn't offended by her refusal to see him. His message included a telephone number with a Los Angeles area code. It turned out to be a nearby hotel. I decided to just pop by for a chat with him.

When I arrived at the hotel, I asked the front desk clerk if I could have Joseph's room number. They said it was against their policy to give out room numbers, but that he was expected in the main banquet room at any time. So I went there.

As I entered the room, two of his bodyguards drew their weapons and pointed them point-blank at me. Without missing a beat, I asked jokingly, "Um, you wouldn't want to get rid of the evidence, would you?" I was referring to me and my DNA.

Seemingly surprised to see me, Joseph told his men to stand down, then walked over to hug me. He motioned for his bodyguards to step back and let us have some privacy to speak.

"My mother won't be coming to see you, she's not feeling up to it."

"I just had some things I wanted to discuss with her is all," he said, "and while I was in town, I thought I'd call on her."

"I thought I would stop by to let you know she wouldn't be coming so you wouldn't spend time waiting for her. I should probably be the one to do all the discussions in the future, since she's unwilling."

"That would be great. I can spend some more time with you," Joseph said. "I thought maybe we could sit down together and have dinner sometime."

"In public? You're not concerned about the press seeing us together? What has changed?"

Unfortunately, our discussion was interrupted by guests who were beginning to enter the banquet room. I excused myself and left for home.

But it seemed that bad luck was becoming the houseguest-from-Hell who wouldn't leave. The next morning, Sam and Uncle Red got into a huge spat, and Sam left for a few days. It took some intervention on our parts to get them back together. Uncle Red and Sam had never been mad at each other for very long before, that I knew of, so it was hard to see Uncle Red unhappy. They had been together for many years with no harsh words spoken between them. Uncle Red and Sam never divulged the basis of the disagreement, and that was okay since I didn't consider it to be any of our business anyway. I was just glad that Sam returned and the drama was soon over.

I agreed to meet Joseph for dinner, privately of course, and we had a good time talking about how we wanted to remain in each other's lives. We had a nice dinner and then agreed that we would get together again soon.

Meanwhile, the tabloids were relentlessly writing about the alleged connection between Zoë and me. Joseph called again to ask if I knew who was fueling the stories, that he would deal with them himself. After telling him I had no idea, Joseph said he believed me. That made my day that he would trust my answer. But that was the least of my problems. The relentless anger gods were indignant, and waiting for us in South Dakota.

Just as we closed one bad chapter in our lives, another one was about to be unleashed onto us. We received a distraught telephone call from Anita, and she told Adam to come quickly - Dakota was dying. Adam and I immediately hopped a flight to be with Dakota. When we reached the hospital, the doctors told us that she had a rare blood disease with no known cure.

Adam and I sat vigil at Dakota's bedside along with Anita and Adam's mother all through the night, and when she awoke, we tried reassuring her that she was going to be okay. However, her fever was so high she couldn't stay conscious for very long.

The next day, a doctor admitted that they'd made a mistake and he now said it was a virus, not a blood disease. Later that day, he came back and said she'd been poisoned. We were livid and Adam was frantic to get a correct diagnosis for her. The doctor said that whatever it was, it was too advanced for them to decipher because it kept rapidly changing its bilocular structure.

They advised us to contact a physician highly knowledgeable in this field of study, a Dr. Schiesser from Switzerland. Adam spoke to him on the telephone and Dr. Schiesser agreed to arrive at Dakota's hospital within thirty-six hours.

Adam and I hadn't had any sleep for about two days so we went back to the hotel. I went in to take a shower. I guess I was in there a long time because Adam came in to check on me. I was huddling in the corner of the shower with the water running while holding a wash cloth to my face - crying. Adam stepped in, clothes and all, turned off the water, and held me for a while during my cry. I had no idea how long I'd been in there, but he convinced me to dry off and jump into bed. He then sent for some dinner and a nice stiff bottle of scotch. I curled up in a soft fluffy robe while Adam combed and dried my hair for me. We held each other all night. I felt that I should have been comforting him, but it was just like Adam to be comforting me.

The next morning as we arrived at the hospital, I told Adam I would join him in a minute, that I wanted to stop at the hospital gift shop for a moment. I purchased a few colorful cheery balloons along with some children's books to read to Dakota. I knew the only ones they had were too young for a ten-year-old, but I thought I could make it fun anyway.

I spent most of my time in Dakota's room, largely staying out of the way of Adam and Anita so they could talk with the doctors. I put my chair between her bed and the window so I'd be out of the way of the doctors and nurses assessing her. I sat with Dakota when it was allowed, reading to her. When I would finish one book, I went to another. When I would finish all of them, I started over - one by one. Dakota was very weak now and couldn't sit up. She wanted to help read the stories, but couldn't physically so I would do all of the parts and voices. I tried not to act them out too much, knowing children like to imagine them all on their own.

One evening while reading to her, Adam's mother was knitting in the corner of the room as she sat in a rocking chair they had brought up from the nursery ward. Adam appeared and stood in the doorway and watched us for a while, before saying, "Why don't you go home to the girls, JoJo? I can stay here. All we're going to do is sit around for the next few days anyway. You can't do anything here."

"I can be here for Dakota," I snapped defensively. "She's my daughter now too, you know."

"Hopa Tokala is right, Waeco Wawate Ca," said his mother matriarchally. "Don't send her away. She is filling Dakota's room with good energy and a strong healing spirit." She was impressive - while she spoke, Adam's mother did not miss a beat in her rocking chair or her stitching.

"Fine. I didn't mean anything by it," he said softly and sincerely.

I took a deep breath to change my demeanor and added, "My place is with you. I'll go home when you go home." I went back to reading to Dakota.

Dr. Schiesser arrived and reviewed her blood work. He diagnosed the condition as a poisoning. He said the poison was an advanced one, but had characteristics from other rare poisons that he'd seen before. Dr. Schiesser also reassured us that she would be fine once they gave her some medication and performed a transfusion with some of Adam's blood the following day.

"Where was she the last few days before she became ill?" the doctor asked.

"She's been at home and in school is all," Anita stated.

"Did any other child become ill at school?"

"No, not that I know of. Certainly not like Dakota."

"Did any other person become ill at your house?"

"No."

"I believe that the only way the child could have contracted this was orally. If it were injected, she would have had the symptoms earlier and stronger. She had to have eaten something soon before developing the first symptom. We have to assume at this point, that someone gave her something with this poison in it."

"Someone poisoned my child?! Why?" asked Anita, distraught by the concept.

"Yes, deliberately or accidentally, I don't know. Was the child around any strangers the day she became ill?"

"Yes, but the only stranger near Dakota that day was Mr. Simmons from the mayor's office," said Anita. "It was government day at the school, and there were many people from each branch of government there. We assumed that he was checked out and reputable. Mr. Simmons said that he was assigned to her class. He bought all of the children in her class an ice cream cone. They all ate the ice cream and no one else was sick. She only had a little stomachache that night so I just thought Dakota was sick because she had too much junk food that day."

"Is there anyone who would want to do her harm?" asked Adam.

"No, not at all," answered Adam's mother. "Dakota is

the sweetest girl and all of her classmates love her."

The doctor left and Adam got up to call the mayor's office. He found out that no one by that name ever represented that office.

"What did the man look like?" I asked.

"Well, I can show you. They all had a picture taken while standing at the ice cream truck." Anita pulled out a pack of photographs from her purse, flipped to one and all of us looked at it. "He's looking away, but you can still see him," Anita added.

All of a sudden, I felt my stomach flicker. This guy was familiar in some way, but I couldn't put my finger on it. I began to feel the hair on the back of my neck starting to prickle. What was it? That name wasn't familiar, but I knew I'd seen him somewhere before. I thought, "Yeah, that was the same guy standing in back of Joseph in one of his photographs on the wall of his study at the ranch." I remembered that he had a ear piece in like Tracy wears. I kept this to myself until Adam and I got back to our hotel room.

"You're quiet. You're not still mad at me are you?" Adam asked solemnly.

I answered, "I was never mad at you - a little hurt, but never mad. And that's not what I was pondering."

"What are you pondering?"

"Adam, I have something I have to tell you," I said cautiously. He sat down on the bed. Adam seemed shell-shocked from everything going on, but listened to me nonetheless. "I've been mulling something over in my head and I may be way off-base here, but I have to say this to see if it sounds as ridiculous out loud as it does in my head. When I was in Joseph's study, there were a million photographs on the walls. I was in there for a long time so I amused myself with looking at some of them. There was a guy in one of the photographs who I think is one of Joseph's security men. I'm pretty sure this is the same guy who was at Dakota's school - this Mr. Simmons."

"Why would he be involved with a bunch of Native American children in a private school or the mayor's office in South Dakota - far from Texas?"

"I don't know how the guy got in or what he said to get access to the class - but if he did do this, Joseph has to be told."

"But why would that guy do this to her? What are you thinking?"

"Okay, just hear me out for a minute. Rumors are running rampant that Joseph may run for the Presidency next term. What would you do for your boss to get a dream job of a lifetime? The security man may be getting me out of the picture, at least for a while, so that Joseph can concentrate on running for election. Just a thought."

He immediately got up and stormed over to the phone.

"Adam," I said softly as I put my hand on his, pulling it away from the telephone. "I don't think we should tell anyone else about this just yet. We need to move cautiously. We don't know if Joseph's telephone has been tapped or if this guy is hanging around nearby and could overhear the conversation. We can't take any chances."

Adam nodded.

The next day, the hospital attendant drew a sample of Adam's blood. They needed to be sure it matched Dakota's blood with the same RzRz factor as many Native Americans have. I sat with him and Dakota when they performed the transfusion. We stayed a few extra days just to make sure that Dakota was feeling better, and also so that Adam felt comfortable enough with Dakota's recovery to leave.

When we returned to Los Angeles, the girls were running around crazy to see us. That put a smile on Adam's angelic face again. We rolled around on the family room floor with them. As Adam got up to answer the telephone in the next room, I was amused to see what they probably saw in him - a gentle giant.

"So how's the planning for Lexy's reception coming along, Gamma?" I asked as I got up from the floor. She looked like she was about to come unglued.

"Never bedda," she answered, mocking me for always saying that when things had fallen apart. We laughed.

"Well, since I haven't done my good deed yet today,

what can I do to help?" I asked teasing her.

"Oh, nothing dear, we'll be ready when it gets here," she answered not really paying enough attention to me as I admitted that I hadn't executed my good deed yet that day.

"Why don't you tell me about it and maybe I can fill in any blanks for you."

As Gamma began telling me about the grand soiree, I couldn't help but laugh to myself thinking about the bizarreness of Lexy's requests. The basic setup was generally the same as Tommy's *World Series of Birthdays Extravaganza* party we threw for his eighteenth birthday. Lexy's reception was also going to be held in the Party Barn, but this gathering would include mostly famous people that she knew from Hollywood and London. And it would be done in a yellow butterfly theme, not with baseball decor like Tommy's. Gamma hired the same staff supervisor that oversaw the direction of all our parties, along with many of the same staff positions.

Lexy and Brad came to stay with us a week before the reception and planned to stay for another week after it was over. Brad and Adam spent time together talking, mainly about the perils of being married to an actress. Lexy and I received more than our share of digs from them that week. But it was all in good fun, and we got in a few digs of our own.

As always, no one was allowed in the main house, all the activities were to be in the Party Barn area. Adam and I decided that we needed to move the girls to Mom's suite for added protection in case those who wished us harm knew our routine. I was feeling paranoid with what happened to Dakota, so I also increased the security in Mom's suite by adding one more guard inside the suite with Clara and the girls. Tracy would stay with Adam and I when we were ready to join the party.

I'd given most of the other staff members the night off, except Tracy and Clara. Gampy put his *little babies*, the rottweilers, in Mom's suite to help protect the girls as well.

We had decided to have a mock wedding, since Lexy

and Brad were already married, and a big blowout reception. When her big moment was about to arrive, I snuck over to Lexy's room to see how she was fairing. She looked beautiful. Lexy was in her element. She was dressed in a beautiful ivory antique lace gown with pearls everywhere, it had been designed by our favorite designer, Gemi. The guys would just be wearing black suits. Adam and I would stand up for Lexy and Brad, as we did at their Vegas ceremony. There wouldn't be a real justice of the peace, but a friend doing a skit of Elvis to make it fun. We did the something old, new, borrowed, and blue the night before at the rehearsal dinner, so she wouldn't worry about time getting away from us.

Gamma had commissioned a decorator who strung tiny twinkling lights all around the Party Barn. There were so many of them, that they became the main lighting for the area. We also had candles on the tables for atmosphere.

Lexy wouldn't have anyone walking her up the aisle since her parents wouldn't be there. She would walk in right behind me. I would be wearing a yellow antique dress with yellow butterflies clipped all around me. I made Lexy promise that she wouldn't get mad if I unclipped a few sometime during the evening.

The invitations had gold lettering and yellow butter-flies on them. Lexy found these beautiful candleholders for wedding party favors. She had a three-tiered wedding cake made of white frosting and lemon cake. They decided that they didn't want a groom's cake. The flowers were simple white roses with yellow butterflies made of chiffon clipped to them. The menu was Prime Rib and Chicken Kiev. Lexy wanted mostly champagne, and it continuously flowed from a fountain just outside the disco. Gamma and I made up pouches of bird seed instead of rice.

They were planning on waiting until later to take their honeymoon. Lexy had to go back to work on one more film before she would have some time off.

Since Lexy had four ladies-in-waiting to help with her every need, I left and tiptoed out to the patio to see what was going on at the Party Barn. There were many famous people beginning to arrive. Gamma had arranged for Lexy's favorite band to be there. Since I could hear the music starting to play, I knew the event was almost ready to begin.

I returned to our suite to see how Adam was doing with his tie. He wasn't great with tying them so I hopped up onto a foot stool to help him before getting dressed myself. We went over to Mom's to check on the girls. They were sleeping soundly even with the band's music playing.

I turned to Adam and said, "You look very nice tonight in your handsome suit, Mr. Maguire."

"Thank you."

"Okay, now it's your turn to say something nice about me," I teased. "No, on second thought, I'd rather you put your mouth to work over here." I pulled him close to kiss me.

We gathered in the family room to start the festivities. We marched out to the Party Barn and had the mock wedding. Afterwards, Lexy and Brad did the whole shebang with the tossing of the bouquet and the throwing of the garter. Tommy caught the garter, and I thought Mom was going to have a heart attack as she cried out that her baby was too young to get tied down with marriage.

Lexy gave me a beautiful diamond necklace with a yellow butterfly in the center as my maid of honor gift. Adam received a Native American design of a Turquoise and Opal bangle from Brad. I was so glad that Adam and Brad had become friends. It made it easier to meet up with Lexy since Brad and Adam got along so well.

The reception was wonderful, and it gave Lexy an opportunity to introduce Brad to her side of the world - the acting world. This was quite different from his world of investment banking. Even though they had been married for a while, Brad really hadn't met any of these people. He looked a little overwhelmed at first, but then he didn't seem to care - never taking his eyes off his bride.

The night was long and we were ready to end it so Adam and I snuck out, checked on the girls, and went to our suite. We then decided to leave the girls at Mom's that night because they were sleeping and we didn't want to disturb them. Adam and I retired for the evening and when we awoke the next day, Adam received a call from someone from our past. At least I'd hoped she would have stayed in our past.

~*~¡~*~¡~*~¡~*~¡~*~¡~*~

I was so immersed in telling my story, I hardly noticed when Lydia changed the tapes as the recorder clicked off.

~*~¡~*~¡~*~¡~*~¡~*~¡~*~

Chapter XVIII

The Ultimate Intruder

Adam and I thought we would let the girls sleep in, and we decided to spend some time alone together as we frequently did in the mornings. Just before we were getting ready to sit out on the patio to drink our morning coffee, Adam received a telephone call. A call from *her* - Kelly. Once again, she was intruding on our personal time together with scheduling concerns for his next film. And even though Adam knew that their working relationship was a sore spot with me, he stayed on the telephone for twenty minutes talking to her.

"What did *she* want?"

"Just to let me know what the scheduling was for the film."

"Oh yeah, right. She could have just faxed that information to you."

"Not a big deal," he answered.

"I don't know why you have to keep doing movies with that woman when you know she is trying to ruin our marriage."

"That doesn't mean she's going to - unless we let her."

"Miss Jordan?" Brandy said as she popped her head into the front room to our suite.

Not really comprehending that Brandy was speaking to me, being engrossed in my discussion, I continued, "You are a big star now and you have power on the set. Can't you just have her removed from the film?"

"She has a right to make a living."

"Miss Jordan?" Brandy said again, still without my

knowledge she was standing there or if she needed my input on a scheduling issue.

"Oh, she's just there to make trouble, not make a living. Kelly asked to be on this set only because you were on it," I said somewhat teasing him now.

"Oh really?" he said teasing me right back in a sexy voice.

"Miss Jordan?"

"Yes Brandy, I'm sorry - what is it?"

"You're needed in the family room."

"Okay, we'll be down in a little while," I said to Brandy. I turned back to Adam. "And she knew very well this would upset me..."

"Miss Jordan, I think the both of you need to come right now, please. It's urgent."

"Brandy? Why? What happened?" I asked, as I saw the fear on her face. Adam and I got up immediately and the three of us headed out as Brandy explained that there were police officers who wanted to see us.

As I took each step, things slowed to a snail's pace. Everyone was talking in slow motion even though there seemed to be a million people running in all directions around the family room. Why were police officers at my house? Why was Gamma screaming? What happened?

"I'm sorry, ma'am, but we're here to inform you that your daughter has been kidnapped. We have a ransom note that was left in her crib in the living quarters on the east side of the house. Ma'am? Ma'am?"

I felt sick and disoriented. I looked around the room. "Adam? Adam, where are you?" Everything faded.

"JoJo? JoJo, are you alright?" Adam asked, as he knelt beside me. "JoJo, can you hear me?" He turned to the others and calmly said, "Someone get some water please."

"Adam?" I said groggily. "Tell me this is a dream." I was still lying on the floor looking up at him.

"No, I'm afraid it's real," he said gently. "Are you okay to sit up?"

I nodded as I sat up. A policeman handed me a cup

of water. I took it as I asked him in my coldest most ruthless voice, "What do they want?"

"Here's the note. Please don't take it out of the cellophane casing; we still have to dust it for prints. It basically says they want six million dollars."

"I'm able to read, thank you," I said, but not offensively. I gritted my teeth, and turning to Adam, I finally got the nerve to ask, "Which one?"

"Little Tiff, JoJo," he said, having gotten the information during my unconsciousness.

"Oh, God," I said as I dropped my head down with my eyes closed. "Where are our other babies?" I asked, looking back up at Adam.

"They're safe. Tracy is with them."

I started shaking. I knew we had to get Tiff back soon. If she went into an asthmatic attack, she could suffocate and die. All she would need to do is to get agitated enough. I asked, "How did this happen? They were behind an impenetrable fortress!? Did they happen to take her medication?"

I'm not sure I heard everything the detective had said, but what I could comprehend of it was: "We don't know about the medication yet ma'am, but the whole transaction was recorded on your surveillance tape. Apparently, they subdued the guards by putting pressure on their necks, which made them pass out. They then drugged the guards inside the suite with a spray of some kind. They first sprayed the faces of the dogs that were in the room with whatever was in the spray can and then killed them by strangulation. They nearly decapitated one and there is blood virtually everywhere in the room. They drugged someone else claiming to be your nanny with the spray as well, but she doesn't appear to be harmed. That's about all we know at this point."

"Is everyone else okay? The security? Where's Mom?"

"Yes, everyone involved is being transported to the hospital to be checked out. Your mother does not appear to have been in the living quarters at the time, ma'am. We have agents at the hospital and once your people are released, they will be questioned for any further possible information that they may have."

"How did you know? Who called you?"

"Annie Kobach called in the complaint to 911, ma'am."

"Gamma, why didn't you tell us?"

"I didn't want to waste *any* time, dear. They could have still been on the grounds with her. I sent Brandy to your suite to get you when I returned from the front gate with the police and ambulance, so they would know where to go."

"Good thinking," I said as I stood up and hugged her. "Where is everyone else?"

The detective answered, "They are being interrogated for more information. Ma'am, are you well enough to answer some questions for us?"

"Yes, of course."

"Where were you when this happened?"

"Not knowing when it actually happened, I can't answer that, but Adam and I were in the front room of our suite when Brandy came in and told us. We'd been there all night. I stepped out onto the patio for a moment to see if I needed something other than a sweater this morning. We were getting ready to sit outside for a while. I looked over at the Party Barn to see if they'd started cleaning up yet - just a glance really."

"Did you see or hear anything while you were on the patio?"

"Not that would indicate something was happening over at Mom's. The party area is in the opposite direction to Mom's suite."

"What time did the clean-up crew arrive?"

"Gamma?"

"About six-thirty, mostly."

The police detective turned to Adam, "Did you see or hear anything?"

"No, I was talking on the telephone shortly before Brandy came in."

"Are you two the biological parents to the child, or is there a third party involved with custody?"

"Adam and I are," I said.

"Is this your daughter's doll?" asked the detective. "We found it in her crib wrapped up like a sleeping child. The note was attached to it." He showed all of us a doll that had been stuffed into an evidence bag.

"No, it's not hers. And the doll doesn't belong to any of my other daughters."

"Meaning more children than your other two?"

"Yes, Adam has a daughter from a previous marriage who is not here right now, but she has some of her things here as well," I answered.

"Thank you. That's all the questions we have right now," he concluded. "If we have any more, can we reach you here?" I nodded as the detective leaned over to listen to someone whispering in his ear. "Ma'am, we have a point of entry onto the property. They targeted the east wall. There were fresh tire tracks in the mud and recent scuff marks on the wall. There was also some blood found there."

"BLOOD?!" Adam and I both asked simultaneously.

"Ma'am, we think it's the dog's blood, but we'll have it analyzed. There wasn't any blood found anywhere near the other two children."

"Jordan dear, we've woke everyone in the guest quarters and the police are questioning them now," Gamma informed me. "The police said we could return to our suite so everyone is heading over there if you need us. We'll take Stephie and Beth with us."

"Okay Gamma, that's good - we'll come over later." She left with Stephie, Beth, Tommy, Gampy, Sam and two security guards. Uncle Red stayed with Adam, Tracy and I. I also learned that Mom had left early that morning for an alcoholics in recovery meeting and that she would be back later that morning. The staff was then questioned and were released back to their quarters. I assumed the police asked Lexy and Brad to leave after they were interrogated since those two weren't really a part of the household. I assumed they went to a hotel.

I watched as they interrogated the guests from last night's reception. Each one was questioned, dismissed and then asked to wait in their cars if they had brought any other guest with them before allowing them to leave. It looked humiliating, but I didn't care. If they had any information, I wanted the police to find out what it was.

Adam was holding me one moment, but then standing over by the window the next. I think he just didn't know what to do with himself. I didn't know quite what to do with myself either. I felt like crying, but I wanted to keep a clear head so I could focus on helping them find Tiffany.

Another police officer came in and began whispering something to the detective. "Ma'am, we have some more bad news," the detective told us a moment later. "We found a deceased woman in a field near those tire tracks that we now assume were made by the getaway vehicle. We believe that we've identified her, but we'd like someone to verify identification if they could."

"Uncle Red, would you?"

He nodded. "Of course, Joey - I'll be right back."

Adam was standing, looking out the window, and being very quiet. I knew him well enough to know he was about to explode. Adam was a gentle man, but even he had his breaking point. More police were tracking around the room, and I could sense that made Adam nervous, knowing how he felt about guns in general, but especially in his house.

"Ma'am, the coroner said it appears that the woman we found died from electrocution."

"How can someone die from electrocution in the middle of a field?"

"They found her next to a transformer," the detective said. "We have to assume at this point that's how she was electrocuted."

I could then see Uncle Red's face as he walked back into the room. It was an ash color. Could it have been Mom out there?

"Ma'am, we've identified the victim as Alexandria Sherman-Reger."

That threw me. I froze to process the information, but I couldn't believe it. No, he didn't just say that! He couldn't have. She was just here. I saw Adam start to walk over to me as I sunk to the floor on my knees with my head in my hands. I cried out, "NO! You have to be wrong!"

"Sorry ma'am."

"Uncle Red?" He confirmed it as I sobbed and fell to the floor.

"Oh Lexy!" What was I going to do without her? Lexy was my best friend. My only girlfriend. My savior. She was a brilliant actress. She had just finally found the love of her life. She had her whole life ahead of her. She was funny and kind. She brightened up every day that I spent with her. She was a daughter. She was a granddaughter. She was a wife.

I slowly rose and tried to compose myself before placing a call to Lexy's mother. It was just about the hardest thing I've ever had to do. She was understandably very upset. After a lengthy conversation with her, she asked that I say a few words at Lexy's memorial after they sent her home. I was honored that Lexy's mother would think of me in her time of sorrow. But all that would have to wait, as the detective informed us, the coroner would be holding onto Lexy's body until further notice. There was something suspicious found on her, but they wouldn't say what.

"Has anyone told Brad?"

"Yes ma'am. We contacted him in a guest room here," said the detective."

"Why didn't Brad tell anyone that she was missing?" I asked as I cried.

"He said he was asleep when we called and didn't know she was missing or even gone from the room. But that's all I'm authorized to tell you at this point, ma'am."

~✳~!~✳~!~✳~!~✳~!~✳~!~✳~

I looked over at Lydia who didn't appear to be the least bit sorry for my loss. It was more like she was disappointed that more people hadn't been killed. I hated every minute with her and knew I had to end our interview as quickly as I could.

~✳~!~✳~!~✳~!~✳~!~✳~!~✳~

Chapter XIX

The End of the Beginning

After the officers were finished dusting for prints, the investigators commandeered our suite and set up their telephone tracking-equipment. For the time being, we closed off the room in Mom's suite where the dogs had been slain in. Mom returned and was notified of the awful news, then went over to stay with Gamma and Gampy until we could get the blood cleaned up in her suite. The coroner also took the deceased dogs back to the forensic's lab to test them for clues. Adam and I moved Stephie and Beth back to their bedroom and sat vigil at Tiffany's bedside. I kept crying, thinking this was wrong, this wasn't the way it was suppose to be. My best friend was dead. We had four healthy daughters, and now one was sick from a poison with possible long-term effects that Dakota would have to endure, and another was missing and we didn't know if Tiffany was dead or alive. Adam and I held Stephie and Beth, fed them and played with them. It wasn't until seven long agonizing hours later that the kidnappers finally contacted us with payment instructions.

We had the bank messenger over the money, and Uncle Red made the drop for us, but not before the detectives marked the money. The instructions were to put the money into a locker at the bus station. They posted a guard who loitered around the locker disguised as a transient. However, no one came to claim the money and we heard nothing further from the kidnappers. Each moment that passed was excruciating.

Adam and I went to the family room and told everyone that we needed to go light a candle for Tiffany at the chapel and pray for our daughter, alone. When Tracy said she was going with us, I said I had Adam with me and would feel better if she watched over the other girls and my family with the other two guards.

By that time, the press had the story. When Adam and I went to leave the grounds, they were right outside the gates. We asked Uncle Red to run interference for us in his truck by blocking the media trucks behind us. It gave us the advantage, and we left without being followed.

Adam and I were at the chapel for a while, but then decided to check into a hotel room for the night. We just couldn't bear to go back to that house until all of our children were there. We knew Stephie and Beth were being well cared for by Mom and Gamma, and we needed to spend some time to pray for our other daughters.

Once checked-in at an unostentatious hotel, we called Zoë to see if she knew anything about the mystery man in the photograph with Joseph. She didn't. We asked her not to tell anyone that we had called because Adam and I didn't want to get this man into any trouble if these were all just coincidences and he was innocent after all. That's also why we didn't tell the police about him. Plus, if he was involved, we were scared to tell anyone for fear he would kill Tiff in retaliation.

Adam and I sat there, held each other, and prayed for hours until we received a call from someone who wouldn't identify themselves. That was the tip we were waiting for, the call to go pick up our daughter. They said to come alone and not to tell anyone or Tiffany would suffer for it.

Adam looked over at me and nodded. "Let's go bring our daughter home," he said.

We drove the Land Rover to the airport and flew to Dallas on the longest flight I'd ever taken. We followed the instructions they gave us to the letter. We rode a city bus from the airport to an abandoned warehouse on the other side of town. There, we found our daughter sleeping soundly and unhurt. It was a miracle and the best day of our lives when we found her unharmed and we knew she was coming home. We believed that prayer had rescued our daughter. We went directly to the airport and flew back home to Los Angeles that same day. The news of us being at the airport must have already been out because the press was there at the airport when we arrived. They asked a million questions before Adam, Tiff and I got into the Land Rover.

When Adam and I returned home, we were told that someone had picked up the money from the bus station. There was a collapsible back panel that had been taken off from the locker behind it. The police said that the kidnappers probably had the money minutes after the drop was made. We also heard that there was a shootout at Joseph's Houston ranch, and that everyone present there was killed in the massacre. The authorities said they didn't have any leads as to who may have done it, or if everyone there just killed each other. Adam and I figured that it didn't matter that we didn't tell the police about the man who we suspected because he was amongst the slain at the ranch. Joseph had also been there and was killed, allegedly trying to save our daughter's life according to one of the inspectors. His body was found in a position suggesting that he killed the man who they suspected of kidnapping Tiffany. An officer told us the evidence suggested that Tiffany was being held there for a short while.

Adam and I were so grateful to get our daughter back safely with us. All of our prayers were answered. We also felt grateful that we had each other during that time. We now had an unbreakable bond. We were stronger than ever as a couple. So much so, that Adam called the casting director of his current film and told them he wouldn't be on the same set as Kelly anymore, and she was fired right away. I never asked him to make the call, but did I regret that he did? Hell no.

~✳~¡~✳~¡~✳~¡~✳~¡~✳~¡~✳~

I wasn't sure if it was a mistake telling Lydia that last part, so I quickly changed the subject. I didn't want Adam to get sued knowing he got Kelly fired from the set. That would be all we need, to have her hound us for the next few years in court.

"There have been many rumors surfacing that you and your husband were more involved with the return of your daughter. Was there any truth in that?" Lydia asked.

"Just what I've told you is all. The same people who wrote that Gamma was a madame in a bordello probably wrote that," I answered.

Lydia packed up her things and said, "That was the best story I'd ever heard." She also said her editor would authorize her to run the article as a series over two to three months in their magazine. Lydia also hinted at wanting to be the ghostwriter for my biography when I was ready to write it. I said that this was it and I didn't expect any more *adventures* for a while so there wouldn't be anything more to write about. Not that I would let her write my biography anyway.

Of course, there are still the *teen* years for my children that might warrant some good stories. I would like to believe that the adversities our children might face from growing up wild in Hollywood would not happen, and would simply be a far-off distant illusion. I know there's a possibility of them getting into trouble with relationships, drugs, drinking - all the things rich kids get into trouble over - even with strong morals being taught by Gamma. But with that long into our future, hopping frogs secretly placed in pockets was the only mischief I wanted to witness from them for a good long time.

Lydia said she'd be in touch. Eddie ushered her out, and I watched from the window as she went on her way.

Adam came into the family room, sat on the couch next to me, and asked, "You okay?"

"Never bedda."

"Poured it on a little thick, didn't you - about all that praying and hand-wringing stuff?" He chuckled. "As if that was going to get Tiff back."

I grinned like the Cheshire Cat in *Alice in Wonderland*, thinking about the mysterious disappearing evidence I hid from Lydia. "Serves her right for trashing my family in past articles. That's my story and I'm sticking to it - no matter what the truth is. The end."

Chapter XX

Reality

Of course, that was only *The End* according to the story that I told Lydia. And most of it had been as a load of horse manure. I wasn't about to tell her the whole truth. Partly because I wanted to protect Zoë from the truth and partly because it was just none of Lydia's damn business. But mostly because the real story wasn't repeatable - much less printable. The editors of her magazine just didn't know who they were dealing with when they tried blackmailing me into an interview. I wasn't going to let them or anyone else hurt my family again, and there wasn't anyone creditable left alive on the opposing side to contradict me.

It was actually Mom, not Larry, who gave me the idea for the embellished performance for Lydia. She reminded me of my first play performance; *Harvey-the-Rabbit* - a fallacy, a figment of the imagination, an invisible tale.

You see, deciphering the real story was knowing that Adam and I both had Irish tempers and, we knew early on that we'd take no prisoners from the ordeal. There would be no hostages. I couldn't risk allowing the enemy to come after us again. I couldn't risk any of my children being hurt again. I couldn't risk the police arresting members of my family for something that they hadn't done. I couldn't risk anyone discovering the real story that would possibly have taken their father from my children to be imprisoned for the rest of his life. Not to mention - me. What would any mother have done to secure a safe sanctuary for her children? To make sure that they didn't feel abandoned by their parents? No one will hurt my family and get away with it. I wasn't Pollyanna, nor obtuse, no matter what anyone might think about me. I was tougher and sharper than they gave me credit for - that was their ultimate mistake. Ruthless? No, it was survival. And there wouldn't be any journal entries written here to incriminate us.

It mostly started when I went to visit Joseph in Houston that first time we'd met. That's where the true events drastically began to divert from my story to Lydia, and that's when my life went awry. She had no way of proving that my story to her had detoured. Everything that I had told her was what I wanted the readers of her magazine to know, or what was a matter of record somewhere - whether on a police report, a hospital chart or from eyewitnesses. That was good and that was bad. Bad because I couldn't misrepresent anything about what was on record, so if I wanted to deviate, I would have to be more creative. But good because that way when she verified my story, there was evidence to substantiate and strengthen my credibility. She wasn't omnipotent and Joseph wasn't talking so where I could, I led Lydia down the path where *I* wanted her to go.

~✳~⁚~✳~⁚~✳~⁚~✳~⁚~✳~⁚~✳~

After Mom received her first threatening note from Joseph, Uncle Red and I flew to Houston. We agreed that we would meet back at the hotel after our respective meetings - that first meeting with Joseph. I began to develop a few butterflies in my stomach as I neared my fishing trip about Joseph. I chartered a limo and arrived at Joseph's ranch, where I was ushered into his study. I looked at the photographs cooling my heels for thirty minutes while waiting for him to see me. I decided that was long enough. Even though I wanted to fish around to find out what he was up to with summoning Mom there, I'd had enough. I was about to inform his personal assistant that if Joseph wanted to talk, he'd need to call me to reschedule. Just at that moment, as if he were reading my thoughts, Joseph instructed her to permit me into his office. He walked over to greet me at the door and put his arm around me, hugging me from the side. "Jordan," he said, "welcome. Come sit down and let's talk a while. I hope I didn't keep you waiting too long." It instantly reminded me of Mr. Burton, one of our foster parents. It was that same weird phony feeling that I always got from him.

"You look just like her, Jordan," he said. There was a kind of spooked look in his eyes, like Joseph had just seen a ghost. "A pair of dark glasses and you could have passed yourself off as her," he added.

"Katia. *Her* name is Katia," I said with a smile, knowing that, in me, he must have been looking at that girl he took advantage of thirty years ago. "She wasn't up for making the trip."

"Well, I hope she's feeling okay. I wanted to see your mother to ask why she never told me about you," he explained as I sat there silently. "I think I had a right to know. It was never my intention to intimidate her in any way."

Somehow I got a sense that he wasn't telling the truth. Maybe it was the politician in him, but something was off. I was hoping maybe I was just paranoid because I was so nervous. I wanted to get to know Joseph, but unfortunately for him, my instincts were usually correct. I was instantly defensive thanks to the incongruous words he choose.

"She's fine, thank you," I replied. "I can't answer the question you're raising. I don't know why she never told you, but here I am and it's a done deal now."

"Well, while we're here, I'd like to talk to you about this before we make any announcements to the press. There's no need to place blame, and I wouldn't want them to be too hard on your mother. You know how the tabloids can be about women's mistakes."

"Why would they be hard on *her?*" I asked, fake smiling at him. "It took two of you to make the *mistake*. And what's there to talk about? I'm sure it won't take much investigating for the press to make the connection; they're already inquiring about it. And since when do they wait for anyone's announcements to write what they want, anyway?"

"There's much that needs to be decided, such as the way we'll go public with it. This is a delicate situation, and it'll need to be explained gently."

"The way? What way would that be?"

"Well, I'm a public figure and I have to approach these things carefully. I'd just like you to trust me on this for a while," Joseph said as he smiled that all too familiar kind of smile - a schmoozing smile. Exactly like that old familiar sucking up that Dad did just before he stole something from me.

"*These things*? How many of *these things* have there been?" I asked, not liking where the discussion was going. "With all due respect, I don't know you well enough to trust you. And I have serious trust issues that I learned while growing up. So I wouldn't trust very easily even if I *did* know you better."

"I'm sorry to hear that," Joseph said as if he were ordering dinner from a menu.

As I felt my abandonment issues creeping back in, I said, "Well, this *mistake* has nothing to hide from anyone. This was your faux pas," I said, defending Mom for not telling him about me. "You say you didn't know about me, but you must have had some idea that this *mistake* was a possibility. You do remember having sex with Katia when she was a school girl, right?" Joseph wasn't fooling anyone, I knew he had no intention of letting anyone know about this.

"Yes, but I was an irresponsible kid back then, and I'm an important person today with real responsibilities," Joseph said as if that excused his behavior. He then added, "I'll choose when the time is right and that is not now." He sounded like he was giving an order to one of his staff members. I translated that to mean he was ashamed of my existence. That I, his mistaken offspring, wasn't worthy of others knowing about before his run for the White House.

I thought, "Spoken like a true politician." I knew I wouldn't accomplish anything there, especially since Joseph had just changed the subject from claiming he didn't know about me, to him being irresponsible back then. That way, he was taking no responsibility for this. Neither had anything to do with the other. It was like an old magician's trick - "the hand is quicker than the eye." Joseph also was trying to divert the focus from his *indiscretion* by saying his life's purposes were more important. I'm sure Joseph just wanted to bury this due to what the public *and* what his opponents would do to him before an election - the story could be political homicide for him. I rose while saying, "I've taken enough of your time *Governor*. You can contact me in the future; my mother won't be up to any further discussions regarding this matter." I knew Joseph would push Mom over the edge if he spoke to her as he had just spoken to me.

My back was to the door as Lillian suddenly entered the room and said, "Joey?" I instinctively turned around and answered, "Yes?" As did he. That's when it hit me; Joseph and I had the same name. Lillian looked surprised. Perhaps she too had just realized the name similarity. That made me think of Uncle Red who was the only one who called me Joey, and how I would now associate Joseph-the-bully with my sweet uncle. She never finished speaking, but stepped to the side of the room and smiled waiting for us to finish.

I departed for the hotel moments later. When I saw Uncle Red in the hotel lounge, I vented wildly about Joseph not welcoming me into his family, about his wanting to hide the situation, about having another dominate male try to tell me what I will and won't do. I found it hard to concentrate on what Uncle Red was saying and kept on seething until I realized how insensitive I was being knowing I'd always looked onto Uncle Red as a father and now I was whining about what a complete stranger had said to me.

After Uncle Red and I returned home, Mom confessed she came up with the name for me because it was similar to his. And that she had avoided being too obvious by naming me Josephine or Joline so it wouldn't draw attention to the situation. That way, Mom could always be close to the boy she'd had such a big crush on.

Meanwhile, Adam and I were making progress in improving our life together as husband and wife. We had made peace with the past, and now all of it was in the past - including Jack. But that didn't mean we didn't have our conflicts. I did something stupid that I now regret. This would drive a wedge between us for quite some time. I knew how much he wanted to be successful in his acting career so I tried to make secret deals to get him access to the best Hollywood scripts and parts. When Adam found out, he was crushed. Adam said that he wanted to make it on his own or he didn't want to make it at all.

"I love this work and this is my craft. I want to perfect it all on my own," he blustered. "If all I wanted was fame, then I would be satisfied with just being married to you and living out my days as Mr. *Walsh!*"

Ooo, ouch, that hurt - but he was right. Plus I was glad Adam didn't want to use me for my money or fame. However, I also wanted to help my husband where I could, and I was very powerful in the film industry. Needless to say, Adam was mad that I attempted to use my influence to buy his way in and he said he thought I didn't have any faith in him to succeed.

Chapter XXI

Steering Off Course

We headed for Adam's next film location where the Jack look-alike began to wreak havoc on our personal life. I suspected Adam was still upset with the career-building scheme I had pulled and this Jack look-alike thing wasn't making matters any better. It didn't help when this guy was constantly bombarding Adam with detailed lies of how he and I were *getting along*. That must have been difficult for Adam professionally as well, since they played best friends in the film. And I think it bears repeating that I did feel somewhat better when Eddie *accidently* dumped a tray of Bloody Marys all over the Jack look-alike.

During the special *holiday* that we took driving through Nevada with the girls and their hopping frogs, Adam felt unconstrained enough with me to unfold the circumstances surrounding his father's death. His father died from a gunshot wound, being one reason why Adam hates and won't go near guns. His father was trying to teach eight-year-old Adam how to use a rifle during a hunting trip with other fathers and sons. When Adam and his father were sneaking up on a deer, they stumbled onto a sleeping bear, startling it. The bear reared up while jolting Adam which made him lose control of his rifle, dropping it onto the ground. That's when it accidently fired on his father. The loud blast of the rifle shot scared off the bear, but his father was on the ground critically wounded. The other fathers and sons on the trip were initially on another side of the hill, but when they reached them, none could give aid to Adam's father. The group was out in the wilderness and could not reach a hospital quickly enough to save his father's life. That was the other reason Adam despised guns, he took his father's life with one, no matter how unintentional. Adam said that's why he spent so much time in the wilderness - to ask the spirits why they did this to him. He said he eventually found his answer - they hadn't. Adam and his father were just victims of circumstance that day. That was when his mother taught him to forgive himself for the accident, and to love himself again. That was all the counseling that Adam needed - his family.

When Adam and I returned home, Mom was a big bundle of nerves. She'd received another message from Joseph about meeting with him. This one was sent by special messenger to the house; it had the State of Texas seal on the envelope and the memo was typed on the Governor's letterhead. It read: *Mrs. Walsh: Governor Matthews requires your attendance for a meeting at the West Palms Hotel at 7:00 pm on this upcoming Friday.*

I needed to put an end to Joseph's harassment of her. Mom wasn't going to see him for any reason, and I needed to make sure he knew that. I stuck the memo in my journal in case I needed it later for proof that he was using his office to harass her. After driving over to his hotel and discovering his location, I entered the banquet room where two of his bodyguards drew their weapons on me. Only after Joseph glanced over at a busboy entering the room, did he tell his men to stand down. I told Joseph that Mom wouldn't be coming to see him and that she doesn't come at anyone's beck and call, least of all someone who doesn't have jurisdiction in our state - referring to the State of Texas seal all over his summons. I made it clear that Joseph would need a court ordered writ of compliance and not some demands scratched out on his letterhead for any further communication with her. I wanted Joseph to know that I knew he didn't have any power here, any legal power anyway, and that I knew a few things about the rights of us lowly civilians. I could see the anger bubbling up inside of him as we were interrupted by guests beginning to enter the banquet room, so I left.

I returned home to find that Tracy was seething that I had left without telling her. Adam was not too far behind her in the scolding. I decided not to divulge having stared down the barrel of a gun, well two guns actually. I wished that I *had* brought Tracy along with me. Since she had been a sharp-shooter for the Olympic's team, I knew she could have popped them all. And I also knew exactly how good Tracy was because she was the one who taught me how to shoot several years ago. And I gotta say, I ain't no slouch either.

With that behind me, I needed to regain my focus and concentrate on my life with the only family I needed and wanted, with the exception of Zoë. I felt I didn't need any more distractions about something or someone that no longer mattered. I knew where Joseph was coming from, and it wasn't a loving fatherly kind of place. I made sure Mom stuck around the house for the next few weeks; I didn't want him or one of his henchmen ambushing her somewhere when she least expected it. Mom was often one big raw nerve as it was, and she deserved some peace and happiness.

The next morning, Uncle Red called and he sounded extremely groggy. "Hi Joey, I need your help."

"Anything Uncle Red, what's wrong? And where are you? Sam said you had a meeting with a client and didn't come home last night. He is half out of his mind with worry. Why didn't you call or come home?"

"I don't know what happened, but I need you and Adam to come over here quickly. Don't tell Sam. I'm at the West Palms Hotel, room 237."

That's when it struck me like lightning. Hearing the name of that hotel again, like getting a message sent to me directly from Joseph.

When we arrived at the hotel, there were cops swarming everywhere. They wouldn't let us cross the police lines so we talked to Uncle Red by shouting over them. He wanted us to call an attorney friend of his. That friend met us at the police station an hour later and then went in to represent Uncle Red.

Several hours after we arrived at the police station, we finally got in to see Uncle Red. We spoke to him in an interrogation room after he'd been booked and submitted to a drug test required from a writ of execution. Uncle Red told us his story of the past evening, or what he knew of it. He was found in a hotel room lying next to a known male prostitute who was stabbed to death with a knife still sticking out of his chest. They also found drugs in the room. When they performed a toxicology report on Uncle Red, the police found the drug Rohypnol, also known as GHB, in his system. Uncle Red said that he had no recollection of what happened from the time he was meeting with a client downstairs in the lobby bar to when he was awaken by a screaming maid. He said the maid claimed she entered because it was after check-out time, and then, when she saw all of the blood, she screamed. Uncle Red told us that he'd been set up. He said he would never cheat on Sam or take drugs, much less, murder someone, but we already knew he didn't have it in him to do any of these sinister things.

"Why would someone want to frame me for that man's murder? I only help people; I don't put them behind bars or hurt them, for someone wanting to do *this* to me."

"I don't know, but we will do everything we can to stop this, Uncle Red," I said, reassuring him. "The guy who was found next to you... was this the same guy you met at your meeting?"

"No. I'd never seen either of them before."

"Who was it that you met with?" asked his lawyer friend.

"He said his name was Mr. Rivers, and he needed my help," Uncle Red answered. "When I got to the meeting, we talked a while at a table in the hotel bar, but Mr. Rivers soon said he felt better. Before he left, he said he'd be in touch if anything further was needed."

"Did you have anything to eat or drink while you were in the bar?" his friend inquired.

"Yes, I ordered a beer. However, I only had a sip or two - surely not enough to get me drunk and make me pass out."

"Did you ever leave your drink alone with him during this meeting?" I asked.

"Just for a split second when I went to the bar for a napkin. Mr. Rivers said he was about to cry over his dilemma and was embarrassed. He asked if I'd grab a napkin or two. Why?"

"The police said they found GHB in your system. I'm guessing that's how you consumed it," his lawyer friend answered.

"What did he look like?" Adam prompted.

"Well, what stands out the most to me was that he had a scar above is right eyebrow and snowy white hair."

After our conversation, a police officer came into the interrogation room and took Uncle Red away - to a cell.

The judge wouldn't grant bail and Uncle Red spent the next night in jail. Not surprising, when Sam found out that Uncle Red was being accused of murdering a prostitute he'd spent the night with, he wanted to leave him. Sam was devastated. "We built a good relationship and it's gone in an instant," he simmered, throwing various belongings into a suitcase.

"No, it doesn't have to be over, Sam. Uncle Red loves you very much and was concerned about how you would take this," I said, trying to get him to see things differently. "Does that sound like someone who wants to risk their relationship? You can trust that he's telling the truth; I would stake my life on it. And you know I don't trust that many people, especially to stake my life on just their word. Be here for him, Sam - please? What do you have to lose by just listening to him when he comes home? And he *will* be coming home soon, I assure you."

I was becoming very agitated. Something stunk here. Who was this monster that was making a mess out of our lives? I looked around on Uncle Red's desk, but couldn't find any information about the guy he met with the previous night. I thought maybe he made a notation and then forgot with all that was going on, but no leads were there.

As a family, Adam, Mom, Gamma, Gampy, Sam and I were all up late trying to figure out what to do at this point. We didn't want to involve Tommy, and besides, he was out of town at an away game.

I organized my thoughts out loud. "What do we know so far? We know Uncle Red is innocent. We know someone went to a lot of trouble to frame him - enough to murder someone. We don't know who the client was that met with him. Or why he would do this to him, assuming that Mr. Rivers also put Uncle Red in the bed with the dead guy along with drugging Uncle Red. We know Uncle Red didn't know the dead guy. I've tried to think back to anything that may have happened in any of Uncle Red's cases that would anger someone enough to set him up like this. But Uncle Red mostly handles small stuff, nothing like murder cases where someone would go to jail for a long time if he lost their case. Nothing makes sense. The only one who would do something this mean to him - is Dad, and he's dead." I wasn't ready yet to admit that I was also thinking there was a possibility that Joseph could be involved, so I kept that to myself - but not for very long.

I couldn't believe the timing when early the next day Joseph mysteriously called. He said if I wanted, he could make all of Uncle Red's predicaments go away. He said he could dissolve the whole matter so that no one would ever have to know about it. Uncle Red would be able to walk away scot-free. Joseph would involve a judge he knew to close the police report so the press couldn't find out it was Uncle Red in the room. He gave me some happy-horse-slop about wanting to compensate for the years of being an absentee father. But then, he revealed what the favor would cost me - my silence in our other matter long enough for him to defuse the situation with the press. That would be my price, and he wasn't even hinting around about it. I now felt certain that he did this to Uncle Red. It was time for me to just admit it - Joseph was most likely involved. Even if there weren't all of these coincidences, he as much as confessed. I thought about asking him how he knew about this so quickly, but I figured I wouldn't get a straight answer. Plus I didn't want Joseph to know that I suspected him.

I knew doing what Joseph was asking was wrong, but my heart ached for Uncle Red. "This is blackmail and I won't soon forget it," I thought. But all it would cost me was the time Joseph wanted. I had asked him "how much time," but he couldn't give me an estimation - just said he needed to leave it open-ended. Of course, that's what I was expecting so there was no real big news there. Joseph had even went so far as to deny any responsibility for this recent bad luck. Funny, I never asked if he was involved.

I discussed the offer with Uncle Red and Adam, and they agreed because this was a setup and a very good one. Since someone obviously went to all this trouble and ruthlessness, enough to kill someone to set him up, we believed that Uncle Red would have little chance to prove himself innocent. He knew that first-hand from being an attorney and seeing what circumstantial evidence could do to a case if it was powerful enough. And even though no one saw Uncle Red put the knife into this guy's chest, his fingerprints were all over the knife, the room and the drug paraphernalia - not to mention the fact that he was found lying next to the dead man in a drug-induced state of unconsciousness. Uncle Red wouldn't be getting off with manslaughter for this one. Agreeing to Joseph's offer could also buy us time as well. Time to figure out what was going on here and to find out who the white-haired guy was.

We agreed to let Joseph handle it. I made the call.

Uncle Red was released, and miraculously the arrest paperwork disappeared. By the next day, the case was dismissed due to a lack of evidence. It seems the body of the male prostitute had somehow mystically vanished from the morgue. That began to scare me. I thought Joseph was just going to do a little hocus-pocus and fudge the cause of death or something, but not make the corpse evaporate along with the entire case against Uncle Red. Joseph was more powerful than I gave him credit for. His actions deserved my respect. Respect for how dangerous he was like how I respected one of Adam's knives - not admiration.

There would be no dinners with Joseph, and no closeness. Only contempt and mistrust.

Meanwhile, the tabloids were relentless and continued writing their articles about how they thought there might be a connection between Zoë and I, with the rare blood type coming to light after the plane accident, which no one was actually sure how they got that information. Coincidently, not an instant later, the relentless anger gods were waiting for us in South Dakota.

Chapter XXII

Saving Dakota

After we visited Dakota in the hospital, and after we spoke to Anita about the man who posed as a government official, Adam and I returned to our hotel where I told him of a theory I had. "I've been mulling something over in my head and I may be way off base here, but let me share it with you. When I was in Joseph's study waiting to meet with him, there was a guy in one of the photographs who I think is one of Joseph's men. I'm pretty sure this is the same guy who went to Dakota's school, this Mr. Simmons. I don't know how he got in or what he said to get access to the school children, but if the guy did do this, Joseph is most likely involved. And the guy also fits the description Uncle Red gave us of Mr. Rivers, that he met in the hotel bar."

"I can't see Joseph being involved with a bunch of Native American children in a private school or even the Mayor's office in South Dakota for that matter," said Adam. "You already told Joseph that you weren't going public with your information after Uncle Red's fiasco. Why would he continue with making your life arduous if he had defused the situation?"

"Okay, just hear me out for a minute. You heard the taped conversation I had with the *outsider* about wanting to expose Joseph for statutory rape. Rumors are running rampant that he wants to run for the President's seat next term, the most powerful position in the country, maybe even the world. What would you do to stop a story from ruining your chances of a dream job of a lifetime? It's not just an illegitimate child story anymore; it's a statutory rapist story. That puts a whole new spin on things. The public could forgive one, but not the other. If Joseph can do the math so can the press. They wouldn't have to know about the tape; they just would have to know how old Mom was when I was conceived. And what is the one common denominator in all of these things - the Jack look-alike, Uncle Red's blackout, Dakota's illness?"

"You."

"Yes. These things have happened so quickly, one right after the other and usually immediately after a story in the tabloids about the connection between Zoë and I. Joseph might be planning his defense in the press by discrediting me - as a cheating wife, as someone who covered up a murder, and I'm not sure about Dakota's situation yet, but I'm sure he has something in store to implicate me in that as well. It seems like Joseph's acquiring security for himself before this all gets publicized and he has tied me into all of these things."

"Perhaps, but why doesn't he just kill you and be done with it? You'd be gone and out of his life, no longer an issue. Sorry honey, I'm just playing devil's advocate here," Adam said affectionately.

I winked at Adam knowing he was just helping and answered, "But my proof wouldn't be out of his life, and that's what he's frightened of. Killing me won't be enough. There would still be proof that I was telling the truth in the birth certificates for Mom and me; those certificates would prove our ages. There would also still be proof in the blood tests for Zoë and I that they ran at the hospital before I was prepped for surgery. But discrediting me would be how he could make people believe that proof was not creditable. All he would have to do at that point would be to change the birth records, and it seems as though that would be a cinch for him, knowing how he made Uncle Red's evidence disappear. That way, my copy of the birth certificate would seem like the bogus one when I came forward with it. Then he could make it so I was implemented in switching the hospital records. His people could claim I didn't have the same blood as Zoë and that someone else donated it. Who's going to believe a discredited murderous woman? It's not a matter of silencing me period, but it's a matter of silencing me in the press. He's probably going to make it appear that I latched onto this family only to claim part of his fortune," I added as I paused to regroup my thoughts.

I began tidying up the hotel room as I continued my thoughts. "I don't believe that Joseph had anything to do with the plane crash because his wife and legitimate daughter were on that flight too. But as of right now, I rule nothing out. And who was there to extinguish the evidence on Uncle Red? How did Joseph know about the arrest so fast? And what a coincidence that it happen at the same hotel where I had spoken to Joseph the day before. I'm sure that was his way of letting me know he could get to me at any time."

"I'll kill 'em! I'll kill him with my bare hands if he's involved in hurting Dakota!" Adam shouted, springing suddenly to his feet and storming over to the telephone. I was so engrossed with my summation that I hadn't noticed Adam getting agitated and heated, suspecting Joseph was involved in poisoning his daughter.

"Adam," I said delicately as I gently pulled his hand away from the phone, "I don't think we should tell anyone else about this just yet. We need to move cautiously. Joseph is a very powerful man and if he's involved, we'll have monumental difficulties on our hands. We're going to have to plan our defense, not to mention, our offense very carefully."

He nodded, then added looking me straight in the eyes, "I'll kill 'em."

I said nothing.

The next day, I sat with him and Dakota while they performed a blood transfusion between father and daughter.

Chapter XXIII

Going to the Chapel

When Lexy and Brad came to stay with us a week before the reception, Lexy - seeming upset and nervous - told me that she needed to talk to me privately. During our talk, she said that she had received a call from the parents of the woman who had adopted her child. The callers told her that their daughter and son-in-law died in an automobile accident. While the grandparents had been willed the child, they couldn't raise him. Lexy then said she went to discuss possible new arrangements with Dirk at the Matthews' ranch house. While there, she overheard a mysterious man with white hair talking to a woman, but she hadn't seen the woman. The only thing she could tell me for sure about the woman was that the voice sounded familiar to her. Lexy said it sounded as if they were plotting a kidnapping. She didn't know whose, but the name "Walsh" was mentioned a few times. Lexy said the man said something strange like "Well, I guess the only thing left to do is to decide which baboon we want her to be." And then he laughed about it.

After Lexy left Dirk and Joseph's ranch house, she said she had a strange feeling that her life was in danger because odd things kept happening. The gas in her hotel room was accidently turned on without a flame the night before she was to leave. The taxi she was in was cut off and almost drove over a cliff. And she was nearly run over at the airport by a car speeding through the pedestrians' walkway; the vehicle came so close that it actually did hit her overnight case. Lexy said her taxi driver was so freaked out, he muttered something about her being stalked by the Angel of Death and took off, not even waiting for his tip.

After discussing the kidnapping plot with Adam later that night, we assumed that they were going to attempt to kidnap me. We figured Joseph would somehow try to implicate me in another of his schemes to continue discrediting me. So with that information, we increased security at the house and for Lexy's upcoming reception.

Adam and I decided that we needed to move the girls to Mom's suite for added protection in case Joseph's goons knew our routine. I was feeling paranoid with all the bizarre things happening to the family and the dangerous things Lexy had gone through in Houston so I also increased the security inside Mom's suite and added one more guard outside her suite as well. Tracy would stay nearby Adam and me. Gampy put his *little babies*, the rottweilers, in Mom's suite to help protect the girls too.

The night of Lexy's reception, while changing clothes afterwards in preparation for bed, I discovered what it was that Joseph had in store for me surrounding Dakota's illness. There, in one of my dresser drawers, was a vile of liquid. That shook me to my core. I knew someone from his camp had been in my bedroom. That was very close to my world and to my children. Since it wasn't mine and I'd never seen it before, Adam and I assumed it was probably the same poison that Dakota had consumed. We put the vile in a safe place and planned to get it tested to be sure. I wasn't sure how Joseph planned to put me at the scene, maybe imply that I had paid someone to poison her, but nevertheless, we had to be extra careful from then on.

Even though we had beefed up the security around the girls, we didn't really think they were the target. Adam and I thought we had it all figured out. So we were baffled as to how they knew to look in Mom's suite for our daughters. There was no evidence that any other attempts had been made to gain access to other parts of the grounds so they had to have known we took the girls there, and that was a spur of the moment decision Adam and I made that night. They weren't after Mom because they left the doll behind with the ransom note. That gave us reason to believe that one of the girls was the premeditated target. I had no proof that they knew they took the frailest and neediest child.

When the dogs were killed, I believed they were sending us a message that they could get to any of us at any time and do whatever they wanted to do to us. That was evident when we found Lexy's body. So each moment that passed waiting for word about Tiffany was excruciating.

Adam just sat on the floor next to Tiffany's bed holding her binky; which was the same spot where they had often played for hours at a time. I walked over and sat down next to him. He seemed to be in some sort of shock or trance and didn't say anything or even notice me. We sat in silence for a while and that's when I thought Adam and I needed to go somewhere else where we could talk and not have it on the surveillance monitor or a chance of anyone overhearing us. I thought it best to say we were going to a chapel because nothing else would have been acceptable behavior. I looked over at Adam and said, "We have to get out of here for a while. Why don't we go to the chapel?"

"No, I think I'll just stay here a while longer."

"Adam, look at me," I said. He looked up at me while I spun my eyes up toward the monitor behind me without letting it see me. "Let's just go for a while," I said.

He understood by nodding.

We secretly packed a few things in a duffle bag. While in the closet where there were no monitors watching, I included Tiffany's medication and a fistful of cash from the closet floor safe. We also included the mysterious vile, not wanting the police that were swarming all over the suite to find it. We took the bag through the bathroom and gave it to Eddie where we instructed him to confidentially put it in the Land Rover. We came to the family room and told everyone that we needed to go light a candle for our daughter at the chapel. Alone. When Tracy said she was going with us, I said I had Adam to protect me.

After successfully evading the press at the front gate

of the house, and once Adam and I reached the chapel, we went inside and made sure no one was lurking about. Then Adam sat down in one of the pews. He was looking drained and confused.

I went over to him and said, "We have to get her back."

"We will. They're doing everything they can to get Tiff back."

"No, I'm saying *we* have to get her back."

Adam was silent; he seemed to be numb. He just sat there in silence. I began talking and I couldn't seem to stop. "I'm not just going to sit here and let them do this to me again. Not like Jack. Not like before." Adam looked over at me startled, not knowing what to say. I continued, "I am not going to let them run my life. Adam, are you with me? You know they're going to kill her anyway; they didn't take her medication. They won't care enough to help her when she can't breath. Do you think they'll risk taking her to a hospital when she starts gasping for air? They're going to kill her anyway, just like they did Lexy. Don't we owe it to our daughter to fight back? If Joseph is involved, do you think the police are just going to prance up to his door and ask him to hand Tiffany over? That's probably what he's counting on, that we'll tell the police he has her so they'll think I'm crazy. You know if we don't do something ourselves, it will destroy us. We are vulnerable just sitting by and letting this happen. At least we'll know that we did something, even if it's the wrong thing. If Tiffany is going to die, I want to be there with her. I want to be there *for* her. I want my voice to be the last thing she hears in this world, to know her Mommy loves her, even if they kill me too. I can do that for my daughter, I *will* do that for my daughter. Adam, I did not go through twenty-seven hours of labor just to let her die! You remember when I said, 'My children will never feel abandoned?' We have to go get her. You know that's right."

Adam looked at me and nodded. "You had me on 'we have to get her back.' Let's go bring our daughter home."

Once alone in the Land Rover and driving out of the

chapel parking lot, Adam turned to me and asked, "So you don't want to include Tracy? Why? I think she'd be loyal and wouldn't divulge anything about this."

"I don't completely trust anyone, except you. I know that sounds paranoid, but we can't risk it. Look at all we've had to endure not knowing who it is that's a part of this. And we know that someone in the house had to be involved, how else would they know about us moving the girls to Mom's without trying to look anywhere else for them?"

"You don't think she can be trusted?"

"I wouldn't stake Tiffany's life on it, would you? I know in my mind that Tracy is, but I need to feel in my heart and I don't. The only one I'd risk her life on is you." I paused, then added solemnly, "Adam, something just doesn't sit right about all of this with me. Even if Joseph is involved in doing this and he has all the money in the world, why would he or they be asking for only six million dollars when literally everyone on earth knows we're worth twenty times that and could probably get a hold of twenty times more? If Joseph would want to make the investigators believe a real kidnapper was doing this, why not ask for an appropriate amount of money from your mark?"

"Someone not interested in money? Perhaps they lost sight of their goal because of what they are really going after," he answered, knowing where I was headed with the question.

"Someone screwed up. They made a mistake and now it's our turn to be in control, Adam. Our family is our life and we're going to take it back," I said. I started to have a nagging feeling that there was still something about this that seemed familiar, and the feeling was getting stronger and stronger every time I reviewed the recent episodes.

Adam broke my concentration as he suggested, "We have to establish an alibi. Let's check into a hotel and pay for a week in advance. Then we can put out a do-not-disturb sign on the door so they won't bother us. That way, we can make some phone calls and then go where the clues takes us. No one will know we weren't there the whole time."

As we drove to the hotel, I organized my thoughts out

loud. "We'll call Zoë first. If she does know anything, I think she will tell me. We'll ask her not to say anything. Besides, I'm sure that Lillian has shielded Zoë from the press about Tiffany's kidnapping story because it had something to do with me - 'the illegitimate one,' so Zoë won't know why we are really asking these questions. We'll say it's a surprise for Joseph," I said smirking. "Next, we'll talk to Lillian to see what she might know. I can threaten to take away what she needs the most in order to keep her from telling Joseph that we called, her daughter's *Godsend* - me. I'm sure Lillian will cooperate, especially if she's kept my existence a secret for all these years, for that exact reason - to keep me safe, or rather my blood and organs. But if she doesn't cooperate, you do know what that means? He'll be on to us and so will the police."

"It's our only chance right now to get some information and leads. We have to take that chance," Adam replied.

We did get a few clues from Zoë and Lillian, but not what we were hoping for - Tiffany's whereabouts.

Adam and I knew that if we were going to do this, we would have to go deep undercover. Since both of us were public figures and very recognizable, we would have to transform ourselves with very good disguises so no one would know who we were and what we were doing.

After devising our plan, we headed for a store owned by a friend of mine, a makeup artist specializing in special effects in the movie industry. This was the same guy who I had personally asked to do my makeup for my wedding to Jack. We told him it was for an upcoming masquerade party so we wouldn't get him involved. I asked him to keep it confidential because the press would try to *unmask* us and ruin our ruse. Since he had recently returned from China working on a film, he hadn't heard the news about Tiff's kidnapping, so we hadn't mentioned it to him. He went so far as to dismiss his staff until we had departed and destroyed the paperwork on our cash transaction. He furnished us with wigs and facial prosthetics, along with other appropriate apparatus. I wore a blonde wig and Adam wore a short-haired brown one. His beautiful long black hair would have made him distinctly recognizable, and we were both glad he didn't have to cut it.

With the disguises donned, we then were able to buy new photo IDs, thanks to my experiences with the Mexican underground.

Adam and I went with some information we had received from Zoë. She said her father had been leaving the Austin Governor's mansion and going to their Houston ranch more frequently than usual. We decided to head for Houston.

"We have to leave the Land Rover at the hotel so no one will suspect that we went to the airport," I said. "We'll take a cab to LAX. Then we can pick up a cheap wreck when we get to Houston, and no one will dream it's us. We'll have to get some help from the home-front. All of the phone lines at the house will probably be tapped by the police waiting for a call from the kidnappers, so I'll contact Mom at one of her alcoholics in recovery meetings."

While wearing our disguises, we booked our flight separately so as to not give anyone any reason to think we were *them, that famous couple.* We went to the ticket counter with our fake IDs in hand, paid cash for our coach tickets, and flew the all-nighter to Dallas. When we arrived, Adam purchased a Dallas map, while I obtained a city bus schedule and then tore some pages out of a telephone book for warehouse listings. We separately caught flights to Houston that morning. The flights were agonizing for me, still being squeamish about flying, but I got through it and did manage to sleep a little.

On our way to acquire a car in Houston, Adam and I made up a code. The plan was that if one of us were taken, we could use the code to tell the other one where we were being held. We then acquired a gun and a knife. Since Adam didn't like guns, he insisted that I take the pistol for my protection. Adam knew how to handle himself with a knife; not that he needed it, his hands were lethal weapons.

Houston was my old stomping grounds. We started asking questions to a few of Uncle Red's private-eye buddies he knew about any strange activity in the area, but I knew most of the snitches were out at night not during the day. We didn't get much information.

It was just like Mexico all over again, but that's how I knew we were on to something. Most people didn't like answering questions and others just shrugged. I knew from experience that some people would share what they knew for a price. A big price. And it would have to be bigger than anyone else was paying them. Again and again, I could sense that people wanted to tell me what they knew, just as much as what others were trying so desperately to hide. They seemed scared, very scared. That was good for us because I knew we were getting closer to Tiffany.

Chapter XXIV

The Wicked Baboon

Adam and I both looked tired and drained from being awake most of the night. I was also tired of wearing the prosthetic nose that I'd had on for the past twelve or so hours.

"Let's drive out to the ranch first to see what's going on out there," Adam said as I was somewhat daydreaming about what it was about all of this that seemed familiar to me. "Let's see if we can find out why Joseph needs to be there so much, as Zoë indicated. Listen, are you hungry? You feel like some breakfast? You want to stop on the way to pick something up? JoJo, maybe some fruit?"

"Huh, fruit?"

"Yeah, would you like some fruit?"

"Bananas."

"Bananas? You don't like bananas, remember? Why bananas?"

"Bananas! That's it! Six million in bananas!"

"Sure, why not?" he asked kidding me.

"Someone from the Monkey Murders is in on this," I thought out loud. "They have to be; there's too many coincidences."

"The what?" asked Adam.

"Oh, that's right - you didn't know me then. When Lexy and I did our second movie together, I concocted the Monkey Murders. It was a practical joke I played on the entire cast - even on Lexy," I said as I started to unfold the caper for him. "I bought six stuffed monkeys to match another stuffed one they had for the set rehearsals. The rehearsal monkey was kidnapped and five of the other monkeys were used for bait to extort six million in bananas. Plus one was used as a decoy to frame someone on the set. The 'monkey-napper' was asking for six million in bananas for the return of the original production monkey. Six million, get it?" I paused before continuing. "I guess that was the furthest thing from my mind. I haven't thought about the Monkey Murders in years."

"What happened?"

"I framed the original monkey with a crate of bananas and a bank statement that said he deposited one million in bananas that began with a demand for six million," I answered. Then I began reminiscing more of the events surrounding the murder mystery. "But the original monkey was initially kidnapped, except this monkey's abduction had been staged. Tiffany's kidnapping wasn't staged."

"I meant what happened to the other monkeys?"

"They were all picked off one by one and they all died a horrible death," I said solemnly, realizing even more significance to the monkey's deaths that had on our lives. "Adam, each one died differently. The first was stabbed, like Uncle Red's bedmate. The second one was poisoned, like Dakota. The third monkey was a decoy that I planted in someone's trailer to take the fall for the ruse. As with Tiffany, there was a *decoy* doll in her crib. The fourth was electrocuted, like Lexy. And the last one was hung - Gampy's dogs were strangled, which is basically the same thing." As I looked over wide-eyed at Adam, I added, "The only other one exploded, but it's out of sequence so they may want us to believe that Tiffany is already dead. And there was something that Lexy had said after she overheard a conversation with the mysterious man and woman that was too strange to make sense out of at the time; 'The only thing left to do is to decide which baboon we want her to be.' That means they *are* going to kill her by an explosion of some sort. We have to be careful when going in; they may have the house or the room they're holding her in rigged with explosives."

"We will be. I'll go in first and you'll stay in the car."

"No, we'll go in together. I go where you go, remember?" I said. "Adam, there's something else. I've been thinking about it and I just have to get it out. Scorpions run rampant in this area. If Tiffany is here and gets stung, that might set her off into an asthmatic attack. Sorry, I just didn't want to carry that around inside myself anymore."

Adam leaned over and kissed me. "We'll find her, we're getting closer."

When Adam and I reached Joseph's ranch, he drove around a curve in the road and parked back behind some trees. We then needed a diversion for the bodyguards and staff that might be in the house. We lit a small fire on the road near the woods so that it would appear the woodlands were on fire. It was actually far enough away from the brush not to catch the whole area on fire. We waited until some people ran toward the fire and then snuck in. Adam and I skirted around everyone we saw and searched for any clues. One of the places we searched was Joseph's desk in his private office.

"Adam, look," I whispered, "I found something. This is Millie's name and telephone number - she worked on the Monkey Murders set. What would Joseph be doing with her number if she weren't involved? Millie was the set designer who I set up to take the fall for the disappearance of the original monkey."

"I thought you said the monkey did it?"

"I'll explain later, let's get out of here."

Adam and I searched as much of the house as we could without running the risk of being caught. Unfortunately, we couldn't get to the upper level. As we snuck out, I came across a photograph on the wall in the hallway. "Adam," I whispered pointing at the man standing in back of Joseph in the photo. He had a scar above is right eyebrow and snowy white hair. It was the Mr. Simmons who appeared in the photograph with Dakota at her school, and he also matched the description Uncle Red gave us of Mr. Rivers.

As we drove away, I noticed that Millie's telephone

area code indicated that she lived in Austin. We decided to drive the two hundred mile trip to see what we could learn from her. Adam and I went to the library and looked up her telephone number in the reverse telephone-number directory. We then drove to the house and sat in the car nearby waiting for someone to enter or exit the place. There was no activity for about an hour. The two of us weren't even sure it was the right place, but we waited. We were in the middle of deciding what to do next when someone drove up and got out. It was two large men who just walked into the unlocked house without knocking.

"This may not be Millie's place if these guys can just walk in unannounced," Adam said, commenting about their actions.

"Now what?" I asked.

"Let's see if the men bring anything out with them - say for instance, a small child."

We waited for twenty minutes and I could see that Adam was getting antsy. Then the men came out, but they had nothing with them. Adam said it was time to go in. The plan was that he would approach the front door and act like he was lost and in need of directions. Adam looked very different with his short brown hair and a mustache so hopefully Millie wouldn't recognize him from his films even though she was also in the film industry. We hoped the disguise would throw her off long enough for Adam to get Millie to open the door. Adam put on some gloves and made his way to her house.

Once Adam had Millie in front of him behind the slightly ajar door, he pushed his way in. I came up behind him and entered.

"Where is my baby?" I screamed.

"Walsh? You look different..."

"Where is my baby?" I repeated, interrupting her, ignoring what she was saying about my appearance.

"I don't have your baby," Millie said unconvincingly.

We searched the house, but didn't find Tiff. We did find evidence, however, that she'd had a child there.

Adam had Millie by the collar and about an inch off

the floor, somewhat choking her. "Where is she?" he demanded.

Millie then coughed out, "I thought it was a practical joke and that they weren't really going to kidnap anyone, just a dolly belonging to her. And I was scared to do anything about it when they gave me a real kid to hang onto."

"Gee, I don't know - maybe call the police," Adam fired back.

"She's always had it out for me," said Millie pointing at me.

"You're going to turn this around on me so it's my fault you're a kidnapper? You wicked woman. Just know this, I reward those who help me and eliminate those who don't."

"Where is our baby?!" Adam shrieked.

"They have her at the Matthews ranch."

"Liar! We were just there and she wasn't!"

"Those guys said they just spoke to their boss there and that's where she is - I swear."

"Who were those guys and what were they doing here?"

"They were here to, well, to..."

"Spit it out!"

"To pay me."

"You're going with us," said Adam.

"What?! I'm not going anywhere," blistered Millie.

"It's either us or the police. Or perhaps we'll just tell the Matthews boys you squealed on them and let them take care of you like they did a friend of ours who is now lying on a slab at the morgue. So, which is it *wicked* woman?" Adam demanded to know, mocking Millie with my title of her.

She tried to fight Adam, but he subdued Millie and duck-taped her hands and feet together. He then swiftly put her in the back seat of our car. All three of us made the trip back to the Matthews ranch and parked in the same place as we had before. Adam duck-taped Millie's mouth and then duck-taped her to a nearby tree. I said I was impressed and a little scared he knew how to do that.

"Yeah, maybe we can try that when we get home," he

teased. "This is going to be very dangerous - are you up for it?" He looked at me seriously. "You can always go back to the car. I'll bring her out."

"No way are you getting to do this all by yourself. We stay together, remember?" I said with confidence.

Chapter XXV

Taking Back My Life

We made our way into Joseph's ranch house. It seemed more deserted than the last time. No domestic staff was within our sight. That gave us reason to pause. Why would a Governor's house be void of security? Then we saw a guard standing just inside of a room toward the front of the house. It was this Mr. Rivers or Mr. Simmons guy with the white hair. He swung around as he drew his gun and said, "We've been expecting you."

Adam was close enough to the guy to swing a foot around him, and he knocked the gun out of the white-haired man's hand while demanding, "Where's my daughter?!"

This all came about so quickly, I barely saw what happened.

"Maybe she's in the same place I put your blonde bimbo friend," he said, backing up seemingly to stall for time. "The blonde wasn't easy to kill, a little trickier with that high voltage," he said, taunting Adam.

"I've come to get my daughter!" Adam reiterated.

While pulling a knife from his boot area, the white-haired man responded, "Over my dead body." He began waving the knife at Adam. Again, Adam swung his body around and kicked the man with such a great force that the guy crashed to the floor with his face downward. Adam quickly knelt down and put his other knee into the guy's back so he couldn't move.

I wanted to help by shooting him or something, but it all happened so fast that I wouldn't have gotten a good aim.

Also, I didn't want to shoot Adam by mistake, and have him die the same death as his father. So I stayed out of it.

"Acceptable," Adam said as he reached around and grabbed the man's chin, snapping his neck. After it snapped, the guard never made another sound.

After I saw Adam kill him with his bare hands, I stared right at him in amazement. At first, I think he thought I was disgusted or appalled that he could kill someone. But then I smirked and said, "You know, on some level, I thought all that Nam stuff was a load of crap, but I gotta say, I'm impressed." I knew that was shallow, but I didn't care. The menace deserved to die for what he did to us, to our family, to Lexy, to Tiffany, to Uncle Red, and to Gampy's *little babies*. The list was infinite.

We walked down the hallway toward the stairs and were ambushed by two guards. One lunged at us before Adam took him down with his knife. I could see that the other guard had a gun in his hand, so I emptied the clip in my gun into him. I released the clip and it clanged to the floor. Then I removed another clip from my pocket and loaded it into the gun.

"Who are you - Dirty Harriet? Nice shooting," Adam teased.

"You can thank Tracy for that," I answered.

We looked around for any other surprises. Adam and I were sure that the noise from the gunfire would bring out anyone else at the ranch. We continued up the stairs to the upper level, and as I turned the corner, I could hear child-like whimpering. I walked to the doorway of the room where the sound was coming from, and came upon Joseph clutching Tiffany. Assuming he heard my earlier gunshots, Joseph appeared prepared for our arrival by smiling nefariously at me as I walked in. I raised my gun straight out and pointed it directly at him. My face turned cold and stoic. Adam hadn't reached the doorway yet, but saw my reaction which gave him a warning that Joseph was in the room. Joseph was standing in front of an opened sliding glass door. He was clenching Tiffany by the scruff of the neck of her pajamas. He then brought her within inches of the balcony's edge. Tiff was calm, but she began whining after she saw me. She had her arms out for her mommy.

"You shoot me, I'll toss her off," Joseph said, threatening me.

Adam walked up and entered the room, sidestepping toward the balcony with his knife out and ready. I tried to focus and not pay too much attention to what Tiffany wanted or even my impulse to look directly into her eyes. I knew that would only slow me down and give her reason to start crying, which would only worsen her medical condition.

Adam was defenseless to help her. Joseph was goading me as he began swinging Tiff over the thirty-foot drop. He ordered me to lower the gun and told Adam to put down his knife and back away. We both complied. I lowered my gun, but I hadn't dropped it. I tried concealing it by stepping behind a high-back chair. I then tried distracting Joseph by talking to get his mind off what Adam was doing - which was moving toward a window off the balcony.

"That's not actually blowing her up, Joseph. Why deviate from the plan you had going? Now the police are going to think it's a poor job of a copycat."

"Don't you think the insides of her body will explode if I dropped her off this balcony?" he said with malice.

"I'll trade myself for my baby, Joseph," I said. "That's what you wanted anyway, wasn't it? You can destroy the evidence - me. But you have to let her go free. If you kill her, you know we're going to kill you just like we killed your henchmen." I wanted Joseph to know that we were capable of killing and that he no longer had backup to help him. "Let her go, Joseph, and you walk out of here unharmed," I said as I eased my way to the adjacent side of the room so Adam would be on Joseph's blind side.

"Shut up, I'm calling the shots here," Joseph barked angrily. "You know nothing about what I want..." I let him ramble, positioning myself further over so he would lose total sight of Adam. "...You know nothing about how important I am. I'll be the ruler of this country soon and you're not going to ruin that for me. You were never suppose to be allowed to live. Had Lillian told me, you wouldn't have. But I'll deal with her later. Perhaps she'll have an accident and I'll get the sympathy vote for being a widower," he said snorting. "I guess I should have been more careful when I killed that pregnant woman thirty years ago," Joseph said as he taunted me by showing what appeared to be a gun nestled in his belt.

"Kill the wrong woman, did you *Pops*?" I asked mockingly.

"Apparently so - I thought I'd killed your mother with you still inside her."

"You couldn't even remember what she looked like from a few months earlier? Well, that explains the ghostly look I got from you during our first meeting," I said, keeping his thoughts busy on me. "Zoë would be dead right now if you'd had - ever consider that?"

"Casualties of war, my dear," Joseph raved like a madman passionately. "Women are only born to bred rulers, but I have a son who will carry on the family name. And there's a bigger picture here." As Joseph spoke insanely, he took a step closer allowing Tiffany a margin of safety.

"Bigger than family?" I asked hostilely.

"If you have to ask that, you'll never understand the answer," he responded sarcastically. "Now, all I have to do is complete my framing of you for the kidnapping. I'll place your dead bodies amongst all this evidence and then simply leave. That way, you won't have any credibility for what you may have already blabbed to the press. And with those disguises you're wearing, the police will think you didn't want anyone to know that you were here. Why else would you be wearing them? No one would be wearing disguises to save their child - they'd want the world to know they had. Then, all that's left to do will be to make various adjustments on a few documents. And don't worry, I'll take care of your mother for you, and this time I won't get confused."

As Joseph kept ranting and focusing his attention on me, Adam had exited the open window on the opposite side of the room and positioned himself on the balcony to secure Tiffany's safety. Suddenly, Adam managed to grab her away from Joseph. Realizing that he had no leverage over us anymore, Joseph stepped into the room toward me while reaching down toward his belt. And just after I knew Tiffany was safely out of my gunshot range, I lifted my arm straight out and fired my gun. The blast exploded into Joseph's chest. Cold. Ruthless. Precise.

I stood there for a moment before realizing that our threat no longer existed. Then I walked toward him as my arm lowered, stopped and stood over him while saying, "I guess I'm a chip off the old block after all, hey *Pops*? Boom, exploded." That's when I reached down to him and checked for a pulse. Not to find one, but to make sure there wasn't one.

I took Tiffany from Adam's arms and hugged her close. I assessed her condition, and since she was wheezing a little, I gave her some medicine.

Before taking our daughter out of that horrible place, Adam and I had to make a few adjustments. I wiped my gun clean, along with the empty gun clip that was on the floor in the hallway and the one that I loaded into the gun. Adam pressed the white-haired guy's right hand all around the gun and clips before tossing the gun off the balcony and dropping the empty clip on the floor. Adam hadn't touched the knife with his bare hands, so we then pressed the white-haired guy's prints on it, making it appear that he killed both of the other guards who had ambushed us in the hallway. After tossing the white-haired man off the balcony, we turned Joseph's body around. It then appeared that the white-haired guy had shot Joseph, forcing him to fall backwards off the balcony, breaking his neck in the process.

Once in the car, Adam turned to me and asked with concern, "How are you doing?"

I smiled over at him while I held our daughter close and said, "Never bedda." I made a quick pre-arranged call to Mom before we drove the four-hour drive from Houston to the Dallas airport. We wiped the wreck clean of fingerprints, then abandoned it in the long-term parking lot. Since we didn't use our real names to purchase the car, no one would know it belonged to us. We removed our disguises and hopped onto a flight home.

Adam insisted that he get to hold Tiffany at least a

little while once on the flight home. I laughed and said, "Have mercy on my heart," and gave her to him. She slept in his arms until we reached Los Angeles.

We got our facts and story straight before we had disembarked in L.A. We were soon spotted by the press. They surrounded us and speared a million questions at us. We quickly jumped into the Land Rover, but not before responding, "We found her in an abandoned warehouse in Dallas."

We went straight to the hospital to get Tiffany checked out. She was a little upset, but perfect in every other way.

When we returned to the house, the police were still there with their tracking equipment set up. The detective asked us some questions as we secured our daughter's bedroom and got her into bed.

"Where have you been for the past few days?" he asked. "We had just heard from a news source that you were staying at a nearby hotel, but we hadn't had a chance to check out those facts yet to see if it was true or if you were kidnapped too."

"Adam and I needed to have some time alone to pray for our daughter so we went to the chapel," I answered. "We knew everyone at home was safe so we then decided to check into a hotel here in Los Angeles to get some clarity about everything that was happening. Adam doesn't like guns and so many of your officers had one, that we just couldn't come back here."

"How did you know where your daughter was?"

"An anonymous telephone caller."

"How do you think they knew where you were?"

"On the way to the hotel, we stopped and made a telephone call to a 'not so uncorrupted source' we knew from a friend of a friend of a friend - if you know what I mean. Actually, I don't even know the guy's name, but the word is that if the crime was done in Los Angeles, this guy knows about it. Anyway, he came out to the hotel and spoke to us in the parking lot. We gave him our room number and asked the guy to call with any information about Tiffany. After about an hour, we received an anonymous call in our hotel room. The caller said to go to Dallas to get our daughter, but we had to wait forty-eight hours before leaving. They told us not to tell anyone, especially the police. Then the caller told us Tiffany's location, and said their people would kill Tiff if we deviated from these instructions at all. Then the caller hung up. Since we knew you had everything under control here, we figured we would at least attempt to locate her."

"Where did you find your daughter?"

"At an abandoned warehouse on the other side of Dallas. They had us take a bus there. I don't remember exactly, but here are the directions they gave us," I said as I passed the detective the notepad from the Los Angeles hotel room.

"Is she okay? Do you want us to call an ambulance to have her checked out?"

"No thank you, we just got back from the hospital. That's the first place we took her."

I'm not sure he believed my story. However, they packed up their equipment and left.

After our ordeal and with Tiffany now back home with her family, Gamma wasted no time in fixing us all dinner - we talked about the great aroma. Gampy was in his workshop sharpening the blades on Adam's knives. Mom and Uncle Red were in the family room having a bonfire with wigs, IDs and other assorted apparatus.

Chapter XXVI

Justice for Lexy

You see, the police never had to perform an investigation on Adam and I after that day, because we were at the Los Angeles hotel when the massacre took place at the ranch, right? Well, our doubles were. My phone calls were placed to Mom at her alcoholics in recovery meetings about staging our alibis. Mom dressed up in my clothes, plus a large floppy hat and big round dark sunglasses that hid most of her face. It was Joseph who actually gave me the idea when he said I could be her double with only some dark glasses. Uncle Red, with his dark skin like Adam's, donned a long black wig we left at the hotel room for him which we got from my makeup artist friend. We left the hotel key in the Land Rover we left in the hotel parking lot. Our doubles were seen at the hotel a couple of times during those few days to establish our alibis. They only appeared briefly and from a distance as to not be bombarded by the press surrounding Tiffany's kidnapping. Mom and Uncle Red wore hats and glasses also to appear as though the real Jordan and Adam would be shrouding themselves from the press.

We had mapped out our every move for our fabricated story of reaching our daughter in Dallas. We located a warehouse from the telephone pages and a Dallas map with the city bus routes for the warehouse. We even had a notepad we took from the Los Angeles hotel with their logo complete with written instructions from the anonymous fictitious kidnapper. We took the notepad with us to Dallas and I wrote the instructions down once we gathered information in Dallas just in case they questioned us about it; we would have the details straight. We also had Mom call us at the hotel from a payphone so there would be a record of it at the hotel switchboard - AKA, our call from the anonymous caller.

After we secured Tiffany's safety, we made our prearranged call to Mom and Uncle Red at the hotel and had them drive to the airport in the Land Rover and park it in the long-term parking. Then they purchased round-trip plane tickets in our names, and flew to Dallas being seen in their Jordan and Adam disguises. Once in the terminal at the Dallas airport, they went into their respective bathrooms, changed clothes and removed their wigs. The four of us met for just an instant to exchange clothing, identifications, car keys and airplane tickets, and then they disappeared. We hung out at the airport just long enough after they arrived to simulate the pick up of our daughter from the bus schedule time frame. Mom's excuse for being away from the house was her meetings that she needed more now than ever because of Tif's disappearance. And Uncle Red still had clients to see.

I had called Larry to have the press at the airport so we could establish witnesses that would put us there, coming off a flight from Dallas, and to make a short statement of where we had found Tiffany. We jumped into the Land Rover that was at the airport, right where Mom and Uncle Red said they left it.

Later that week, the police told us of the ranch massacre. We appeared shocked and appalled at such violence, as if we didn't know anything about any dead bodies.

The police discovered the inside source that we suspected was there at the house. They found out that the supervisor for the party events deposited one million dollars into an investment account, but oddly not with the marked money from the kidnapper's ransom. Sam later told us that the supervisor had given him some wedding cake and told him that he didn't want the girls to think they were being left out of the festivities. He asked if Sam would go and give it to them. That's when the supervisor probably observed Sam going into Mom's suite with it. Sam said it seemed innocent enough.

Millie was the one who wrote the ransom note that was found in Tiffany's crib; in fact, her fingerprints were all over it. However, the police didn't know that until they found Millie and fingerprinted her because her prints were not on file with them. Adam said that after hearing this, he didn't feel so bad about leaving her there duct-taped to the tree to ward off creatures, even the ones who carried guns and shot her in the head while being taped to that tree. The money that the police found at her house was also unmarked.

We had abolished everyone involved with Lexy's murder, along with the rest of the wrongdoers against us.

Chapter XXVII

Saving My Best Friend's Soul

Once Tiffany was back with us and the paperwork was concluded a few days later, they released Lexy's body. We never did find out what was on her body which was so mysterious that they wouldn't release her earlier. I was grateful for it though; the stall gave me a chance to say good-bye to my friend. Otherwise, I would have been too preoccupied with Tiffany's ordeal to have attended Lexy's funeral. I guess since the case was closed, they didn't need to release any further information - including what was on Lexy.

Lexy's Mom released her body to our care so we could bring her home. Adam and I flew Lexy's body back to London, back to her home, back to her family. It was time to go bury our friend. We made arrangements for the funeral home to assume her casket from the airport. Adam and I then checked into our hotel and had a quiet evening. I knew it was going to be emotional the following day.

Lexy's mother was sobbing and standing over the casket when we arrived for the funeral. We walked in, and as Adam sat down, I went up to Lexy's mother and gave her a hug. She hugged me tight and said how happy Lexy would be knowing I was there. That about sent me over the edge, but I knew I had to be strong for Lexy. I went over and sat down next to Adam. Suddenly, I leaned over and whispered to him in a panic, "Where are my notes? I have to have my notes. I don't know how I will focus on talking and not falling apart up there if I don't have my notes."

"You'll be fine - just say what's in your heart," he said compassionately.

"That's what I mean - if I do that, I'll fall apart."

When it was my turn to speak, I walked up to the podium, my legs shaking. I put my hand in my pocket and found the notes. "What can I say about Lexy?" I began. "Just that she was there for *every single* main event of my life. She was more than just there; she was a sister. She was there for my first big movie role. She was there the first time I went to the Acclamation Awards. She was there for countless birthdays. She was there when I met my first love. She was right beside me when I was to marry my first love. She was there when I fell apart over the loss of him. She was there when my girls were born - right there in the delivery room coaching me on - of course, we had to resuscitate her a few times, but she was *there*. One of my daughters even bares her name. Lexy was my maid of honor when I married my husband, Adam. She was there for me when Foxy, my beloved dog of fourteen years, passed away. She was the kind of person who was always there when her friends needed her. She never left my side for one minute." I turned and looked up toward heaven before adding, "Bye Pookie."

I cried most of the way back from London. Poor Adam, he didn't know what to do for me. In fact, I didn't know what I wanted him to do for me. I sat there and stared out the window at nothing. I thought of Lexy, I thought of our good times together. I thought of her beautiful smile. I thought of her beautiful heart - a heart so beautiful that she was probably trying to save her namesake when she died. Then Adam and I started talking about how Lexy died. She was electrocuted based on the events of the Monkey Murders and that was premeditated, which made me feel Lexy was killed for more than just being there at the wrong place. She knew what could ruin the chances for Joseph's son to follow in his father's footsteps. The same thing that brought Joseph down. A child. An innocent child. I'm sure that if Joseph knew where Lexy's son was all those years growing up, he'd have killed him too. That's probably the only thing that saved

the boy - Dirk's embarrassment from the event and unwilling-
ness to stay involved with his son. Adam and I wanted to do
something honorable for Lexy to repay her for everything that
she'd done for us. Near the end of the plane ride, I turned
and looked upward to say, "Thanks Lexy, I owe you everything. We will take care of Aidan, your son." Adam smiled
and nodded.

It didn't take long before more trouble found us again.
Dirk vowed that he would seek his revenge, even though he
said he couldn't prove we had anything to do with his
father's death. He said he felt it and would make sure we felt
his sting. We didn't know what he had in store for us, but if
he was anything like his father, we would probably have to
nip that in the bud as well. Dirk came into our lives full force
now. He would show up wherever we were, like a stalker.
Fortunately, Adam and I didn't leave the grounds very often
so we didn't have to put up with his glares.

One of the more minor offenses Dirk cooked up was
that he'd make digs at Tommy by calling me Sissy. Tommy
seethed over that - Sissy was his name for me and he didn't
want Dirk to taint it for him.

Then when Dirk caught wind of us trying to adopt
Aidan, he petitioned the courts for custody. This child was
about to be used as a pawn. Dirk claimed he knew nothing
of the birth and the original adoption and that he had father's
rights. I knew better - not only did he know, but Dirk also
paid for everything when Lexy had dropped out of sight in
Hollywood. I knew because I visited Lexy and even helped
deliver her baby. Dirk was there briefly just to sign the
adoption papers, giving the child away.

I knew Adam and I had to be clever to do what was
right for Lexy's son. We sought the help of one of the police
officers who set up the telephone tracing equipment when
Tiffany was taken. He gave me a wiring device for recording
conversations. If Dirk was anything like his father, I knew he
would be arrogant enough to implicate himself. Dirk agreed
to meet me, secretly, in the parking basement of an apartment building. He was pompous and sneered at me when I

approached.

"You will never get custody of that kid," he boasted.

"Maybe, maybe not. What do you think Lexy would have wanted? You told her to take care of it when his adoptive parents died."

"I don't care what *Lexy* would have wanted," Dirk said mocking her to taunt me.

"And what about your mother? Have you told her she's a grandmother?"

"She knows and she doesn't care. What are you doing here? What do you want? Oh, just forget it - you won't get whatever you're wanting so don't bother."

"Is that right?" I said sarcastically. "And what about Zoë?"

"What about her?"

"Does she know that you fathered a child, then abandoned it - only to come back and use it as a pawn in a sick revenge plot against me?"

"Well, you think highly of yourself. Who cares about you? Who says I'm doing this for revenge?"

"The county clerk you bribed."

"How do you know about that?"

"I have my sources. So, no denials - no big show of outrage?"

"You have no proof I did anything."

"I don't have to have proof. I can just withhold any further medical help from Zoë ever again. How's that sound? One life for another. Her liver is still unstable."

"I'll take that chance just to piss you off."

"That's quite a risk. You'd forfeit your sister's life for a son you don't want or care about only to piss me off? How about I tell Zoë about this? How do you think she'll react?"

"It doesn't matter. She'll never believe you over me," Dirk said as he turned to walk away.

"Will she believe you over you?" I asked as he turned to see that I was showing him the wire I was wearing.

Just then, Adam and the officer jumped out of the van we parked there prior to the meeting.

Shortly thereafter when hearing the tape played by the

police officer, the county clerk admitted Dirk paid her $100,000 to destroy the paperwork on Aidan's first adoption so he could get custody. She copped a plea and Dirk was arrested for bribery. We figured it was her because I knew he was aware of his son and she was the clerk who was assigned to handle the paperwork. The officer also suspected her of wrong-doing in other cases and was thrilled when we came to him for the sting.

Adam, Uncle Red and I went to court. The judge asked for our petition statement for temporary custody toward the final adoption of Aidan. Then the judge asked why I wanted custody, more in-depth than what was written on our petition.

I stood and stated, "Thank you, your honor. I'm very familiar with the court's procedures on custody. As you might know, I was a ward of the courts when I was about Aidan's age, so I know the feelings that he is experiencing about all of this, and I believe we can make a compassionate transition for him. And also, we made a promise to his biological mother, Alexandria Sherman-Reger - and our friendship was legendary. With the deepest respect your honor, that promise to care for Lexy's son, keep him safe, and make sure he knows he's loved is a higher statute to us than any other."

Fortunately for Adam and I, the judge was amused and also so moved by my allegiance to Lexy that he granted us temporary custody. Final adoption would be postponed until we could be assessed by the courts through visits from a social worker. It was one of the happiest times of my life. I was so pleased that I could do this for Lexy after all she had done for me. I had kept my promise to her.

I had to collect myself for a moment. I didn't want Aidan to see this crazed woman crying over him after all that he'd been through. I then walked over to him at the back of the courtroom, and sat in an adjacent chair to his. "Hi Aidan, how are you?" I asked with a gentle smile on my face.

He shrugged with his head down, staring at his feet while swinging them back and forth. The ten-year-old seemed confused as to where he was and why.

I introduced Aidan to everyone. "I'm Jordan and this is my husband, Adam. See that nice man over there? He's my Uncle Red. He helped all of us in court today. Would it be okay if we all went out in the hall to talk a while?"

He nodded, then asked, "Can Nanna come with us?"

"Of course she can, and she can stay as long as you want her to."

We walked out to the hall and sat down on one of the benches. "Aidan, do you know why you are here today?"

He shook his head from side to side.

"You are here because your parents are gone now and Nanna isn't able to care for you. We are here asking the judge if it would be okay if we took you home with us. I know it sounds scary because I was in your shoes when I was about your age."

That got Aidan's attention, and he looked up from the ground and asked, "Really, what did you do wrong?"

"Wrong? Oh sweetie, I didn't do anything wrong to be there back then, and you didn't do anything wrong either to be here today. You aren't being punished for anything, Aidan. Is that what you thought?"

"Yes," he said putting his head back down.

"No. Sometimes bad things happen to nice people. I know because that's what happened to your parents and that's what happened to a real good friend of ours. And that is why we are here today. You didn't do anything wrong. Aidan - Adam and I would like you to come home with us to be a part of our family now."

"Why?"

"Well, for many reasons. For one, I made a promise to someone close to me that I would keep you safe. Another reason is I think you are a pretty nice kid and I want to help you just as someone once helped me when I needed it."

"Who?"

"My grandparents. They adopted my brother and I when we needed help and when we needed a home. And for all the other reasons we can tell you over time because I don't want you getting overwhelmed with details right now.

You have enough to handle with having a new home to go to. Would you like to come see our house and maybe you'll stay a while and make it your home too?"

"Do you have enough room for me?"

"Yes," I answered smiling, "we have miles of room, and even if we didn't, we'd make room." Then I paused as I looked out the front door through the glass at the press hovering there. I added, "Aidan, there are a lot of people who are interested in what's going on in here today and they are outside waiting to see us. I wanted you to know that because it may seem a little scary to someone not expecting it. They'll have cameras that make bright flashes and they'll be asking you questions. We won't be talking to them today, instead we'll just go straight to the car and get in. Would it be okay if I held your hand to the car?" I asked.

He nodded.

We all walked out of the courthouse together. After we said good-bye to Nanna, I asked Aidan, "How do you feel about little sisters? You'll have lots of them."

"No brothers?" he asked teasing me a little.

"Not yet," I said looking at Adam, teasing him.

And while the press surrounded us and shouted their questions, I continued talking to Aidan as if we were alone so it would keep his mind off their aggressiveness. "We have dogs, cats and bunnies and even some horses."

Aidan's eyes got brighter as we all started to get into the car. Adam pulled me closer to him from the driver's seat as Uncle Red got Aidan belted in behind us. I leaned over to Adam and said, "Have mercy on my heart."

"No, no, you can't use that now - that's my line," Adam said as he kissed me. He added, "Let's take our son home, shall we?"

I nodded to Adam as the paparazzi snapped furiously into the car at us.

Aidan's eyes were as wide as saucers when he saw the house and even wider when he saw his room. He asked, "Do we live at this hotel or do we have to work here?"

Adam and I just smiled at each other. I said, "This is our home, Aidan. The only work you'll be doing here is homework."

He scrunched up his nose at my comment.

Mom settled Aidan into his new room. She was in her element, fussing over Aidan as she did with Tommy as a boy. Meanwhile, Adam called Dakota and told her she had a new brother now only a few months older than her. Dakota was thrilled, but then asked if she could still have the responsibility for caring for her younger sisters like she was taught. Adam told her it was her duty to and that Aidan and her could both do it together. He added that since Aidan was older, it was his responsibility to watch over all of them, including her. I think Dakota was happy that she didn't lose much seniority while gaining another sibling.

The court-ordered social worker didn't waste any time and made a visit the same day we brought Aidan home. We gave her a tour of our house and of Aidan's room, barely ahead of getting Aidan settled into his new room himself. We granted her unfettered access to speak to anyone on the grounds, and told her she would have that courtesy during any of her visits.

We had to explain to the social worker the situation regarding Mom's suite. Without getting too deep into the back story on the kidnapping, we basically said that the suite would be off limits to Aidan for now. The room where the dogs were slain in was being gutted and remodeled. We were also having every other place where the blood had touched removed and reconstructed.

Of all the animals, Aidan said he liked Pasta the best. He said this was because he would laugh the most when she licked his toes. I think the ten-year-old went without his socks purposely just to get the giggles that first day. Snuggles liked Aidan the best of all of us in just the short time since she met him. She would bring Aidan her ball and place it down in front of him. I don't know if Snuggles was just jealous of the time he spent with Pasta, or what, but she wouldn't let anyone else touch that ball but him.

The first night, Aidan had a hard time feeling comfortable enough to fall asleep. I meandered over to his room to check on him. I could hear him crying. I popped my head into his room and said, "Hi Aidan honey, how are you doing?"

He sat up in bed and shrugged.

I sat down in the chaise lounge chair in his room and asked, "Would you like to sit with me a while?"

He said okay and sat down next to me. I pulled the afghan off the back of the chair and laid it over Aidan while I talked to him. He soon fell asleep. I felt so comfortable there, that I too, fell asleep. I awoke in the morning to the sound of Adam's voice and with him tenderly kissing me.

"There you are - I wondered where you ran off to. I hate waking up without you," he whispered.

"I'm right here, with your son," I said smiling up at him. I swear I heard Adam giggle a little when I said the word "son" to him.

Aidan woke and smiled at us. "I'm glad both of you are here."

Adam smiled widely and off they went together. Adam said something about teaching his son how to shave. "What?!" I asked as they laughed at me. I was hoping that Adam was kidding and that they went to brush their teeth or something sane. But they were bonding and that was good.

Gampy was feeling depressed about his *little babies*, so Gamma went down to the animal shelter and adopted a few more *little babies* for him. The household was all in attendance when she presented them to him. "These aren't to replace those you lost," Gamma explained to him, "because you can't replace loved ones - but to give you the ability to provide others with love and care. I know that is too mushy for you, but it's true."

Gampy blushed, and after the dogs began jumping and romping with him, he was smiling for the first time since that horrible day.

One day soon thereafter, I finally got a moment to sit down and just do nothing. I was feeling run-down and just wanted to sit and watch the children play. I looked over at Aidan playing with Pasta and Snuggles, and I couldn't believe what I saw. With all that was going on, I hadn't noticed it.

"Wow, you look just like her," I said, not even knowing I had spoken the words out loud.

"Like who?" Aidan asked.

"Your mother."

"You knew my mother?"

"Yes, I knew the mother who gave birth to you."

"Is that the nice lady you told me about - that bad things happened to?"

"Yes, she was my best friend."

"Will you tell me about her sometime?"

"I'll start every single one of your days telling you something about her," I answered. "Starting with, she was so special to me, that your sister Tiffany has her middle name." I felt tears starting to form. Just then, Gamma entered the family room and looked at my watering eyes.

"Jordan dear, are you okay?"

"Never bedda, Gamma," I said after taking a deep breath. "I'm just enjoying being with my children." But that wasn't entirely true. Beyond the tears, physically, I had been feeling extremely nauseous in the past few weeks. It's no wonder, in all of the excitement recently, I had failed to notice that my body was changing. Then, a few days ago, I did know something was amiss - enough to administer a home pregnancy test. Yep, I was pregnant again. When I told Gamma, she beamed.

I asked her, "Does this qualify as a good deed today, Gamma?"

She laughed and said, "Yes, in a big way!"

I tried to find a different manner in which to tell Adam about the baby this time, rather than just blurting it out like last time. I was dreaming up something more romantic, and into about my fourth month of pregnancy, I came up with something fun. I had Gamma do the sneaky stuff for me. We filled the Party Barn with lavender roses. I had Brandy type up a menu with a baby food theme: baby back ribs, baby spring vegetables, baby-shaped pasta and baby chocolate souffles, and we positioned the menus on

Adam's place setting. Gamma also tied little booties to the backs of our chairs and had Eddie serve us sparkling cider. I put a tiny rubber ducky in Adam's glass, along with pacifiers as beverage charms around the stems of the glasses.

Adam let me sit there at the table for an hour trying to get him to notice the baby theme, but he was just teasing me - he really had noticed it at the beginning of the evening. "What a nefarious trick to play on a pregnant woman," I said as we laughed. Then the rest of the family joined us for our *baby* party.

"Don't you think I know every inch of my wife's body? I probably knew before you did," Adam said as I had a surprised look on my face. "So when do you think this one happened?" he asked nonchalantly continuing to eat his dinner.

"I'm thinking just around the time we came back from your last film - don't you remember?" I asked as I leaned over toward him so others couldn't hear me. "If it's a girl, we'll name her *Golden Wheat*," I whispered in his ear hintingly.

"Ohhhh, yeah, mummm. That was soooo..."

"Adam!" I said as everyone laughed.

"I already know what I'm going to name him," he announced.

"Oh, this should be good," I sarcastically responded as my arms were folded while staring at him. "What do you mean *you* name him? And what do you mean *him*?"

"Yep, his name will be Flannagan Adam Maguire?"

"You want to name our son Flannagan Maguire?!"

"Why? What's wrong with that?"

"What do you mean what's wrong with that? That's an Irish alcoholic just waiting to grow up." Everyone laughed. "Flannagan? I can see a *huge* therapy bill in his future."

"Yeah, okay - we'll talk."

"And aren't you closer to your Native American roots than the Irish ones? Even if it's a boy, at least *Golden Wheat* would sound authentically Native without sending the poor kid into therapy."

Adam nodded while eating his souffle. "Yes, but

you're Irish too, ya know."

"Never in my life did I think I would have six kids. We are so lucky."

"What makes you think we're stopping at six?" Adam said just before jumping out of my reach. "I had my mind set on a baseball team that Tommy would coach after his retirement." Everyone laughed, especially Tommy - except me, of course.

"You sure have an awful lot to say for someone who won't be giving birth," I added as I mocked being pregnant by waddling up to the dessert table for the second time. We had a wonderful time that night. Everyone was happy, everyone was healthy, and everyone was home safe.

Aidan appeared to be feeling more like a part of the family. We had pampered him at first, but then slowly let that fade. We didn't want him to feel like he stood out. Aidan was one of the family and everyone was treated equally. He had asked what he should call everyone. I told him he should decide what he felt most comfortable with. Since we were all equal, he said he wanted to call everyone what everyone else was calling everyone. That felt good to me.

In addition to teaching my children that knowledge is the most powerful tool they would ever possess, I filled my days with teaching my children things I learned from Gamma in my childhood. This included good manners, cooking and charitable good deeds. One day he asked me, "Mom, why do I need to do all of this homework - I don't want to."

"Well, Aidan honey, let's ask the magic mirror. Come over here, and stand in front of the mirror and answer this question... What is it called when a butterfly flaps its wings in England that can distort the stir of the earth's waterways to form a hurricane off the coast of Florida?"

"Huh?" he asked as Adam walked in and stood behind both of us facing the mirror.

"No, don't ask me - ask the magic mirror," I instructed.

"I don't get it," Aidan said as he looked into the mirror with a scrunched up face. Then he asked the mirror, "What's the answer?"

"Only you can answer that, Aidan," I told him. "However, while we're here, I want you to look at your face when you say that. Is that the face you want to have the rest of your life, all scrunched up like that? Because when someone else asks you a question that you don't know the answer to, that's the face they're going to see. Or would you rather have a face like this?" I exaggerated my smile widely and continued as we both were still looking into the mirror, "Why yes, Mrs. Maguire, that's called the butterfly effect." I then gave Aidan both expressions as examples - smiling, scrunching, smiling, scrunching.

Finally, he said, "I want Dad's face," pointing at Adam who was smiling at all of our silly faces we were making.

"That's a very nice choice, Aidan, and what a beautiful angelic face it is," I said smiling at Adam.

I didn't want all of the other children to feel left out with all the gifts the new baby was already receiving, even before the birth. So I bought all four of my daughters hair brushes with lilac-scented handles just like Gampy bought Gamma and I years ago. And Adam and I gave Aidan an all-in-one Swiss Army knife. He loved it. I wasn't sure I wanted him to have a knife yet, but I trusted Adam to deal with it. And he did, teaching Aidan how to respect its sharpness. I thought maybe Dakota might think we were favoring Aidan by giving him a different kind of gift, a grown-up gift, but she is a girly-girl and loved her hair brush. I also secretly included some makeup in Dakota's gift and knew Adam would have had a melt-down if he even suspected she was growing up without his permission.

This time, we decided that it was Adam's turn to determine whether or not we'd find out the sex of the baby beforehand, and he said no. So we waited. That about killed Gamma. She's a planner. She loves to plan everything about everything. She even had lists to organize her lists. Gamma kept complaining that she wouldn't have enough time to decorate the nursery in the traditional blues or pinks. I told her to just use both because with my luck, Adam would give me one of each. Adam about fainted when he heard me say that - only because it would get him closer to his baseball team.

When Adam asked me what I was getting him for his birthday that year, I said nothing and just looked at him while pointing to my stomach. He laughed and said, "How did you know? That's exactly what I wanted."

But I did manage to get him a little something. Still it was very difficult trying to think of the right gift for him. I mean, what do you get a guy who has everything? But I knew his family was the most important thing to Adam, so I commissioned a painter to paint one gigantic mural on the arcade room walls representing everyone's life in the house. There were many different poses of us. There was one with Adam and I sipping make-believe tea at a tea party with our four daughters, who had daisies and tiger lilies in their hair. Another was him with Aidan playing catch. There was one with all of the children letting frogs hop off their hands while a rainbow spanned behind them. There was one with Adam holding his not-yet-born baby in his arms as he looked down at the bundle with his angelic face. And there was one of just the two of us standing together in a field of golden wheat next to a scarecrow with its scarf waving in the wind, and another of us dancing with our triplets hobbling in a circle around us. I also included about six others with our children that symbolized special moments in our lives. All the rest of the family was in the background somewhere and it was sort of a game for Adam to find them. Some of them were standing behind trees, lying under park benches, or wherever. There was one with Pasta and Snuggles rolling on the grass, wiggling upside down and waggling their tails. I even had him paint Foxy up in the clouds. Foxy Lady had a halo on her head and was wagging her tail as Lexy petted her. Gampy's *little babies* were also sitting close by them. The mural was magical. Adam loved it. In fact, he teared up after he saw everyone looking back at him in the walls.

When Gamma asked what I wanted for my thirtieth birthday, I joked, "A big I.V. full of pain-killing drugs for the birth of this Tyrannosaurus growing inside of me."

All she said was, "If you didn't want to ferment the

Merlot, you shouldn't have let that winemaker plant his vineyard." Then Gamma smiled, commenting about how befitting and clever she was.

"No Gamma, wine ain't gonna be strong enough for this occasion," I bantered as I found just enough energy to hop out of the way of her stinging kitchen towel snap, even as big as I was.

Adam and I attended the Acclamation Awards that year with Tracy close by while entering and exiting the auditorium. Well, I "waddled to them" was more like it at seven months pregnant. I had been out of the public-eye for months tending to and enjoying my family instead of working, and it was a shock to many at the ceremony to see how much my stomach had expanded. We were both up for awards. Mine was first. I was up for a film I did a year ago January. I had decided at the time to do one more film before my hiatus officially began. The story was much like my story with Jack. I had poured everything into the role that I had to give. I don't know if Adam ever made the connection.

I won the Ack Award for Best Supporting Actress. After arriving at the podium, I said, "Sorry *we* took so long to get up here," as I tried to figure out which way to position my stomach. That gave the audience time to laugh at my joke. Then I took a deep breath. "This isn't my first Acclamation Award, even though it's the first that I've won. Lexy bequeathed hers to me and now she and I have two. We were best friends and what was mine was hers. I want to thank my family and friends, my five and a half children, and I'll get demolished if I don't thank Larry Wozowski, my agent. Dakota honey, we miss you. I also want to thank my dear sweet husband, Adam, for being there with me in every step of this journey called life. You're amazing." I blew him a kiss and exited the stage while hurrying back to my seat for his nomination announcement.

By now, Adam had made quite a name for himself in Hollywood on his own without my help. He won Best Actor for his film with the Jack look-alike. That's when I knew he *was* a great actor. If Adam could pull off making people believe that he was that jerk's best friend, he could do anything. Adam had a wonderful speech prepared that he wouldn't let me hear before that night. When he reached the podium, Adam said, "I want to thank the cast and crew from the film. I want to thank my wonderful agent for getting me such great scripts. I want to also thank my family and friends for supporting me. And Dakota, we miss you. But I want to especially thank my wife, JoJo, for proving every single day that there is a merciful God smiling down on us. Have mercy on my heart, I love you."

I was an elated emotional mess, and my hormones were taking over my body. Adam had never been so vocal about his feelings before, especially in public. People were all looking back at me and smiling at his public display of affection through his wonderful words, and I was crying like a baby. It was a good night, but all Adam and I kept thinking was that we wanted to spend it with our family at home.

"I finally won an Ack Award," I said to Lexy's award sitting on our mantel at home. "When Larry sent me that script, he said it was going to win me my Ack Award. He was right." I set my Acclamation Award right next to Lexy's, then Adam set his on the other side. He said we would both stand beside her forever. I wept at his good heart.

It all kind of made me wonder - if we didn't have the adversity of Jack in our lives, would we have done as well with our respective roles?

As my due date approached, I knew this would be a much harder birth for me, even though Dr. Easton *promised* I was only having a single-birth baby. That's because Lexy wasn't there to coach me. Okay... there to humor me with distractions so the pain wouldn't be as bad. That made me sad so I decided to tell Aidan about the day he was born to take my mind off it.

"I was there the day you were born, and you were amazing."

"How so?"

"You weren't expected for another couple of weeks, but you were in such a big hurry. Kind of like the way you are now," I teased. "You had tons of hair, and I swear I even saw that you had some teeth already."

"Better to bite you with, my dear," Aidan said as he showed his teeth and pretended to be the wolf in the *Little Red Riding Hood* tale.

I talked and played with my children for hours that day. I knew the laughter of my children was what I needed to help me make it through the birth of our next child.

As I was wheeled into the delivery room and the family looked on, everyone gave me their good thoughts. That was when a candy-striper added, "Good luck."

I couldn't resist, so I responded, "If it was about luck, I'd be giving birth spinning on the roulette table at the Bellagio."

I think I would have had more energy with Lexy being there though. But Adam was there with all the energy in the world. This was his first time in the delivery room of all six of his children. He had been too squeamish to watch Dakota being born, he was incapacitated when the girls were born and didn't know Aidan when he was born, so he was all for being there this time.

What an amazing man! Adam did good for his first time. Only fainted once. That's much better than Lexy did. I guess it's true about what they say; you don't really remember the pain and exhaustion from the first one, but I did from this one. Seemed like I gave birth to six this time if I judged by how tired I was. I slept for fifteen hours straight after he was born.

And yep, wouldn't you know it - we named him Flannagan Adam Maguire. Aidan kept high-fiving everyone in the waiting room that it came out a boy. I don't know who was happier - Aidan, Adam, Uncle Red, Sam, Tommy or Gampy. Maybe they all thought it was high time the playing field had been evened. In any case, I decided I was going to call him AJ for Adam Junior, and see if anyone else picked up on it. To me, Flannagan sounded like a sixty-year-old boozer who should be hanging out in a mahogany smoke-filled bar.

Chapter XXVIII

Abolishing the Nightmare

I began to have nightmares again. This time, of that horrible day in Texas. I started re-living the events in my sleep state and that's when it was all dredged up for me again. After much thought and talking to Adam about it, I decided to analyze it and I came to some conclusions. I figured if I organized the events in my mind and understood what everything meant, I could file them away in the back of my mind and I would be rid of the dreams forever.

Much of what I thought about Joseph's motivations were speculation. I often thought it was all fueled by his wanting to become the most powerful man in the free world, but who knows with a madman like him. He tried beating us down, making us weak and vulnerable. That's when he struck, when we were intimidated and confused.

The Jack-look-alike, we assumed, was the first of Joseph's tactics to discredit me. He used my vulnerability for my first love and Adam's insecurities to get me into a scandal. At that point, it was all about making me appear questionable if I did go public with the truth about him. I think in some ways, Joseph wanted to break up my marriage to prove he was in control of my life, and to prevent me from crossing him. I hoped the Jack look-alike got a truck load of money from Joseph because he was black-listed in Hollywood once the word was out he tried to get between Adam and I. Even the actors who may not have been our best friends, or were even jealous of us, turned against the Italian. You don't behave like that in their backyard, not in Hollywood. Adam asked Quincy, who was suppose to be starring with him in that movie, why he was a no-show. Quincy explained that he was fired without cause. We had to assume Joseph arranged it.

The second of Joseph's tactics purely angered me. He hurt someone dear to me. He was beginning to show his ruthlessness and took a human life to do it, when he set up Uncle Red for murder. Uncle Red never hurt anyone in his life. He was only kind and helped people. He chose his profession to aid people when they were most vulnerable and took whatever they could afford as payment, not what he demanded like some attorneys. Uncle Red was even chastised for this by his parents because he was so different than his conniving brother. Trusting Joseph on exterminating Uncle Red's arrest records was my first tactical error in judgement, following my heart to help someone close to me when I knew it would come back to bite me in the butt. Joseph was setting me up to take the fall for extinguishing the evidence against Uncle Red. This was when I knew we shouldn't take any prisoners at the end.

The third of his tactics was just plain evil. Joseph made an innocent girl sick to save his political career. Dakota may always have complications from the poison. She is the sweetest girl and didn't deserve any of this. But I guess that was Joseph's MO - to prey on sweet innocent victims. I see the look in Adam's eyes when he watches Dakota now. It's more of a "sorry, I wish I had stopped him before he hurt you" kind of look. It broke my heart that Joseph changed this relationship. They are still close but Adam became more protective over her more than with his other children. I guess because he doesn't see her every day and can't be next to her every day, even though he calls her every night. We're still working on Anita to come live with us, but she hasn't agreed yet. Dakota will always need access to her father's blood to stay well. This was when Adam knew he *wouldn't* take any prisoners at the end.

Joseph also killed my best friend. I do not know what to say about that. It hurt me to my core. She was my first and only girlfriend. I was so lucky to have found her and lucky that she loved me too. Lexy was talented. She was gifted, and not only as an actress, but as someone who was brave and courageous. She was kind and generous. She was a wife. She was a daughter. She was a mother. She was Lexy. I'm going to miss her desperately. I still get excited about calling Lexy to tell her what happened in a day. It takes me a few moments to realize that I can't. And the strange part is that I don't seem to be getting any closer to realizing it with each episode in my life. Joseph took her from me, and for that alone, I wished that I could have killed him twenty times over. I now regret not plugging every bullet from that gun into him. Not that Joseph would have been any more dead; just that it would have made me feel better. But that would have made the police suspicious as the scene would have appeared to involve a crime of passion rather than what it was - self-defense. And defense against future harm.

Joseph hurt my daughter Tiffany, and he didn't have any qualms about the idea of killing her. I just hope Tiff never remembers being lost and alone those few days in her young life. Adam and I decided that we will never bring it up again until it's necessary. Until, of course, the press asks her about it, and we know they will someday. But until that day, Tiff will be safe and unknowledgeable about the whole ordeal. We took the kids to an amusement park the same week, so that Tiffany might think it was all a bad merry-go-round ride. Since she slept the whole way back from Dallas, she won't remember being on an airplane. All Tiffany knows is that she was in the safe strong arms of her Daddy.

Joseph killed defenseless animals too. Gampy's *little babies* were drugged unconscious and out of the kidnapper's way, and they couldn't hurt a fly - much less the kidnappers. They didn't have to kill them. I think they did it just to be cruel and make some sort of sick point. They could have just tied nooses around their necks to bring the point home about the hung monkey symbolism. But really, why would they care about those precious dogs? I guess they figured that they'd already killed a person, so what was a few dogs? When I remember the look in Gampy's eyes when he saw them, it still makes me cry. I'd never seen him so hurt before. I'd never seen him cry before.

In addition, Joseph knew he could torment Mom at any given moment. He was important and powerful, and she nearly went back into the bottle because of him. I'm not going as far as to blame Joseph for her drinking problem in the first place, that would be ludicrous because we all have to take responsibility for our own actions. No buts, no how-evers - I'll leave it at that. I destroyed the memo Joseph sent Mom that I had stuck into my journal, since I told Lydia we received a telephone call message instead. Mom was a jewel during the time of tension with Joseph. She never cracked once. She's proud of herself too, I think. Mom's stronger now than she's ever been. She said something the other day about being interested in writing mystery novels. Good for her.

I have to wonder - why did Joseph choose the monkey murders when he knew I would figure it out? Maybe because he wanted the press and police to think it was me who was reenacting this all along from a plan I had devised years ago. Surely Millie would have seen the similarity and stopped it if she realized he was mimicking them, knowing I would eventually figure it out - leading me to her. Maybe Joseph wanted to set her up if I escaped the blame. I have to think that either Millie's stupidity got her killed or she was really more involved than she admitted. Whichever it was, the wild animals who killed her knew Millie had to be expelled to cover their tracks. No matter, she would no longer be a threat to us.

I'd heard that the *outsider* from my taped conversation who got the information about Joseph had died in a freak one-vehicle accident shortly before we went after Tiffany. I don't know if Joseph had anything to do with that one, but it was curious timing. As a result of the death, we never had to address the issue of the context of the conversation going public. Even if the *outsider* or anyone else did the math and realized Mom was underage, Joseph wasn't around to be charged with anything now and it would just be a matter of gossip.

Tracy was never implicated in the kidnapping and knows nothing of what we did. I hadn't felt bad about excluding her - not wanting to make her an accomplice in any way. I know she would have been loyal and stood by us no matter what, but I was glad we didn't have to visit that scenario. Tracy's still the best shot I've ever seen, but I'm closing the gap between us.

My only regret was that I couldn't kill Joseph as many times as he took something from us and left destruction in its place. Lexy's death, Tiffany's trauma, Uncle Red's torment, Dakota's ravished body, Gampy's *little babies'* demise, Mom's persecution, Zoë's right to have an authentic righteous father, Adam's peace of mind for the safety of his children and the honesty of his wife's fidelity, the list is infinite. I didn't feel the least bit guilty about what I did. Perhaps I should have, but I'll save that for my shrink's couch - if I ever feel my conscience cannot handle what has happened.

Now was the time to celebrate with the family. The next couple of weeks were eventful. I began to think of all the things that happened.

Along with moving past my bad dreams, Adam and I now have an unbreakable bond. We are stronger than ever. We vowed not to keep secrets from one another anymore. Nothing. Whatever we were feeling or thinking, we would spill it. I gotta say, Adam has become more vocal and puts his feeling right out there. Not every wife can say that about her husband.

I told Lydia about the special *holiday* that Adam, the girl and I took - along with Clara and Eddie - driving through Nevada because I wanted people to understand that we were a family, and not just a Hollywood power couple. We were a loving family that could have a great time together when we were away from people who tried to sabotage our happiness. I also included it because Adam and I both had careers to think about and all of this press about the Matthews family connection wasn't doing our work life any good. So I told Lydia about our adventures with chirping grasshoppers, rainbows, hopping frogs, bonnets of tiger lilies, and fool's gold in the river. It was just good PR to show a human side to us.

Zoë only knew Joseph as a loving father and I won't give him the satisfaction of distorting her image of him. She will never know what a monster I spared her from. I am happy that she will have fond memories of him. He at least did that right. I'm guessing it really wasn't Joseph though, but Lillian who built a positive image of Joseph for Zoë. Nevertheless, I was happy for that. I knew what it was like to have a bad father, actually two bad fathers, and I didn't want that for her. And it was also so the world wouldn't chastise her for Joseph's sins. This was the main reason Adam and I didn't admit we were there at the ranch that day and just claimed self-defense or justifiable homicide. I didn't want Zoë to know I killed our father - for whatever reason.

I don't think Lillian was involved in Joseph's antics. I think she was just mesmerized by becoming First Lady someday. And she did love her daughter enough to keep her safe for many years by keeping my identity a secret. That way she could access my rare blood type for her if and when she needed it. Lillian and I came to an agreement, actually many agreements. But one was that I wouldn't ever take away her *Godsend* if she would never tell Zoë about the real Joseph. Oddly enough, it was Lillian who saved my life all those years ago by not telling Joseph I was still alive. Mom said that Lillian probably kept tabs on me just in case something like an airplane crash would happen. And speaking of which, they finally determined the cause of what killed so many. One hundred and seventeen people - passengers including crew members - were onboard our flight that crashed, and ninety-two made it off alive. All but two fatalities were of people seated over the wings. Most of them died from the fuel burning. The news reports said that the airlines had installed low-altitude wind-shear detection equipment in all of the commercial cockpit aircrafts, however, it did not help on that day. The debris from the plane spread over the entire runway and sheared a corner piece off one terminal. Fortunately it was a new terminal that was just being built, and no one was hurt in that building. The whole middle-section of the airplane was burned out like a bombed section of Beirut. I've heard some of the burn victims are still trying to recover, physically. I'm sure we're all still trying to recover spiritually. They designed a memorial for the fallen victims in a park located in Los Angeles. Adam and I attended the annual memorial service for the victims.

Tommy seemed a little shy about bringing his new girlfriend around. That was enough to relentlessly punish him for not telling us who he was dating, and for not bringing her by to meet the family. I asked him if she had two heads or fourteen toes, and stuff like that. A girl's gotta have some fun. Tommy should have known better. It would have been a whole lot easier to just tell us, than it would be to endure my practical jokes. He finally did bring her to the house to meet everyone, and Tommy was right, he did find someone nice. It was Zoë. That's what she was doing on the plane the day of the accident - flying to see Tommy play ball. Lillian thought she and Zoë were in L.A. for a shopping trip and to see friends, but Zoë planned to ditch her mother for a while to see Tommy. He knew the story Mom told me about how he and I had different fathers. He didn't tell us about them dating because he worried I would think it was too weird being his sister *and* being Zoë's sister. Zoë heard the story from him and that's how she knew to call me "sis" when she woke from the accident. I also guess that was why Tommy was hanging around the hospital after the crash and disappeared for hours after I'd returned home.

Zoë and I have become very good friends, sisters, and finally, sisters-in-laws when she married Tommy in a small ceremony on February 14th - the girls' second birthday. Some thought the pairing was weird, but I thought it made perfect sense and that there was no one better suited for him. Zoë was already a part of the family. Zoë said that she did manage to remember some of the things I told her that night, but wanted me to repeat the story someday. For one, she wanted to know more about Tommy growing up. She said it was also because she wanted to know some of what to expect after her children were born. I guessed Tommy hadn't told her much about himself. You know how guys can be. Even though Zoë inherited many millions of dollars when her father's estate was settled, and Tommy had the trust fund I had secured for him years ago, they still wanted to live at the house with us, and loved it there. We loved having them there too.

The last I heard, after Dirk got out of jail, he squandered most of his inheritance away. Zoë was understanding toward him, but fortunately refused to give him the money he demanded from her. Poor guy, Dirk actually had to get a job and work for a living. Knowing the father troubles I'd had, we had no intention nor obligation to let Dirk see Aidan, which became irrelevant since he never asked to see him. Adam was the best father Aidan could have drawn anyway. My heart would always skip a beat from pride when I heard Adam teaching Aidan the ways of his native ancestors, the ways of the earth, and about respecting the earth. Adam rarely called Aidan by name, he called him *son*. And, of course, Adam's Mom gave all of the children Native American names.

Zoë mentioned that Lillian was feeling a bit lonely with Joseph being dead, Dirk off doing God knows what, and her daughter living behind a fortress. Zoë suggested that we might invite Lillian to live at the house with us in the suite she and Tommy had since there was lots of room for her. I didn't have a problem with it and I could never say no to Zoë, but I did ask her if it would be okay if we all took a vote on it. After all, I wasn't the only person living at the house, and it was everyone's home. The vote was unanimous. Aidan was happy to get another grandmother that lived so close by.

And with all of the happiness the married couples were feeling, Uncle Red and Sam thought it was high time they got in on it too. They had a commitment ceremony of their own and were married by a friend of theirs. Of course, it wasn't legal, but we never dreamed of treating them like it wasn't. And, of course, Gamma got to plan it and was in her element again. I'm not sure she understood much about it, being from her generation and all, but she was happy for them.

I had a heck of a time trying to explain to Aidan that his Aunt Zoë was really his Aunt Zoë.

Chapter XXIX

My Other "Godsend"

*D*ear *Journal: Something hit me just before drifting off to sleep tonight. The first of the events in the Monkey Murders was the kidnapping of the original monkey. That couldn't have signified Tiffany being kidnapped and held for ransom as I earlier assumed because she represented the monkey that was blown up. So who was the original monkey? Joseph? No because the monkey was ultimately framed at the end and Joseph was not framed. Jack's kidnapping happened before anything else, that might make it the original one. That event got me out of circulation in the press for a year and a half while nothing more destructive happened in my world during that time. Could Joseph have set up Jack's disappearance too, and was content just having me out of the limelight during my time looking for Jack? Did changing my name to Mel Kobach for the production company after I returned from Mexico buy me some time without Joseph attacking me? No, I made a few more films after returning to Los Angeles using my real name, so I'm not sure Jack's abduction was Joseph's doing, or why else would he not continue to attack me while returning to my acting.*

Jack was kidnapped as was the original prop monkey, but the monkey staged his own kidnapping. Did Jack? Maybe Jack and Joseph were both in on it together, like Millie and Millie.

As I was lying there wide awake thinking about it all, other questions came to me.

What would someone do for three million dollars that didn't already have millions dollars? Unlike Joseph who had twenty times that amount. So who got the money that Jack's father paid? Jack never could tell the Federalies where the prison was. He had always wanted to sail around the world, wouldn't that have given him more of a tan weathered look than being inside of a prison? Who was Jack really talking about when I overheard him on the telephone making what I thought was our honeymoon plans?

I needed to slip out of bed for a moment to go into the closet where I kept my old journal. After the plane accident, I wanted and needed a fresh journal - that one having smelt like jet fuel. I had to find something - I needed to find that journal entry. It was bugging the hell out of me that I hadn't remembered a tiny detail with all of the wedding planning and excitement going on at that time. I found the old journal entry that I was searching for and I confirmed what I had been thinking.

Jack had seen me in a bikini and SCUBA gear prior to telling the person on the telephone that he "couldn't wait for the first time to see her in a bikini under her SCUBA gear." We were at the villa in the South of France the time we first made love. While there, we SCUBA dived. I had forgotten that. Since it wasn't me he was referring to, who was he talking about? With my luck, it was probably Kelly. Not that I'm serious about that suggestion because they don't even know each other, but it would fit the timing perfectly.

As I sat in bed, I began to think of other incidences that happened.

Should I go ask the ticket agents at the Acapulco airport if there was another flight out that day before the twin-engine flight was chartered? Jack said there wasn't. Should I go ask Buck if he'd checked the bathroom before boarding the flight home to see if Jack was really where he said he was, taken ill and in the men's room? Surely he would have. Should I ask Gamma about the prenup argument she'd had with Jack the week before our engagement party? She never did tell me what that was all about. Did Jack run out of funds and extort money from his father? Surely, he knew I would have given him anything. Did Jack burn through the three million dollars and that's why he came back to me? If so, who killed the pilot if there were no Mexicans posing as Federalies storming the plane? Was the pilot even *killed at all, as Jack said? Should I go to the Acapulco airport and ask to charter a twin-engine airplane? Who would I get? And if Jack wasn't at a prison, what happened to the plane? Why didn't they ever find it?*

I'm not sure I even want to know these answers. I would have had to put a lot of trust in Jack to believe his story. Am I that obtuse? Or maybe I should just forget about it, and I was probably just reading way too much into it. I had irrevocably and permanently said good-bye to Jack and all that we ever were. It felt good. It felt like I had lifted a hundred pounds off my shoulders, so why was Jack's story still nagging at me. Maybe it was just a case of indigestion from eating burritos for dinner, and it was all just like Jack said it was.

Although, why would Jack tell Adam that I had died in the airplane crash when it would have been so easy to expose the lie. Was it to kidnap me and take me away like he went away? Was Jack planning something before Adam found me? Was that why he kept looking at the door to see if Adam would move away from it so he could steal me away or to somehow convince me to leave with him?

As I paused from writing for a moment. I looked over at Adam while pondering to myself... Should I share my thoughts with Adam? Or should I just keep them to myself? We promised to never keep secrets from one another again - that's what hurt our relationship in the first place. Yet, I didn't want Adam to think that I was obsessing about Jack again. I also had the fear that Adam would go after Jack if he did fake his death, because I knew my husband was capable of killing. I wasn't sure not stopping Adam was such a bad thing because of the hell I went through for a year and a half in Mexico while being separated from my family - possibly all for nothing.

I am looking at Adam, now sleeping soundly - innocently. I have no questions about him. No doubts about his love for me. We have no trust issues between us. He is my other Godsend. How lucky was I to escape that bridge of death with Jack, to live in paradise with Adam? How fortunate was I to have crossed that burning bridge before the flames would have devoured me forever? Goodnight Journal and good-bye. I'll be destroying you in a firey blaze along with your predecessor. Sorry about that, but I can't take the chance that you'll betray me.

Adam woke to my heating the room up with my firey journals just as I was tossing the last page into the fireplace. He asked, "What are you doing over there?"

I answered not wanting him to know what I was really doing. "I was cold so I thought I would warm up with a fire."

"It's summer, Jordan. How could it be too cold?"

"I know, but you keep the thermostat at ninety below in here and I was cold."

"Well, come here. I'll keep you warm."

The next morning, I slid out of bed and walked into the nursery to see my big boy. But instead of finding AJ, there was just a rubber ducky in his crib. That meant someone in the house had him. The ducky had been my idea to be used as a signal within the family, that way we wouldn't panic that one of our children was lost again. I knew he was safe.

As I stood in the shower, I began to think about the previous night's questions. I stepped out and glanced outside to discover Adam and Aidan hitting baseballs in the batting cages. I dressed and then meandered to the kitchen like a woman on a mission, and as the scent of Gamma's world-famous cinnamon buns drove me closer to them, I organized my questions.

"Morning, Gamma. Where is everyone?"

"Morning, dear - how did you sleep?"

"Not great, and you?" I said as I tried to sneak away a cinnamon bun before getting my hand slapped.

"I'm not done with those yet - sit. Your grandfather is where he usually is, working in his hobby shop. Your mother and brother are off somewhere together, I didn't really understand what they said they were doing. Zoë and Lillian are with AJ in their suite. Your husband and other son Aidan are out hitting baseballs. And your daughters are in the play area outside with Clara. I haven't seen your uncles yet this morning."

I chuckled a bit, not yet used to hearing Sam being referred to as my uncle. "How do you keep tabs on everyone like that?" I said, smiling. "It must be a gift or something." I sat there silently for a few moments before continuing the conversation with her. "Gamma, if I asked you something, would you be honest with me?"

"Of course, dear," she said. Then without missing a beat, she added, "No, I don't think you should change the color of your hair to orange. No, nothing should be pierced this week, especially in those areas which aren't allowed to be viewed in public. And yes, no matter how hard you try not to, you're getting older along with the rest of us." She turned and grinned at me.

I chuckled at Gamma's jokes and then responded, "You're just full of wit this morning, aren't you? What kind of plants did you brew in your tea this morning, Gamma?" Then I blurted out, "I wanted to know if you suggested a prenup to Jack just before we were to be married."

Gamma turned and peered at me with a serious look. "Whatever made you think of that?" she asked looking shocked. "Please don't tell me that you and Adam are having problems."

"No, we're fine, and you didn't answer my question. Did you?"

"Well, I don't know if I can remember that far back."

"Please try, I think you know what I'm asking. Please tell me the truth. What were the two of you fighting about just before our engagement party?"

Gamma glanced outside, I think to figure out where Adam was. Then she came over and sat down beside me. She looked at me and said, "I think some things are best kept in the past, Jordan dear."

I shook my head from side to side and then responded, "I think that's for me to decide in this case, Gamma. Please, I need some answers and I'm starting with you. I'm not going to let this drop no matter where I have to go for the answers."

"Okay dear - yes, we were arguing that day. I never cared much for him, you know that. We were arguing because I had seen Jack with someone else the week before. I confronted Jack and he had said it was just a friend he was taking to lunch. However, they were not acting like *just friends*. He gave her something - a present, some kind of jewelry. I told Jack that I saw him give her something and said how I thought it was inappropriate after he had just proposed to you. Would you like me to continue, dear?"

I nodded. "How did you see this? Were you spying on him for some reason?" I asked gently, as to not be accusing her of any wrongdoing.

"No, not really. They were seated at the window table of the restaurant near my hairdressers, and anyone could have seen them. It was shameful the way they were carrying on. After approaching Jack about this, I asked why he wanted to marry you if he was seeing other girls. Jack denied it at first, but then said he was Italian and it's acceptable in his culture. I then asked if he was only marrying you for your money. He answered, 'It doesn't hurt.' I told him that he needed to prove his love and the best way would be to sign a prenup. Jack laughed and said you would never make him sign one. He also said he would never marry you if you asked him to sign one."

"Then maybe you should have insisted that we have a prenup, since you didn't want me to marry him," I said smiling, sort of kidding with her.

Gamma smiled back then grew more serious as she continued. "He said he would win an Acclamation Award for the best performance of a hurt shocked husband-to-be that ever lived. And he said that you would believe him over me and if you didn't, he would sue you for breach of commitment or something like that."

"And you believed that I could believe him over you?" I asked surprised that she would be taken in by that.

"No. But then Jack said that he would marry you and have other women on the side out of spite if I didn't stay out of your lives. I didn't want to see you hurt, I knew how much you loved him. I thought maybe I was overreacting and I should just stay out of it."

"Gamma, no offense, but had you told me, I may have

broken up with him and wouldn't have had to go through what I did for so many years."

"I'm sorry - I thought it was for the best."

"Did you think he ever really loved me?"

"No."

"Thanks Gamma, was that all of it?"

"Yes, as far as I can remember. If I remember anything else, I'll tell you."

"Thanks," I said before I hugged her, snatched a cinnamon bun and left. I trotted outside to watch Adam and Aidan a while, pondering what Gamma had said. Adam took a break and jogged over to me. He sat beside me on the grass with Pasta and Snuggles hopping around us like bunnies.

"Hi JoJo," Adam said warmly while he gave me a kiss. "What's on your mind? No, don't try to hide it. I know you well enough to know something is rolling around up there." Adam tapped his finger on my forehead, teasing me.

"Yeah, but I haven't composed it all yet, enough to put words to it. Give me a while to ponder it," I answered deciding to change the subject. "You looked good out there. You're all hot and sweaty, mumm," I teased. We kissed again as Aidan covered his eyes and squawked about our public display of affection.

"I'm going to go out of town for a few days on business for the production company," I told Adam.

"I thought you put that on hold for now. Can't your replacement handle it?"

"Not this time. I'm the only one who can cover this one. It won't take me long to scout out some locations."

"Where is it?"

"Well, we're looking at a few different locations and it's complicated right now," I replied. "That's why I have to handle it. I'll let you know when we've decided on something." I noticed that he was looking away. I knew that look; it meant that he knew I was sidestepping his questions.

"You taking Tracy?" Adam asked as he watched Aidan bat.

"I don't know yet, maybe."

"Yes," he said as he looked at me. "We still don't

know if we're completely out of danger yet, especially with that psychopath, Dirk, running around out there." He looked back at Aidan again and added. "So yes you are."

"Okay, then yes I am. Why did you ask if you weren't going to give me a choice?" I teased. I pulled off his right shoe and sock and Pasta started licking his foot.

Adam jabbered something in Lakota at me as I ran into the house snickering.

I packed a bag and advised Tracy that we were headed out of town. I decided to wait until I got to the airport to make our reservations instead of using Brandy. Eddie dropped Adam, Tracy and I off at our LAX terminal, and Adam said good-bye at the ticket counter. And, I made sure my husband secretly pinched my behind this time before he returned to the limo. I decided to take a flight through Dallas so Adam or anyone else who was interested in my travel plans would not know where we were really headed. Then Tracy and I caught a flight to Acapulco.

After we checked into our hotel in Mexico and rented a car, the two of us headed back to the airport. I needed to ask a few questions there. I finally found someone who was working back when Jack and Buck were there. Apparently they'd had a high rate of employee turnover and informants were scarce. The ticket agent remembered that there had been a scheduled flight to Los Angeles that had left Acapulco after Buck's flight and before the chartered flight that Jack hired. The ticket agent remembered something else - that flight left only minutes before Jack's chartered flight. They only remembered that information because they had been wanting the airlines to move the departure time for years. I also asked if he'd heard of any freelance pilots getting killed near Mazatlan around that time. He said no. I asked to speak to any of those freelance pilots that were around then and he said there were only two, and one was a woman. The only one around at the time for us to speak with was the woman. It turns out that she was an older woman and the opposite of Jack's type - broke and aging. The woman knew nothing about him. That was a bust.

Tracy and I decided to go and have some lunch before returning to speak to the male pilot who was expected that afternoon.

A few hours later, I approached the male pilot alone. Tracy was standing far enough away that she wouldn't be able to overhear our conversation. "Hola, ¿cómo estás tú? You speak English? Can I ask you a few questions?"

"Well, that was three. And I guess it would all depend on the questions, honey."

"Have you ever seen this man?" I asked as I showed the pilot a photograph of Jack.

"What's it worth to me?" he asked, not looking at the photo yet.

I pulled five hundred dollars out of my pocket, gave it to him folded up, and repeated, "Ever seen this man?"

"Oh, yeah, that guy. Fickled guy, has an accent. Yeah - what about him?"

"When's the first time you laid eyes on him?"

"Oh, well, it must be about eight years now when he first chartered a flight from me."

"That long ago - how would you still remember him?"

"Because that was the year of the crickets, honey - well, the summer of the crickets, anyway. We had such a bad cricket problem that they would get into the planes and bug the hell out of people - excuse the pun." He paused and gave me a grin. "The crickets were everywhere. I remember him being so squeamish about them that I secretly named him *cricketman*. I also remember him because he's been here on and off since then. I've seen him around."

"Anything unusual about him that you remember? Did he seem sick to you or unsteady on his feet?"

"Sick? Not physically, but he was a bit of a loon. Unusual? You mean besides the fact that he had me file a flight plan for Los Angeles, paid me for that fare, and then decided he wanted to make a stop prior to getting there? Yep, a loon."

"It was his idea to make the stop?"

"Yeah. We can't just make those decisions last minute

unless it's an emergency landing. But since he paid me in advance and paid me well, I did what he asked. The weirdest part was that he decided to stay and not finish to his destination. So I just flew back to Acapulco to get another fare and pocketed the money he gave me."

"Where did you drop him off?"

"On a deserted airstrip close to Mazatlan."

"Why didn't you radio the tower to tell them?"

"Because what we were doing was illegal - that is, making a stop without it being an emergency, and I wasn't getting my license pulled for nobody. And if you repeat that, I'll deny it."

"Did you see if anyone was there to meet him?"

"Yeah, some blonde broad in a jeep. Couldn't miss her - a brick house if you know what I mean."

"When's the last time you saw him?"

"Just last month. I saw him cruising through the airport hanging onto that same broad."

"Thanks, you've been very helpful."

"Anytime, honey."

"And this is for not repeating our conversation to anyone," I said as I handed him another five hundred dollars.

"Sure thing, honey," he said, with a big smile. "I never saw you and we can do business anytime you want."

Once Tracy and I got back to our hotel and went into our respective rooms, I called Larry. "Hi, listen - can you fax me a photograph to my hotel?" I asked. "Do you think you can get a hold of a photo of her? Thanks Larry."

After receiving the fax from Larry, I went back to speak to the pilot. I handed him a hundred dollar bill and asked, "Is this the blonde broad?"

"Yep, that's the one," he said immediately. "If you hang around, she should be here next week. She comes by here to pick up some packages every Tuesday morning."

"Thanks, pal," I said before handing him another hundred dollar bill.

I decided to use the time before the woman's return to

the airport to pose some questions to others who were involved. So we flew to Italy to visit Jack's father at his villa. Before Tracy and I drove out to the villa, I hired an interpreter. The three of us arrived, made our hellos, and then Jack's father invited us to sit with him a while. After we made some small talk, he asked, "Why have you come here?"

"I think I may have found the ones who kidnapped your son in Mexico, but I have to ask you some questions. Who did you give the three million dollars to?"

"We wired the money to the Mexican International Bank in Acapulco - and it wasn't three million, it was six million."

There was that number again - six. Why six? Was there some big cosmic joke out there that kept giving me the number six? Was it a sign or something? And six wasn't even my favorite number. "I'm sorry I must have misunderstood when I heard it was three million. Are you sure it was Acapulco? Because he was kidnapped near Mazatlan."

He said he was positive so I finished up quickly and excused myself. I had to make sure I was back in Mexico in time to do some more errands and to see the blonde broad on Tuesday. So we didn't waste any time in Italy and took the first flight out to the states for our next stop.

Visiting Buck was next on my list. So Tracy and I flew to Nashville where he lived. I decided to surprise him. That way, if Buck were to tell Jack that I'd been there, I would be gone by the time they could do anything about it. Buck's house was much bigger than the last one he'd had when Jack and he were starting out in racing. Funny, Buck hadn't won any major events that I knew of to put him in a house like that.

After making small talk for a moment, I asked Buck, "Did you happen to check the men's room before boarding the flight home to see if Jack was in there?" I wanted to find out if Jack really was where he said he was, and Buck had no way of knowing that Jack told me that he was in the men's room.

"Ah yeah, I think so. Yeah I did," he said, not so

convincingly.

"Where do you think he could have wondered off to?"

"I'm not sure. Why are you asking questions after all this time?"

"I may have found out who kidnapped him."

Buck appeared surprised.

"Have you seen Jack since he's been back?"

"No."

I knew he had. Jack and Buck were photographed together in Vegas when we saw Jack there at Lexy's wedding. It wasn't until I returned home after the wedding that I saw an article about Jack "getting his life back," accompanied by the photo that had Buck in a background shot.

We wrapped up our conversation, and I said good-bye to Buck, then Tracy and I headed out. Since Jack would soon know I was asking questions, we immediately hopped a flight back to Acapulco.

After Tracy and I arrived, we got a hotel for the night. Early the next morning, we drove back over to the airport to wait for the blonde broad. I walked over to the waiting area, donned sunglasses and a big floppy touristy-hat, and there I sat - waiting. Tracy was standing at a distance nearly. After about forty-five minutes, the broad showed up. I walked over to her and said, "Hello Kelly. Small world. How are you?" I asked. "Gone on any dives lately?"

She looked surprised to see me. "What? What are you doing here?"

"I was just about to ask you the same question. And all this time, I thought you were hot for Adam. Silly me. So how's Jack been lately?"

"Have you lost your mind? I don't know what you are talking about."

"Oh, sure you do, Kelly. You were seen here with him just last month."

Kelly tried turning the tables on me, saying, "Well, I don't know anything about any Jack, but Adam and I have seen each other plenty of times this year."

"Doubtful - he wouldn't even do a movie with you and

you want me to believe you've seen him? Not a chance."

"Why do you think he did that? Because you were getting too close to finding out about us."

Ignoring her comment, I asked, "Did Jack run out of funds and extort money from his father? Did Jack burn through that money and that's why he came back to me?"

"I don't know what you are babbling about. You must have lost your mind," Kelly said right before she walked away.

I didn't waste any time. We drove right over to the loading docks where I knew Kelly was headed to pick up her packages.

"Hello again," I said sarcastically greeting her. "Funny how I know where you're going to be before you do - isn't it?" Looking visibly upset and frazzled, she grabbed her packages and left.

Again, I didn't waste any time. We drove straight over to the Mexican International Bank there in Acapulco where we went inside and waited.

"Hello again," I said cheerfully to Kelly. "Funny how we keep running into one another - isn't it?"

Kelly looked even more upset this time and asked, "What are you doing - stalking me or something?"

"I was here first, as well as the other two places so how could I be stalking you?" After Kelly got in line, I stood behind her. She was seething and walked out of line to the deposit slip supply desk in the center of the bank. I got out of line and followed her.

"What are you doing here?" she whispered loudly.

"I'm going to follow you everywhere you go. I'm going to be your shadow until the end of time. All you have to do is answer some questions and I'm outta here."

"What?!"

"Let's step outside," I said as others were starting to watch our performance. After we were out of earshot from them, I asked, "Where did you meet Jack?"

"I don't know any Jack."

"Okay Kelly, until the end of time, remember? I have the time, how about you? I also have the money to take you down. I will make sure that everyone here in this town knows what a criminal you are. Kidnapping is illegal, you know, and you are the only one who can be implemented in Jack's kidnapping. You were the one who drove him away in your jeep that day," I said smiling, knowing I had her cornered.

"I didn't do anything and you can't prove that."

"Oh, but I can," I claimed. "I've spoken to Jack's pilot, an eyewitness to your crime and he's fingered you - with this." I showed her a picture of herself. "How else do you think I knew where and when to find you?"

She looked nervous. "Okay, but I didn't kidnap anyone. I met Jack just before you two were suppose to get married. *He* pursued me."

"I don't doubt that. You didn't give him money, did you?" I asked sarcastically.

"He loved me, not you. He flew me to Mazatlan when he was suppose to be with you during some school graduation thing - that's how much he loved me. Jack wanted to marry me, but he said he needed to marry you to secure our future. I was against it, but he said he would make it up to me."

"How?" I asked coldly.

"Jack said he would eventually leave you and marry me. After that, we could sail around the world together. But I didn't like his idea and didn't want him to even touch you again. That's when I came up with a plan so that we could be together and expel you from the equation."

"His kidnapping. But he never got any money from me then. Are you saying that you two were behind the kidnapping of my daughter? That's the only money I've ever paid out."

"No, but thanks for the idea. We *did* try to extort money from you, but you were out of town living in Mazatlan somewhere. We didn't know where exactly and we couldn't find you. I tried for six months to get the information from someone at your house, but they wouldn't tell me where you were and just wanted to take messages. We then decided to just send a ransom note to your house, but no one ever responded. That's when we decided to extort the money from his father instead."

I was stunned. Gamma lied to me. She said that was all that she knew. They had received a ransom demand for Jack's return and they just ignored it. For all they knew, Jack could have been killed and they didn't care that I was going through hell. "Why did Jack come back to me if he was suppose to be so happy with you - to get more money?"

"I don't know, I guess. But I can tell you that we broke up because of you."

"How could that be?"

"He never stopped talking about you, or rather your money. I put up with it for four years as we sailed around together off the coast here," she said.

"Why did you go after Adam?"

"You ruined my life. That's when I decided it was payback time. I heard about you spending time with Adam on the set in San Antonio from a friend who had worked on the film. I then decided to get on the set of Adam's next picture to start an affair with him and take him away from you. And I had him. He was sleeping with me when you showed up. Another week and he wouldn't have even cared about you or those brats of yours."

I didn't let her rattle me. "Yeah, whatever - then what? If Jack had millions of dollars, why did he come back?"

"He burned through most of that, so he was still hanging around down here, something about a rich heiress in town. I hooked up with him again about a year and a half later and told him you were even richer than before. That's when he decided to go back to you - for the money. Jack saw that you were back doing movies, and I know that's the only reason he wanted to be back with you - to be back in that lifestyle. He didn't love you, you know," she said to hurt me.

"Yeah, got that - thanks for the tip," I said sarcastically. "When was the last time you saw Jack?"

"Last month. You never understood him at all. Jack needs a certain lifestyle, but he loved me."

"Yeah, I used to say that, but good for you Kelly - he's all yours." I turned and left her standing there. Tracy eyed

Kelly with distrust, and then followed me to our rental car.

As I sat on the plane to Los Angeles, I could feel my face turning red. I was angry. How could I have been so stupid? I was feeling humiliated. Jack used me right from the start - just like Joseph used Mom. How naive and trusting of us!

After learning my lesson the last time I lost my Irish temper, I decided to let it cool down a bit before speaking. By the time we got home, it was dinnertime. When I entered the house, everyone was at the table eating. Hellos came from around the diningroom as I made my greeting. Adam stood up, greeted, then kissed me before offering me his chair.

Eddie was quick to add, "Miss Jordan, I would have picked you up at the airport but I was never notified."

"Yes, I know, Eddie - we took a cab," I replied. "Adam, can I see you for a moment?"

We went to our suite and into our bedroom. I didn't waste any time before saying, "I finally figured out how to tell you what's been on my mind."

Adam said he wanted a hug first. Then he said, "You've been gone for almost a week, and I've gotten no calls from you. Where have you been? I was worried." We hugged and I didn't want to let him go. I feared it may be the last hug I would get from him. Adam sat on the bed to listen to what I had to say.

"The night before I left town, I was writing in my journal and realized that Jack may not have been kidnapped."

"Is that why you had a bonfire with your two journals in our fireplace that night?"

"Yes. I destroyed any and all evidence of what we'd done and everything that I've thought since I've known Jack. There was just too much information in them. I know we promised to never keep secrets from one another again because that's what hurt our relationship in the first place. However, I didn't want you to think I was obsessing about Jack again. I went to Mexico to find some answers. I also went to Italy to speak to Jack's parents, and to Nashville to speak to Buck."

"You went to Italy?!"

"Yes."

"That's it - just yes?"

"I know it was wrong of me not to tell you, but I had to find the answers. To be honest, I really didn't know how to tell you about the real intent of my trip."

"Not only did you not tell me - you lied to me."

"Yes, but I had to in order to clarify things. I deserved some answers."

"So you lied to me to spare my feelings, when all you did was hurt them in the end." He paused. "You said it was business."

"Yes. There was some business, but yes I did lie," I confessed. Then I blurted, "Did you ever sleep with Kelly?"

"What? You're turning this around on me?"

"No, it's just a question. Did you?"

"No, not even close. I couldn't even look at anyone else back then. You broke my heart. I was obsessed with thinking about you after our time together in San Antonio. I couldn't even work, much less date. Why ask me that now?"

I told Adam about what Kelly said - that they were sleeping together. I also told him about Jack not being kidnapped, about him trying to extort money from me, and about Kelly's involvement with Jack. I told Adam no one at the house told me that they received a ransom note. "Kelly wanted to take you away from me because of Jack talking about me all the time when they were together. I didn't want you going after him because of what I suspected. We didn't need any more trouble."

"You broke our trust."

"Yes."

He began to leave the room.

"Adam."

He turned around and said, "If I would have done this to you, would you have forgiven me? If I would have run off with Kelly somewhere?"

"I didn't run off with Jack - I didn't even see him."

"Yes you did - that's all you saw."

"Okay, I get what you're saying, but I'm not obsessing

about him - I swear," I said sincerely. "I just needed some answers to move past this once and for all. We need to finish this." As I stood up to leave, I added, "Shall we go finish this once and for all?"

Adam followed me and together we summoned Gamma, Gampy, Mom and Uncle Red into the family room. I shut the door.

"Well Gamma - anything you want to tell me before we get started?" I said, trying to control my anger.

"No dear, I don't know what you're asking me."

"Mom and Uncle Red weren't even living with us in the Hollywood Hills house so that leaves you and Gampy who knew about the ransom note. I know the truth. How could you have done this to me?" I was hoping she would just fess up.

"What are you talking about, dear?" asked Gamma.

"Someone here lied to me. They knew about Jack being alive all along because there was a ransom note sent to the house."

Gamma and Mom gasped. "Someone knew all along?" Gamma asked, stunned. "I'm sure that's not true, dear - it couldn't be."

Adam walked over to the window and stared out. That's what he did when he was upset. I knew Adam was tired of hearing about Jack. I knew he thought all of this was over.

"Did you think I wouldn't find out?" I said looking at Gamma. "I had a right to know that you received a ransom note from Jack's kidnappers. And on top of that, no one told me or did anything about it."

"No, I'm sure you're mistaken - no one here did that," Gamma profusely stated.

"I did."

I swung around and said, "What?"

"I did it," said Gampy. "It was me who received the ransom note from the kidnappers. No one else here knew anything about it. It was all me." As he spoke, Gampy was standing stiffly, as if in front of a firing squad. "I received it about six months after Jack went missing. I thought it was odd that they had waited so long to contact us. I was quite certain that he was no good because I knew about the argument he'd had with Annie before the engagement party. That wasn't the only reason I thought he was no good. I'd seen other signs along the way." We all sat down to listen to his story. "I knew Jack wasn't dead and I knew that he hadn't been kidnapped. You see, I had proof in a photograph of him after the abduction. Proof that he was quite alive. After I received the ransom note, I tried contacting you, Jordan, but you were not in your Mexico apartment. So I decided to do some investigating after I took a second look at the payment instructions. The kidnapper demanded that the ransom money be sent to an Acapulco bank. This seemed strange to me. I would have thought they would be in Mazatlan where Jack disappeared. So I hired a private investigator to do some digging there in Acapulco, and sure enough, he found Jack about a year after he went missing. Apparently, he had been out sailing and that's what took the investigator so long to find him."

"Yeah, I learned about the bank in Acapulco," I acknowledged. "I confronted Jack's father about the details of his payment, and that's where they sent the money. That's when I knew for sure that the kidnapping was all a ruse."

Gampy went on to tell us more of his explanation. He said, "Lexy knew too. I sent her down to Mazatlan to help bring you back, Jordan. She was furious at Jack for doing this, but she was also furious at me for not telling you. Lexy demanded that we stop keeping this a secret and tell you. Just about the time we decided to tell you, you came home."

"You should have told her," Adam said cutting him off. "She's been mourning a phantom - someone who hadn't even existed. Jordan would never be in love with a man like that, had she known his true worth. That wasn't fair to her or to me."

I continued the scolding. "You know how I feel about men taking my control away. I would have never thought you could do this to me. It was my right to know and not your right to protect me against him. You only did this because you thought I would have taken Jack back. But guess what?

I'm not that stupid. If I had been told what Gamma and you knew, I would have dropped him like a hot rock. But no one bothered to tell me, and I spent years grieving for someone who wasn't even dead - not to mention, wasn't worth my time or tears."

"I'm sure your grandfather was just looking out for your best interests, dear," said Gamma, trying to defend him and to bring peace back into the room.

"It wasn't his choice to make - it was mine," I said simmering.

"You were on the road to recovery, you had gotten over him and moved on," Gampy reminded me. "I didn't want to be the one to take that all away from you."

I was numb. All I could think to say was "We all have a lot of things to think about, and we all have some forgiving to do. I need some time." I left the room.

Adam popped his head into our bedroom about an hour later. "Do you want me here?" he asked.

I was lying on the bed, and I turned to look at him. "I'm the one who needs to be forgiven," I said. "Why would I not want you here? I love you more than you'll ever know. I'm sorry I hurt you. I'm sorry I broke your heart after our time together in San Antonio. You're such a good man and it breaks my heart just knowing that you were hurt."

Adam shrugged and looked down like Aidan always had when he doesn't know what to say. He then walked over to me and then pulled a lavender rose out from behind him then offered it to me.

I smiled and accepted the rose.

He sat down on the bed next to me, then asked, "Do you think you'll be able to forgive your grandfather for not telling you?"

"Yes, I already have, but not if it were anyone else though. Gampy and Gamma took Tommy and me in when we needed them the most. Tommy and I could have been a ward of the state forever, and lived with people like the Burtons our whole childhood. Even worse - not living together as a family and never really knowing each other. How could I ever stay mad at them? I truly understand where he was at with not telling me. I was there just a few short days ago, yet I can't help but to think that all of this could have been avoided if he had just told me about it when it happened. The funny thing is that what Jack did had no correlation to the Monkey Murders, that was purely Joseph's plot, but that's how I discovered Jack's scam. There *are* a few people that I won't be forgiving, though. There *are* a few people who need some payback over this and I *am* going to seek revenge." I looked at Adam, then continued, "On Jack... and on Kelly."

Adam smirked and asked, "How?"

"You'll see. I won't keep secrets from you about the important things, but I can still have some mystery about me, can't I?"

"Yes."

"That's it - just yes?"

"Yes, and this," he said before he kissed me. "Are we good then?"

"Never bedda."

"Have mercy on my heart, woman"

"Let's go tell Gampy he's forgiven."

I debated whether or not to just let Tracy handle Jack and Kelly in her own "Olympic team" kind of way. And after she knew the truth about them - she conveyed that would have delighted her to *handle* them. But then I thought of something else that would be more fitting.

"Lydia, hello - this is Jordan Walsh. I've got some more of that juicy gossip you like so much. Can we do lunch?"

Adam and I celebrated our third anniversary by reading Lydia's article in the Newsmonger Magazine. She began the article with the headlines, **Jack Rebello May Wish He Were Dead - Again.** She told the readers that he had scammed me all during our relationship, including the theft of the condo, and his affairs with other women. Then he scammed the authorities by faking his own kidnapping. She went on to write that he scammed his father out of six million dollars after attempting and failing to scam me for the ransom. Of course, Lydia had to use the word "alleged" so she couldn't be sued. It was all out there. Even *more* than I had told her. Who knew the media would be my friend after all?

The last I heard, Jack's father had been sent a copy of Lydia's article - anonymously, of course. And as a result, he disowned Jack and removed him from his will. That was the least of Jack's problems though. He, along with Kelly, were indicted for extortion and a truckload of other offenses. Since Jack committed the crimes in Mexico, he was extradited there to face the charges. He would spend time in a Mexican prison after all. And he didn't have my money, nor his father's, to help him out of this one. Justice. If nothing else, Gamma was happy!

"Hell hath no fury like a woman scorned," I said to Adam. He smiled, knowing our problems with Jack was truly over and we now had closure. He also jokingly commented that he would never cross me, now knowing what I was capable of.

Something hit me just before drifting off to sleep tonight. If Jack faked his own death, could Dad have faked his? Death would have gotten him away from all the people who he owed money to - including the raunchy casting company that he swindled. No one from the family ever got an opportunity to identify Dad's body. What was the accidental connection that was made by the police that gave them reason to believe he was Uncle Red's brother when the body was found? He had a fake ID on him with another name, so how did they know to contact Uncle Red? Should I ask Uncle Red who the buddy was that he spoke to at the police station that made the connection and how? Maybe I should ask Uncle Red again if we could exhume Dad's body to have it moved here.

Could *he* have been the original monkey? The police never did find the six million dollars we paid the kidnappers with the marked money.

The End

Ordering Information

CMS Enterprises
Orders at http://www.cyndiemstyles.com
ISBN 0-9768170-0-4
$14.95 plus $2.30 shipping/handling (CA residents 8.25% tax)
More titles available

✂ ---

CMS Enterprises
Orders at http://www.cyndiemstyles.com
ISBN 0-9768170-0-4
$14.95 plus $2.30 shipping/handling (CA residents 8.25% tax)
More titles available

✂ ---

CMS Enterprises
Orders at http://www.cyndiemstyles.com
ISBN 0-9768170-0-4
$14.95 plus $2.30 shipping/handling (CA residents 8.25% tax)
More titles available

✂ ---

CMS Enterprises
Orders at http://www.cyndiemstyles.com
ISBN 0-9768170-0-4
$14.95 plus $2.30 shipping/handling (CA residents 8.25% tax)
More titles available

✂ ---

CMS Enterprises
Orders at http://www.cyndiemstyles.com
ISBN 0-9768170-0-4
$14.95 plus $2.30 shipping/handling (CA residents 8.25% tax)
More titles available

www.ingramcontent.com/pod-product-compliance
Lightning Source LLC
Chambersburg PA
CBHW031430240626
47154CB00001B/273